The Adventures of

Mᴿ VERDANT GREEN

The Adventures of
MR VERDANT GREEN

BY

CUTHBERT BEDE B.A.

With illustrations by the author

INTRODUCED BY
ANTHONY POWELL

'A COLLEGE JOKE TO CURE THE DUMPS'
SWIFT

Oxford New York Toronto Melbourne
OXFORD UNIVERSITY PRESS
1982

Oxford University Press, Walton Street, Oxford OX2 6DP

London Glasgow New York Toronto
Delhi Bombay Calcutta Madras Karachi
Kuala Lumpur Singapore Hong Kong Tokyo
Nairobi Dar es Salaam Cape Town
Melbourne Auckland

and associate companies in
Beirut Berlin Ibadan Mexico City

Introduction © Anthony Powell 1982

First published, in three parts, 1853, 1854, 1857
First published as an Oxford University Press paperback
with Anthony Powell's introduction 1982

British Library Cataloguing in Publication Data
Bede, Cuthbert
The adventures of Mr. Verdant Green.
– (Oxford paperbacks)
I. Title
823'8[F] PR4161.B/
ISBN 0-19-281331-5

Printed in Great Britain by
Richard Clay (The Chaucer Press) Ltd
Bungay, Suffolk

ER

CONTENTS

Cuthbert Bede.

INTRODUCTION

BY ANTHONY POWELL

I FEEL pretty sure that I first read *The Adventures of Mr Verdant Green: an Oxford Freshman*, by Cuthbert Bede, B.A., at the age of eleven or twelve in 1917, when, the war having brought my parents to Cambridge, we were living in what were normally out-of-college undergraduate rooms, where *Verdant Green* was among the few books. That was quite an appropriate background, though most of the Cambridge colleges were then accommodating army cadets.

I did not understand a great deal of the story, but liked the illustrations drawn by the author himself, and, my sense of the past making me only dimly aware that Oxford must have altered a good deal since those days, accepted the picture as a realistic one. The vision never wholly faded, and notwithstanding the few vestigial traces that survived into the 1920s, undergraduates in the flesh turned out in many respects an anti-climax. From this initial reading I always retained the fact that scholars of Merton are known as postmasters.

Two points must be underlined: that the author of *Verdant Green* was never himself an Oxford undergraduate (nor even an Oxford don), and that his name was not Cuthbert Bede. He was called Edward Bradley, and fell in love with Oxford from the outside. This passion might be compared with Kipling's for the Army, both writers finding the same fascination in technical detail, and, Bradley especially, satirising as much as romanticising the institutions and types that had won their hearts.

Son of a surgeon from a Worcestershire family of long clerical (and perceptibly literary) tradition, the Revd Edward Bradley (1827–1889) was educated at Kidderminster Grammar School and University College, Durham. Durham students in the Middle Ages had been associated with Trinity College, Oxford, since when several serious efforts had been made to establish a College in Durham itself, but these were unsuccessful until 1832. In short Durham University was new, but by no means 'redbrick'.

Bradley graduated B.A. in 1848, Licentiate of Theology the following year. He was still too young to be ordained, and it was then that
the Oxford experience took place. He seems to have studied at Oxford
for about a year, and certainly made many undergraduate friends.

After he took orders there was a curacy at Glatton-with-Holme in
Huntingdonshire, the first of a procession of poetic names which were
to be his incumbencies: Bobbington in Staffordshire; Detton-with-
Caldecote in Huntingdonshire; Stretton in Rutland; finally Lenton-
with-Hanby in Lincolnshire. Bradley was a hard-working, resource-
ful, popular clergyman, whose capabilities as a writer brought him into
contact with a London world of books and journalism. He would
sometimes raise quite large sums of money for his churches by lectur-
ing on such subjects as 'Wit and Humour'. At a rather less gilded level
there is perhaps a touch of a latter-day Sydney Smith.

Bradley wrote under the name Cuthbert Bede because the two
patron saints of Durham are St Cuthbert and the Venerable Bede. He
was not forgetful of his own *alma mater* in other respects either, calling
his elder son by the former Christian name, and including a warmly
reminiscent descriptive passage when Verdant Green passes through
Durham to stay with friends in the North of England. One regrets that
Bradley never produced a novel about being a Durham undergraduate, which would have made an invaluable contribution to docu-
menting the 'campus' life of a new university at that date.

Bradley wrote novels, verse, miscellaneous pieces for a great many
periodicals, including *Punch*, *All the Year Round*, *the Illustrated London News*, *the Boy's Own Paper*, lots more. His occasional writings
have gone the way of most journalism, and he had no gift as a poet,
though he claims to have reintroduced into England the double-
acrostic. As a novelist he was influenced no doubt by Dickens,
Thackeray, Surtees, Marryat, and he contributed a few quite bright
ideas of his own, but he is without much sense of construction or
development of narrative.

Nearer and Dearer (1857), for instance, opens with a promising
situation. Two young men, bored by finding themselves snowbound
in a country house, have a bet about persuading a hitherto unknown
pupil at a neighbouring Academy for Young Ladies to grant a lock of
her hair. One of the young men calls at the school, and asks for Miss

Smith, saying he is her brother, taking a chance that there will be a girl of that surname; also risking (an embarrassment not emphasized) that Miss Smith might be revealed as less than ravishingly beautiful. It turns out that a pretty Miss Smith is indeed employed as a junior mistress. Her real brother has been in India since she was a small child, so that she at once embraces the impostor. All is going well, when the genuine brother arrives. Something might have been made out of this, but Bradley cannot sustain his story. All ends happily, but rather flatly.

Bradley may have seen *The Adventures of Oxymel Classic, Esq.: Once an Oxford Scholar* (anon., 1768); otherwise *Verdant Green* seems to have inaugurated the subsequently proliferating 'Oxford novel' – T. Hughes's *Tom Brown at Oxford* (1861), *The Hypocrite* (1898) by C. Ranger-Gull (the Oxford section wonderfully Ninetyish, the story ending in suicide), Beerbohm's *Zuleika Dobson* (1911), Book Three of *Sinister Street* (1914), by Compton Mackenzie, *Making Conversation* (1931), by Christine Longford (about a woman's college), *Gaudy Night* (1935), by Dorothy L. Sayers – to mention only a few of a long line of Oxford novels, many of interest as period pieces.

Bradley's manuscript had considerable difficulty in finding a publisher. When this was done the work first appeared in three instalments: *Adventures* (1853); *Further Adventures* (1854); *Married and Done For* (1857). All were then bound up together in the last year, and sold in one volume. By 1870 *Verdant Green* had gone to 100,000 copies; sales doubled when the book was issued in sixpenny format. Bradley made only £350 out of the whole transaction, so that his publishers could congratulate themselves on their astuteness.

Twenty years later Bradley attempted a sequel in *Little Mr Bouncer, and His Friend, Verdant Green* (1878). This pendant to the earlier work usually gets rather a bad press. Certainly *Little Mr Bouncer* lacks the full impact of the original, but the author – curiously unchanged once back in his old element – has something to say in the Oxford sections (only about half the book), and these additional Verdant Green trimmings are worth a glance, especially for contemporary language.

Bradley was in the habit of illustrating his novels, and for *Verdant Green* the author's own pictures are beyond question a *sine qua non*. This fact is re-inforced by the Boy's Holiday Library edition (1900), with four plates only, by M. Bede Hewerdine, whose style suggests a hardened illustrator of school stories who has here felt it necessary to impose a faint touch of Pre-Raphaelitism via Walter Crane. The only conceivable reason for choosing Hewerdine (if not a pseudonym) must have been in his middle name.

As a comic draughtsman Bradley might be defined as less professional than Thackeray but funnier, being free of a self-conscious archness of comment that Thackeray's line so often conveys. John Betjeman used many of the *Verdant Green* pictures with good effect throughout *An Oxford University Chest* (1938), something Bradley – and Verdant Green himself – would have appreciated from a future Poet Laureate.

The theme of *Verdant Green* is the classical one of the innocent young man who is taken in by everyone he meets; Oxford providing an ideal setting for hoaxes and swindles perpetrated on a novice. The hero, only son among several daughters of a Warwickshire squire, has on his mother's insistence not attended a public school. His father, never having been to a university, is not greatly drawn to them either, but is persuaded by the local parson, whose own son is already up at Oxford.

'The next question to be decided was, to which of the three Universities should he go – to Oxford, Cambridge, or Durham . . . . Mr Green at once put Durham aside, on account of its infancy, and its want of *prestige* that attaches to the names of the two great Universities.'

Cambridge was next ruled out, Mr Green having heard that 'the great Newton' had been 'horsed' as a Cambridge undergraduate, and fearing such severe discipline might continue at that University. In fact very little is known about Newton's Cambridge days, Mr Green's misapprehension evidently referring to John Aubrey's note about Milton being whipped while at Christ's; interesting in the implication that Verdant Green's father had read, if incorrectly remembered, Malone's selection from the *Brief Lives* (1813).

Oxford therefore it had to be. The local parson arranged for entrance to Brazenface College, the name presumably designating Brasenose, though B.N.C. is also mentioned quite often in the book; once as housing 'a very gentlemanly set'. This was before the period when Brasenose came to be thought of as a predominantly athletic college, its early-nineteenth century reputation having more the sort of distinction Jowett was to achieve for Balliol; that was probably intended by Bradley to be also the Brazenface tone.

Going up at Easter (in what would come to be looked on as a 'by-term' now that the academic year begins in October) Verdant Green travels with his father in a stage-coach, thereby dating the moment to before September 1852, by which time the railway had taken over, coaches ceased to run. Fellow passengers include several under-graduates destined to play a part in Verdant Green's Oxford life, their behaviour heralding what he is in for.

To the great alarm of Green *père* one of these young men, Four-in-hand Fosbrooke (a nickname borrowed without acknowledgement by Galsworthy for Four-in-hand Forsyte in *The Forsyte Saga*), for some miles of the journey takes over the reins from the coachman, causing the vehicle to rock ominously from side to side while (in a phrase from *Little Mr Bouncer*) Fosbrooke is 'tooling the tits'.

Verdant Green, matriculating with a minimum of formality, settles down to be an 'Oxford man'. The undergraduate generation portrayed is that of the late 1840s, early 1850s. Sweeping changes, institutional and social, were to take place in the University very soon, though still short of those to follow in the 1870s. The previous Oxford decade had undergone the heart-searchings of the Tractarian Movement; while Matthew Arnold (Balliol) had won the Newdigate with a poem on Cromwell; a few years later (about the date when the complete *Verdant Green* was published) Swinburne (Balliol) would be proclaiming rampant atheism to the Old Mortality Society.

Verdant Green contains no hint of any such fierce intellectual life. The furthest anyone goes in that direction is for a 'Reading Man', anxious to earn a good degree, to object when the *cornet-à-pistons* or the drum are played too continuously under the window when he is attempting to work.

In *Little Mr Bouncer*, however, there does occur the expression 'aesthetical tastes', one certainly current by the late '70s, though perhaps questionable at the date of Verdant Green's Oxford residence. In any case aestheticism is not invoked in connection with what was later to be known as an 'aesthete'. On the contrary, the phrase is applied to the Hon. Blucher Boots, a raffish young man devoted to racing, who is found in the middle of the morning wearing a 'scarlet Turkish fez' with a crimson-and-blue striped dressing-gown. His rooms are decorated with Landseer prints, Parian statuettes, 'pretty feminine inanities', but horses rather than the arts preoccupy the owner, who tries to ensnare Verdant Green into 'making a book' on the Derby.

More in the ancestry of aesthetes-to-be – though O.U.D.S. aesthetes might be held to have fallen into a rather special category of their own – is the stage-struck Foote (St John's) in *Verdant Green*, known as 'Footelights' on account of his theatrical obsessions. Foote's rooms are hung with 'water-colour drawings by Cattermole, Cox, Fripp, Hunt, and Frederick Tayler' (all still holding their market reasonably well, especially Cox), making a background for suits of armour, Etruscan vases, a Gothic lectern. Foote was accustomed to give imitations of Keane and other famous actors; a trapdoor into the wine-cellar providing an aperture for representing Hamlet in Ophelia's grave.

Another potential aesthete, this time of a gastronomic order, is promised by Towlinson, who always brings into Hall a bottle of *The King of Oude's Sauce* (doubtless a shrewdly-named chutney, Oude then being in the news), but Towlinson, like Blucher Boots, turns out to be sporting in his tastes, belonging, in fact, to a 'bad set' that indulged in cock-fighting.

At this period St Mary's Hall (known as Skimmery) had not yet been absorbed into Oriel, and Worcester was referred to by more centrally situated colleges as Botany Bay. Noblemen still wore gold tassels on their mortar-board caps (a punishment for drunkenness, Verdant Green was told), hence the term tuft-hunter for a snob. When he speaks of the 'Oxford Snobocracy', however, Bradley means what he calls elsewhere the *profanum vulgus*, 'snob' (shoemaker) still denoting a person of lower social status, rather than one over-keen on associating with those of higher rank.

All classes are derided equally by Bradley: rackety aristocrats; prosy dons; pilfering servants; rapacious tradesmen; shady loafers. Verdant Green's scout, Filcher, lives up to his surname, while Mrs Tester, the bedmaker (a female adjunct to become obsolete, then come into fashion again in recent times), is perpetually in need of lumps of sugar soaked in brandy to cure her spasms.

Owing to his spectacles Verdant Green is at once known as Gig-lamps, possibly the earliest instance in print of this subsequently stereotyped nineteenth-century nickname for the bespectacled. Although prototype of all duffers at sport, and pitilessly ragged, he seems to have been generally popular. There is perhaps a slight ambiguity here, which the author never wholly resolves. If Verdant Green were quite so maladroit as represented, would he have gone down well with the 'hearties' in his college?

In rather the same way, after abject failure as dog-owner, horseman, archer, cricketer, fencer, boxer, skater, oar, Verdant Green in the end manages to sit a horse reasonably well, and actually rows in the Brazenface Torpid (second College boat). Could he have so far adjusted himself? Perhaps he could, his innocence and doggedness exerting an invincible charm. His actual allowance is never mentioned, but it seems possible that he was fairly well off, which may have helped. At least his father supplied him with solid silver plate (with crest and motto *Semper virens*), most of which seems to have been 'mislaid' in due course by Filcher.

After his first 'wine' Verdant Green appears to have found no difficulty in joining in with his friends' drinking, and he at once took to smoking, a habit marred only by an occasion when he was lured into inhaling a giant cigar made up of cabbage leaves, brown paper, and refuse tobacco. The convincing account of a hangover suggests that Bradley himself was familiar with those dire symptoms.

Much of Oxford undergraduate life of the period was for the not too fastidious. Over the river from Christ Church meadows lay a field where an itinerant hawker patrolled with a cage of live rats slung on his back. These could be released at sixpence a time for under-graduates to try out the sporting proclivities of their dogs. There were also the recurrent 'Town and Gown' scrimmages, which dated back to the Middle Ages, when medieval undergraduates had been known to lose their lives in these light-hearted rags.

Verdant Green takes part in the time-honoured Town and Gown brawl on the night of the Fifth of November – 'the Saturnalia of Guy-Fawkes' – when his undergraduate acquaintances engage the services of The Putney Pet, a London prize-fighter, to stiffen their ranks in what must have been at times fairly demanding encounters. On this particular evening hostilities are sparked off by a 'slang rhyme of peculiar offensiveness used to a Wadham gentleman'. We may safely assume that the verses in question included the word Sodom, but it is not clear how the townsmen knew that particular undergraduate came from Wadham College; the assumption perhaps causing trouble with someone who was in fact not a Wadhamite.

At the height of the battle we are told that 'a cowardly fellow was using his heavy-heeled boots on the body of a prostrate under-graduate', but 'to the credit of the Town, be it said, they discarded bludgeons and stones, and fought, in John Bull fashion, with their fists'. The Senior Proctor, felled in the mêlée, is rescued by The Pet. The prize-fighter had agreed to wear a mortar-board for the festivities, but could not be induced to assume a gown – even a short commoner's gown – for fear of cramping his pugilistic style. Accordingly the Proctor, once safe behind a College gate, immediately taxes his rescuer with failure to be in correct academic attire.

Muted in modern terms, the subject of sex is not altogether ignored. Indeed one feels that Bradley knew a great deal more than he was prepared to set down on paper. Incidentally his picture of Verdant Green kissing a maid on the stairs on his return from Oxford (p. 130), which appears in some impressions of the book, was omitted from others. Had it caused disapproval? If so, from what quarter?

Verdant Green, walking one day down the High, is attracted by a girl who looks French; and French she turns out to be. Willing to try every sport at least once, 'he stalked this little deer to her lair'. The lair turns out to be a 'fancy hosiery warehouse'; and he spends the next fortnight buying odds and ends he does not in the least want in order to chat with her. One suspects that Madamoiselle Mouslin de Laine (like several of the dons, the waiter at the *Mitre* with a face 'like half a sliced muffin', Filthy Lucre, the dog-seller) may be drawn from life, if only because a French girl employed in an Oxford haberdasher's otherwise sounds so improbable.

The word 'deer' is used again by the author, possibly with a similar connotation in his mind. Verdant Green, on a walk one morning, 'strolled round the neatly-kept potato-gardens denominated the Parks, looking in vain for the deer that have never been there, and finding them represented only by nursery-maids – and others'. But

who were the Others thus separated by a dash? Were they young men
hoping to scrape acquaintance with the nursery-maids, or could tarts
be picked up between the potato-gardens?

There is a further hint of undercover sex, though only in reading-
matter. Verdant Green falls into the habit of taking a punt out on to
the Cherwell, where lounge other undergraduates 'with their legs up
and a weed in their mouth, reading the latest novel, or some less
immaculate work'. But, since novels in those days were apt to be
denigrated as a 'waste of time', is an erotic book implied?

Verdant Green himself seems to have been strongly drawn to the
opposite sex. On the occasion of the Northumberland visit to the
country house of an Oxford friend's parents he immediately falls in
love with one of the girls also staying there; and behaves with notable
bravery when she is threatened by a dangerous bull. (Bulls seem to
have been very much on Bradley's mind, because a similar incident
with another bull takes place only a few pages later.) Unlike most
novels of the period no difficulties whatever are raised by either family
about the young couple becoming engaged.

Once again, since Verdant Green has no apparent job in prospect,
we are led to wonder whether the Green family were not a great deal
richer than generally indicated. It is agreed, reasonably enough, that
the wedding should not be celebrated for two years. Even so, when
Verdant Green formally takes his B.A. degree, he is a married man.
That might well happen today, even more probably at an American
college; but surely a married Oxford undergraduate would have been
very unusual in the 1850s? Perhaps there were sides to Verdant Green
underplayed by the author, and, from what they knew of their son, his
parents were only too thankful to have him married and settled. Indeed the many stories about Verdant Green's vigorous sex life may
have been the reason for his being found so acceptable by his more
dissipated acquaintances.

The naturalist John George Wood (1827–1889) has been put forward as model for Verdant Green's Oxford friend Henry Bouncer
(hero of the sequel). Wood, also a surgeon's son, was one of the
undergraduate companions of Bradley's Oxford interlude, the friendship kept up all their lives, which occupied exactly the same span of
years. Wood, well known in his day as a popular rather than rigorously

scientific writer on his subject, had been at Oxford one of the Merton postmasters; became a clergyman; married; and throughout his life produced a flow of books on natural history, sometimes diverging to other matters like *The Boy's Own Treasury of Sports and Pastimes* (1866).

This looks rather like one of those not uncommon occasions when a character in a novel is automatically identified with someone known to be associated with the author, the parallel drawn with little or no regard to actual resemblance. Wood is described as a 'weakly' child, devoted from his earliest years to natural history, a parson whose churches were noted for their choral services. He may well have been small and noisy, it is true, but one doubts whether even as an under-graduate he ever behaved quite like Bouncer, ceaselessly blowing a post-horn, two rampageous terriers always at his heels, almost illiterate, and cribbing in his exams to avoid being 'plucked'.

Incidentally Bouncer, whose mother, a widow, wishes him to read for the bar, is represented on one page of the book as having been educated at Eton; on another, at Harrow. At first sight this duality might seem improbable, but it must be remembered that Matthew Arnold was at school both at Rugby and Winchester; Trollope at both Winchester and Harrow. Perhaps Bouncer was indeed that rare bird an Old Etonian Old Harrovian.

Bradley has an observant eye, and is well read. One must regret that he represents an early example of that only too common modern aberration of saying Frankenstein instead of Frankenstein's Monster, but against that he perceptively draws attention to the 'impossible gownsman' in Turner's *View of Oxford, from Ferry Hincksey*. When he quotes Tweedledum and Tweedledee they are from John Byrom ('Christians, awake! Salute the happy morn'), rather than Lewis Car-roll's *Alice*. There are informative vignettes like Verdant Green's visit as a tourist to Blenheim, showing how far from recent is the Stately Home industry, and how much more exorbitant in the past; a servant taking the sightseer a short way, then handing him on to a series of other flunkies with the words: 'I don't go any further, sir; half-a-crown!'

In his *Notes sur l'Angleterre* (1872) the French philosopher and historian Hippolyte Taine employs *Aventures de M. Verdant Green, illustré par l'auteur* as one of the keys to English university life. Taine (whose investigations in England had taken place in the 1860s, when in some respects Oxford was already changed in tone from the Verdant Green period), records the hero's 'passion naissante pour une grisette', concluding from all he had heard and read that in English universities drunkenness was more permissible than libertinism. Taine (incidentally, an admirer of Casanova's *Memoirs*) found the novel 'un petit roman assez gai'; no doubt an excellent example of his own theories as to 'la race, le milieu et le moment'.

When towards the end of the century Gladstone (Christ Church) found himself in Oxford after an interval of many years, the veteran Oxonian was appalled by the slovenly aspect of the bowler-hatted undergraduates. He himself had been up about twenty years before Verdant Green, in whose day there would still probably have been little to find fault with in the way of undergraduate turn-out. One wonders what either of them would think on returning to an Oxford where Town and Gown are indistinguishable; even male and female sometimes requiring a second look. An updated *Verdant Green* might achieve something amusing and penetrating in the way of satire.

PART I

CHAPTER I

Mr Verdant Green's Relatives and Antecedents.

IF you will refer to the unpublished volume of *Burke's Landed Gentry*, and turn to letter G, article 'GREEN', you will see that the Verdant Greens are a family of some respectability and of considerable antiquity. We meet with them as early as 1096, flocking to the Crusades among the followers of Peter the Hermit, when one of their name, Greene surnamed the Witless, mortgaged his lands in order to supply his poorer companions with the sinews of war. The family estate, however, appears to have been redeemed and greatly increased by his great-grandson, Hugo de Greene, but was again jeoparded in the year 1456, when Basil Greene, being commissioned by Henry the Sixth to enrich his sovereign by discovering the philosopher's stone, squandered the greater part of his fortune in unavailing experiments; while his son, who was also infected with the spirit of the age, was blown up in his laboratory when just on the point of discovering the elixir of life. It seems to have been about this time that the Greenes became connected by marriage with the equally old family of the Verdants; and, in the year 1510, we find a Verdant Greene as Justice of the Peace for the County of Warwick, presiding at the trial of three decrepid old women, who, being found guilty of transforming themselves into cats, and in that shape attending the nightly assemblies of evil spirits, were very properly pronounced by him to be witches, and were burnt with all due solemnity.

In tracing the records of the family, we do not find that any of its members attained to great eminence in the state, either in the counsels of the senate or the active services of the field; or that they amassed any unusual amount of wealth or landed property. But we may perhaps ascribe these circumstances to the fact of finding the Greens, generation after generation, made the dupes of more astute minds, and when the hour of danger came, left to manage their own affairs in the best way they could – a way that commonly ended in their mismanagement and total confusion. Indeed, the idiosyncrasy of the family appears to have been so well known, that we continually meet with them performing the character of catspaw to some monkey who had seen and understood much more of the world than they had – putting their hands to the fire, and only finding out their mistake when they had burned their fingers.

In this way the family of the Verdant Greens never got beyond a certain point either in wealth or station, but were always the same unsuspicious, credulous, respectable, easy-going people in one century as another, with the same boundless confidence in their fellow-creatures, and the same readiness to oblige society by putting their names to little bills, merely for form's and friendship's sake. The Vavasour Verdant Green, with the slashed velvet doublet and point-lace fall, who (having a well-stocked purse) was among the favoured courtiers of the Merry Monarch, and who allowed that monarch in his merriness to borrow his purse, with the simple IOU of 'Odd's fish! you shall take mine to-morrow!' and who never (of course) saw the sun rise on the day of repayment, was but the prototype of the Verdant Greens in the full-bottomed wigs, and buckles and shorts of George I's day, who were nearly beggared by the bursting of the Mississippi Scheme and South-Sea Bubble; and these, in their turn, were duly represented by their successors. And thus the family character was handed down with the family nose, until they both re-appeared (according to the veracious chronicle of Burke, to which we have referred) in

'VERDANT GREEN, of the Manor Green, Co. Warwick, Gent., who married Mary, only surviving child of Samuel Sappey, Esq., of Sapcot Hall, Co. Salop; by whom he has issue, one son, and three daughters: Mary, VERDANT, Helen, Fanny.'

Mr Burke is unfeeling enough to give the dates when this bunch of Greens first made their appearance in the world; but these dates we withhold, from a delicate regard to personal feelings, which will be duly appreciated by those who have felt the sacredness of their domestic hearth to be tampered with by the obtrusive impertinences of a census-paper.

It is sufficient for our purpose to say that our hero, Mr Verdant Green, junior, was born much in the same way as other folk. And although pronounced by Mrs Toosypegs˙his nurse, when yet in the first crimson blush of his existence, to be 'a perfect progidy, mum, which I ought to be able to pronounce, 'avin nuss'd a many parties through their trouble, and bein aweer of what is doo to a Hinfant', yet we are not aware that his *début* on the stage of life, although thus applauded by such a *clacqueur* as the indiscriminating Toosypegs, was announced to the world at large by any other means than the notices in the county papers, and the six-shilling advertisement in *The Times*.

'Progidy' though he was, even as a baby, yet Mr Verdant Green's nativity seems to have been chronicled merely in this everyday manner, and does not appear to have been accompanied by any of those more monstrous phenomena, which in earlier ages attended the production of a *genuine* prodigy. We are not aware that Mrs Green's favourite Alderney spoke on that occasion, or conducted itself otherwise than as unaccustomed to public speaking as usual. Neither can we verify the assertion of the intelligent Mr Mole the gardener, that the plaster Apollo in the Long Walk was observed to be bathed in a profuse perspiration, either from its feeling compelled to keep up the good old classical custom, or because the weather was damp. Neither are we bold enough to entertain an opinion that the chickens in the poultry-yard refused their customary food; or that the horses in the stable shook with trembling fear; or that any thing, or any body, saving and excepting Mrs Toosypegs, betrayed any consciousness that a real and genuine prodigy had been given to the world.

However, during the first two years of his life, which were passed chiefly in drinking, crying, and sleeping, Mr Verdant Green met with as much attention, and received as fair a share of approbation, as usually falls to the lot of the most favoured of infants. Then Mrs Toosypegs again took up her position in the house, and his reign was over. Faithful to her mission, she pronounced the new baby to be *the* 'progidy', and she was believed. But thus it is all through life; the new baby displaces the old; the second love supplants the first; we find fresh friends to shut out the memories of former ones; and in nearly everything we discover that there is a Number 2 which can put out of joint the nose of Number 1.

Once more the shadow of Mrs Toosypegs fell upon the walls of Manor Green; and then her mission being accomplished, she passed away for ever; and our hero was left to be the sole son and heir, and the prop and pride of the house of Green.

And if it be true that the external forms of nature exert a hidden but powerful sway over the dawning perceptions of the mind, and shape its thoughts to harmony with the things around, then most certainly ought Mr Verdant Green to have been born a poet; for he grew up amid those scenes whose immortality is that they inspired the soul of Shakespeare with his deathless fancies!

The Manor Green was situated in one of the loveliest spots in all Warwickshire, a county so rich in all that constitutes the picturesqueness of a true English landscape. Looking from the drawing-room windows of the house, you saw in the near foreground the pretty French garden, with its fantastic parti-coloured beds, and its broad gravelled walks and terrace; proudly promenading which, or perched on the stone balustrade, might be seen perchance a peacock flaunting his beauties in the sun. Then came the carefully kept gardens, bounded on the one side by the Long Walk and a grove of shrubs and oaks; and on the other side by a double avenue of stately elms, that led through velvet turf of brightest green, down past a little rustic lodge, to a gently sloping valley, where were white walls and rose-clustered gables of cottages peeping out from the embosoming trees, that betrayed the village beauties they seemed loth to hide. Then came the grey church-tower, dark with shrouding ivy; then another clump of stately elms, tenanted by cawing rooks; then a yellow stretch of bright meadow-land, dappled over with browsing kine knee-deep in grass and flowers; then a deep pool that mirrored all, and shone like silver; then more trees with floating shade, and homesteads rich in wheat-stacks; then a willowy brook that sparkled on merrily to an old mill-wheel, whose slippery stairs it lazily got down, and sank to quiet rest in the stream below; then came, crowding in rich profusion, wide-spreading woods and antlered oaks; and golden gorse and purple heather; and sunny orchards, with their dark-green waves that in Spring foamed white with blossoms; and then gently swelling hills that rose to close the scene and frame the picture.

Such was the view from the Manor Green. And, full of inspiration as such a scene was, yet Mr Verdant Green never accomplished (as far as poetical inspiration was concerned) more than an 'Address to the Moon,' which he could just as well have written in any other part of the country, and which, commencing with the noble aspiration,

> O moon, that shinest in the heaven so blue,
> I only wish that I could shine like you!

and terminating with one of those fine touches of nature which rise superior to the trammels of ordinary versification,

> But I to bed must be going soon,
> So I will not address thee more, O moon!

will no doubt go down to posterity in the Album of his sister Mary.

For the first fourteen years of his life, the education of Mr Verdant Green was conducted wholly under the shadow of his paternal roof, upon principles fondly imagined to be the soundest and purest for the formation of his character. Mrs Green, who was as good and motherly a soul as ever lived, was yet (as we have shown) one of the Sappeys of Sapcot, a family that were not renowned either for common sense or worldly wisdom, and her notions of a boy's education were of that kind laid down by her favourite poet, Cowper, in his 'Tirocinium', that we are

> Well-tutor'd *only* while we share
> A mother's lectures and a nurse's care;

and in her horror of all other kind of instruction (not that she admitted Mrs Toosypegs to her counsels), she fondly kept Master Verdant at her own apron-strings. The task of teaching his young idea how to shoot was committed chiefly to his sisters' governess, and he regularly took his place with them in the school-room. These daily exercises and mental drillings were subject to the inspection of their maiden-aunt, Miss Virginia Verdant, a first cousin of Mr Green's, who had come to visit at the Manor during Master Verdant's infancy, and had remained there ever since; and this generalship was crowned with such success, that her nephew grew up the girlish companion of his sisters, with no knowledge of boyish sports, and no desire for them.

The motherly and spinsterial views regarding his education were favoured by the fact that he had no playmates of his own sex and age; and since his father was an only child, and his mother's brothers had died in their infancy, there were no cousins to initiate him into the mysteries of boyish games and feelings. Mr Green was a man who only cared to live a quiet, easy-going life, and would have troubled himself but little about his neighbours, if he had had any; but the Manor Green lay in an agricultural district, and, saving the Rectory, there was no other large house for miles around. The rector's wife, Mrs Larkyns, had died shortly after the birth of her first child, a son, who was being educated at a public school; and this was enough, in Mrs Green's eyes, to make a too intimate acquaintance between her boy and Master Larkyns a thing by no means to be desired. With her favourite poet she would say,

> For public schools, 'tis public folly feeds;

and, regarding them as the very hotbeds of all that is wrong, she would turn a deaf, though polite, ear to the rector whenever he said, 'Why don't you let your Verdant go with my Charley? Charley is three years older than Verdant, and would take him under his wing.' Mrs Green would as soon think of putting one of her chickens under the wing of a hawk, as intrusting the innocent Verdant to the care of the scapegrace Charley; so she still persisted in her own system of education, despite all that the rector could advise to the contrary.

As for Master Verdant, he was only too glad at his mother's decision, for he partook of all her alarm about public schools, though from a different cause. It was not very often that he visited at the Rectory during Master Charley's holidays; but when he did, that young gentleman favoured him with such accounts of the peculiar knack the second master possessed of finding out all your tenderest places when he licked a feller for a false quantity that, by Jove! you couldn't sit down for a fortnight without squeaking; and of the jolly mills they used to have with the town cads, who would lie in wait for you, and half kill you if they caught you alone; and of the fun it was to make a junior form fag for you, and do all your dirty work; that

Master Verdant's hair would almost stand on end at such horrors, and he would gasp for very dread lest such should ever be *his* dreadful doom.

And then Master Charley would take a malicious pleasure in consoling him, by saying, 'Of course, you know, you'll only have to fag for the first two or three years; then – if you get into the fourth form – you'll be able to have a fag for yourself. And it's awful fun, I can tell you, to see the way some of the fags get riled at cricket! You get a feller to give you a few balls, just for practice, and you hit the ball into another feller's ground; and then you tell your fag to go and pick it up. So he goes to do it, when the other feller sings out, "Don't touch that ball, or I'll lick you!" So you tell the fag to come to you, and you say, "Why don't you do as I tell you?" And he says, "Please, sir!" and then the little beggar blubbers. So you say to him, "None of that, sir! Touch your toes!" We always make 'em wear straps on purpose. And then his trousers go tight and beautiful, and you take out your strap and warm him! And then he goes to get the ball, and the other fellow sings out, "I told you to let that ball alone! Come here, sir! Touch your toes!" So he warms him too; and then we go on all jolly. It's awful fun, I can tell you!'

Master Verdant would think it awful indeed; and, by his own fireside, would recount the deeds of horror to his trembling mother and sisters, whose imagination shuddered at the scenes from which they hoped their darling would be preserved.

Perhaps Master Charley had his own reasons for making matters worse than they really were; but, as long as the information he derived concerning public schools was of this description, so long did Master Verdant Green feel thankful at being kept away from them. He had a secret dread, too, of his friend's superior age and knowledge; and in his presence felt a bashful awe that made him glad to get back from the Rectory to his own sisters; while Master Charley, on the other hand, entertained a lad's contempt for one that could not fire off a gun, or drive a cricket-ball, or jump a ditch without falling into it. So the Rectory and the Manor Green lads saw but very little of each other; and while the one went through his public-school course, the other was brought up at the women's apron-string.

But though thus put under petticoat government, Mr Verdant

Green was not altogether freed from those tyrants of youth the dead languages. His aunt Virginia was as learned a Blue as her esteemed ancestress in the court of Elizabeth, the very Virgin Queen of Blues; and under her guidance Master Verdant was dragged with painful diligence through the first steps of the road that was to take him to Parnassus. It was a great sight to see her sitting stiff and straight – with her wonderfully undeceptive 'false front' of (somebody else's) black hair, graced on either side by four sausage-looking curls – as, with spectacles on nose and dictionary in hand, she instructed her nephew in those ingenuous arts which should soften his manners, and not permit him to be brutal. And, when they together entered upon the romantic page of Virgil (which was the extent of her classical reading), nothing would delight her more than to declaim their sonorous Arma-virumque-cano lines, where the intrinsic qualities of the verse sur-passed the quantities that she gave to them.

Fain would Miss Virginia have made Virgil the end and aim of an educational existence, and so have kept her pupil entirely under her own care; but, alas! she knew nothing further; she had no acquaintance with Greek, and she had never flirted with Euclid; and the rector persuaded Mr Green that these were indispensable to a boy's educa-tion. So, when Mr Verdant Green was (in stable language) 'rising' sixteen, he went thrice a week to the Rectory, where Mr Larkyns bestowed upon him a couple of hours, and taught him to conjugate τύπτω, and get over the *Pons Asinorum*. Mr Larkyns found his pupil not a particularly brilliant scholar, but he was a plodding one; and, though he learned slowly, yet the little he did learn was learned well.

Thus the Rectory and the home studies went hand and hand, and continued so, with but little interruption, for more than two years; and Mr Verdant Green had for some time assumed the *toga virilis* of stick-up collars and swallow-tail coats, that so effectually cut us off from the age of innocence; and the small family festival that annually celebrated his birthday had just been held for the eighteenth time, when

A change came o'er the spirit of *his* dream.

CHAPTER II

Mr Verdant Green is to be an Oxford-man.

ONE day when the family at the Manor Green had assembled for luncheon, the rector was announced. He came in and joined them, saying, with his usual friendly *bonhomie*, 'A very well-timed visit, I think! Your bell rang out its summons as I came up the avenue. Mrs Green, I've gone through the formality of looking over the accounts of your clothing-club, and, as usual, I find them correctness itself; and here is my subscription for the next year. Miss Green, I hope that you have not forgotten the lesson in logic that Tommy Jones gave you yesterday afternoon?'

'Oh, what was that?' cried her two sisters; who took it in turns with her to go for a short time in every day to the village-school which their father and the rector had established: 'Pray tell us, Mr Larkyns! Mary has said nothing about it.'

'Then', replied the rector, 'I am tongue-tied, until I have my fair friend's permission to reveal how the teacher was taught.'

Mary shook her sunny ringlets, and laughingly gave him the required permission.

'You must know, then,' said Mr Larkyns, 'that Miss Mary was giving one of those delightful object lessons, wherein she blends so much instructive –'

'I'll trouble you for the butter, Mr Larkyns,' interrupted Mary, rather maliciously.

The rector was grey-headed, and a privileged friend. 'My dear,' he said, 'I was just giving it you. However, the object-lesson was going on; the subject being *Quadrupeds* which Miss Mary very properly explained to be "things with four legs". Presently, she said to her class, "Tell me the names of some quadrupeds?" when Tommy Jones, thrusting out his hand with the full conviction that he was making an important suggestion, exclaimed, "Chairs and tables!" That was turning the tables upon Miss Mary with a vengeance!'

During luncheon the conversation glided into a favourite theme with Mrs Green and Miss Virginia – Verdant's studies: when Mr Larkyns, after some good-natured praise of his diligence, said, 'By the way, Green, he's now quite old enough, and prepared enough for matriculation: and I suppose you are thinking of it.'

Mr Green was thinking of no such thing. He had never been at college himself, and had never heard of his father having been there; and having the old-fashioned, what-was-good-enough-for-my-father-is-good-enough-for-me sort of feeling, it had never occurred to him that his son should be brought up otherwise than he himself had been. The setting-out of Charles Larkyns for college, two years before, had suggested no other thought to Mr Green's mind, than that a university was the natural sequence of a public school; and since Verdant had not been through the career of the one, he deemed him to be exempt from the other.

The motherly ears of Mrs Green had been caught by the word 'matriculation', a phrase quite unknown to her; and she said, 'If it's vaccination that you mean, Mr Larkyns, my dear Verdant was done only last year, when we thought the small-pox was about; so I think he's quite safe.'

Mr Larkyn's politeness was sorely tried to restrain himself from giving vent to his feelings in a loud burst of laughter; but Mary gallantly came to his relief by saying, 'Matriculation means, being entered at a university. Don't you remember, dearest mamma, when Mr Charles Larkyns went up to Oxford to be matriculated last January two years?'

'Ah, yes! I do now. But I wish I had your memory, my dear.'

And Mary blushed, and flattered herself that she succeeded in looking as though Mr Charles Larkyns and his movements were objects of perfect indifference to her.

So, after luncheon, Mr Green and the rector paced up and down the long-walk, and talked the matter over. The burden of Mr Green's discourse was this: 'You see, sir, I don't intend my boy to go into the Church, like yours; but, when anything happens to me, he'll come into the estate, and have to settle down as the squire of the parish. So I don't exactly see what would be the use of sending him to a university, where, I dare say, he'd spend a good deal of money – not that I should grudge that, though – and perhaps not be quite such a good lad as he's always been to me, sir. And, by George! (I beg your pardon,) I think his mother would break her heart to lose him; and I don't know what we should do without him, as he's never been away from us a day, and his sisters would miss him. And he's not a lad, like your Charley, that could fight his way in the world, and I don't think he'd be altogether happy. And as he's not got to depend upon his talents for his bread and cheese, the knowledge he's got at home, and from you sir, seems to me quite enough to carry him through life. So, altogether, I think Verdant will do very well as he is, and perhaps we'd better say no more about the matriculation.'

But the rector *would* say more; and he expressed his mind thus: 'It is not so much from what Verdant would learn in Latin and Greek, and such things as make up a part of the education, that I advise your sending him to a university; but more from what he would gain by mixing with a large body of young men of his own age, who represent the best classes of a mixed society, and who may justly be taken as fair samples of its feelings and talents. It is formation of character that I regard as one of the greatest of the many great ends of a university system; and if for this reason alone, I should advise you to send your future country squire to college. Where else will he be able to meet with so great a number of those of his own class, with whom he will have to mix in the after changes of life, and for whose feelings and tone a college-course will give him the proper key-note? Where else can he learn so quickly in three years – what other men will perhaps be striving for through life without attaining – that self-reliance which will enable him to mix at ease in any society, and to feel the equal of its members? And, besides all this – and each of these points in the education of a young man is, to my mind, a strong one, – where else could he be more completely "under tutors and governors", and more thoroughly under *surveillance*, than in a place where college-laws are no respecters of persons, and seek to keep the wild blood of youth within its due bounds? There is something in the very atmosphere of a university that seems to engender refined thoughts and noble feelings; and lamentable indeed must be the state of any young man who can pass through the three years of his college residence, and bring away no higher aims, no worthier purposes, no better thoughts, from all the holy associations which have been crowded around him. Such advantages as these are not to be regarded with indifference; and though they come in secondary ways, and possess the mind almost imperceptibly, yet they are of primary importance in the formation of character, and may mould it into the more perfect man. And as long as I had the power, I would no more think of depriving a child of mine of such good means towards a good end, than I would of keeping him from anything else that was likely to improve his mind or affect his heart.'

Mr Larkyns put matters in a new light; and Mr Green began to think that a university career might be looked at from more than one point of view. But as old prejudices are not so easily overthrown as the lath-and-plaster erections of mere newly-formed opinion, Mr Green was not yet won over by Mr Larkyns's arguments. 'There was my father,' he said, 'who was one of the worthiest and kindest men living; and I believe he never went to college, nor did he think it necessary that I should go; and I trust I'm no worse a man than my father.'

'Ah! Green,' replied the rector; 'the old argument! But you must not judge the present age by the past; nor measure out to *your* son the same degree of education that your father might think sufficient for *you*. When you and I were boys, Green, these things were thought of very differently to what they are in the present day; and when your father gave you a respectable education at a classical school, he did all that he thought was requisite to form you into a country gentleman, and fit you for that station in life you were destined to fill. But consider what a progressive age it is that we live in; and you will see that the standard of education has been considerably raised since the days when you and I did the "propria quæ maribus" together; and that when he comes to mix in society, more will be demanded of the son than was expected from the father. And besides this, think in how many ways it will benefit Verdant to send him to college. By mixing more in the world, and being called upon to act and think for himself, he will gradually gain that experience without which a man cannot arm himself to meet the difficulties that beset all of us, more or less, in the battle of life. He is just of an age when some change from the narrowed circle of home is necessary. God forbid that I should ever speak in any but the highest terms of the moral good it must do every young man to live under his mother's watchful eye, and be ever in the company of pure-minded sisters. Indeed I feel this more perhaps than many other parents would, because my lad, from his earliest years, has been deprived of such tender training, and cut off from such sweet society. But yet, with all this high regard for such home influences, I put it to you, if there will not grow up in the boy's mind, when he begins to draw near to man's estate, a very weariness of all this, from its very sameness; a surfeiting, as it were, of all these delicacies, and a longing for something to break the monotony of what will gradually become to him a humdrum horse-in-the-mill kind of country life? And it is just at this critical time that college life steps in to his aid. With his new life a new light bursts upon his mind; he finds that he is not the little household-god he had fancied himself to be; his word is no longer the law of the Medes and Persians, as it was at home; he meets with none of those little flatteries from partial relatives, or fawning servants, that were growing into a part of his existence; but he has to bear contradiction and reproof, to find himself only an equal with others, when he can gain that equality by his own deserts; and, in short, he daily progresses in that knowledge of himself, which, from the *gnothiseauton* days down to our own, has been found to be about the most useful of all knowledge; for it gives a man stability of character, and braces up his mental energies to a healthy enjoyment of the business of life. And so, Green I would advise you, above all things, to let Verdant go to college.

Much more did the rector say, not only on this occasion, but on others; and the more frequently he returned to the charge, the less resistance were his arguments met with; and the result was, that Mr Green was fully persuaded that a university was the proper sphere for his son to move in. But it was not without many a pang and much secret misgiving that Mrs Green would consent to suffer her beloved Verdant to run the risk of those dreadful contaminations which she imagined would inevitably accompany every college career. Indeed, she thought it an act of the greatest heroism (or, if you object to the word, heroineism,) to be won over to say 'yes' to the proposal; and it was not until Miss Virginia had recited to her the deeds of all the mothers of Greece and Rome who had suffered for their children's sake, that Mrs Green would consent to sacrifice her maternal feelings at the sacred altar of duty.

When the point had been duly settled, that Mr Verdant Green was to receive a university education, the next question to be decided was, to which of the three Universities should he go? To Oxford, Cambridge, or Durham? But this was a matter which was soon determined upon. Mr Green at once put Durham aside, on account of its infancy, and its wanting the *prestige* that attaches to the names of the two great Universities. Cambridge was treated quite as summarily, because Mr Green had conceived the notion that nothing but mathematics were ever thought or talked of there; and as he himself had always had an abhorrence of them from his youth up, when he was hebdomadally flogged for not getting-up his weekly propositions, he thought that his son should be spared some of the personal disagreeables that he himself had encountered; for Mr Green remembered to have heard that the great Newton was horsed during the time that he was a Cambridge undergraduate, and he had a hazy idea that the same indignities were still practised there.

But the circumstance that chiefly decided Mr Green to choose Oxford as the arena for Verdant's performances was, that he would have a companion, and, as he hoped, a mentor, in the rector's son, Mr Charles Larkyns, who would not only be able to cheer him on his first entrance, but also would introduce him to select and quiet friends, put him in the way of lectures, and initiate him into all the mysteries of the place; all which the rector professed his son would be glad to do, and would be delighted to see his old friend and playfellow within the classic walls of Alma Mater.

Oxford having been selected for the university, the next point to be decided was the college.

'You cannot', said the rector, 'find a much better college than Brazenface, where my lad is. It always stands well in the class-list, and keeps a good name with its tutors. There are a nice gentlemanly set of men there; and I am proud to say that my lad would be able to introduce Verdant to some of the best. This will of course be much to his advantage. And besides this, I am on very intimate terms with Dr Portman, the Master of the college; and, if they should not happen to be very full, no doubt I could get Verdant admitted at once. This too will be of advantage to him; for I can tell you that there are secrets in all these matters, and that at many colleges that I could name, unless you knew the principal, or had some introduction or other potent spell to work with, your son's name would have to remain on the books two or three years before he could be entered; and this, at Verdant's age, would be a serious objection. At one or two of the colleges, indeed, this is almost necessary, under any circumstances, on account of the great number of applicants; but at Brazenface there is not this over-crowding; and I have no doubt, if I write to Dr Portman, but what I can get rooms for Verdant without much loss of time.'

'Brazenface be it then!' said Mr Green, 'and I am sure that Verdant will enter there with very many advantages; and the sooner the better, so that he may be the longer with Mr Charles. But when must his – his what-d'ye-call-it, come off?'

'His matriculation?' replied the rector. 'Why, although it is not usual for men to commence residence at the time of their matricula-tion, still it is sometimes done. And as my lad will, if all goes on well, be leaving Oxford next year, perhaps it would be better, on that account, that Verdant should enter upon his residence as soon as he has matriculated.'

Mr Green thought so too; and Verdant, upon being appealed to, had no objection to this course, or, indeed, to any other that was decided to be necessary for him; though it must be confessed, that he secretly shared somewhat of his mother's feelings as he looked forward into the blank and uncertain prospect of his college life. Like a good and dutiful son, however, his father's wishes were law; and he no more thought of opposing them, than he did of discovering the North Pole, or paying off the National Debt.

So all this being duly settled, and Mrs Green being entirely won over to the proceeding, the rector at once wrote to Dr Portman, and in due time received a reply to the effect that they were very full at Brazenface, but that luckily there was one set of rooms which would be vacant at the commencement of the Easter term; at which time he should be very glad to see the gentleman his friend spoke of.

Portraits of

MR. VERDANT GREEN AND HIS FAMILY.

1. Mr. Green, senior.
2. Miss Virginia Verdant.
3. Mrs. Green.
4. Mr. Verdant Green.
5. Miss Helen Green.
6. Miss Fanny Green.
7. Miss Mary Green.

CHAPTER III

Mr Verdant Green leaves the Home of his Ancestors.

THE time till Easter passed very quickly, for much had to be done in it. Verdant read up most desperately for his matriculation, associating that initiatory examination with the most dismal visions of plucking, and other college tortures.

His mother was laying in for him a new stock of linen, sufficient in quantity to provide him for years of emigration; while his father was busying himself about the plate that it was requisite to take, buying it brand-new, and of the most solid silver, and having it splendidly engraved with the family crest, and the motto 'Semper virens'.

Infatuated Mr Green! If you could have foreseen that those spoons and forks would have soon passed – by a mysterious system of loss which undergraduate powers can never fathom – into the property of Mr Robert Filcher, the excellent, though occasionally erratic, scout of your beloved son, and from thence have melted, not 'into thin air', but into a residuum whose mass might be expressed by the equivalent of coins of a thin and golden description – if you could but have foreseen this, then, infatuated but affectionate parent, you would have been content to have let your son and heir represent the ancestral wealth by mere electro-plate, albata, or any sham that would equally well have served his purpose!

As for Miss Virginia Verdant, and the other woman portion of the Green community, they fully occupied their time until the day of separation came, by elaborating articles of feminine workmanship, as *souvenirs*, by which dear Verdant might, in the land of the strangers, recall visions of home. These were presented to him with all due state on the morning of the day previous to that on which he was to leave the home of his ancestors.

All the articles were useful as well as ornamental. There was a purse from Helen, which, besides being a triumph of art in the way of bead decoration, was also, it must be allowed, a very useful present, unless one happened to carry one's riches in a *porte-*

monnaie. There was a pair of braces from Mary, worked with an ecclesiastical pattern of a severe character – very appropriate for academical wear, and extremely effective for all occasions when the coat had to be taken off in public. And there was a watch-pocket from Fanny, to hang over Verdant's night-capped head, and serve as a depository for the golden mechanical turnip that had been handed down in the family, as a watch, for the last three generations. And there was a pair of woollen comforters knit by Miss Virginia's own fair hands; and there were other woollen articles of domestic use, which were contributed by Mrs Green for her son's personal comfort. To these, Miss Virginia thoughtfully added an infallible recipe for the toothache, an infliction to which she was a martyr, and for the general relief of which in others she constituted herself a species of toothache missionary; for, as she said, 'You might, my dear Verdant, be seized with that painful disease, and not have me by your side to cure it:' which it was very probable he would not, if college rules were strictly carried out at Brazenface.

All these articles were presented to Mr Verdant Green with many speeches and great ceremony; while Mr Green stood by, and smiled benignantly upon the scene, and his son beamed through his glasses (which his defective sight obliged him constantly

to wear) with the most serene aspect.

It was altogether a great day of preparation, and one which it was well for the constitution of the household did not happen very often; for the house was reduced to that summerset condition usually known in domestic parlance as 'upside down.' Mr Verdant Green personally superintended the packing of his goods; a performance which was only effected by the united strength of the establishment. Butler, Footman, Coachman, Lady's-maid, House-maid, and Buttons were all pressed into the service; and the coachman, being a man of some weight, was found to be of great use in effecting a junction of the locks and hasps of over-filled book-boxes. It was astonishing to see all the amount of literature that Mr Verdant Green was about to convey to the seat of learning: there was enough to stock a small Bodleian. As the owner stood with his hands behind him, placidly surveying the scene of preparation, a meditative spectator might have possibly compared him to the hero of the engraving 'Moses going to the fair', that was then hanging just over his head; for no one could have set out for the great Oxford booth of this Vanity Fair with more simplicity and trusting confidence than Mr Verdant Green.

When the trunks had at last been packed, they were then, by the

thoughtful suggestion of Miss Virginia, provided each with a canvas covering, after the manner of the luggage of females, and labelled with large direction-cards filled with the most ample particulars concerning their owner and his destination.

It had been decided that Mr Verdant Green, instead of reaching Oxford by rail, should make his *entrée* behind the four horses that drew the Birmingham and Oxford coach – one of the few four-horse coaches that still ran for any distance* and which, as the more pleasant means of conveyance, was generally patronised by Mr Charles Larkyns in preference to the rail; for the coach passed within three miles of the Manor Green, whereas the nearest railway was at a much greater distance, and could not be so conveniently reached. Mr Green had determined upon accompanying Verdant to Oxford, that he might have the satisfaction of seeing him safely landed there, and might also himself form an acquaintance with a city of which he had heard so much, and which would be doubly interesting to him now that his son was enrolled a member of its University. Their seats had been secured a fortnight previous; for the rector had told Mr Green that so many men went up by the coach, that unless he made an early application, he would altogether fail in obtaining places; so a letter had been dispatched to the 'Swan' coach-office at Birmingham, from which place the coach started, and two outside seats had been put at Mr Green's disposal.

The day at length arrived, when Mr Verdant Green for the first time in his life (on any important occasion) was to leave the paternal roof; and it must be confessed that it was a proceeding which caused him some anxiety, and that he was not sorry when the carriage was at the door to bear him away, before (shall it be confessed?) his tears had got the mastery over him. As it was, by the judicious help of his sisters, he passed the Rubicon in courageous style, and went through the form of breakfast with the greatest hilarity, although with several narrow escapes of suffocation from choking. The thought that he was going to be an Oxford MAN fortunately assisted him in the preservation of that tranquil dignity and careless ease which he considered to be the necessary adjuncts of the manly character, more especially as developed in that peculiar biped he was about to be transformed into; and Mr Verdant Green was enabled to say 'Good-bye' with a firm voice and undimmed spectacles.

All crowded to the door to have a last shake of the hand; the maidservants peeped from the upper windows; and Miss Virginia sobbed out a blessing, which was rendered of a striking and original character by being mixed up with instructions never to forget what she had

* This well-known coach ceased to run between Birmingham and Oxford in the last week of August 1852, on the opening of the Birmingham and Oxford Railway.

taught him in his Latin grammar, and always to be careful to guard
against the toothache. And amid the good-byes and write-oftens that
usually accompany a departure, the carriage rolled down the avenue
to the lodge, where was Mr Mole the gardener, and also Mrs Mole,
and, moreover, the Mole olive-branches, all gathered at the open gate

to say farewell to the young master. And just as they were about to
mount the hill leading out of the village, who should be there but the
rector lying in wait for them and ready to walk up the hill by their side,
and say a few kindly words at parting. Well might Mr Verdant Green
begin to regard himself as the topic of the village, and think that going
to Oxford was really an affair of some importance.

They were in good time for the coach; and the ringing notes of the
guard's bugle made them aware of its approach some time before they
saw it rattling merrily along in its cloud of dust. What a sight it was
when it did come near! The cloud that had enveloped it was discovered

to be not dust only, but smoke from the cigars, meerschaums, and short clay pipes of a full complement of gentlemen passengers, scarcely one of whom seemed to have passed his twentieth year. No bonnet betokening a female traveller could be seen either inside or out; and that lady was indeed lucky who escaped being an inside passenger on the following day. Nothing but a lapse of time, or the complete re-lining of the coach, could purify it from the attacks of the four gentle-men who were now doing their best to convert it into a divan; and the consumption of tobacco on that day between Birmingham and Oxford must have materially benefited the revenue. The passengers were not limited to the two-legged ones, there were four-footed ones also. Sporting dogs, fancy dogs, ugly dogs, rat-killing dogs, short-haired dogs, long-haired dogs, dogs like muffs, dogs like mops, dogs of all colours and of all breeds and sizes, appeared thrusting out their black noses from all parts of the coach. Portmanteaus were piled upon the roof; gun-boxes peeped out suspiciously here and there; bundles of sticks, canes, foils, fishing-rods, and whips, appeared strapped together in every direction; while all round about the coach, 'Like a swarth Indian with his belt of beads', hat-boxes dangled in leathery profusion. The Oxford coach on an occasion like this was a sight to be remembered.

A 'Wo-ho-ho, my beauties!' brought the smoking wheelers upon their haunches; and Jehu, saluting with his elbow and whip finger, called out in the husky voice peculiar to a dram-drinker, 'Are you the two houtside gents for Hoxfut?' To which Mr Green replied in the affirmative; and while the luggage (the canvas-covered, ladylike look of which was such a contrast to that of the other passengers) was being quickly transferred to the coach-top, he and Verdant ascended to the places reserved for them behind the coachman. Mr Green saw at a glance that all the passengers were Oxford men, dressed in every variety of Oxford fashion, and exhibiting a pleasing diversity of Ox-ford manners. Their private remarks on the two new-comers were, like stage 'asides', perfectly audible.

'Decided case of governor!' said one.

'Undoubted ditto of freshman!' observed another.

'Looks ferociously mild in his gig-lamps!' remarked a third, allud-ing to Mr Verdant Green's spectacles.

'And jolly green all over!' wound up a fourth.

Mr Green, hearing his name (as he thought) mentioned, turned to the small young gentleman who had spoken, and politely said, 'Yes, my name is Green; but you have the advantage of me, sir.'

'Oh! have I?' replied the young gentleman in the most affable manner, and not in the least disconcerted; 'my name's Bouncer; I remember seeing you when I was a babby. How's the old woman?' And without waiting to hear Mr Green loftily reply. 'Mrs Green – my WIFE, sir – is quite well – and I do NOT remember to have seen you, or ever heard your name, sir!' – little Mr Bouncer made some most unearthly noises on a post-horn as tall as himself, which he had brought for the delectation of himself and his friends, and the alarm of every village they passed through.

'Never mind the dog, sir,' said the gentleman who sat between Mr Bouncer and Mr Green; 'he won't hurt you. It's only·his play; he always takes notice of strangers.'

'But he is tearing my trousers,' expostulated Mr Green, who was by no means partial to the 'play' of a thoroughbred terrier.

'Ah! he's an uncommon sensible dog,' observed his master; 'he's always on the look-out for rats everywhere. It's the Wellington boots that does it; he's accustomed to have a rat put into a boot, and he worries it out how he can. I dare say he thinks you've got one in yours.'

'But I've got nothing of the sort, sir; and I must request you to keep your dog . . .'. A violent fit of coughing, caused by a well-directed volley of smoke from his neighbour's lips, put a stop to Mr Green's expostulations.

'I hope my weed is no annoyance?' said the gentleman; 'if it is, I will throw it away.'

To which piece of politeness Mr Green could, of course, only reply, between fits of coughing, 'Not in the least, I – assure you – I am very fond – of tobacco – in the open air.'

'Then I dare say you'll do as we are doing, and smoke a weed yourself,' said the gentleman, as he offered Mr Green a plethoric cigar-case. But Mr Green's expression of approbation regarding tobacco was simply theoretical; so he treated his neighbour's offer as magazine editors do the MSS. of unknown contributors – it was 'declined with thanks'.

Mr Verdant Green had already had to make a similar reply to a like proposal on the part of his left-hand neighbour, who was now expressing violent admiration for our hero's top-coat.

'Ain't that a good style of coat, Charley?' he observed to his neighbour. 'I wish I'd seen it before I got this over-coat! There's something sensible about a real, unadulterated top-coat; and there's a style in the way in which they've let down the skirts, and put on the velvet collar and cuffs regardless of expense, that really quite goes to one's heart. Now I dare say the man that built that', he said, more particularly addressing the owner of the coat, 'condescends to live in a village, and waste his sweetness on the desert air, while a noble field might be found for his talent in a University town. That coat will make quite a sensation in Oxford. Won't it, Charley?'

And when Charley, quoting a popular actor (totally unknown to our hero), said, 'I believe you, my bo-oy!' Mr Verdant Green began to feel quite proud of the abilities of their village tailor, and thought what two delightful companions he had met with. The rest of the journey further cemented (as he thought) their friendship; so that he was fairly astonished when, on meeting them the next day, they stared him full in the face, and passed on without taking any more notice of him. But freshmen cannot learn the mysteries of college etiquette in a day.

However, we are anticipating. They had not yet got to Oxford, though, from the pace at which they were going, it appeared as if they would soon reach there; for the coachman had given up his seat and the reins to the box-passenger, who appeared to be as used to the business as the coachman himself; and he was now driving them, not only in a most scientific manner, but also at a great pace. Mr Green was not particularly pleased with the change in the four-wheeled government; but when they went down a hill at a quick trot the heavy luggage making the coach rock to and fro with the speed his fears increased painfully. They culminated as the trot increased into a canter, and then broke into a gallop as they swept along the level road at the bottom of the hill, and rattled up the rise of another. As the horses walked over the brow of the hill, with smoking flanks and jingling harness, Mr Green recovered sufficient breath to expostulate with the coachman for suffering – 'a mere lad', he was about to say, but fortunately checked himself in time – for suffering any one else than the regular driver to have the charge of the coach.

'You never fret yourself about that, sir,' replied the man; 'I knows my bis'ness, as well as my dooties to self and purprietors, and I'd never go for to give up the ribbins to any party but wot had showed hisself fitted to 'andle 'em. And I think I may say this for the genelman as has got 'em now, that he's fit to be fust vip to the Queen herself; and I'm proud to call him my poople. Why, sir – if his honour here will pardon

me for makin' so free - this 'ere gent is Four-in-hand Fosbrooke, of which you *must* have heerd on.'

Mr Green replied that he had not had that pleasure.

'Ah! a pleasure you *may* call it, sir, with perfect truth,' replied the coachman; 'but, lor bless me, sir, weer *can* you have lived?'

The 'poople' who had listened to this, highly amused, slightly turned his head, and said to Mr Green, 'Pray don't feel any alarm, sir; I believe you are quite safe under my guidance. This is not the first time by many that I have driven this coach – not to mention others; and you may conclude that I should not have gained the *sobriquet* to which my worthy friend has alluded without having *some* pretensions to a knowledge of the art of driving.'

Mr Green murmured his apologies for his mistrust – expressed perfect faith in Mr Fosbrooke's skill – and then lapsed into silent meditation on the various arts and sciences in which the gentlemen of the University of Oxford seemed to be most proficient, and pictured to himself what would be his feelings if he ever came to see Verdant driving a coach! There certainly did not appear to be much probability of such an event; but can any *pater familias* say what even the most carefully brought up young Hopeful will do when he has arrived at years of indiscretion?

Altogether, Mr Green did not particularly enjoy the journey. Besides the dogs and cigars, which to him were equal nuisances, little Mr Bouncer was perpetually producing unpleasant post-horn effects, – which he called 'sounding his octaves' – and destroying the effect of the airs on the guard's key-bugle, by joining in them at improper times and with discordant measures. Mr Green, too, could not but perceive that the majority of the conversation that was addressed to himself and his son (though more particularly to the latter), although couched in politest form, was yet of a tendency calculated to 'draw them out' for the amusement of their fellow-passengers. He also observed that the young gentlemen severally exhibited great capacity for the beer of Bass and the porter of Guinness, and were not averse even to liquids of a more spirituous description. Moreover, Mr Green remarked that the ministering Hebes were invariably addressed by their Christian names, and were familiarly conversed with as old acquaintances – most of them receiving direct offers of marriage, or the option of putting up the banns on any Sunday in the middle of the week – while the inquiries after their grandmothers and the various members of their family circles were both numerous and gratifying. In all these verbal encounters little Mr Bouncer particularly distinguished himself.

Woodstock was reached: 'Four-in-hand Fosbrooke' gave up the reins to the professional Jehu; and at last the towers, spires and domes of Oxford appeared in sight. The first view of the City of Colleges is always one that will be long remembered. Even the railway traveller, who enters by the least imposing approach, and can scarcely see that he is in Oxford before he has reached Folly Bridge, must yet regard the city with mingled feelings of delight and surprise as he looks across the Christ Church Meadows and rolls past the Tom Tower. But he who approaches Oxford from the Henley Road, and looks upon that unsurpassed prospect from Magdalen Bridge, or he who enters the city, as Mr Green did, from the Woodstock Road, and rolls down the shady avenue of St Giles', between St John's College and the Taylor Buildings, and past the graceful Martyrs' Memorial, will receive impressions such as probably no other city in the world could convey.

As the coach clattered down the Cornmarket, and turned the corner by Carfax into High Street, Mr Bouncer, having been compelled, in deference to University scruples, to lay aside his post-horn, was consoling himself by chanting the following words, selected probably in compliment to Mr Verdant Green:

> To Oxford, a Freshman so modest,
>   I enter'd one morning in March;
> And the figure I cut was the oddest—
>   All spectacles, choker, and starch.
> > Whack fol lol, lol iddity, &c.
>
> From the top of 'the Royal Defiance',
>   Jack Adams, who coaches so well,
> Set me down in these regions of science,
>   In front of the Mitre Hotel.
> > Whack fol lol, lol iddity, &c.
>
> 'Sure never man's prospects were brighter,'
>   I said, as I jumped from my perch;
> 'So quickly arrived at the Mitre,
>   Oh, I'm sure to get on in the Church!'
> > Whack fol lol, lol iddity, &c.

By the time Mr Bouncer finished these words, the coach appropriately
drew up at the *Mitre*, and the passengers tumbled off amid a knot of
gownsmen collected on the pavement to receive them. But no sooner
were Mr Green and our hero set down, than they were attacked by a

horde of the aborigines of Oxford, who, knowing by vulture-like sagacity the aspect of a freshman and his governor, swooped down upon them in the guise of impromptu porters, and made an indiscriminate attack upon the luggage. It was only by the display of the greatest presence of mind that Mr Verdant Green recovered his effects, and prevented his canvas-covered boxes from being carried off in the wheel-barrows that were trundling off in all directions to the various colleges.

But at last all were safely secured. And soon, when a snug dinner had been discussed in a quiet room, and a bottle of the famous (though I have heard some call it 'in-famous') Oxford port had been produced, Mr Green, under its kindly influence, opened his heart to his son, and gave him much advice as to his forthcoming University career; being, of course, well calculated to do this from his intimate acquaintance with the subject.

Whether it was the extra glass of port, or whether it was the nature of his father's discourse, or whether it was the novelty of his situation, or whether it was all these circumstances combined, yet certain it was that Mr Verdant Green's first night in Oxford was distinguished by

a series, or rather confusion, of most remarkable dreams, in which bishops, archbishops, and hobgoblins elbowed one another for precedence; a beneficent female crowned him with laurel, while Fame lustily proclaimed the honours he had received, and unrolled the class-list in which his name had first rank.

Sweet land of visions, that will with such ease confer even a *treble* first upon the weary sleeper, why must he awake from thy gentle thraldom, to find the class-list a stern reality, and Graduateship too often but an empty dream!

CHAPTER IV

Mr Verdant Green becomes an Oxford Undergraduate.

MR VERDANT GREEN arose in the morning more or less refreshed and after breakfast proceeded with his father to Brazenface College to call upon the Master; the porter directed them where to go, and they sent up their cards. Dr Portman was at home, and they were soon introduced to his presence.

Instead of the stern, imposing-looking personage that Mr Verdant Green had expected to see in the ruler among dons, and the terror of offending undergraduates, the master of Brazenface was a mild-looking old gentleman, with an inoffensive amiability of expression and a shy, retiring manner that seemed to intimate that he was more alarmed at the strangers than they had need to be at him. Dr Portman seemed to be quite a part of his college, for he had passed the greatest portion of his life there. He had graduated there, he had taken Scholarships there, he had even gained a prize-poem there; he had been elected a Fellow there, he had become a Tutor there, he had been Proctor and College Dean there; there, during the long va-cations, he had written his celebrated 'Disquisition on the Greek Particles', afterwards published in eight octavo volumes; and finally, there he had been elected Master of his college, in which office, honoured and respected, he appeared likely to end his days. He was unmarried; perhaps he had never found time to think of a wife; perhaps he had never had the courage to propose for one; perhaps he had met with early crosses and disappointments, and had shrined in his heart a fair image that should never be displaced. Who knows? for dons are mortals, and have been undergraduates once.

The little hair he had was of a silvery white, although his eyebrows retained their black hue; and to judge from the fine fresh-coloured features and the dark eyes that were now nervously twinkling upon Mr Green, Dr Portman must, in his more youthful days, have had an ample share of good looks. He was dressed in an old-fashioned reverend suit of black, with knee-breeches and gaiters, and a massive

watch-seal dangling from under his waistcoat, and was deep in the
study of his favourite particles. He received our hero and his father
both nervously and graciously, and bade them be seated.

'I shall al-ways,' he said, in monosyllabic tones, as though he were
reading out of a child's primer – 'I shall al-ways be glad to see any of
the young friends of my old col-lege friend Lar-kyns; and I do re-joice
to be a-ble to serve you, Mis-ter Green; and I hope your son, Mis-ter,
Mis-ter Vir—— Vir-gin-ius,'...

'Verdant, Dr Portman,' interrupted Mr Green, suggestively, 'Verdant.'

'Oh! true, true, true! and I do hope that he will be a ve-ry good
young man, and try to do hon-our to his col-lege.'

'I trust he will, indeed, sir,' replied Mr Green; 'it is the great wish
of my heart. And I am sure that you will find my son both quiet and
orderly in his conduct, regular in his duties, and always in bed by ten
o'clock.'

'Well, I hope so too, Mis-ter Green,' said Dr Portman, monosyllabi-cally; 'but all the young gen-tle-men do pro-mise to be reg-u-lar and or-der-ly when they first come up, but a term makes a great dif-fer-ence. But I dare say my young friend Mis-ter Vir-gin-ius,' . . .

'Verdant,' smilingly suggested Mr Green.

'I beg your par-don,' apologised Dr Portman; 'but I dare say that he will do as you say, for in-deed my friend Lar-kyns speaks well of him.'

'I am delighted – proud!' murmured Mr Green, while Verdant felt himself blushing up to his spectacles.

'We are ve-ry full,' Dr Portman went on to say, 'but as I do ex-pect

great things from Mis-ter Vir-gin——Verdant, Verdant, I have put some rooms at his ser-vice; and if you would like to see them, my ser-vant shall show you the way.' The servant was accordingly summoned, and received orders to that effect; while the Master told Verdant that he must, at two o'clock, present himself to Mr Slowcoach, his tutor, who would examine him for his matriculation.

'I am sor-ry, Mis-ter Green,' said Dr Portman, 'that my en-gage-ments will pre-vent me from ask-ing you and Mis-ter Virg—Ver-dant, to dine with me to-day; but I do hope that the next time you come to Ox-ford I shall be more for-tu-nate.'

Old John, the Common-room man, who had heard this speech made to hundreds of 'governors' through many generations of fresh-men, could not repress a few pantomimic asides, that were suggestive of anything but full credence in his master's words. But Mr Green was delighted with Dr Portman's affability, and perceiving that the inter-view was at an end, made his *congé*, and left the Master of Brazenface to his Greek particles.

They had just got outside when the servant said, 'Oh, there is the scout! *Your* scout, sir!' at which our hero blushed from the conscious-ness of his new dignity; and, by way of appearing at his ease, inquired the scout's name.

'Robert Filcher, sir,' replied the servant; 'but the gentlemen always call 'em by their Christian names.' And beckoning the scout to him, he bade him show the gentlemen to the rooms kept for Mr Verdant Green; and then took himself back to the Master.

Mr Robert Filcher might perhaps have been forty years of age, perhaps fifty; there was cunning enough in his face to fill even a century of wily years; and there was a depth of expression in his look, as he asked our hero if *he* was Mr Verdant Green, that proclaimed his custom of reading a freshman at a glance. Mr Filcher was laden with coats and boots that had just been brushed and blacked for their respective masters; and he was bearing a jug of Buttery ale (they are renowned for their ale at Brazenface) to the gentleman who owned the pair of 'tops' that were now flashing in the sun as they dangled from the scout's hand.

'Please to follow me, gentlemen,' he said; 'it's only just across the quad. Third floor, No. 4 staircase, fust quad; that's about the mark, *I* think, sir.'

Mr Verdant Green glanced curiously round the Quadrangle, with its picturesque irregularity of outline, its towers and turrets and battle-ments, its grey time-eaten walls, its rows of mullioned heavy-headed windows, and the quiet cloistered air that spoke of study and reflec-tion; and perceiving on one side a row of large windows, with great buttresses between, and a species of steeple on the high-pitched roof, he made bold (just to try the effect) to address Mr Filcher by the name assigned to him at an early period of his life by his godfathers and godmothers, and inquired if that building was the chapel.

'No, sir,' replied Robert, 'that there's the 'All, sir, *that* is – where you dines, sir, leastways when you ain't 'Æger', or elseweer. That at the top is the lantern, sir, *that* is; called so because it never has no candle in it. The chapel's the hopposite side, sir. Please not to walk on the grass, sir; there's a fine agin it, unless you're a Master. This way if *you* please, gentlemen!' Thus the scout beguiled them, as he led them to an open doorway with a large 4 painted over it; inside was a door on either hand, while a coal-bin displayed its black face from under a staircase that rose immediately before them. Up this they went, following the scout (who had vanished for a moment with the

boots and beer); and when they had passed the first floor, they found the ascent by no means easy to the body or pleasant to the sight. The once white-washed walls were coated with the uncleansed dust of the three past terms; and where the plaster had not been chipped off by flying porter-bottles or the heels of Wellington boots, its surface had afforded an irrestistable temptation to those imaginative under-graduates who displayed their artistic genius in candle-smoke cartoons of the heads of the University, and other popular and unpopular characters. All Mr Green's caution, as he crept up the dark, twisting staircase, could not prevent him from crushing his hat against the low, cobwebbed ceiling, and he gave vent to a very strong but quiet anathema, which glided quietly and audibly into the remark, 'Con-founded awkward staircase, I think!'

'Just what Mr Bouncer says,' replied the scout, 'although he don't reach so high as you, sir; but he *do* say, sir, when he comes home pleasant at night from some wine-party, that it *is* the aukardest stair-case as was ever put before a gentleman's legs. And he *did* go so far, sir, as to ask the Master, if it wouldn't be better to have a staircase as would go up of hisself, and take the gentlemen up with it, like one as they has at some public show in London – the Call-and-see-em, I think he said.'

'The Colosseum, probably,' suggested Mr Green. 'And what did Dr Portman say to that, pray?'

'Why he said, sir – leastways so Mr Bouncer reported – that it worn't by no-means a bad idea, and that p'raps Mr Bouncer'd find it done in six months' time, when he come back again from the country. For you see, sir, Mr Bouncer had made hisself so pleasant, that he'd been and got the porter out o' bed, and corked his face dreadful; and then, sir, he'd been and got a Hinn-board from somewhere out of the town, and hung it on the Master's private door; so that when they went to early chapel in the morning, they read as how the Master was 'licensed to sell beer by retail', and 'to be drunk on the premises.' So when the Master came to know who it was as did it, which in course the porter told him, he said as how Mr Bouncer had better go down into the country for a year, for change of hair, and to visit his friends.'

'Very kind indeed of Dr Portman,' said our hero, who missed the moral of the story, and took the rustication for a kind forgiveness of injuries.

'Just what Mr Bouncer said, sir,' replied the scout, 'he said it *were* pertickler kind and thoughtful. This is his room, sir; he come up on'y yesterday.' And he pointed to a door, above which was painted in white letters on a black ground, 'BOUNCER.'

'Why', said Mr Green to his son, 'now I think of it, Bouncer was the name of that short young gentleman who came with us on the coach yesterday, and made himself so – so unpleasant with a tin horn.'

'That's the gent, sir,' observed the scout; 'that's Mr Bouncer, agoing the complete unicorn, as he calls it. I dare say you'll find him a pleasant neighbour, sir. Your rooms is next to his.'

With some doubts of these prospective pleasures, the Mr Greens, père et fils, entered through a double door painted over the outside with the name of 'SMALLS', to which Mr Filcher directed our hero's attention by saying, 'You can have that name took out, sir, and your own name painted in. Mr Smalls has just moved hisself to the other quad, and that's why the rooms is vacant, sir.'

Mr Filcher then went on to point out the properties and capabilities of the rooms, and also their mechanical contrivances.

'This is the hoak, this 'ere outer door is, sir, which the gentlemen sports, that is to say, shuts, sir, when they're a readin'. Not as Mr Smalls ever hinterfered with his constitootion by too much 'ard study sir; he only sported his hoak when people used to get troublesome about their little bills. Here's a place for coals, sir, though Mr Smalls, he kept his bull-terrier there, which was agin the regulations, as *you* know, sir.' (Verdant nodded his head, as though he were perfectly aware of the fact.) 'This ere's your bed-room, sir. Very small, did you say, sir? Oh, no, sir; not by no means! *We* thinks that in college reether a biggish bed-room, sir. Mr Smalls thought so, sir, and he's in his second year, *he* is.' (Mr Filcher thoroughly understood the science of 'flooring' a freshman.)

'This is *my* room, sir, this is, for keepin' your cups and saucers, and wine-glasses and tumblers, and them sort o' things, and washin' 'em up when you wants 'em. If you likes to keep your wine and sperrits here, sir – Mr Smalls always did – you'll find it a nice cool place, sir: or else here's this 'ere winder-seat; you see, sir, it opens with a lid, 'andy for the purpose.'

'If you act upon that suggestion, Verdant,' remarked Mr Green aside to his son, 'I trust that a lock will be added.'

There was not a superfluity of furniture in the room; and Mr Smalls having conveyed away the luxurious part of it, that which was left had more of the useful than the ornamental character; but as Mr Verdant

Green was no Sybarite, this point was but of little consequence. The window looked with a sunny aspect down upon the quad, and over the opposite buildings were seen the spires of churches, the dome of the Radcliffe, and the gables, pinnacles, and turrets of other colleges. This was pleasant enough: pleasanter than the stale odours of the Virginian weed that rose from the faded green window-curtains, and from the old Kidderminster carpet that had been charred and burnt into holes with the fag-ends of cigars.

'Well, Verdant,' said Mr Green, when they had completed their inspection, 'the rooms are not so very bad, and I think you may be able to make yourself comfortable in them. But I wish they were not so high up. I don't see how you can escape if a fire was to break out, and I am afraid collegians must be very careless on these points. Indeed, your mother made me promise that I would speak to Dr Portman about it, and ask him to please to allow your tutor, or somebody, to see that your fire was safely raked out at night; and I had intended to have done so, but somehow it quite escaped me. How your mother and all at home would like to see you in your own college room!' And the thoughts of father and son flew back to the Manor Green and its occupants, who were doubtless at the same time thinking of them.

Mr Filcher then explained the system of thirds, by which the furniture of the room was to be paid for; and, having accompanied his future master and Mr Green downstairs, the latter accomplishing the descent not without difficulty and contusions, and having pointed out the way to Mr Slowcoach's rooms, Mr Robert Filcher relieved his feelings by indulging in a ballet of action, or *pas d'extase*; in which poetry of motion he declared his joy at the last valuable addition to Brazenface and his own perquisites.

Mr Slowcoach was within, and would see Mr Verdant Green. So that young gentleman, trembling with agitation, and feeling as though he would have given pounds for the staircase to have been as high as that of Babel, followed the servant upstairs, and left his father, in almost as great a state of nervousness, pacing the quad below. But it was not the formidable affair, nor was Mr Slowcoach the formidable man, that Mr Verdant Green had anticipated; and by the time that he had turned a piece of *Spectator* into Latin, our hero had somewhat recovered his usual equanimity of mind and serenity of expression: and the construing of half a dozen lines of Livy and Homer, and the answering of a few questions, was a mere form; for Mr Slowcoach's long practice enabled him to see in a very few minutes if the freshman before him (however nervous he might be) had the usual average of abilities, and was up to the business of lectures. So Mr Verdant Green was soon dismissed, and returned to his father radiant and happy.

CHAPTER V

Mr Verdant Green matriculates, and makes a sensation.

As they went out at the gate, they inquired of the porter for Mr Charles Larkyns, but they found that he had not yet returned from the friend's house where he had been during the vacation; whereupon Mr Green said that they would go and look at the Oxford lions, so that he might be able to answer any of the questions that should be put to him on his return. They soon found a guide, one of those wonderful people to which show-places give birth, and of whom Oxford can boast a very goodly average; and under this gentleman's guidance Mr Verdant Green made his first acquaintance with the fair outside of Alma Mater.

The short, thick stick of the guide served to direct attention to the various objects he enumerated in his rapid career. 'This here's Christ

Church College', he said, as he trotted them down St Aldate's, 'built by Card'nal Hoolsy four underd feet long and the famous Tom Tower as tolls wun underd and wun hevery night that being the number of stoodents on the foundation;' and thus the guide went on, perfectly independent of the artificial trammels of punctuation, and not particular whether his hearers understood him or not: that was not *his* business. And as it was that gentleman's boast that he 'could do the alls, collidges, and principal hedifices in a nour and a naff', it could not be expected but that Mr Green should take back to Warwickshire otherwise than a slightly confused impression of Oxford.

When he unrolled that rich panorama before his 'mind's eye', all its component parts were strangely out of place. The rich spire of St Mary's claimed acquaintance with her poorer sister at the cathedral. The cupola of the Tom Tower got into close quarters with the huge dome of the Radcliffe, that shrugged up its great round shoulders at the intrusion of the cross-bred Græco-Gothic tower of All Saints. The theatre had walked up to St Giles' to see how the Taylor Buildings agreed with the University galleries; while the Martyrs' Memorial had stepped down  to Magdalen Bridge, in time to see the college taking a walk in the Botanic Gardens. The Schools and the Bodleian had set their back against the stately portico of the Clarendon Press; while the antiquated Ashmolean had given place to the more modern Townhall. The time-honoured, black-looking front of University College had changed into the cold cleanliness of the 'classic' *façade* of Queen's. The two towers of All Souls – whose several stages seem to be pulled out of each other like the parts of a telescope – had, somehow, removed themselves from the rest of the building, which had gone, nevertheless, on a tour to Broad Street; behind which, as every one knows, are the Broad Walk and the Christ Church meadows. Merton Chapel had got into *New* quarters; and Wadham had gone to Worcester for change of air. Lincoln had migrated from near Exeter to Pembroke; and Brasenose had its nose quite put out of joint by St John's. In short, if the maps of Oxford are to be trusted, there had been a general *pousset* movement among its public buildings.

But if such a shrewd and practised observer as Sir Walter Scott, after a week's hard and systematic sight-seeing, could only say of Oxford, 'The time has been much too short to convey to me separate and distinct ideas of all the variety of wonders that I saw: my memory only at present furnishes a grand but indistinct picture of towers, and chapels, and oriels, and vaulted halls, and libraries, and paintings', – if Sir Walter Scott could say this after a week's work, it is not to be wondered at that Mr Green, after so brief and rapid a survey of the city at the heels of an unintelligent guide, should feel himself slightly confused when, on his return to the Manor Green, he attempted to give a slight description of the wonderful sights of Oxford.

There was *one* lion of Oxford, however, whose individuality of expression was too striking either to be forgotten or confused with the many other lions around. Although (as in Byron's *Dream*)

> A mass of many images
> Crowded like waves upon

Mr Green, yet clear and distinct through all there ran

> The stream-like windings of that glorious street*

to which one of the first critics of the age† has given this high testimony of praise: 'the High Street of Oxford has not its equal in the whole world.'

Mr Green could not, of course, leave Oxford until he had seen his beloved son in that elegant cap and preposterous gown which constitute the present academical dress of the Oxford undergraduate; and

* Wordsworth, *Miscellaneous Sonnets*.
† Dr Waagen, *Art and Artists in England*.

to assume which, with a legal right to the same, matriculation is first necessary. As that amusing and instructive book, the *University Statutes*, says in its own delightful and unrivalled canine Latin, '*Statutum est, quod nemo pro Studente, seu Scholari, habeatur, nec ullis Universitatis privilegiis, aut beneficiis*' (the cap and gown, of course, being among these) '*gaudeat, nisi qui in aliquod Collegium vel Aulam admissus fuerit, et intra quindenam post talem admissionem in matriculam Universitatis fuerit relatus.*' So our hero put on the required white tie and then went forth to complete his proper costume.

There were so many persons purporting to be 'Academical robemakers' that Mr Green was some little time in deciding who should be the tradesman favoured with the order for his son's adornment. At last he fixed upon a shop, the window of which contained a more imposing display than its neighbours of gowns, hoods, surplices, and robes of all shapes and colours, from the black velvet-sleeved Proctor's to the blushing gorgeousness of the scarlet robe and crimson silk sleeves of the D.C.L.

'I wish you', said Mr Green, advancing towards a smirking individual, who was in his shirt-sleeves and slippers, but in all other respects was attired with great magnificence – 'I wish you to measure this gentleman for his academical robes, and also to allow him the use of some to be matriculated in.'

'Certainly, sir,' said the robe-maker, who stood bowing and smirking before them – as Hood expressively says,

> Washing his hands with invisible soap,
> In imperceptible water –

'certainly, sir, if you wish it; but it will scarcely be necessary, sir; as our custom is so extensive, that we keep a large ready-made stock constantly on hand.'

'Oh, that will do just as well,' said Mr Green; 'better, indeed. Let us see some.'

'What description of robe would be required?' said the smirking gentleman, again making use of the invisible soap; 'a scholar's?'

'A scholar's!' repeated Mr Green, very much wondering at the question, and imagining that all students must of necessity be also scholars; 'yes, a scholar's, of course.'

A scholar's gown was accordingly produced: and its deep, wide sleeves, and ample length and breadth, were soon displayed to some advantage on Mr Verdant Green's tall figure. Reflected in a large mirror, its charms were seen in their full perfection; and when the delighted Mr Green exclaimed, 'Why, Verdant, I never saw you look so well as you do now!' our hero was inclined to think that his father's words were the words of truth, and that a scholar's gown was indeed becoming. The *tout ensemble* was complete when the cap had been added to the gown; more especially as Verdant put it on in such a manner that the polite robe-maker was obliged to say, 'The hother way, if you please, sir. Immaterial perhaps, but generally preferred. In fact, the shallow part is *always* the forehead – at least, in Oxford, sir.'

While Mr Green was paying for the cap and gown (N.B. the money of governors is never refused), the robe-maker smirked, and said, 'Hexcuse the question; but may I hask, sir, if this is the gentleman that has just gained the Scotland Scholarship?'

'No, replied Mr Green. 'My son has just gained his matriculation, and, I believe, very creditably; but nothing more, as we only came here yesterday.'

'Then I think, sir,' said the robe-maker, with redoubled smirks – 'I think, sir, there is a leetle mistake here. The gentleman will be hinfringing the University statutes, if he wears a scholar's gown and hasn't got a scholarship; and these robes 'll be of no use to the gentleman, yet awhile at least. It will be an undergraduate's gown that he requires, sir.'

It was fortunate for our hero that the mistake was discovered so soon, and could be rectified without any of those unpleasant consequences of iconoclasm to which the robe-maker's infringement of the 'statues' seemed to point; but as that gentleman put the scholar's gown on one side, and brought out a commoner's, he might have been heard to mutter, 'I don't know which is the freshest, the freshman or his guv'nor.'

When Mr Verdant Green once more looked in the glass, and saw hanging straight from his shoulders a yard of blueish-black stuff, garnished with a little lappet, and two streamers whose upper parts were gathered into double plaits, he regretted that he was not indeed a scholar, if it were only for the privilege of wearing so elegant a gown. However, his father smiled approvingly, the robe-maker smirked judiciously; so he came to the gratifying conclusion that the commoner's gown was by no means ugly, and would be thought a great deal of at the Manor Green when he took it home at the end of the term.

Leaving his hat with the robe-maker, who, with many more smirks and imaginary washings of the hands, hoped to be favoured with the gentleman's patronage on future occasions, and begged further to trouble him with a card of his establishment – our hero proceeded with his father along the High Street, and turned round by St Mary's, and so up Catte Street to the Schools, where they made their way to the classic 'Pig-market,'* to await the arrival of the Vice-Chancellor.

When he came, our freshman and two other white-tied fellow-freshmen were summoned to the great man's presence; and there, in the ante-chamber of the Convocation House,† the edifying and imposing spectacle of Matriculation was enacted. In the first place, Mr

---

* The reason why such a name has been given to the Schools' quadrangle may be found in the following extract from *Ingram's Memorials:* 'The schools built by Abbot Hokenorton being inadequate to the increasing wants of the University, they applied to the Abbot of Reading for stone to rebuild them; and in the year 1532 it appears that considerable sums of money were expended on them; but they went to decay in the latter part of the reign of Henry VIII. and during the whole reign of Edward VI. The change of religion having occasioned a suspension of the usual exercises and scholastic acts in the University, in the year 1540 only two of these schools were used by determiners, and within two years after none at all. The whole area between these schools and the divinity school was subsequently converted into a garden and *pig-market;* and the schools themselves, being completely abandoned by the masters and scholars, were used by glovers and laundresses.'

† '*In apodyterio domui congregationis.*'

Verdant Green took divers oaths, and sincerely promised and swore that he would be faithful and bear true allegiance to her Majesty Queen Victoria. He also professed (very much to his own astonishment) that he did 'from his heart abhor, detest, and abjure, as impious and heretical, that damnable doctrine and position, that princes ex-communicated or deprived by the pope, or any authority of the see of Rome, may be deposed or murdered by their subjects, or any other whatsoever.' And, having almost lost his breath at this novel 'position', Mr Verdant Green could only gasp his declaration, 'that no foreign prince, person, prelate, state, or potentate, hath, or ought to have, any jurisdiction, power, superiority, pre-eminence, or authority, ecclesias-tical or spiritual, within this realm.' When he had sufficiently recovered his presence of mind, Mr Verdant Green inserted his name in the University books as 'Generosi filius natu maximus', and then signed his name to the Thirty-nine Articles – though he did not endanger his matriculation, as Theodore Hook did, by professing his readiness to sign forty if they wished it! Then the Vice-Chancellor concluded the performance by presenting to the three freshmen (in the most liberal manner) three brown-looking volumes, with these words; 'Scitote vos in Matriculam Universitatis hodie relatos esse, sub hac conditione, nempe ut omnia Statuta hoc libro comprehensa pro virili observetis.' And the ceremony was at an end, and Mr Verdant Green was a matriculated member of the University of Oxford. He was far too nervous – from the weakening effect of the popes, and the excom-municate princes, and their murderous subjects – to be able to trans-late and understand what the Vice-Chancellor had said to him, but he thought his present to be particularly kind; and he found it a copy of the University Statutes, which he determined forthwith to read and obey.

Though if he had known that he had sworn to observe statutes which required him, among other things, to wear garments only of a black or 'subfusk' hue; to abstain from that absurd and proud custom of walking in public *in boots*, and the ridiculous one of wearing the hair long;* statutes, moreover, which demanded of him to refrain from all taverns, wine-shops, and houses in which they sold wine or any other

* See the *Oxford Statutes, tit. xiv. 'De vestitu et habitu scholastico.'*

drink, and the herb called *nicotiana* or 'tobacco'; not to hunt wild beasts with dogs or snares or nets; not to carry crossbows or other 'bombarding' weapons, or keep hawks for fowling; not to frequent theatres or the strifes of gladiators; and only to carry a bow and arrows for the sake of honest recreation;* if Mr Verdant Green had known that he had covenanted to do this, he would, perhaps, have felt some scruples in taking the oaths of matriculation. But this by the way.

Now that Mr Green had seen all that he wished to see, nothing remained for him but to discharge his hotel bill. It was accordingly called for, and produced by the waiter, whose face by a visitation of that complaint against which vaccination is usually considered a safeguard – had been reduced to a state resembling the interior half of a sliced muffin. To judge from the expression of Mr Green's features as he regarded the document that had been put into his hand, it is probable that he had not been much accustomed to Oxford hotels; for he ran over the several items of the bill with a look in which surprise contended with indignation for the mastery, while the muffin-faced waiter handled his plated salver, and looked fixedly at nothing.

Mr Green, however, refraining from observations, paid the bill; and, muffling himself in greatcoat and travelling-cap, he prepared

* *Ditto, tit. xv. 'De moribus conformandis.'*

himself to take a comfortable journey back to Warwickshire, inside the Birmingham and Oxford coach. It was not loaded in the same way that it had been when he came up by it, and fellow-passengers were of a very different description; and it must be confessed that, in the absence of Mr Bouncer's tin horn, the attacks of intrusive terriers, and the involuntary fumigation of himself with tobacco (although its presence was still perceptible within the coach), Mr Green found his journey *from* Oxford much more agreeable than it had been *to* that place. He took an affectionate farewell of his son, somewhat after the manner of the 'heavy fathers' of the stage; and then the coach bore him away from the last lingering look of our hero, who felt anything but heroic at being left for the first time in his life to shift for himself.

His luggage had been sent up to Brazenface, so thither he turned his steps, and with some little difficulty found his room. Mr Filcher had partly unpacked his master's things, and had left everything uncom-

fortable and in 'the most admired disorder', and Mr Verdant Green sat himself down upon the 'practicable' window-seat, and resigned himself to his thoughts. If they had not already flown to the Manor Green, they would soon have been carried there; for a German band, just outside the college-gates, began to play 'Home, sweet home', with that truth and delicacy of expression which the wandering minstrels of Germany seem to acquire intuitively. The sweet melancholy of the simple air, as it came subdued by distance into softer tones, would have power-

fully affected most people who had just been torn from the bosom of their homes, to fight, all inexperienced, the battle of life; but it had such an effect on Mr Verdant Green, that – but it little matters saying *what* he did; many people will give way to feelings in private that they would stifle in company; and if Mr Filcher on his return found his master wiping his spectacles, why that was only a simple proceeding which all glasses frequently require.

To divert his thoughts, and to impress upon himself and others the fact that he was an Oxford MAN our freshman set out for a stroll; and as the unaccustomed feeling of the gown about his shoulders made him feel somewhat embarrassed as to the carriage of his arms, he stepped into a shop on the way and purchased a light cane, which he considered would greatly add to the effect of the cap and gown. Armed with this weapon, be proceeded to disport himself in the Christ Church meadows, and promenaded up and down the Broad Walk.

The beautiful meadows lay green and bright in the sun; the arching
trees threw a softened light, and made a chequered pavement of the
great Broad Walk; 'witch-elms *did* counter-change the floor' of the
gravel-walks that wound with the windings of the Cherwell; the droop-
ing willows were mirrored in its stream; through openings in the trees
there were glimpses of grey old college-buildings; then came the walk
along the banks, the Isis shining like molten silver, and fringed around
with barges and boats; then another stretch of green meadows; then

a cloud of steam from the railway-station; and a background of gently-
rising hills. It was a cheerful scene, and the variety of figures gave life
and animation to the whole.

Young ladies and unprotected females were found in abundance,
dressed in all the engaging variety of light spring dresses; and, as may
be supposed, our hero attracted a great deal of their attention, and
afforded them no small amusement. But the unusual and terrific
appearance of a spectacled gownsman with a cane produced the
greatest alarm among the juveniles, who imagined our freshman to be
a new description of beadle or Bogy, summoned up by the exigencies

of the times to preserve a rigorous discipline among the young people; and, regarding his cane as the symbol of his stern sway, they harassed their nursemaids by unceasingly charging at their petticoats for protection.

Altogether, Mr Verdant Green made quite a sensation.

CHAPTER VI

Mr Verdant Green dines, breakfasts, and goes to Chapel.

OUR hero dressed himself with great care, that he might make his first appearance in Hall with proper *éclat*; and, having made his way towards the lantern-surmounted building, he walked up the steps and under the groined archway with a crowd of hungry undergraduates who were hurrying in to dinner. The clatter of plates would have alone been sufficient to guide his steps; and, passing through one of the doors in the elaborately-carved screen that shut off the passage and the buttery, he found himself within the hall of Brazenface. It was of noble size, lighted by lofty windows, and carried up to a great height by an open roof, dark (save where it opened to the lantern) with great oak beams, and rich with carved pendants and gilded bosses. The ample fire-places displayed the capaciousness of those collegiate mouths of 'the wind-pipes of hospitality', and gave an idea of the dimensions of the kitchen-ranges. In the centre of the hall was a huge plate-warmer, elaborately worked in brass with the college arms. Founders and benefactors were seen, or suggested, on all sides; their arms gleamed from the windows in all the glories of stained glass; and their faces peered out from the massive gilt frames on the walls, as though their shadows loved to linger about the spot that had been benefited by their substance. At the further end of the hall a deep bay-window threw its painted light upon a dais, along which stretched the table for the dons; Masters and Bachelors occupied side-tables; and the other tables were filled up by the undergraduates; everyone, from the don downwards, being in his gown.

Our hero was considerably impressed with the (to him) singular character of the scene; and from the 'Benedictus benedicat' grace-before-meat to the 'Benedicto benedicamur' after-meat, he gazed curiously around him in silent wonderment. So much indeed was he wrapped up in the novelty of the scene, that he ran a great risk of losing his dinner. The scouts fled about in all directions with plates, and glasses, and pewter dishes, and massive silver mugs that had gone round the tables for the last two centuries, and still no one waited upon Mr Verdant Green. He twice ventured to timidly say, 'Waiter!' but as no one answered to his call, and as he was too bashful and occupied with his own thoughts to make another attempt, it is probable that he would have risen from dinner as unsatisfied as when he sat down, had

not his right-hand companion (having partly relieved his own wants) perceived his neighbour to be a freshman, and kindly said to him, 'I think you'd better begin your dinner, because we don't stay here long. What is your scout's name?' And when he had been told it, he turned to Mr Filcher and asked him, 'What the doose he meant by not waiting on his master?' which, with the addition of a few gratuitous threats, had the effect of bringing that gentleman to his master's side, and reducing Mr Verdant Green to a state of mind in which gratitude to his companion and a desire to beg his scout's pardon were confusedly blended. Not seeing any dishes upon the table to select from, he referred to the list, and fell back on the standard roast-beef.

'I am sure I am very much obliged to you,' said Verdant, turning to his friendly neighbour. 'My rooms are next to yours, and I had the pleasure of being driven by you on the coach the other day.'

'Oh!' said Mr Fosbrooke, for it was he; 'ah, I remember you now! I suppose the old bird was your governor. *He* seemed to think it anything but a pleasure, being driven by Four-in-hand Fosbrooke.'

'Why, pap – my father – is rather nervous on a coach,' replied Verdant: 'he was bringing me to college for the first time.'

'Then you are the man that has just come into Smalls' old rooms? Oh, I see. Don't you ever drink with your dinner? If you don't holler for your rascal, he'll never half wait upon you. Always bully them well at first, and then they learn manners.'

So, by way of commencing the bullying system without loss of time, our hero called out very fiercely 'Robert!' and then, as Mr Filcher glided to his side, he timidly dropped his tone into a mild 'Glass of water, if you please, Robert.'

He felt rather relieved when dinner was over, and retired at once to his own rooms; where making a rather quiet and sudden entrance, he found them tenanted by an old woman, who wore a huge bonnet tilted on the top of her head, and was busily and dubiously engaged at one of his open boxes. 'Ahem!' he coughed, at which note of warning the old lady jumped round very quickly, and said – dabbing curtseys where there were stops, like the beats of a conductor's *bâton* – 'Law bless me, sir. It's beggin your parding that I am. Not seein' you a comin' in. Bein' 'ard of hearin' from a hinfant. And havin' my back turned. I was just a puttin' your things to rights, sir. If you please, sir, I'm Mrs. Tester. Your bedmaker, sir.'

'Oh, thank you,' said our freshman, with the shadow of a suspicion that Mrs Tester was doing something more than merely 'putting to rights' the pots of jam and marmalade, and the packages of tea and coffee, which his doting mother had thoughtfully placed in his box as a provision against immediate distress. 'Thank you.'

'I've done my rooms, sir,' dabbed Mrs Tester. 'Which if thought agreeable, I'd stay and put these things in their places. Which it certainly is Robert's place. But I never minds putting myself out. As I always perpetually am minded. So long as I can obleege the gentlemen.'

So, as our hero was of a yielding disposition, and could, under skilful hands, easily be moulded into any form, he allowed Mrs Tester to remain, and conclude the unpacking and putting away of his goods, in which operation she displayed great generalship.

'You've a deal of tea and coffee, sir,' she said, keeping time by curtseys. 'Which it's a great blessin' to have a mother. And not to be left dissolute like some gentlemen. And tea and coffee is what I mostly lives on. And mortial dear it is to poor folks. And a package the likes of this, sir, were a blessin' I should-never even dream on.'

'Well, then,' said Verdant, in a most benevolent mood, 'you can take one of the packages for your trouble.'

Upon this, Mrs Tester appeared to be greatly overcome. 'Which I once had a son myself,' she said. 'And as fine a young man as you are, sir. With a strawberry mark in the small of his back. And beautiful red whiskers, sir, with a tendency to drink. Which it were his rewing, and took him to be enlisted for a sojer. When he went across the seas to the West Injies. And was took with the yaller fever, and buried there. Which the remembrance, sir, brings on my spazzums. To which I'm an hafflicted martyr, sir. And can only be heased with three spots of brandy on a lump of sugar. Which your good mother, sir, has put a bottle of brandy. Along with the jam and the clean linen, sir. As though a purpose for my complaint. Ugh! oh!'

And Mrs Tester forthwith began pressing and thumping her sides in such a terrific manner, and appeared to be undergoing such internal agony, that Mr Verdant Green not only gave her brandy there and then, for her immediate relief – 'which it heases the spazzums deerectly, bless you,' observed Mrs Tester, parenthetically – but also told her where she could find the bottle, in case she should again be attacked when in his rooms; attacks which, it is needless to say, were repeated at every subsequent visit. Mrs Tester then finished putting away the tea and coffee, and entered into further particulars about her late son; though what connection there was between him and the packages of tea, our hero could not perceive. Nevertheless he was much interested with her narrative, and thought Mrs Tester a very affectionate, motherly sort of woman; more especially, when (Robert having placed his tea-things on the table) she showed him how to make the tea; an apparently simple feat that the freshman found himself perfectly unable to accomplish. And then Mrs Tester made a final dab, and her exit, and our hero sat over his tea as long as he could, because it gave an idea of cheerfulness; and then, after directing Robert to be sure not to forget to call him in time for morning chapel, he retired to bed.

The bed was very hard, and so small, that, had it not been for the wall, our hero's legs would have been visible (literally) at the foot; but despite these novelties, he sank into a sound rest, which at length passed into the following dream. He thought that he was back again at dinner at the Manor Green, but that the room was curiously like the hall of Brazenface, and that Mrs Tester and Dr Portman were on either side of him, with Mr Fosbrooke and Robert talking to his sisters; and that he was reaching his hand to help Mrs Tester to a packet of tea, which her son had sent them from the West Indies, when he threw over a wax-light, and set every thing on fire; and that the parish engine came up; and that there was a great noise, and a loud hammering; and,

'Eh? yes! oh! the half-hour is it? Oh, yes! thank you!' And Mr Verdant Green sprang out of bed much relieved in mind to find that the alarm of fire was nothing more than his scout knocking vigorously at his door, and that it was chapel-time.

'Want any warm water, sir?' asked Mr Filcher, putting his head in at the door.

'No, thank you,' replied our hero; 'I – I –'

'Shave with cold. Ah! I see, sir. It's much 'ealthier, and makes the 'air grow. But anything as you *does* want, sir, you've only to call.'

'If there is anything that I want, Robert,' said Verdant, 'I will ring.'

'Bless you, sir,' observed Mr Filcher, 'there ain't no bells never in colleges! They'd be rung off their wires in no time. Mr Bouncer, sir, he uses a trumpet like they does on board ship. By the same token, that's it, sir!' And Mr Filcher vanished just in time to prevent little Mr Bouncer from finishing a furious solo, from an entirely new version of *Robert le Diable*, which he was giving with novel effects through the medium of a speaking-trumpet.

Verdant found his bed-room inconveniently small; so contracted, indeed, in its dimensions, that his toilette was not completed without his elbows having first suffered severe abrasions. His mechanical tur-

nip showed him that he had no time to lose; and the furious ringing of a bell, whose noise was echoed by the bells of other colleges, made him dress with a rapidity quite unusual, and hurry down stairs and across quad to the chapel steps, up which a throng of students were hastening. Nearly all betrayed symptoms of having been aroused from their sleep without having had any spare time for an elaborate toilette;

and many, indeed, were completing it, by thrusting themselves into surplices and gowns as they hurried up the steps.

Mr Fosbrooke was one of these; and when he saw Verdant close to him, he benevolently recognised him, and said, 'Let me put you up to a wrinkle. When they ring you up sharp for chapel, don't you lose any time about your absolutions – washing, you know; but just jump into a pair of bags and Wellingtons; clap a top-coat on you, and button it up to the chin, and there you are, ready dressed in the twinkling of a bed-post.'

Before Mr Verdant Green could at all comprehend why a person should jump into two bags, instead of dressing himself in the normal manner, they went through the ante-chapel, or 'Court of the Gentiles', as Mr Fosbrooke termed it, and entered the choir of the chapel through a screen elaborately decorated in the Jacobean style, with pillars and arches, and festoons of fruit and flowers, and bells and pomegranates. On either side of the door were two men, who quickly glanced at each one who passed, and as quickly pricked a mark against

his name on the chapel lists. As the freshman went by, they made a careful study of his person, and took mental daguerreotypes of his features. Seeing no beadle, or pew-opener (or, for the matter of that, any pews), or anyone to direct him to a place, Mr Verdant Green quietly took a seat in the first place that he found empty, which happened to be the stall on the right hand of the door. Unconscious of the trespass he was committing, he at once put his cap to his face and knelt down; but he had no sooner risen from his knees, than he found an imposing-looking don, as large as life and quite as natural, who was staring at him with the greatest astonishment, and motioning him to immediately 'come out of that!' This our hero did with the greatest speed and confusion, and sank breathless on the end of the nearest bench; when just as, in his agitation, he had again said his prayer, the service fortunately commenced, and somewhat relieved him of his embarrassment.

Although he had the glories of Magdalen, Merton, and New College chapels fresh in his mind, yet Verdant was considerably impressed with the solemn beauties of his own college chapel. He admired its harmonious proportions, and the elaborate carving of its decorated tracery. He noted everything: the great eagle that seemed to be spreading its wings for an upward flight – the pavement of black and white marble – the dark canopied stalls, rich with the later work of Grinling Gibbons – the elegant tracery of the windows; and he lost himself in a solemn reverie as he looked up at the saintly forms through which the rays of the morning sun streamed in rainbow tints.

But the lesson had just begun; and the man on Verdant's right appeared to be attentively following it. Our freshman, however, could not helping seeing the book, and, much to his astonishment, he found it to be a Livy, out of which his neighbour was getting up his morning's lecture. He was still more astonished, when the lesson had come to an end, by being suddenly pulled back when he attempted to rise, and finding the streamers of his gown had been put to a use never intended for them, by being tied round the finial of the stall behind him – the silly work of a boyish gentleman, who, in his desire to play off a practical joke on a freshman, forgot the sacredness of the place where college rules compelled him to show himself on morning parade.

Chapel over, our hero hurried back to his rooms, and there, to his great joy, found a budget of letters from home; and surely the little items of intelligence that made up the news of the Manor Green had never seemed to possess such interest as now! The reading and re-reading of these occupied him during the whole of breakfast-time; and Mr Filcher found him still engaged in perusing them when he came to clear away the things. Then it was that Verdant discovered the extended meaning that the word 'perquisites' possesses in the eyes of a scout; for, to a remark that he had made, Robert replied in a tone of surprise, 'Put away these bits o' things as is left, sir!' and then added, with an air of mild correction, 'you see, sir, you's fresh to the place, and don't know that gentlemen never likes that sort o' thing done *here*, sir; but you gets your commons, sir, fresh and fresh every morning and evening, which must be much more agreeable to the 'ealth than a heating of stale bread and such like. No, sir!' continued Mr Filcher, with a manner that was truly parental, 'no sir!' you trust to

me, sir, and I'll take care of your things, I will.' And from the way that he carried off the eatables, it seemed probable that he would make good his words. But our freshman felt considerable awe of his scout, and murmuring broken accents that sounded like 'ignorance – customs – University,' he endeavoured, by a liberal use of his pocket-handkerchief, to appear as if he were not blushing.

As Mr Slowcoach had told him that he would not have to begin lectures until the following day, and as the Greek play fixed for the lecture was one with which he had been made well acquainted by Mr Larkyns, Verdant began to consider what he could do with himself; when the thought of Mr Larkyns suggested the idea that his son Charles had probably by this time returned to college. He determined therefore at once to go in search of him; and looking out a letter which the rector had commissioned him to deliver to his son, he inquired of Robert, if he was aware whether Mr Charles Larkyns had come back from his holidays.

''Ollidays, sir?' said Mr Filcher. 'Oh! I see, sir! Vacation, you mean, sir. Young gentlemen as is *men*, sir, likes to call their 'ollidays by a different name to boys, sir. Yes, sir, Mr Charles Larkyns, he come up last arternoon, sir; but he and Mr Smalls, the gent as he's been down with this vacation, the same as had these rooms, sir, they didn't come to 'All, sir, but went and had their dinners comfortable at the Star, sir; and very pleasant they made theirselves; and Thomas, their scout, sir, has had quite a horder for sober-water this morning, sir.'

With somewhat of a feeling of wonder how one scout contrived to know so much of the proceedings of gentlemen who were waited on by another scout, and wholly ignorant of his allusion to his fellow-servants' dealings in soda-water, Mr Verdant Green inquired where he could find Mr Larkyns; and as the rooms were but just on the other side of the quad., he put on his hat, and made his way to them. The scout was just going into the room, so our hero gave a tap at the door and followed him.

CHAPTER VII

Mr Verdant Green calls on a Gentleman who
'is licensed to sell'.

MR VERDANT GREEN found himself in a room that had a pleasant
look-out over the gardens of Brazenface, from which a noble chestnut
tree brought its pyramids of bloom close up to the very windows. The
walls of the room were decorated with engravings in gilt frames, their
variety of subject denoting the catholic taste of their proprietor. 'The
start for the Derby', and other coloured hunting prints, showed his
taste for the field and horse-flesh; Landseer's 'Distinguished Member
of the Humane Society', 'Dignity and Impudence', and others,
displayed his fondness for dog-flesh; while Byron beauties, 'Amy Rob-
sart', and some extremely *au naturel* pets of the ballet, proclaimed his
passion for the fair sex in general. Over the fireplace was a mirror (for
Mr Charles Larkyns was not averse to the reflection of his good-looking
features, and was rather glad than otherwise of 'an excuse for the glass'),
its frame stuck full of tradesmen's cards and (unpaid) bills, invites, 'bits
of pasteboard' pencilled with a mystic 'wine', and other odds and ends
– no private letters though! Mr Larkyns was too wary to leave his
'family secrets' for the delectation of his scout. Over the mirror was
displayed a fox's mask, gazing vacantly from between two brushes;
leaving the spectator to imagine that Mr Charles Larkyns was a second
Nimrod, and had in some way or other been intimately concerned in the
capture of these trophies of the chase. This supposition of the
imaginative spectator would be strengthened by the appearance of a list
of hunting appointments (of the past season) pinned up over a list of
lectures, and not quite in character with the tabular views of
prophecies, kings of Israel and Judah, and the Thirty-nine Articles,
which did duty elsewhere on the walls, where they were presumed to be
studied in spare minutes – which were remarkably spare indeed.

The sporting character of the proprietor of the rooms was further
suggested by the huge pair of antlers over the door, bearing on their
tines a collection of sticks, whips, and spurs; while to prove that Mr

Larkyns was not wholly taken up by the charms of the chase, fishing-rods, tandem-whips, cricket-bats, and Joe Mantons, were piled up in odd corners; and single-sticks, boxing-gloves, and foils, gracefully arranged upon the walls, showed that he occasionally devoted himself to athletic pursuits. An ingenious wire-rack for pipes and meer-schaums, and the presence of one or two suspicious-looking boxes, labelled 'collorados', 'regalia', 'lukotilla', and with other unknown words, seemed to intimate that, if Mr Larkyns was no smoker himself, he at least kept a bountiful supply of 'smoke' for his friends; but the perfumed cloud that was proceeding from his lips as Verdant entered the room, dispelled all doubts on the subject.

He was much changed in appearance during the somewhat long interval since Verdant had last seen him, and his handsome features had assumed a more manly, though perhaps a more rakish look. He was lolling on a couch in the *negligé* attire of dressing-gown and slippers, with his pink striped shirt comfortably open at the neck. Lounging in an easy chair opposite to him was a gentleman clad in tartan-plaid, whose face might only be partially discerned through the glass bottom of a pewter, out of which he was draining the last draught. Between them was a table covered with the ordinary appointments for a breakfast, and the extra-ordinary ones of beer-cup and soda-water. Two Skye terriers, hearing a strange footstep, immediately barked out a challenge of 'Who goes there?' and made Mr Larkyns aware that an intruder was at hand.

Slightly turning his head, he dimly saw through the smoke a spectacled figure taking off his hat, and holding out an envelope; and without looking further, he said, 'It's no use coming here, young man, and stealing a march in this way! I don't owe *you* anything; and if I did, it is not convenient to pay it. I told Spavin not to send me any more of his confounded reminders; so go back and tell him that he'll find it all right in the long-run, and that I'm really going to read this term, and shall stump the examiners at last. And now, my friend, you'd better make yourself scarce and vanish! You know where the door lies!'

Our hero was so confounded at this unusual manner of receiving a friend, that he was some little time before he could gasp out, 'Why, Charles Larkyns – don't you remember me? Verdant Green!'

Mr Larkyns, astonished in his turn, jumped up directly, and came

to him with outstretched hands. ''Pon my word, old fellow,' he said,
'I really beg you ten thousand pardons for not recognising you; but
you are so altered – allow me to add, improved, – since I last saw you;
you were not a bashaw of two tails, then, you know; and, really,
wearing your beaver up, like Hamlet's uncle, I altogether took you for
a dun. For I am a victim of a very remarkable monomania. There are
in this place wretched beings calling themselves tradesmen, who
labour under the impression that I owe them what they facetiously
term little bills; and though I have frequently assured their messen-
gers, who are kind enough to come here to inquire for Mr Larkyns,
that that unfortunate gentleman has been obliged to hide himself from
persecution in a convent abroad, yet the wretches still hammer at my
oak, and disturb my peace of mind. But bring yourself to an anchor,
old fellow! This man is Smalls; a capital fellow, whose chief merit
consists in his devotion to literature; indeed, he reads so hard that he
is called a *fast* man. Smalls! let me introduce my friend Verdant Green,
a freshman – ahem! – and the proprietor, I believe, of your old rooms'.

Our hero made a profound bow to Mr Smalls, who returned it with great gravity, and said he 'had great pleasure in forming the acquaintance of a freshman like Mr Verdant Green', which was doubtless quite true; and he then evinced his devotion to literature by continuing the perusal of one of those vivid and refined accounts of 'a rattling set-to between Nobby Buffer and Hammer Sykes', for which *Tintinnabulum's Life* is so justly famous.

'I heard from my governor,' said Mr Larkyns, 'that you were coming up; and in the course of the morning I should have come and looked you up; but the – the fatigues of travelling yesterday,' continued Mr Larkyns, as a lively recollection of the preceding evening's symposium stole over his mind, 'made me rather later than usual this morning. Have you done anything in this way?'

Verdant replied that he had breakfasted, although he had not done any thing in the way of cigars, because he never smoked.

'Never smoked! Is it possible!' exclaimed Mr Smalls, violently interrupting himself in the perusal of *Tintinnabulum's Life*, while some private signals were rapidly telegraphed between him and Mr Larkyns; 'ah! you'll soon get the better of that weakness! Now, as you're a freshman, you'll perhaps allow me to give you a little advice. The Germans, you know, would never be the deep readers that they are, unless they smoked; and I should advise you to go to the Vice-Chancellor as soon as possible, and ask him for an order for some weeds. He'd be delighted to think you are beginning to set to work so soon!' To which our hero replied, that he was much obliged to Mr Smalls for his kind advice, and if such were the customs of the place, he should do his best to fulfil them.

'Perhaps you'll be surprised at our simple repast, Verdant,' said Mr Larkyns; 'but it's our misfortune. It all comes of hard reading and late hours: the midnight oil, you know, must be supplied, and *will* be paid for; the nervous system gets strained to excess, and you have to call in the doctor. Well, what does he do? Why, he prescribes a regular course of tonics; and I flatter myself that I am a very docile patient, and take my bitter beer regularly, and without complaining.' In proof of which Mr Charles Larkyns took a long pull at the pewter.

'But you know, Larkyns,' observed Mr Smalls, 'that was nothing to my case, when I got laid up with elephantiasis on the biceps of the lungs, and had a fur coat in my stomach!'

'Dear me!' said Verdant sympathisingly; 'and was that also through too much study?'

'Why, of course!' replied Mr Smalls; 'it couldn't have been anything else – from the symptoms, you know! But then the sweets of learning surpass the bitters. Talk of the pleasures of the dead languages, indeed! why, how many jolly nights have you and I, Larkyns, passed "down among the dead men!"'

Charles Larkyns had just been looking over the letter which Verdant had brought him, and said, 'The governor writes that you'd like me to put you up to the ways of the place, because they are fresh to you, and you are fresh (ahem! very!) to them. Now, I am going to wine with Smalls to-night, to meet a few nice, quiet, hard-working men (eh, Smalls?), and I dare say Smalls will do the civil, and ask you also.'

'Certainly!' said Mr Smalls, who saw a prospect of amusement;

'delighted, I assure you! I hope to see you – after Hall, you know, – but I hope you don't object to a very quiet party?'

'Oh, dear no!' replied Verdant; 'I much prefer a quiet party; indeed, I have always been used to quiet parties; and I shall be very glad to come.'

'Well, that's settled then,' said Charles Larkyns; 'and, in the mean time, Verdant, let us take a prowl about the old place, and I'll put you up to a thing or two, and show you some of the freshman's sights. But you must go and get your cap and gown, old fellow, and then by that time I'll be ready for you.'

Whether there are really any sights in Oxford that are more especially devoted, or adapted, to its freshmen, we will not undertake to affirm; but if there are, they could not have had a better expositor than Mr Charles Larkyns, or a more credible visitor than Mr Verdant Green.

His credibility was rather strongly put to the test as they turned into the High Street, when his companion directed his attention to an individual on the opposite side of the street, with a voluminous gown, and enormous cocked hat profusely adorned with gold lace. 'I suppose you know who that is, Verdant? No! Why, that's the Bishop of Oxford! Ah, I see, he's a very different-looking man to what you had expected; but then these university robes so change the appearance. That is his official dress, as the Visitor of the Ashmolean!'

Mr Verdant Green having 'swallowed' this, his friend was thereby enabled, not only to use up old 'sells', but also to draw largely on his invention for new ones. Just then, there came along the street, walking in a sort of young procession – the Vice-Chancellor, with his Esquire- and Yeoman-bedels. The silver maces, carried by these latter gentlemen, made them by far the most showy part of the procession, and accordingly Mr Larkyns seized the favourable opportunity to point out the foremost bedel, and say, 'You see that man with the poker and loose cap? Well, that's the Vice-Chancellor.'

'But what does he walk in procession for?' inquired our freshman.

'Ah, poor man!' said Mr Larkyns, 'he's obliged
to do it. "Uneasy lies the head that wears a
crown," you know; and he can never go anywhere,
or do anything, without carrying that poker, and
having the other minor pokers to follow him.
They never leave him, not even at night. Two of
the pokers stand on each side his bed, and relieve
each other every two hours. So, I need hardly say,
that he is obliged to be a bachelor.'

'It must be a very wearisome office,' remarked
our freshman, who fully believed all that was told
to him.

'Wearisome, indeed; and that's the reason why they are obliged to
change the Vice-Chancellors so often. It would kill most people, only
they are always selected for their strength – and height,' he added, as a
brilliant idea just struck him. They had turned down Magpie Lane, and
so by Oriel College, where one of the fire-plug notices had caught Mr
Larkyns' eye. 'You see that,' he said; 'well, that's one of the plates they
put up to record the Vice's height. F. P. 7 feet, you see: the initials of his
name – Frederick Plumptre!'

'He scarcely seemed so tall
as that,' said our hero,
'though certainly a tall man.
But the gown makes a dif-
ference, I suppose.'

'His height was a very
lucky thing for him, how-
ever,' continued Mr Larkyns.
'I dare say when you have
heard that it was only those
who stood high in the University that were elected to rule
it, you little thought of the
true meaning of the term?'

'I certainly never did,' said the freshman, innocently; 'but I knew that the customs of Oxford must of course be very different from those of other places.'

'Yes, you'll soon find that out,' replied Mr Larkyns, meaningly. 'But here we are at Merton, whose Merton ale is as celebrated as Burton ale. You see the man giving in the letters to the porter? Well, he's one of their principal men. Each college does its own postal department; and at Merton there are fourteen postmasters,* for they get no end of letters there.'

'Oh, yes!' said our hero, 'I remember Mr Larkyns – your father, the rector, I mean – telling us that the son of one of his old friends had been a postmaster of Merton; but I fancied that he had said it had something to do with a scholarship.'

'Ah, you see, it's a long while since the governor was here and his memory fails him,' remarked Mr Charles Larkyns, very unfilially. 'Let us turn down the Merton fields, and round into St Aldate's. We may perhaps be in time to see the Vice come down to Christ Church.'

'What does he go there for?' asked Mr Verdant Green.

'To wind up the great clock, and put big Tom in order. Tom is the bell that you hear at nine each night; the Vice has to see that he is in proper condition, and, as you have seen, goes out with his pokers for that purpose.'

On their way, Charles Larkyns pointed out, close to Folly Bridge, a house profusely decorated with figures and indescribable ornaments, which he informed our freshman was Blackfriars' Hall, where all the men who had been once plucked were obliged to migrate to; and that Folly Bridge received its name from its propinquity to the Hall. They were too late to see the Vice-Chancellor wind up the clock of Christ Church; but as they passed by the college, they met two gownsmen

* Exhibitioners of Merton College are called 'postmasters'.

who recognised Mr Larkyns by a slight nod. 'Those are two Christ Church men,' he said, 'and noblemen. The one with the Skye-terrier's coat and eye-glass is the Earl of Whitechapel, the Duke of Minories's son. I dare say you know the other man. No! Why, he is Lord Thomas Peeper, eldest son of the Lord Godiva who hunts our county. I knew him in the field.'

'But why do they wear *gold* tassels to their caps?' inquired the freshman.

'Ah,' said the ingenious Mr Larkyns, shaking his head; 'I had rather you'd not have asked me that question, because that's the disgraceful part of the business. But these lords, you see, they *will* live at a faster

pace than us commoners, who can't stand a champagne breakfast above once a term or so. Why, those gold tassels are the badges of drunkenness!'*

'Of drunkenness! dear me!'

'Yes, it's very sad, isn't it?' pursued Mr Larkyns; 'and I wonder that Peeper in particular should give way to such things. But you see how they brazen it out, and walk about as coolly as though nothing had happened. It's just the same sort of punishment', continued Mr Larkyns, whose inventive powers increased with the demand that the freshman's gullibility imposed upon them – 'it is just the same sort of thing that they do with the Greenwich pensioners. When *they* have been transgressing the laws of sobriety, you know, they are made marked men by having to wear a yellow coat as a punishment; and our dons borrowed the idea, and made yellow tassels the badges of intoxication. But for the credit of the University, I'm glad to say that you'll not find many men so disgraced.'

They now turned down the New Road, and came to a strongly

* As 'Tufts' and 'Tuft-hunters' have become 'household words', it is perhaps need-less to tell anyone that the gold tassel is the distinguishing mark of a nobleman.

castellated building, which Mr Larkyns pointed out (and truly) as Oxford Castle or the Gaol; and he added (untruly), 'if you hear Botany-Bay College* spoken of, this is the place that's meant. It's a delicate way of referring to the temporary sojourn that any undergrad has been forced to make there, to say that he belongs to Botany-Bay College.'

They now turned back, up Queen Street and High Street, when, as they were passing All Saints', Mr Larkyns pointed out a pale, intellectual looking man who passed them, and said, 'That man is Cram, the patent safety. He's the first coach in Oxford.'

'A coach!' said our freshman, in some wonder.

'Oh, I forgot you didn't know college-slang. I suppose a royal mail is the only gentleman coach that *you* know of. Why, in Oxford, a coach means a private tutor, you must know; and those who can't afford a coach, get a cab – *alias* a crib, – *alias* a translation. You see, Verdant, you are gradually being initiated into Oxford mysteries.'

'I am, indeed,' said our hero, to whom a new world was opening.

They had now turned round by the west end of St Mary's, and were passing Brasenose; and Mr Larkyns drew Verdant's attention to the

brazen nose that is such a conspicuous object over the entrance-gate. 'That', said he, 'was modelled from a cast of the Principal feature of the first Head of the college; and so the college was named Brazen-nose.† The nose was formerly used as a place of punishment for any misbehaving Brazennosian, who had to sit upon it for two hours, and was not

---

* A name given to Worcester College, from its being the most distant college.

† Although we have a great respect for Mr Larkyns, yet we strongly suspect that he is intentionally deceiving his friend. He has, however, the benefit of a doubt, as the authorities differ on the origin and meaning of the word Brasenose, as may be seen by the following notices, to the last two of which the editor of *Notes and Queries* has directed our attention:

'This curious appellation, which, whatever was the origin of it, has been perpetuated by the symbol of a brazen nose here and at Stamford, occurs with the modern orthography, but in one undivided word, so early as 1278, in an inquisition now printed in *The Hundred Rolls*, though quoted by Wood from the manuscript record.' – *Ingram's Memorials of Oxford*.

'There is a spot in the centre of the city where Alfred is said to have lived, and which

countenanced until he had done so. These punishments were so frequent that they gradually wore down the nose to its present small dimensions.

'This round building,' continued Mr Larkyns, pointing to the Radcliffe, 'is the Vice-Chancellor's house. He has to go each night up to that balcony on the top, and look round to see if all's safe. Those heads,' he said, as they passed the Ashmolean, 'are supposed to be the twelve Cæsars; only there happen, I believe, to be thirteen of them. I think that they are the busts of the original Heads of Houses.'

Mr Larkyns' inventive powers having been now somewhat exhausted, he proposed that they should go back to Brazenface and have some lunch. This they did; after which Mr Verdant Green wrote to his mother a long account of his friend's kindness, and the trouble he had taken to explain the most interesting sights that could be seen by a Freshman.

'Are you writing to your governor, Verdant?' asked the friend, who had made his way to our hero's rooms, and was now perfuming them with a little tobacco-smoke.

'No; I am writing to my mama – mother, I mean!'

'Oh! to the missis!' was the reply; 'that's just the same. Well, had you not better take the opportunity to ask them to send you a proper certificate that you have been vaccinated, and had the measles favourably?'

may be called the native place or river-head of three separate societies still existing, University, Oriel, and Brasenose. Brasenose claims his palace, Oriel his church, and University his school or academy. Of these, Brasenose College is still called in its formal style "the King's Hall", which is the name by which Alfred himself, in his laws, calls his palace; and it has its present singular name from a corruption of *brasinium*, or *brasin-huse*, as having been originally located in that part of the royal mansion, which was devoted to the then important accommodation of a brew-house.' – From a Review of *Ingram's Memorials* in the *British Critic*, vol. xxiv. p. 139.

'Brasen Nose Hall, as the Oxford antiquary has shown, may be traced as far back as the time of Henry III, about the middle of the thirteenth century; and early in the succeeding reign, 6th Edward I, 1278, it was known by the name of Brasen Nose Hall, which peculiar name was undoubtedly owing, as the same author observes, to the circumstances of a nose of brass affixed to the gate. It is presumed, however, that this conspicuous appendage of the portal was not formed of the mixed metal which the word now denotes, but the genuine produce of the mine; as is the nose, or rather face, of a lion or leopard still remaining at Stamford, which also gave name to the edifice it adorned. And hence, when Henry VIII debased the coin by an alloy of *copper*, it was a common remark or proverb, that "Testons were gone to Oxford, to study in *Brasen* Nose."' – *Churton's Life of Bishop Smyth*, p. 227.

'But what is that for?' inquired our Freshman, always anxious to learn. 'Your father sent up the certificate of my baptism, and I thought that was the only one wanted.'

'Oh,' said Mr Charles Larkyns, 'they give you no end of trouble at these places; and they require the vaccination certificate before you go in for your responsions – the Little-go, you know. You need not mention my name in your letter as having told you this. It will be quite enough to say that you understand such a thing is required.'

Verdant accordingly penned the request; and Charles Larkyns smoked on, and thought his friend the very beau-ideal of a Freshman. 'By the way, Verdant,' he said, desirous not to lose any opportunity, 'you are going to wine with Smalls this evening; and – excuse me mentioning it – but I suppose you would go properly dressed – white tie, kids, and that sort of thing, eh? Well! ta, ta, till then. "We meet again at Philippi!"'

Acting upon the hint thus given, our hero, when Hall was over, made himself uncommonly spruce in a new white tie, and spotless kids, and as he was dressing, drew a mental picture of the party to which he was going. It was to be composed of quiet, steady men, who were such hard readers as to be called 'fast men'. He should therefore hear some delightful and rational conversation on the literature of ancient Greece and Rome, the present standard of scholarship in the University, speculations on the forthcoming prize-poems, comparisons between various expectant class-men, and delightful topics of a kindred nature; and the evening would be passed in a grave and sedate manner; and after a couple of glasses of wine had been leisurely

sipped, they should have a very enjoyable tea, and would separate for an early rest, mutually gratified and improved. This was the nature of Mr Verdant Green's speculations; but whether they were realised or no, may be judged by transferring the scene a few hours later to Mr Smalls's room.

Mr Verdant Green's Morning Reflections are not so pleasant as his Evening Diversions.

MR SMALLS'S room was filled with smoke and noise. Supper had been cleared away; the glasses were now sparkling on the board, and the wine was ruby bright. The table, moreover, was supplied with spirituous liquors and mixtures of all descriptions, together with many varieties of 'cup' – a cup which not only cheers, but occasionally inebriates; and this miscellany of liquids was now being drunk on the premises by some score and a half gentlemen, who were sitting round the table, and standing or lounging about in various parts of the room. Heading the table sat the host, loosely attired in a neat dressing-gown of crimson and blue, in an attitude which allowed him to swing his legs easily, if not gracefully, over the arm of his chair, and to converse cheerfully with Charles Larkyns, who was leaning over the chair back. Visible to the naked eye, on Mr Smalls's left hand, appeared the white tie and full evening dress which decorated the person of Mr Verdant Green.

A great consumption of tobacco was going on, not only through the medium of cigars, but also of meerschaums, short 'dhudheens' of envied colour, and the genuine yard of clay; and Verdant, while he was scarcely aware of what he was doing, found himself, to his great amazement, with a real cigar in his mouth, which he was industriously sucking, and with great difficulty keeping alight. Our hero felt that the unexpected exigencies of the case demanded from him some sacrifice; while he consoled himself by the reflection that, on the homœopathic principle of 'likes cure likes', a cigar was the best preventive against any ill effects arising from the combination of the thirty gentlemen who were generating smoke with all the ardour of lime-kilns or young volcanoes, and filling Mr Smalls' small room with an atmosphere that was of the smoke, smoky. Smoke produces thirst; and the cup, punch, egg-flip, sherry-cobblers, and other liquids, which had been so liber- ally provided, were being consumed by the members of the party as though it had been their drink from childhood; while the conversation was of a kind very different to what our hero had anticipated, being for the most part vapid and unmeaning, and (must it be confessed?) occasionally too highly flavoured with improprieties for it to be faithfully recorded in these pages of most perfect propriety.

The literature of ancient Greece and Rome was not even referred to; and when Verdant, who, from the unusual combination of the smoke and liquids, was beginning to feel extremely amiable and talkative, made a reflective observation (addressed to the company generally) which sounded like the words 'Nunc vino pellite curas, Cras ingens',* he was immediately interrupted by the voice of Mr Bouncer, crying out, 'Who's that talking shop about engines? Holloa, Giglamps!' – Mr Bouncer, it must be observed, had facetiously adopted the *sobriquet* which had been bestowed on Verdant and his spectacles on their first appearance outside the Oxford coach, – 'Holloa, Giglamps, is that you ill-treating the dead languages? I'm ashamed of you!

* Horace, car. i., od. vii.

a venerable party like you ought to be above such things. There! don't blush, old feller, but give us a song! It's the punishment for talking shop, you know.'

There was an immediate hammering of tables and jingling of glasses, accompanied with loud cries of 'Mr Green for a song! Mr Green! Mr Gig-lamps's song!' – cries which nearly brought our hero to the verge of idiotcy.

Charles Larkyns saw this, and came to the rescue. 'Gentlemen,' he said, addressing the company, 'I know that my friend Verdant *can* sing, and that, like a good bird, he *will* sing. But while he is mentally looking over his numerous stock of songs, and selecting one for our amusement, I beg to fill up our valuable time, by asking you to fill up a bumper to the health of our esteemed host Smalls (*vociferous cheers*) – a man whose private worth is only to be equalled by the purity of his milk-punch and the excellence of his weeds (*hear, hear*). Bumpers, gentlemen and no heel-taps! and though I am sorry to interfere with Mr Fosbrooke's private enjoyments, yet I must beg to suggest to him that he has been so much engaged in drowning his personal cares in the bowl over which he is so skilfully presiding, that my glass has been allowed to sparkle on the board empty and useless.' And as Charles Larkyns held out his glass towards Mr Fosbrooke and the punch-bowl, he trolled out, in a rich, manly voice, old Cowley's anacreontic:

> Fill up the bowl then, fill it high!
> Fill all the glasses there! For why
> Should every creature drink but I?
> Why, man of morals, tell me why?

By the time that the 'man of morals' had ladled out for the company, and that Mr Smalls's health had been drunk and responded to amid uproarious applause, Charles Larkyns's friendly diversion in our hero's favour had succeeded, and Mr Verdant Green had regained his confidence, and had decided upon one of those vocal efforts which, in the bosom of his own family, and to the pianoforte accompaniment of his sisters, was accustomed to meet with great applause. And when he had hastily tossed off another glass of milk-punch (merely to clear his throat), he felt bold enough to answer the spirit-rappings which were again demanding 'Mr Green's song!' It was given much in the following manner:

Mr Verdant Green (*in low plaintive tones, and fresh alarm at hearing the sounds of his own voice*). 'I dreamt that I dwe-elt in mar-arble halls, with . . .'

Mr Bouncer (*interrupting*). 'Spit it out, Gig-lamps! Dis child can't hear whether it's Maudlin Hall you're singing about, or what.'

Omnes. 'Order! or-*der!* Shut up, Bouncer!'

Charles Larkyns (*encouragingly*). 'Try back, Verdant: never mind.'

Mr Verdant Green (*tries back, with increased confusion of ideas, resulting principally from the milk-punch and tobacco*). 'I dreamt that I dwe-elt in mar-arble halls, with vassals and serfs at my si-hi-hide; and – and – I beg your pardon, gentlemen, I really forget – oh, I know! – and I also dre-eamt, which ple-eased me most – no, that's not it . . .'

Mr Bouncer (*who does not particularly care for the words of a song, but only appreciates the chorus*). 'That'll do, old feller! We aint pertickler – (*rushes with great deliberation and noise to the chorus*) 'That you lo-oved me sti-ill the sa-ha-hame – chorus, gentlemen!'

Omnes (*in various keys and time*). 'That you lo-oved me sti-ill the same.'

Mr Bouncer (*to Mr Green, alluding remotely to the opera*). 'Now, my Bohemian gal, can't you come out to-night? Spit us out a yard or two more, Gig-lamps.'

Mr Verdant Green (*who has again taken the opportunity to clear his throat*). 'I dreamt that I dwe-elt in mar-arble – no! I beg pardon! sang that (*desperately*) – that sui-uitors sou-ught my hand, that knights on their (*hic*) ben-ended kne-e-ee – had (*hic*) riches too gre-eat to' – (*Mr Verdant Green smiles benignantly upon the company*) – 'Don't rec'lect anymo.'

Mr Bouncer (*who is not to be defrauded of the chorus*). 'Chorus, gentlemen! – That you'll lo-ove me sti-ill the sa-a-hame!'

Omnes (*ad libitum*). 'That you'll lo-ove me sti-ill the same!'

Though our hero had ceased to sing, he was still continuing to clear his throat by the aid of the milk-punch, and was again industriously sucking his cigar, which he had not yet succeeded in getting half through, although he had re-lighted it about twenty times. All this was observed by the watchful eyes of Mr Bouncer, who, whispering to his

neighbour, and bestowing a distributive wink on the company generally, rose and made the following remarks:

'Mr Smalls, and gents all: I don't often get on my pins to trouble
you with a neat and appropriate speech; but on an occasion like the
present, when we are honoured with the presence of a party who has
just delighted us with what I may call a flood of harmony (*hear, hear*) –
and has pitched it so uncommon strong in the vocal line, as to considerably take the shine out of the woodpecker-tapping, that we've
read of in the pages of history (*hear, hear*: "*Go it again, Bouncer!*") –
when, gentlemen, I see before me this old original Little Wobbler –
need I say that I allude to Mr Verdant Green? – (*vociferous cheers*) –
I feel it a sort of, what you call a privilege, d'ye see, to stand on my pins,
and propose that respected party's jolly good health (*renewed cheers*).
Mr Verdant Green, gentlemen, has but lately come among us, and is,
in point of fact, what you call a freshman; but, gentlemen, we've
already seen enough of him to feel aware that – that Brazenface has
gained an acquisition, which – which – (*cries of "Tally-ho! Yoicks!
Hark forrud!"*) Exactly so, gentlemen: so, as I see you are all anxious
to do honour to our freshman, I beg, without further preface, to give
you the health of Mr Verdant Green! With all the honours. Chorus,
gents!'

> For he's a jolly good fellow!
> For he's a jolly good fellow!!
> For he's a jolly good f-e-e-ell-ow!!!
> Which nobody can deny!

This chorus was taken up and prolonged in the most indefinite
manner; little Mr Bouncer fairly revelling in it, and only regretting
that he had not his post-horn with him to further contribute to the
harmony of the evening. It seemed to be a great art in the singer of the
chorus to dwell as long as possible on the third repetition of the word
'fellow,' and in the most defiant manner to pounce down on the bold
affirmation by which it is followed; and then to lyrically proclaim that,
not only was it a way they had in the Varsity to drive dull care away,
but that the same practice was also pursued in the army and navy for
the attainment of a similar end.

When the chorus had been sung over three or four times, and Mr

Verdant Green's name had been proclaimed with equal noise, that gentleman rose (with great difficulty), to return thanks. He was understood to speak as follows:-

'Genelum anladies (*cheers*) - I meangenelum. ("*That's about the ticket, old feller!" from Mr Bouncer.*) Customd syam plic speakn, I -

I - (*hear, hear*) - feel bliged drinkmyel. I'm fresman, genelum, and prow title (*loud cheers*). Myfren Misserboucer, fallowme callm myfren! ("*In course, Gig-lamps, you do me proud, old feller.*") Myfren Misserboucer seszime fresman - prow title, sureyou (*hear, hear*). Genelmun, werall jolgoodfles, anwe wogohotillmorrin! ("*We won't, we won't! not a bit of it!*") Gelmul, I'm fresmal, an namesgreel, gelmul (*cheers*). Fanyul dousmewor, herescardinpock 'lltellm! Misser Verdalgreel, Braseface, Oxul fresmal, anprowtitle! (*Great cheering and rattling of glasses, during which Mr Verdant Green's coat-tails are made the receptacles for empty bottles, lobsters' claws, and other miscellaneous articles.*) Misserboucer said was fresmal. If Misserboucer wantsultme ("*No, no!*"), herescardinpocklltellm namesverdalgreel, Braseface! Not shameofitgelmul! prowtitle! (*Great applause.*) I doewaltilsul Misserboucer! thenwhysee sultme? thaswaw Iwaltknow! (*Loud cheers, and roars of laughter, in which Mr Verdant Green suddenly joins to the best of his ability.*) I'm anoxful fresmal, gelmul, 'fmyfrel Misserboucer loumecallimso. (*Cheers and laughter, in which Mr Verdant Green feebly joins.*) Anweerall jolgoodfles, anwe wogohotilmorril, an I'm fresmal, gelmul, anfanyul dowsmewor - an I - doefeel quiwell!'

This was the termination of Mr Verdant Green's speech, for after making a few unintelligible sounds, his knees suddenly gave way, and with a benevolent smile he disappeared beneath the table.

Half an hour afterwards two gentlemen might have been seen, bearing with staggering steps across the moonlit quad the huddled form of a third gentleman, who was clothed in full evening dress, and appeared incapable of taking care of himself. The two first gentlemen set down their burden under an open doorway, painted over with a large 4; and then, by pulling and pushing, assisted it to guide its steps up a narrow and intricate staircase, until they had gained the third floor, and stood before a door, over which the moonlight revealed, in newly-painted white letters, the name of 'MR VERDANT GREEN.'

'Well, old feller,' said the first gentleman, 'how do you feel now after "Sich a getting up stairs?"'

'Feel much berrer now,' said their late burden; 'feel quite comfurble! Shallgotobed!'

'Well, Gig-lamps,' said the first speaker, 'and By-by won't be at all a bad move for you. D'ye think you can unrig yourself and get between the sheets, eh, my beauty?'

'Its allri, allri!' was the reply; 'limycandle!'

'No, no,' said the second gentleman, as he pulled up the window blind, and let in the moonlight; 'here's quite as much light as you want. It's almost morning.'

'Sotis,' said the gentleman in the evening costume; 'anlittlebirds beginsingsoon! Ilike littlebirds sing! jollittlebirds!' The speaker had suddenly fallen upon his bed, and was lying thereon at full length with his feet on the pillow.

'He'll be best left in this way,' said the second speaker, as he removed the pillow to the proper place, and raised the prostrate gentleman's head; 'I'll take off his choker and make him easy about the neck, and then we'll shut him up and leave him. Why the beggar's asleep already!' And so the two gentlemen went away, and left him safe and sleeping.

It is conjectured, however, that he must have got up shortly after this, and finding himself with his clothes on, must have considered that a lighted candle was indispensably necessary to undress by; for when Mrs Tester came at her usual early hour to light the fires and prepare the sitting-rooms, she discovered him lying on the carpet embracing the coal-scuttle, with a candle by his side. The good woman raised him, and did not leave him until she had, in the most motherly manner, safely tucked him up in bed.

*

Clink, clank! clink, clank! tingle, tangle! tingle, tangle! Are demons smiting ringing hammers into Mr Verdant Green's brain, or is the

dreadful bell summoning him to rise for morning chapel?

Mr Filcher put an end to the doubt by putting his head in at the bedroom door, and saying, 'Time for chapel, sir! Chapel,' thought Mr Filcher; 'here is a chap ill, indeed! – Bain't you well, sir? Restless you look!'

Oh, the shame and agony that Mr Verdant Green felt! The desire to bury his head under the clothes, away from Robert's and everyone else's sight; the fever that throbbed his brain and parched his lips, and made him long to drink up Ocean; the eyes that felt like burning lead; the powerless hands that trembled like a weak old man's; the voice that came in faltering tones that jarred the brain at every word! How he despised himself; how he loathed the very idea of wine; how he resolved never, never to transgress so again! But perhaps Mr Verdant Green was not the only Oxford freshman who has made this resolution.

'Bain't you well, sir?' repeated Mr Filcher, with a passing thought that freshmen were sadly degenerating, and could not manage their three bottles as they did when he was first a scout: 'bain't you well, sir?'

'Not very well, Robert, thank you. I – my head aches, and I'm afraid I shall not be able to get up for chapel. Will the Master be very angry?'

'Well, he *might* be, you see, sir,' replied Mr Filcher, who never lost an opportunity of making anything out of his master's infirmities; 'but if you'll leave it to me, sir, I'll make it all right for you, *I* will. Of course you'd like to take out an *æger*, sir; and I can bring you your commons just the same. Will that do, sir?'

'Oh, thank you; yes, anything. You will find five shillings in my waistcoat-pocket, Robert; please to take it; but I can't eat.'

'Thank'ee sir,' said the scout, as he abstracted the five shillings; 'but you'd better have a bit of somethin', sir – a cup of strong tea, or somethin'. Mr Smalls, sir, when he were pleasant, he always had beer, sir; but p'raps you ain't been used to bein' pleasant, sir, and slops might suit you better, sir.'

'Oh, anything, anything!' groaned our poor, unheroic hero, as he turned his face to the wall, and endeavoured to recollect in what way he had been 'pleasant' the night before. But, alas! the wells of his memory had, for the time, been poisoned, and nothing clear or pure could be drawn therefrom. So he got up and looked at himself in the glass, and scarcely recognized the tangled-haired, sallow-faced wretch, whose bloodshot eyes gazed heavily at him from the mirror. So he nervously drained the water-bottle, and buried himself once more among the tossed and tumbled bed-clothes.

The tea really did him some good, and enabled him to recover sufficient nerve to go feebly through the operation of dressing; though it was lucky that nature had not yet brought Mr Verdant Green to the necessity of shaving, for the handling of a razor might have been attended with suicidal results, and have brought these veracious memoirs and their hero to an untimely end.

He had just sat down to a second edition of tea, and was reading a letter that the post had brought him from his sister Mary, in which she said, 'I dare say by this time you have found Mr Charles Larkyns a very *delightful* companion, and I *am sure* a very *valuable* one; as, from what the rector says, he appears to be so *steady*, and has such *nice quiet* companions' – our hero had read as far as this, when a great noise just without his door caused the letter to drop from his trembling hands; and, between loud *fanfares* from a posthorn, and heavy thumps upon the oak, a voice was heard, demanding 'Entrance in the Proctor's name.'

Mr Verdant Green had for the first time 'sported his oak.' Under any circumstances it would have been a mere form, since his bashful politeness would have induced him to open it to any comer; but, at the dreaded name of the Proctor, he sprang from his chair, and while impositions, rustications, and expulsions rushed tumultuously through his disordered brain, he nervously undid the springlock, and admitted – not the Proctor, but the 'steady' Mr Charles Larkyns and his 'nice quiet companion', little Mr Bouncer, who testified his joy at the success of their *coup d'état*, by blowing on his horn loud blasts that might have been borne by Fontarabian echoes, and which rang through poor Verdant's head with indescribable jarrings.

'Well, Verdant,' said Charles Larkyns, 'how do you find yourself this morning? You look rather shaky.'

'He ain't a very lively picter, is he?' remarked little Mr Bouncer, with the air of a connoisseur; 'peakyish you feel, don't you, now, with a touch of the mulligrubs in your collywobbles? Ah, I know what it is, my boy.'

It was more than our hero did; and he could only reply that he did not feel very well. 'I – I had a glass of claret after some lobster-salad, and I think it disagreed with me.'

'Not a doubt of it, Verdant,' said Charles Larkyns very gravely; 'it would have precisely the same effect that the salmon always has at a public dinner – bring on great hilarity, succeeded by a pleasing delirium, and concluding in a horizontal position, and a demand for soda-water.'

'I hope,' said our hero, rather faintly, 'that I did not conduct myself in an unbecoming manner last night; for I am sorry to say that I do not remember all that occurred.'

'I should think not, Gig-lamps. You were as drunk as a besom,' said little Mr Bouncer, with a side wink to Mr Larkyns, to prepare that gentleman for what was to follow. 'Why, you got on pretty well till old Slowcoach came in, and then you certainly did go it, and no mistake!'

'Mr Slowcoach!' groaned the freshman. 'Good gracious! is it possible that *he* saw me? I don't remember it.'

'And it would be lucky for you if *he* didn't,' replied Mr Bouncer.

'Why his rooms, you know, are in the same angle of the quad as Smalls's; so, when you came to shy the empty bottles out of Smalls's window at *his* window . . .'

'Shy empty bottles! Oh!' gasped the freshman.

'Why, of course, you see, he couldn't stand that sort of game – it wasn't to be expected; so he puts his head out of the bedroom window – and then, don't you remember crying out, as you pointed to the tassel of his night-cap sticking up straight on end, "Tally-ho! Unearth'd at last! Look at his brush!" Don't you remember that, Gig-lamps?'

'Oh, oh, no!' groaned Mr Bouncer's victim; 'I can't remember – oh, what *could* have induced me!'

'By Jove, you *must* have been screwed! Then I dare say you don't remember wanting to have a polka with him, when he came up to Smalls's rooms?'

'A polka! Oh dear! Oh no! Oh!'

'Or asking him if his mother knew he was out – and what he'd take for his cap without the tassel; and telling him that he was the joy of your heart – and that you should never be happy unless he'd smile as he was wont to smile, and would love you then as now – and saying all sorts of bosh? What, not remember it! "Oh, what a noble mind is here o'erthrown!" as some cove says in Shakspeare. But how screwed you *must* have been, Gig-lamps!'

'And do you think', inquired our hero, after a short but sufficiently painful reflection – 'do you think that Mr Slowcoach will – oh! – expel me?'

'Why, it's rather a shave for it,' replied his tormentor; 'but the best thing you can do is to write an apology at once: pitch it pretty strong in the pathetic line – say, it's your first offence, and that you'll never be a naughty boy again, and all that sort of thing. You just do that, Gig-lamps, and I'll see that the note goes to – the proper place.'

'Oh, thank you!' said the freshman; and while, with equal difficulty from agitation both of mind and body, he composed and penned the note, Mr Bouncer ordered up some buttery beer, and Charles Larkyns prepared some soda-water with a dash of brandy, which he gave Verdant to drink, and which considerably refreshed that gentleman. 'And I should advise you,' he said, 'to go out for a constitutional; for walking-time's come, although you have but just done your breakfast.

A blow up Headington Hill will do you good, and set you on your legs again.'

So Verdant, after delivering up his note to Mr Bouncer, took his friend's advice, and set out for his constitutional in his cap and gown, feeling afraid to move without them, lest he should thereby trespass some law. This, of course, gained him some attention after he had crossed Magdalen Bridge; and he might have almost been taken for the original of that impossible gownsman who appears in Turner's well-known 'View of Oxford, from Ferry Hincksey', as wandering-

Remote, unfriended, solitary, *slow* -

in a corn-field, in the company of an umbrella!

Among the many pedestrians and equestrians that he encountered, our freshman espied a short and very stout gentleman, whose shovel-hat, short apron, and general decanical costume, proclaimed him to be a don of some importance. He was riding a pad-nag, who ambled placidly along, without so much as hinting at an outbreak into a canter; a performance that, as it seemed, might have been attended with disastrous consequences to his rider. Our hero noticed that the trio of undergraduates who were walking before him, while they passed others, who were evidently dons, without the slightest notice (being in mufti), yet not only raised their hats to the stout gentleman, but also separated for that purpose, and performed the salute at intervals of about ten yards. And he further remarked that while the stout gentleman appeared to be exceedingly gratified at the notice he received, yet that he had also very great difficulty in returning the rapid salutations; and only accomplished them and retained his seat by catching at the pommel of his saddle, or the mane of his steed - a proceeding which the pad-nag seemed perfectly used to.

Mr Verdant Green returned home from his walk, feeling all the better for the fresh air and change of scene; but he still looked, as his

neighbour, Mr Bouncer, kindly informed him, 'uncommon seedy and doosid fishy about the eyes', and it was some days even before he had quite recovered from the novel excitement of Mr Smalls's 'quiet party'.

CHAPTER IX

*Mr Verdant Green attends Lectures, and, in despite of
Sermons, has dealings with Filthy Lucre.*

OUR freshman, like all other freshmen, now began to think seriously of work, and plunged desperately into all the lectures that it was
possible for him to attend, beginning every course with a zealousness
that showed him to be filled with the idea that such a plan was
eminently necessary for the attainment of his degree; in all this in every
respect deserving the Humane Society's medal for his brave plunge
into the depths of the Pierian spring, to fish up the beauties that had
been immersed therein by the poets of old. When we say that our
freshman, like other freshmen, 'began' this course, we use the verb
advisedly; for, like many other freshmen who start with a burst in
learning's race, he soon got winded, and fell back among the ruck. But
the course of lectures, like the course of true love, will not always run
smooth, even to those who undertake it with the same courage as Mr
Verdant Green.

The dryness of the daily routine of lectures, which varied about as
much as the steak-and-chop, chop-and-steak dinners of ancient
taverns, was occasionally relieved by episodes, which, though not
witty in themselves, were yet the cause of wit in others; for it takes but
little to cause amusement in a lecture-room, where a bad construe; or
the imaginative excuses of late-comers; or the confusion of some young
gentleman who has to turn over the leaf of his Greek play and finds
it uncut; or the pounding of the same gentleman in the middle of the
first chorus; or his offensive extrication therefrom through the medium
of some Cumberland barbarian; or the officiousness of the same barbarian to pursue the lecture when every one else has, with singular
unanimity, 'read no further' – all these circumstances, although perhaps dull enough in themselves, are nevertheless productive of some
mirth in a lecture-room.

But if there were often late-comers to the lectures, there were
occasionally early-goers from them. Had Mr Four-in-hand Fosbrooke

an engagement to ride his horse Tearaway in the amateur steeple-chase, and was he constrained, by circumstances over which (as he protested) he had no control, to put in a regular appearance at Mr Slowcoach's lectures, what was it necessary for him to do more than to come to lecture in a long greatcoat, put his handkerchief to his face as though his nose were bleeding, look appealingly at Mr Slowcoach, and, as he made his exit, pull aside the long greatcoat, and display to his admiring colleagues the snowy cords and tops that would soon be pressing against Tearaway's sides, that gallant animal being then in waiting, with its trusty groom, in the alley at the back of Brazenface? And if little Mr Bouncer, for astute reasons of his own, wished Mr

Slowcoach to believe that he (Mr B) was particularly struck with his (Mr S's) remarks on the force of $\kappa\alpha\tau\acute{\alpha}$ in composition, what was to prevent Mr Bouncer from feigning to make a note of these remarks by the aid of a cigar instead of an ordinary pencil?

But besides the regular lectures of Mr Slowcoach, our hero had also the privilege of attending those of the Revd Richard Harmony. Much learning, though it had not made Mr Harmony mad, had, at least in conjunction with his natural tendencies, contributed to make him extremely eccentric; while to much perusal of Greek and Hebrew MSS. he probably owed his defective vision. These infirmities, instead of being regarded with sympathy, as wounds received by Mr Harmony in the classical engagements in the various fields of literature, were, to Mr Verdant Green's surprise, much imposed upon; for it was a favourite pastime with the gentlemen who attended Mr Harmony's lectures, to gradually raise up the lecture table by a concerted action, and when Mr Harmony's book had nearly reached to the level of his nose, to then suddenly drop the table to its original level; upon which

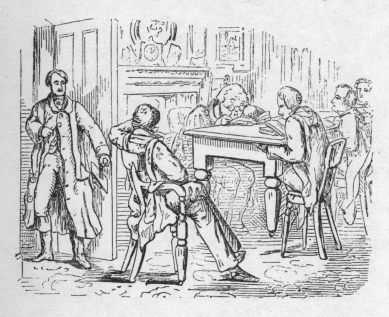

Mr Harmony, to the immense gratification of all concerned, would rub his eyes, wipe his glasses, and murmur, 'Dear me! dear me! how my head swims this morning!' And then he would perhaps ring for his servant, and order his usual remedy, an orange, at which he would suck abstractedly, nor discover any difference in the flavour even when a lemon was surreptitiously substituted. And thus he would go on through the lecture, sucking his orange (or lemon), explaining and expounding in the most skilful and lucid manner, and yet, as far as the 'table-movement' was concerned, as unsuspecting and as witless as a little child.

Mr Verdant Green not only (at first) attended lectures with exem-

plary diligence and regularity, but he also duly went to morning and evening chapel; nor, when Sundays came, did he neglect to turn his feet towards St Mary's to hear the University sermons. Their effect was as striking to him as it probably is to most persons who have only been accustomed to the usual services of country churches. First, there was the peculiar character of the congregation: down below, the Vice-

Chancellor in his throne, overlooking the other dons in their stalls (being 'a complete realisation of stalled Oxon!' as Charles Larkyns whispered to our hero), who were relieved in colour by their crimson or scarlet hoods; and then, 'upstairs,' in the north and the great west galleries, the black mass of undergraduates; while a few ladies' bonnets and heads of male visitors peeped from the pews in the aisles, or looked out from the curtains of the organ-gallery, where, 'by the kind permission of Dr Elvey', they were accommodated with seats, and watched with wonder, while

> The wild wizard's fingers,
>   With magical skill,
> Made music that lingers
>   In memory still.

Then there was the bidding-prayer, in which Mr Verdant Green was somewhat astonished to hear the long list of founders and benefactors, 'such as were, Philip Pluckton, Bishop of Iffley; King Edward the Seventh; Stephen de Henley, Earl of Bagley, and Maud his wife; Nuneham Courtney, knight,' with a long et-cetera; though, as the preacher happened to be a Brazenface man, our hero found that he was 'most chiefly bound to praise Clement Abingdon, Bishop of Jericho, and founder of the college of Brazenface; Richard Glover, Duke of Woodstock; Giles Peckwater, Abbot of Osney; and Binsey Green, Doctor of Music – benefactors of the same.'

Then there was the sermon itself; the abstrusely learned and classical character of which, at first, also astonished him, after having been so long used to the plain and highly practical advice which the rector, Mr Larkyns, knew how to convey so well and so simply to his rustic hearers. But as soon as he had reflected on the very different characters of the two congregations, Mr Verdant Green at once recognized the appropriateness of each class of sermons to its peculiar hearers; yet he could not altogether drive away the thought, how the generality of those who had on previous Sundays been his fellow-worshippers would open their blue Saxon eyes, and ransack their rustic brains, as to 'what *could* ha' come to rector,' if he were to indulge in Greek and Latin quotations – *somewhat* after the following style. 'And though this interpretation may in these days be disputed, yet we shall find that it was once very generally received. For the learned St Chrysostom is very clear on this point, where he says, "Arma virumque cano, rusticus expectat, sub tegmine fagi", of which the words of Irenæus are a confirmation – ὀτοτοτοιο, παπαπεραξ, πολυφλοίσβοιο θαλάσσης.' Our hero, indeed, could not but help wondering what the fairer portion of the congregation made of these parts of the sermons, to whom, probably, the sentences just quoted would have sounded as full of meaning as those they really heard.

*

'Hallo, Gig-lamps!' said the cheery voice of little Mr Bouncer, as he looked one morning into Verdant's rooms, followed by his two bull-terriers; 'why don't you sport something in the dog line? Something in the bloodhound or tarrier way. Ain't you fond o' dogs?'

'Oh, very!' replied our hero. 'I once had a very nice one – a King Charles.'

'Oh!' observed Mr Bouncer, 'one of them beggars that you have to feed with spring-chickens, and get up with curling tongs. Ah! they're all very well in their way, and do for women and carriage-exercise; but give *me* this sort of thing!' and Mr Bouncer patted one of his villanous-looking pets, who wagged his corkscrew tail in reply. 'Now, these are beauties, and no mistake! What you call useful and ornamental; ain't you, Buzzy? The beggars are brothers; so I call them Huz and Buz – Huz his first-born, you know, and Buz his brother.'

'I should like a dog,' said Verdant; 'but where could I keep one?'

'Oh, anywhere!' replied Mr Bouncer confidently. 'I keep these beggars in the little shop for coal, just outside the door. It ain't the law, I know; but what's the odds as long as they're happy? *They* think it no end of a lark. I once had a Newfunland, and tried *him* there; but the obstinate brute considered it too small for him, and barked himself in such an unnatural manner, that at last he'd got no wool on the top of his head – just the place where the wool ought to grow, you know; so I swopped the beggar to a Skimmery* man for a regular slap-up set of pets of the ballet, framed and glazed, petticoats and all, mind you. But about your dog, Gig-lamps: that cupboard there would be just the ticket; you could put him under the wine-bottles, and then there'd be

* Oxford slang for 'St. Mary's Hall.'

wine above and whine below. *Videsne puer?* D'ye twig, young 'un? But if you're squeamish about that, there are heaps of places in the town where you could keep a beast.'

So, when our hero had been persuaded that the possession of an animal of the terrier species was absolutely necessary to a University man's existence, he had not to look about long without having the void filled up. Money will in most places procure anything, from a grant of arms to a pair of wooden legs; so it is not surprising if, in Oxford, such an every-day commodity as a dog can be obtained through the medium of 'filthy lucre', for there was a well-known dog-fancier and proprietor, whose surname was that of the rich substantive just mentioned, to which had been prefixed the 'filthy' adjective, probably for the sake of euphony. As usual, Filthy Lucre was clumping with his lame leg up and down the pavement just in front of the Brazenface gate, accompanied by his last 'new and extensive assortment' of terriers of every variety, which he now pulled up for the inspection of Mr Verdant Green.

'Is it a long-aird dawg, or a smooth 'un, as you'd most fancy,' inquired Mr. Lucre. 'Har, sir!' he continued, in a flattering tone, as he saw our hero's eye dwelling on a Skye terrier; 'I see you're a gent as *does* know a good style of dawg, when you see 'un! It ain't often as you see a Skye sich as that, sir! Look at his colour, sir, and the way he looks out of his 'air! He answers to the name of Mop, sir, in consek-vence of the length of his 'air; and he's cheap as dirt, sir, at four-ten! It's a throwin' of him away at the price; and I shouldn't do it, but I've got more dawgs than I've room for; so I'm obligated to make a sacrifice. Four-ten sir! Ad the distemper, and everythink, and a reg'lar good 'un for the varmin.'

His merits also being testified to by Mr Larkyns and Mr Bouncer (who was considered a high authority in canine matters), and Verdant also liking the quaint appearance of the dog, Mop eventually became his property, for 'four-ten' *minus* five shillings, but *plus* a pint of Buttery-beer, which Mr Lucre always pronounced to be customary 'in all dealins whatsumever atween gentlemen'. Verdant was highly gratified at possessing a real University dog, and he patted Mop, and said, 'Poo dog! poo Mop! poo fellow then!' and thought what a pet his sisters would make of him when he took him back home with him for the holi – the Vacation!

Mop was for following Mr Lucre, who had clumped away up the street; and his new master had some difficulty in keeping him at his heels. By Mr Bouncer's advice, he at once took him over the river to the field opposite the Christ Church meadows, in order to test his rat-killing powers. How this could be done out in the open country, our hero was at a loss to know, but he discreetly held his tongue, for he was gradually becoming aware that a freshman in Oxford must live to learn, and that, as with most men, *experientia docet*.

They had just been punted over the river, and Mop had been restored to *terra firma*, when Mr Bouncer's remark of 'There's the cove that'll do the trick for you!' directed Verdant's attention to an individual, who, from his general appearance, might have been first cousin to 'Filthy Lucre', only that his live stock was of a different description. Slung from his shoulders was a large but shallow wire cage, in which were about a dozen doomed rats, whose futile endeavours to make their escape by running up the sides of their prison were regarded with the most intense earnestness by a group of terriers, who gave way to various phases of excitement. In his hand he carried

a smaller circular cage, containing two or three rats for immediate use.
On the receipt of sixpence, one of these was liberated; and a few yards
start being (sportsmanlike) allowed, the speculator's terrier was then
let loose, joined gratuitously, after a short interval, by a perfect pack
in full cry, with a human chorus of 'Hoo rat! Too loo! loo dog!' The
rat turned, twisted, doubled, – became confused, was overtaken, and,
with one grip and a shake, was dead; while the excited pack returned
to watch and jump at the wire cages until another doomed prisoner was
tossed forth to them. Gentlemen on their way for a walk were thus
enabled to while away a few minutes at the noble sport, and indulge
themselves and their dogs with a little healthy excitement; while the
boating costume of other gentlemen showed that they had for a while
left aquatic pursuits, and had strolled up from the river to indulge in
'the sports of the fancy'.

Although his new master invested several sixpences on Mop's
behalf, yet that ungrateful animal, being of a passive temperament of
mind as regarded rats, and a slow movement of body, in consequence
of his long hair impeding his progress, rather disgraced himself by

allowing the sport to be taken from his very teeth. But he still further disgraced himself, when he had been taken back to Brazenface, by howling all through the night in the cupboard where he had been placed, thereby setting on Mr Bouncer's two bull-terriers, Huz and Buz, to echo the sounds with redoubled fury from their coal-hole quarters; thus causing loss of sleep and a great outlay of Saxon expletives to all the dwellers on the staircase. It was in vain that our hero got out of bed and opened the cupboard-door, and said, 'Poo Mop! good dog, then!' it was in vain that Mr Bouncer shied boots at the coal-hole, and threatened Huz and Buz with loss of life; it was in vain that the tenant of the attic, Mr Sloe, who was a reading-man, and sat up half the night, working for his degree – it was in vain that he opened his door, and mildly declared (over the banisters), that it was impossible to get up Aristotle while such a noise was being made; it was in vain that Mr Four-in-hand Fosbrooke, whose rooms were on the other side of Verdant's, came and administered to Mop severe punishment with a tandem-whip (it was a favourite boast with Mr Fosbrooke, that he could flick a fly from his leader's ear); it was in vain to coax Mop with chicken-bones: he would neither be bribed nor frightened; and after a deceitful lull of a few minutes, just when everyone was getting to sleep again, his melancholy howl would be raised with renewed vigour, and Huz and Buz would join for sympathy.

'I tell you what, Gig-lamps,' said Mr Bouncer the next morning; 'this game 'll never do. Bark's a very good thing to take in its proper way, when you're in want of it, and get it with port wine; but when you get it by itself and in too large doses, it ain't pleasant, you know. Huz and Buz are quiet enough, as long as they're let alone; and I should advise you to keep Mop down at Spavin's stables, or somewhere. But first, just let me give the brute the hiding he deserves.'

Poor Mop underwent his punishment like a martyr; and in the course of the day an arrangement was made with Mr Spavin for Mop's board and lodging at his stables. But when Verdant called there the next day, for the purpose of taking him for a walk, there was no Mop to be found; taking advantage of the carelessness of one of Mr Spavin's men, he had bolted through the open door, and made his escape. Mr Bouncer, at a subsequent period, declared that he met Mop in the company of a well-known Regent-street fancier; but, however that may be, Mop was lost to Mr Verdant Green.

Mr Verdant Green reforms his Tailors' Bills and runs up others. He also appears in a rapid act of Horsemanship, and finds Isis cool in Summer.

THE state of Mr Verdant Green's outward man had long offended Mr Charles Larkyns' more civilised taste; and he one day took occasion delicately to hint to his friend, that it would conduce more to his appearance as an Oxford undergraduate, if he foreswore the primitive garments that his country-tailor had condemned him to wear, and adapted the 'build' of his dress to the peculiar requirements of university fashion.

Acting upon this friendly hint, our freshman at once betook himself to the shop where he had bought his cap and gown, and found its proprietor making use of the invisible soap and washing his hands in the imperceptible water, as though he had not left off that act of imaginary cleanliness since Verdant and his father had last seen him.

'Oh, certainly, sir; an abundant variety,' was his reply to Verdant's question, if he could show him any patterns that were fashionable in Oxford. 'The greatest stock hout of London, I should say, sir, decidedly. This is a nice unpretending gentlemanly thing, sir, that we make up a good deal!' and he spread a shaggy substance before the freshman's eyes.

'What do you make it up for?' inquired our hero, who thought it more nearly resembled the hide of his lamented Mop than any other substance.

'Oh, morning garments, sir! Reading and walking-coats, for erudition and the promenade, sir! Looks well with vest of the same material, sprinkled down with coral currant buttons! We've some sweet things in vests, sir; and some neat, quiet trouserings, that I'm sure would give satisfaction.' And the tailor and robe-maker, between washings with the invisible soap, so visibly 'soaped' our hero in what is understood to be the shop-sense of the word, and so surrounded him with a perfect irradiation of aggressive patterns of oriental gorgeousness, that Mr Verdant Green became bewildered, and finally made choice of one of the unpretending gentlemanly Mop-like coats, and 'vest and trouserings' of a neat, quiet, plaid-pattern, in red and green, which, he was informed, were all the rage.

When these had been sent home to him, together with a neck-tie of Oxford-blue from Randall's, and an immaculate guinea Lincoln-and-Bennett, our hero was delighted with the general effect of the costume; and after calling in at the tailor's to express his approbation, he at once sallied forth to 'do the High', and display his new purchases. A drawn silk bonnet of pale lavender, from which floated some bewitching ringlets, quickly attracted our hero's attention; and the sight of an arch, French-looking face, which (to his short-sighted imagination) smiled upon him as the young lady rustled by, immediately plunged him into the depths of first-love. Without the slightest encouragement being given him, he stalked this little deer to her lair, and, after some difficulty, discovered the enchantress to be Mademoiselle Mouslin de Laine, one of the presiding goddesses of a fancy hosiery warehouse. There, for the next fortnight – until which immense period his ardent passion had not subsided – our hero was daily to be seen purchasing articles for which he had no earthly use, but fully recompensed for his outlay by the artless (ill-natured people said, artful) smiles, and engaging, piquant conversation of mademoiselle. Our hero, when reminded of this at a subsequent period protested that he had thus acted merely to improve his French, and only conversed with mademoiselle for educational purposes. But we have our doubts. *Credat Judæus!*

About this time also our hero laid the nest-eggs for a very promising brood of bills, by acquiring an expensive habit of strolling into shops, and purchasing 'an extensive assortment of articles of every description', for no other consideration than that he should not be called upon to pay for them until he had taken his degree. He also decorated the walls

of his rooms with choice specimens of engravings: for the turning over of portfolios at Ryman's, and Wyatt's, usually leads to the eventual turning over of a considerable amount of cash; and our hero had not yet become acquainted with the cheaper circulating-system of pictures, which gives you a fresh set every term, and passes on your old ones to some other subscriber. But, in the meantime, it is very delightful, when you admire any thing, to be able to say, 'Send that to my room!' and to be obsequiously obeyed, 'no questions asked', and no payment demanded; and as for the future, why – as Mr Larkyns observed, as they strolled down the High – 'I suppose the bills *will* come in some day or other, but the governor will see to them; and though he may grumble and pull a long face, yet he'll only be too glad you've got your degree, and, in the fulness of his heart, he will open his cheque-book. I dare say old Horace gives very good advice when he says, 'carpe diem', but when he adds, 'quam minimum credula postero,'* about 'not giving the least credit to the succeeding day', it is clear that he never looked forward to the Oxford tradesmen and the credit-system. Do you ever read Wordsworth, Verdant?' continued Mr Larkyns, as they stopped at the corner of Oriel Street, to look in at a spacious range of shop windows, that were crowded with a costly

* Car. i, od. xi.

and glittering profusion of *papier maché* articles, statuettes, bronzes, glass and every kind of 'fancy goods' that could be classed as 'art-workmanship'.

'Why, I've not read much of Wordsworth myself,' replied our hero; 'but I've heard my sister Mary read a great deal of his poetry.'

'Shows her taste,' said Charles Larkyns. 'Well, this shop – you see the name – is Spiers'; and Wordsworth, in his sonnet to Oxford, has immortalised him. Don't you remember the lines? –

> O ye Spiers of Oxford! your presence overpowers
> The soberness of reason!*

---

* We suspect that Mr Larkyns is again intentionally deceiving his freshman friend; for on looking into our Wordsworth (*Misc. Son*. iii. 2) we find that the poet does *not* refer to the establishment of Messrs Spiers and Son, and that the lines, truly quoted, are,

> 'O ye *spires* of Oxford! domes and towers!
> Gardens and groves! Your presence', &c.

We blush for Mr Larkyns!

It was very queer that Wordsworth should ascribe to Messrs Spiers all the intoxication of the place; but then he was a Cambridge man, and prejudiced. Nice shop, though, isn't it? Particularly useful, and no less ornamental. It's one of the greatest lounges of the place. Let us go in and have a look at what Mrs Caudle calls the articles of bigotry and virtue.'

Mr Verdant Green was soon deeply engaged in an inspection of those *papier-maché* 'remembrances of Oxford' for which the Messrs Spiers are so justly famed; but after turning over tables, trays, screens, desks, albums, portfolios, and other things – all of which displayed views of Oxford from every variety of aspect, and were executed with such truth and perception of the higher qualities of art, that they formed in themselves quite a small but gratuitous Academy exhibition – our hero became so confused among the bewildering allurements around him, as to feel quite an *embarras de richesses*, and to be in a state of mind in which he was nearly giving Mr Spiers the most extensive (and expensive) order which probably that gentleman had ever received from an undergraduate. Fortunately for his purse, his attention was somewhat distracted by perceiving that Mr Slowcoach was at his elbow, looking over inkstands and reading-lamps, and also by Charles Larkyns calling upon him to decide whether he should have the cigar-case he had purchased emblazoned with the heraldic device of the Larkyns's, or illuminated with the Euripidean motto,

$$\text{Τὸ βακχικὸν δώρημα λαβέ, σε γὰρ φιλῶ.}$$

When this point had been decided, Mr Larkyns proposed to Verdant that he should astonish and delight his governor by having the Green arms emblazoned on a fire-screen, and taking it home with him as a gift. 'Or else', he said, 'order one with the garden view of Brazenface, and then they'll have more satisfaction in looking at that than at one of those offensive cockatoos, in an arabesque landscape, under a bronze sky, which usually sprawls over everything that is *papier-maché*. But you won't see that sort of thing here; so you can't well go wrong, whatever you buy.' Finally, Mr Verdant Green (N.B. Mr Green, senior, would have eventually to pay the bill) ordered a fire-screen to be prepared with the family-arms, as a present for his father; a ditto, with the view of his college, for his mother; a writing-case, with the High Street view, for his aunt; a netting-box, card-case, and a model of the Martyrs' Memorial, for his three sisters; and having thus bountifully remembered his family-circle, he treated himself with a modest paper-knife, and was treated in return by Mr Spiers with a perfect *bijou* of art, in the shape of 'a memorial for visitors to Oxford', in which the chief glories of that city were set forth in gold and colours, in the most attractive form, and which our hero immediately posted off to the Manor Green.

'And now, Verdant,' said Mr Larkyns, 'you may just as well get a hack, and come for a ride with me. You've kept up your riding, of course.'

'Oh, yes – a little!' faltered our hero.

Now, the reader may perhaps remember, that in an early part of our veracious chronicle we hinted that Mr Verdant Green's equestrian performances were but of a humble character. They were, in fact, limited to an occasional ride with his sisters when they required a cavalier; but on these occasions, the old cob which Verdant called his own was warranted not to kick, or plunge, or start, or do any thing derogatory to its age and infirmities. So that Charles Larkyns's proposition caused him some little nervous agitation; nevertheless, as he was ashamed to confess his fears, he, in a moment of weakness, consented to accompany his friend.

'We'll go to Symonds', said Mr Larkyns; 'I keep my hack there; and you can depend upon having a good one.'

So they made their way to Holywell Street, and turned under a gateway, and up a paved yard, to the stables. The upper part of the yard was littered down with straw, and covered in by a light, open roof; and in the stables there was accommodation for a hundred horses. At the back of the stables, and separated from the Wadham Gardens by a narrow lane, was a paddock; and here they found Mr Fosbrooke, and one or two of his friends, inspecting the leaping abilities of a fine hunter, which one of the stable-boys was taking backwards and forwards over the hurdles and fences erected for that purpose.

The horses were soon ready, and Verdant summoned up enough courage to say, with the Count in *Mazeppa*, 'Bring forth the steed!' And when the steed was brought, in all the exuberance of (literally) animal spirits, he felt that he was about to be another Mazeppa, and perform feats on the back of a wild horse; and he could not help saying to the ostler, 'He looks rather – vicious, I'm afraid!'

'Wicious, sir,' replied the groom; 'bless you, sir! she's as sweet-tempered as any young ooman you ever paid your intentions to. The mare's as quiet a mare as was ever crossed; this ere's ony her play at comin' fresh out of the stable!'

Verdant, however, had a presentiment that the play would soon become earnest; but he seated himself in the saddle (after a short delirious dance on one toe), and in a state of extreme agitation, not to say perspiration, proceeded at a walk, by Mr Larkyns's side, up Holywell Street. Here the mare, who doubtless soon understood what sort of rider she had got on her back, began to be more demonstrative of the 'fresh'ness of her animal spirits. Broad Street was scarcely broad enough to contain the series of *tableaux vivants* and heraldic attitudes that she assumed. 'Don't pull the curb-rein so!' shouted Charles Larkyns; but Verdant was in far too dreadful a state of mind to understand what he said, or even to know which *was* the curb-rein; and after

convulsively clutching at the mane and the pommel, in his endeavours to keep his seat, he first 'lost his head', and then his seat, and ignominiously gliding over the mare's tail, found that his lodging was on the cold ground. Relieved of her burden, the mare quietly trotted back to her stables; while Verdant, finding himself unhurt, got up, replaced his hat and spectacles, and registered a mental vow never to mount an Oxford hack again.

'Never mind, old fellow!' said Charles Larkyns, consolingly; 'these little accidents *will* occur, you know, even with the best-regulated riders! There were not *more* than a dozen ladies saw you, though you certainly made very creditable exertions to ride over one or two of them. Well! if you say you won't go back to Symond's, and get another hack, I must go on solus; but I shall see you at the Bump-supper to-night! I got old Blades to ask you to it. I'm going now in search of an appetite, and I should advise you to take a turn round the Parks and do the same. *Au reservoir!*'

So our hero, after he had compensated the livery-stable keeper, followed his friend's advice, and strolled round the neatly-kept potato-gardens denominated 'the Parks', looking in vain for the deer that have never been there, and finding them represented only by nursery maids and – others.

*

Mr Blades, familiarly known as 'old Blades' and 'Billy', was a gentleman who was fashioned somewhat after the model of the torso of Hercules; and, as Stroke of the Brazenface boat, was held in high estimation, not only by the men of his own college, but also by the boating men of the University at large. His University existence seemed to be engaged in one long struggle, the end and aim of which was to place the Brazenface boat in that envied position known in aquatic anatomy as 'the head of the river', and in this struggle all Mr Blades's energies of mind and body – though particularly of body – were engaged. Not a freshman was allowed to enter Brazenface, but immediately Mr Blades's eye was upon him; and if the expansion of the upper part of his coat and waistcoat denoted that his muscular development of chest and arms was of a kind that might be serviceable to the great object aforesaid – the placing of the Brazenface boat at the head of the river – then Mr Blades came and made flattering proposals to the new-comer to assist in the great work. But he was also indefatigable, as secretary to his college club, in seeking out all freshmen, even if their thews and sinews were not muscular models, and inducing them to aid the glorious cause by becoming members of the club. A Bump-supper – that is, O ye uninitiated! a supper to commemorate the fact of the boat of one college having, in the annual races, bumped, or touched the boat of another college immediately in its front, thereby gaining a place towards the head of the river – a Bump-supper was a famous opportunity for discovering both the rowing and paying capabilities of freshmen, who, in the enthusiasm of the moment, would put down their two or three guineas, and at once propose their names to be enrolled as members at the next meeting of the club.

And thus it was with Mr Verdant Green, who, before the evening was over, found that he had not only given in his name ('proposed by

Charles Larkyns, Esq., seconded by Henry Bouncer, Esq.'), but that a desire was burning within his breast to distinguish himself in aquatic pursuits. Scarcely anything else was talked of during the whole evening but the prospective chances of Brazenface bumping Balliol and Brasenose, and thereby getting to the head of the river. It was also mysteriously whispered, that Worcester and Christ Church were doing well, and might prove formidable; and that Exeter, Lincoln, and Wadham were very shady, and not doing the things that were expected of them. Great excitement too was caused by the announcement that the Balliol stroke had knocked up, or knocked down, or done something which Mr Verdant Green concluded he ought not to have done; and that the Brasenose bow had been seen with a cigar in his mouth, and also eating pastry in Hall – things shocking in themselves, and quite contrary to all training principles. Then there were anticipations of Henley; and criticisms on the new eight out-rigger that Searle was laying down for the University crew; and comparisons between somebody's stroke and somebody else's spurt; and a good deal of reference to Clasper and Coombes, and Newall and Pococke, who might have been heathen deities for all that our hero knew, and from the manner in which they were mentioned.

The aquatic desires that were now burning in Mr Verdant Green's

breast could only be put out by the water; so to the river he next day went, and, by Charles Larkyns's advice, made his first essay in a 'tub' from Hall's. Being a complete novice with the oars, our hero had no sooner pulled off his coat and given a pull, than he succeeded in catching a tremendous 'crab', the effect of which was to throw him backwards, and almost to upset the boat. Fortunately, however, 'tubs' recover their equilibrium almost as easily as tombolas, and the Sylph did not belie its character; so the freshman again assumed a proper position, and was shoved off with a boathook. At first he made some hopeless splashes in the stream, the only effect of which was to make the boat turn with a circular movement towards Folly Bridge; but Charles Larkyns at once came to the rescue with the simple but energetic compendium of boating instruction, 'Put your oar in deep, and bring it out with a jerk!'

Bearing this in mind, our hero's efforts met with well-merited success; and he soon passed that mansion which, instead of cellars, appears to have an ingenious system of small rivers to thoroughly irrigate its foundations. One by one, too, he passed those house-boats which are more like the Noah's arks of toy-shops than anything else, and sometimes contain quite as original a mixture of animal specimens. Warming with his exertions, Mr Verdant Green passed the University barge in great style, just as the eight was preparing to start; and though he was not able to 'feather his oars with skill and dexterity', like the jolly young waterman in the song, yet his sleight-of-hand performances with them proved not only a source of great satisfaction to the crews on the river, but also to the promenaders on the shore.

He had left the Christ Church meadows far behind, and was beginning to feel slightly exhausted by his unwonted exertions, when he reached that bewildering part of the river termed 'the Gut'. So confusing were the intestine commotions of this gut, that, after passing a chequered existence as an aquatic shuttlecock, and being assailed with a slang-dictionary-full of opprobrious epithets, Mr Verdant Green caught another tremendous crab, and before he could recover himself, the 'tub' received a shock, and, with a loud cry of 'Boat ahead!' ringing in his ears, the University Eight passed over the place where he and the Sylph had so lately disported themselves.

With the wind nearly knocked out of his body by the blade of the bow-oar striking him on the chest as he rose to the surface, our unfortunate hero was immediately dragged from the water, in a condition like that of the child in *The Stranger* (the only joke, by the way, in that most dreary play) 'not dead, but very wet!' and forthwith placed in safety in his deliverer's boat.

'Hallo, Gig-lamps! who the doose had thought of seeing you here, devouring Isis in this expensive way!' said a voice very coolly. And our hero found that he had been rescued by little Mr Bouncer, who had been tacking up the river in company with Huz and Buz and his meerschaum. 'You *have* been and gone and done it now, young man!' continued the vivacious little gentleman, as he surveyed our hero's draggled and forlorn condition. 'If you'd only a comb and a glass in your hand, you'd look distressingly like a cross-breed with a mermaid! You ain't subject to the whatdyecallems – the rheumatics, are you? Because, if so, I could put you on shore at a tidy little shop where you can get a glass of brandy-and-water, and have your clothes dried; and then mamma won't scold.'

'Indeed', chattered our hero, 'I shall be very glad indeed; for I feel – rather cold. But what am I to do with my boat?'

'Oh, the Lively Polly, or whatever her name is, will find her way back safe enough. There are plenty of boatmen on the river who'll see to her and take her back to her owner; and if you got her from Hall's, I dare say she'll dream that she's dreamt in marble halls, like you did,

Gig-lamps, that night at Smalls's, when you got wet in rather a more lively style than you've done to-day. Now I'll tack you up to that little shop I told you of.'

So there our hero was put on shore, and Mr Bouncer made fast his boat and accompanied him; and did not leave him until he had seen him between the blankets, drinking a glass of hot brandy-and-water, the while his clothes were smoking before the fire.

This little adventure (for a time at least) checked Mr Verdant

Green's aspirations to distinguish himself on the river; and he therefore renounced the sweets of the Isis, and contented himself by practising with a punt on the Cherwell. There, after repeatedly over-balancing himself in the most suicidal manner, he at length peacefully settled down into the lounging blissfulness of a 'Cherwell waterlily', and on the hot days, among those gentlemen who had moored their punts underneath the overhanging boughs of the willows and limes, and beneath their cool shade were lying, in *dolce far niente* fashion, with their legs up and a weed in their mouth, reading the last new novel, or some less immaculate work – among these gentlemen might haply have been discerned the form and spectacles of Mr Verdant Green.

CHAPTER XI

Mr Verdant Green's Sports and Pastimes.

ARCHERY was all the fashion at Brazenface. They had as fine a lawn for it as the Trinity men had; and all day long there was somebody to be seen making holes in the targets, and endeavouring to realise the *pose* of the Apollo Belvidere – rather a difficult thing to do, when you come to wear plaid trousers and shaggy coats. As Mr Verdant Green felt desirous not only to uphold all the institutions of the University, but also to make himself acquainted with the sports and pastimes of the place, he forthwith joined the Archery and Cricket Clubs. He at once inspected the manufactures of Muir and Buchanan;

and after selecting from their stores a fancy-wood bow, with arrows, belt, quiver, guard, tips, tassels, and grease-pot, he felt himself to be duly prepared to represent the Toxophilite character. But the sustaining it was a more difficult thing than he had conceived; for although he thought that it would be next to impossible to miss a shot when the target was so large, and the arrow went so easily from the bow, yet our hero soon discovered that even in the first steps of archery there was something to be learnt, and that the mere stringing of his bow was a performance attended with considerable difficulty. It was always slipping from his instep, or twisting the wrong way, or threatening to snap in sunder, or refusing to allow his fingers to slip the knot, or doing something that

was dreadfully uncomfortable, and productive of perspiration; and two or three times he was reduced to the abject necessity of asking his friends to string his bow for him.

But when he had mastered this slight difficulty, he found that the arrows (to use Mr Bouncer's phrase) 'wobbled', and had a predilection for going anywhere but into the target, notwithstanding its size; and unfortunately one went into the body of the Honourable Mr Stormer's favourite Skye ter-rier, though, thanks to its shaggy coat and the bluntness of the arrow, it did not do a great amount of mischief; neverthless, the vials of Mr Stormer's wrath were outpoured upon Mr Verdant Green's head; and such *epea pteroenta* followed the winged arrow, that our hero became

alarmed, and for the time forswore archery practice.

As he had fully equipped himself for arch-ery, so also Mr Verdant Green (on the authority of Mr Bouncer) got himself up for cricket regardless of expense; and he made his first appearance in the field in a straw hat with blue ribbon, and 'flannels', and spiked shoes of perfect propriety. As Mr Bouncer had told him that, in cricket, attitude was every-thing, Verdant, as soon as he went in for his innings, took up what he considered to be a very good position at the wicket. Little Mr Bouncer, who was bowling, delivered the ball with a swiftness that seemed rather astonishing in such a small gentleman. The first ball was 'wide', nevertheless, Verdant (after it had passed) struck at it, raising his bat high in the air, and bringing it straight down to the ground as though it were an executioner's axe. The

second ball was nearer to the mark; but it came in with such swiftness, that, as Mr Verdant Green was quite new to round bowling, it was rather too quick for him, and hit him severely on the – well, never mind, on the trousers.

'Hallo, Gig-lamps!' shouted the delighted Mr Bouncer, 'nothing like backing up; but it's no use assuming a stern appearance; you'll get your hand in soon, old feller!'

But Verdant found that before he could get his hand in, the ball was got into his wicket; and that while

he was preparing for the strike, the ball shot by; and, as Mr Stumps, the wicketkeeper, kindly informed him, 'there was a row in his timber-yard.' Thus Verdant's score was always on the *lucus a non lucendo* principle of derivation, for not even to a quarter of a score did it ever reach; and he felt that he should never rival a Mynn or be a Parr with any one of the 'All England' players.

Besides these out-of-door sports, our hero also devoted a good deal of his time to acquiring indoor games, being quickly initiated into the mysteries of billiards, and plunging headlong into pool. It was in the billiard-room that Verdant first formed his acquaintance with Mr Fluke of Christ Church, well known to be the best player in the University, and who, if report spoke truly, always made his five hun-

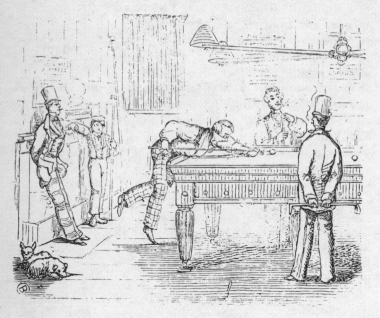

dred a year by his skill in the game. Mr Fluke kindly put our hero 'into the way to become a player'; and Verdant soon found the appren-ticeship was attended with rather heavy fees.

At the wine-parties also that he attended he became rather a greater adept at cards than he had formerly been. 'Van John' was the favourite game; and he was not long in discovering that staking shillings and half-crowns, instead of counters and 'fish', and going odds on the colours, and losing five pounds before he was aware of it, was a very different thing to playing *vingt-et-un* at home with his sisters for 'love' – (though perhaps cards afford the only way in which young ladies at twenty-one will *play* for love).

In returning to Brazenface late from these parties, our hero was sometimes frightfully alarmed by suddenly finding himself face to face with a dreadful apparition, to which, by constant familiarity, he gradually became accustomed, and learned to look upon as the proctor with his marshal and bull-dogs. At first, too, he was on such occasions

greatly alarmed at finding the gates of Brazenface closed, obliging him thereby to 'knock-in', and not only did he apologise to the porter for troubling him to open the wicket, but he also volunteered elaborate explanations of the reasons that had kept him out after time – explanations that were not received in the spirit with which they were

tendered. When our freshman became aware of the mysteries of a gate-bill, he felt more at his ease.

Mr Verdant Green learned many things during his freshman's term, and, among others, he discovered that the quiet retirement of college-rooms, of which he had heard so much, was in many cases an unsubstantial idea, founded on imagination, and built up by fancy. One day that he had been writing a letter in Mr Smalls's rooms, which were on the ground-floor, Verdant congratulated himself that his own rooms were on the third floor, and were thus removed from the possibility of his

friends, when he had sported his oak, being able to get through his window to 'chaff' him; but he soon discovered that rooms upstairs had also objectionable points in their private character, and were not altogether such eligible apartments as he had at first anticipated. First there was the getting up and down the dislocated staircase, a feat which at night was sometimes attended with difficulty. Then, when he had accomplished this feat, there was no way of escaping from the noise of his neighbours. Mr Sloe, the reading-man in the garret above, was one of those abominable nuisances, a peripatetic student, who 'got up' every subject by pacing up and down his limited apartment, and, like the sentry, 'walked his dreary round' at unseasonable hours of the night, at which time could be plainly heard the wretched chuckle, and crackings of knuckles (Mr Sloe's way of expressing intense delight), with which he welcomed some miserable joke of Aristophanes, painfully elaborated by the help of Liddell-and-Scott; or the disgustingly sonorous way in which he declaimed his Greek choruses. This was bad enough at night, but in the day-time there was a still greater nuisance. The rooms immediately beneath Verdant's were possessed by a gentleman whose musical powers were of an unusually limited descrip-

tion, but who, unfortunately for his neighbours, possessed the idea that the cornet-à-piston was a beautiful instrument for picnics, races, boating-parties, and other long-vacation amusements, and sedulously practised 'In my cottage near a wood', 'Away with melancholy', and other airs of a lively character, in a doleful and distracted way, that would have fully justified his immediate homicide, or, at any rate, the confiscation of his offending instrument.

Then, on the one side of Verdant's room, was Mr Bouncer, sounding his octaves, and 'going the complete unicorn', and his bull-terriers, Huz and Buz, all and each of whom were of a restless and loud temperament: while, on the other side, were Mr Four-in-hand Fosbrooke's rooms, in which fencing, boxing, single-stick, and other violent sports were gone through, with a great expenditure of 'Sa-ha! sa-ha!' and stampings. Verdant was sometimes induced to go in, and never could sufficiently admire the way in which men could be rapped with single-sticks without crying out or

flinching; for it made him almost sore even to look at them. Mr Blades, the stroke, was a frequent visitor there, and developed his muscles in the most satisfactory manner.

After many refusals, our hero was at length persuaded to put on the gloves, and have a friendly bout with Mr Blades. The result was as might have been anticipated; and Mr Smalls doubtless gave a very

correct *résumé* of the proceeding (for, as we have before said, he was thoroughly conversant with the sporting slang of *Tintinnabulum's Life*), when he told Verdant, that his claret had been repeatedly tapped, his bread-basket walked into, his day-lights darkened, his ivories rattled, his nozzle barked, his whisker-bed napped heavily, his kissing-trap countered, his ribs roasted, his nut spanked, and his whole person put in chancery, stung, bruised, fibbed, propped, fiddled, slogged, and otherwise ill-treated. So it is hardly to be wondered at if Mr Verdant Green from thenceforth gave up boxing, as a senseless and ungentlemanly amusement.

But while these pleasures (?) of the body were being attended to, the recreation of the mind was not forgotten. Mr Larkyns had proposed

Verdant's name at the Union; and, to that gentleman's great satisfaction, he was not black-balled. He daily, therefore, frequented the reading-room, and made a point of looking through all the magazines and newspapers; while he felt quite a pride in sitting in luxurious state upstairs, writing his letters to the home department on the very best note-paper, and sealing them extensively with the 'Oxford Union' seal; though he could not at first be persuaded that trusting his letters to a wire closet was at all a safe system of postage.

He also attended the Debates, which were then held in the long room behind Wyatt's; and he was particularly charmed with the manner in which vital questions, that (as he learned from the newspapers) had proved stumbling-blocks to the greatest statesmen of the land, were rapidly solved by the embryo statesmen of the Oxford Union. It was quite a sight, in that long picture-room, to see the rows of light iron seats densely crowded with young men – some of whom would perhaps rise to be Cannings, or Peels, or Gladstones – and to hear how one beardless gentleman would call another beardless gentleman his 'honourable friend', and appeal 'to the sense of the House', and address himself to 'Mr Speaker', and how they would all juggle the same tricks of rhetoric as their fathers were doing in certain other debates in a certain other House. And it was curious, too, to mark the points of resemblance between the two Houses; and how the smaller one had, on its smaller scale, its Hume, and its Lord John, and its 'Dizzy', and how they went through the same traditional forms, and preserved the same time-honoured ideas, and debated in the fullest houses, with the greatest spirit and the greatest length, on such points as, 'What course is it advisable for this country to take in regard to the government of its Indian possessions, and the imprisonment of Mr Jones by the Rajah of Humbugpoopoonah?' Indeed, Mr Verdant Green was so excited by this interesting debate, that on the third night of its adjournment he rose to address the House; but being 'no orator as Brutus is', his few broken words were received with laughter, and the honourable gentleman was coughed down.

Our hero had, as an Oxford freshman, to go through that cheerful form called 'sitting in the Schools' – a form which consisted in the following ceremony. Through a door in the right-hand corner of the Schools Quadrangle – Oh, that door! does it not bring a pang into your heart only to think of it? to remember the day when you went in there as pale as the little pair of bands in which you were dressed for your sacrifice; and came out all in a glow and a chill when your examination was over; and posted your bosom-friend there to receive from Purdue the little slip of paper, and bring you the thrilling intelligence that you had passed; or to come empty-handed, and say that you had been plucked! Oh, that door! well might be inscribed there the line which, on Dante's authority, is assigned to the door of another place:

All hope abandon, ye who enter here!

– entering through this door in company with several other unfortunates, our hero passed between two galleries through a passage, by which, if the place had been a circus, the horses would have entered, and found himself in a tolerably large room lighted on either side by windows, and panelled half-way up the walls. Down the centre of this room ran a large green-baize-covered table, on the one side of which were some eight or ten miserable beings who were then undergoing examination, and were supplied with pens, ink, blotting-pad, and large sheets of thin 'scribble-paper', on which they were struggling to impress their ideas; or else had a book set before them, out of which they were construing, or being racked with questions that touched now on one subject and now on another, like a bee among flowers. The large table was liberally supplied with all the apparatus and instruments of torture; and on the other side of it sat the three examiners, as dreadful and formidable as the terrible three of Venice. At the upper end of the room was a chair of state for the Vice-Chancellor, whenever he deigned to personally superintend the torture; to the right and left of which, accommodation was provided for other victims. On the right hand of the room was a small open gallery of two seats (like those seen in infant schools); and here, from 10 in the morning till 4 in the afternoon, with only the interval of a quarter of an hour for luncheon, Mr Verdant Green was compelled to sit and watch the proceedings, his perseverance being attested to by a certificate which he received as a reward for his meritorious conduct. If this 'sitting in the Schools'*

---

* This form has been abolished (1853) under the new regulations.

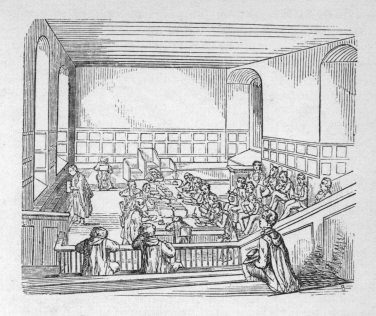

was established as an *in terrorem* form for the spectators, it undoubtedly generally had the desired effect; and what with the misery of sitting
through a whole day on a hard bench with nothing to do, and the agony
of seeing your fellow-creatures plucked, and having visions of the same
prospective fate for yourself, the day on which the sitting took place
was usually regarded as one of those which, 'if 'twere done, 'twere well
it should be done quickly.'

As an appropriate sequel to this proceeding, Mr Verdant Green
attended the interesting ceremony of conferring degrees; where he
discovered that the apparently insane promenade of the Proctor gave

rise to the name bestowed on (what Mr Larkyns called) the equally insane custom of 'plucking',* There too our hero saw the Vice-Chancellor in all his glory; and so agreeable were the proceedings, that altogether he had a great deal of Bliss.†

*When the degrees are conferred, the name of each person is read out before he is presented to the Vice-Chancellor. The Proctor then walks once up and down the room, so that any person who objects to the degree being granted may signify the same by pulling or 'plucking' the Proctor's robes. This has been occasionally done by tradesmen, in order to obtain payment of their 'little bills'; but such a proceeding is very rare, and the Proctor's promenade is usually undisturbed.

†The Revd Philip Bliss, D.C.L., after holding the onerous post of Registrar of the University for many years, and discharging its duties in a way that called forth the unanimous thanks of the University, resigned office in 1853.

CHAPTER XII

Mr Verdant Green terminates his existence as an Oxford Freshman.

'BEFORE I go home', said Mr Verdant Green, as he expelled a volume of smoke from his lips – for he had overcome his first weakness, and now 'took his weed' regularly – 'before I go home, I must see what I owe in the place; for my father said he did not like for me to run in debt, but wished me to settle my bills terminally.'

'What, you're afraid of having what we call bill-ious fever, I suppose, eh?' laughed Charles Larkyns. 'All exploded ideas, my dear fellow. They do very well in their way, but they don't answer; don't pay, in fact; and the shopkeepers don't like it either. By the way, I can show you a great curiosity – the autograph of an Oxford tradesman, *very rare!* I think of presenting it to the Ashmolean.' And Mr Larkyns

opened his writing-desk, and took therefrom an Oxford pastrycook's bill, on which appeared the magic word, 'Received.'

'Now, there is one thing', continued Mr Larkyns, 'which you really must do before you go down, and that is to see Blenheim. And the best thing that you can do is to join Fosbrooke and Bouncer and me, in a trap to Woodstock tomorrow. We'll go in good time, and make a day of it.'

Verdant readily agreed to make one of the party; and the next morning, after a breakfast in Charles Larkyns's rooms, they made their way to a side street leading out of Beaumont Street, where the dog-cart was in waiting. As it was drawn by two horses, placed in tandem fashion, Mr Fosbrooke had an opportunity of displaying his Jehu powers; which he did to great advantage, not allowing his leader to run his nose into the cart, and being enabled to turn sharp corners without chipping the bricks, or running the wheel up the bank.

They reached Woodstock after a very pleasant ride, and clattered up its one long street to the principal hotel; but Mr Fosbrooke whipped into the yard to the left so rapidly, that our hero, who was not much used to the back seat of a dog-cart, flew off by some means at

a tangent to the right, and was consequently degraded in the eyes of the inhabitants.

After ordering for dinner everything that the house was enabled to supply, they made their way in the first place (as it could only be seen between 11 and 1) to Blenheim; the princely splendours of which were not only costly in themselves, but, as our hero soon found, costly also to the sightseer. The doors in the *suite* of apartments were all opposite to each other, so that, as a crimson cord was passed from one to the other, the spectator was kept entirely to the one side of the room, and merely a glance could be obtained of the Raffaelle, the glorious Rubens's,* the Vandycks, and the almost equally fine Sir Joshuas. But even the glance they had was but a passing one, as the servant trotted them through the rooms with the rapidity of locomotion and explanation of a Westminster Abbey verger; and he made a fierce attack on Verdant, who had lagged behind, and was short-sightedly peering at the celebrated 'Charles the First' of Vandyck, as though he had lingered in order to surreptitiously appropriate some of the tables, couches, and other trifling articles that ornamented the rooms. In this way they went at railroad pace through the *suite* of rooms and the library – where the chief thing pointed out appeared to be a grease-mark on the floor made by somebody at somebody else's wedding-breakfast – and to the chapel, where they admired the ingenuity of the sparrows and other birds that built about Rysbrach's monumental mountain of marble to the memory of the Duke and Duchess of Marlborough; and then to the so-called 'Titian room' (shade of mighty Titian, forgive the insult!), where they saw the Loves of the Gods represented in the most unloveable manner,† and where a flunkey lounged lazily at the door, and, in spite of Mr Bouncer's expostulatory 'chaff', demanded half-a-crown for the sight.

Indeed, the sightseeing at Blenheim seemed to be a system of half-crowns. The first servant would take them a little way, and then say, 'I don't go any further, sir; half-a-crown!' and hand them over to servant number two, who, after a short interval, would pass them on (half-a-crown!) to the servant who showed the chapel (half-a-crown!), who would forward them on to the 'Titian' Gallery (half-a-crown!), who would hand them over to the flower-garden (half-a-crown!), who would entrust them to the rose-garden (half-a-crown!), who would give them up to another, who showed parts of the Park, and the rest of it. Somewhat in this manner an Oxford party sees Blenheim (the

---

* Dr Waagen says that the Rubens collection at Blenheim is only surpassed by the royal galleries of Munich, Vienna, Madrid, and Paris.

† The ladies alone would repel one by their gaunt ugliness, their flesh being apparently composed of the article on which the pictures are painted - leather. The only picture not by 'Titian' in this room is a Rubens – 'the Rape of Proserpine' – to see which is well worth the half-crown *charged* for the sight of the others.

present of the nation); and Mr Verdant Green found it the most expensive showplace he had ever seen.

Some of the Park, however, was free (though they were two or three times ordered to 'get off the grass'); and they rambled about among the noble trees, and admired the fine views of the Hall, and smoked their weeds, and became very pathetic at Rosamond's Spring. They then came back into Woodstock, which they found to be like all Oxford towns, only rather duller perhaps, the principal signs of life being some fowls lazily pecking about in the grass-grown street, and two cats sporting without fear of interruption from a dog, who was too much overcome by the *ennui* of the place to interfere with them.

Mr Bouncer then led the way to an inn, where the bar was presided over by a young lady, 'on whom', he said, 'he was desperately sweet', and with whom he conversed in the most affable and brotherly manner, and for whom also he had brought, as an appropriate present, a Book of Comic Songs; 'for', said the little gentleman, 'hang it! she's a girl of what you call *mind*, you know! and she's heard of the opera, and begun the piano – though she don't get much time, you see, for it in the bar – and she sings regular slap-up, and no mistake!'

So they left this young lady drawing bitter beer for Mr Bouncer, and

otherwise attending to her adorer's wants, and endeavoured to have a game of billiards on a wooden table that had no cushions, with curious cues that had no leathers. Slightly failing in this difficult game, they strolled about till dinner-time, when Mr Verdant Green became mysteriously lost for some time, and was eventually found by Charles Larkyns and Mr Fosbrooke in a glover's shop, where he was sitting on a high stool, and basking in the sunshiny smiles of two 'neat little glovers'. Our hero at first feigned to be simply making purchases of Woodstock gloves and purses, as *souvenirs* of his visit, and presents for his sisters; but in the course of the evening, being greatly 'chaffed' on the subject, he began to exercise his imagination, and talk of the 'great fun' he had had – though what particular fun there may be in smiling amiably across a counter at a feminine shopkeeper who is selling you gloves, it is hard to say: perhaps Dr Sterne could help us to an answer.

They spent altogether a very lively day; and after a rather protracted sitting over their wine, they returned to Oxford with great hilarity, Mr Bouncer's post-horn coming out with great effect in the stillness of the moonlight night. Unfortunately their mirth was somewhat checked when they had got as far as Peyman's Gate; for the Proctor, with mistaken kindness, had taken the trouble to meet them there, lest they should escape him by entering Oxford by any devious way; and the marshal and the bull-dogs were at the leader's head just as Mr Fosbrooke was triumphantly guiding them through the turnpike. Verdant gave up his name and that of his college with a thrill of terror, and nearly fell off the drag from fright, when he was told to call upon the Proctor the next morning.

'Keep your pecker up, old feller!' said Mr Bouncer, in an encouraging tone, as they drove into Oxford, 'and don't be down in the mouth about a dirty trick like this. He won't hurt you much, Gig-lamps! Gate and chapel you; or give you some old Greek party to write out; or send you down to your mammy for a twelve-month; or some little trifle of that sort. I only wish the beggar would come up our staircase! if Huz, and Buz his brother, didn't do their duty by him, it would be doosid odd. Now, don't you go and get bad dreams, Gig-lamps! because it don't pay; and you'll soon get used to these sort of things; and what's the odds, as long as you're happy? I like to take things coolly, I do.'

To judge from Mr Bouncer's serenity, and the far-from-nervous manner in which he 'sounded his octaves', *he* at least appeared to be thoroughly used to 'that sort of things', and doubtless slept as tranquilly as though nothing wrong had occurred. But it was far different with our hero, who passed a sleepless night of terror as to his probable fate on the morrow.

And when the morrow came, and he found himself in the dreaded presence of the constituted authority, armed with all the power of the law, he was so overcome, that he fell on his knees and made an abject spectacle of himself, imploring that he might not be expelled, and bring down his father's grey hairs in the usually quoted manner. To his immense relief, however, he was treated in a more lenient way; and as the term had nearly expired, his punishment could not be of long duration; and as for the impositions, why, as Mr Bouncer said, 'Ain't there coves to *barber*ize 'em* for you, Gig-lamps?'

Thus our freshman gained experience daily; so that by the end of the term, he found that short as the time had been, it had been long enough for him to learn what Oxford life was like, and that there was in it a great deal to be copied, as well as some things to be shunned. The freshness he had so freely shown on entering Oxford had gradually yielded as the term went on; and, when he had run halloing the Brazenface boat all the way up from Iffley, and had seen Mr Blades realise his most sanguine dreams as to 'the head of the river', and when, from the gallery of the theatre, he had taken part in the licensed saturnalia of the Commemoration, and had cheered for the ladies in pink and blue, and even given 'one more' for the very Proctor who had so lately

* Impositions are often performed by deputy.

interfered with his liberties; and when he had gone to a farewell pass-party (which Charles Larkyns did *not* give), and had assisted in the other festivities that usually mark the end of the academical year – Mr Verdant Green found himself to be possessed of a considerable ac-quisition of knowledge of a most miscellaneous character; and on the authority, and in the figurative eastern language of Mr Bouncer, 'he was sharpened up no end, by being well rubbed against university bricks. So, goodbye, old feller!' said the little gentleman, with a kind remembrance of imaginary individuals, 'and give my love to Sairey and the little 'uns.' And Mr Bouncer 'went the complete unicorn', for the last time in that term, by extemporising a farewell solo to Verdant which was of such an agonising character of execution, that Huz, and Buz his brother, lifted up their noses and howled.

'Which they're the very moral of Christyuns, sir!' observed Mrs Tester, who was dabbing her curtseys in thankfulness for the large amount with which our hero had 'tipped' her. 'And has ears for moosic, sir. With grateful thanks to you, sir, for the same. And it's obleeged I feel in my'art. Which it reelly were like what my own son would do, sir. As was found in drink for his rewing. And were took to the West Injies for a sojer. Which he were – ugh! oh, oh! Which you be'old me a hafflicted martyr to these spazzums, sir. And how I am to get through them doorin' the veecation. Without a havin' 'em eased by a-goin' to your cupboard, sir. For just three spots o'brandy on a lump o' sugar, sir. Is a summut as I'm afeered to think on. Oh! ugh!' Upon which Mrs Tester's grief and spasms so completely overcame her, that our hero presented her with an extra half-sovereign, wherewith to purchase the medicine that was so peculiarly adapted to her complaint. Mr Robert Filcher was also 'tipped' in the same liberal manner; and our hero completed his first term's residence in Brazen-face by establishing himself as a decided favourite.

Among those who seemed disposed to join in this opinion was the Jehu of the Warwickshire coach, who expressed his conviction to our delighted hero, that 'he wos a young gent as had much himproved hisself since he tooled him up to the 'Varsity with his guvnor.' To fully deserve which high opinion, Mr Verdant Green tipped for the box-seat, smoked more than was good for him, and besides finding the coachman in weeds, drank with him at every 'change' on the road.

The carriage met him at the appointed place, and his luggage (no longer encased in canvas, after the manner of females) was soon transferred to it; and away went our hero to the Manor Green, where he was received with the greatest demonstrations of delight. Restored to the bosom of his family, our hero was converted into a kind of domestic idol; while it was proposed by Miss Mary Green, seconded by Miss

Fanny, and carried by unanimous acclamation, that Mr Verdant Green's University career had greatly enhanced his attractions.

The opinion of the drawing-room was echoed from the servants'-hall, the ladies' maid in particular being heard freely to declare, that 'Oxford College had made quite a man of Master Verdant!'

As the little circumstance on which she probably grounded her encomium had fallen under the notice of Miss Virginia Verdant, it may have accounted for that most correct-minded lady being more reserved in expressing her opinion of her nephew's improvement than were the rest of the family; but she nevertheless thought a great deal on the subject.

'Well, Verdant!' said Mr Green, after hearing divers anecdotes of his son's college-life, carefully prepared for home-consumption; 'now tell us what you've learnt in Oxford.'

'Why,' replied our hero, as he reflected on his freshman's career, 'I have learnt to think for myself, and not to believe everything that I hear; and I think I could fight my way in the world; and I can chaff a cad...'

'Chaff a cad! oh!' groaned Miss Virginia to herself, thinking it was something extremely dreadful.

'And I have learnt to row – at least, not quite; but I can smoke a weed – a cigar, you know. I've learnt that.'

'Oh, Verdant, you naughty boy!' said Mrs Green, with maternal fondness. 'I was sadly afraid that Charles Larkyns would teach you all his wicked school habits!'

'Why, mama,' said Mary, who was sitting on a footstool at her brother's knee, and spoke up in defence of his college friend; 'why, mama, all gentlemen smoke; and of course Mr Charles Larkyns and Verdant must do as others do. But I dare say, Verdant, he taught you more useful things than that, did he not?'

'Oh, yes,' replied Verdant; 'he taught me to grill a devil.'

'Grill a devil!' groaned Miss Virginia. 'Infatuated young man!'

'And to make shandy-gaff and sherry-cobbler, and brew bishop and egg-flip: oh, it's capital! I'll teach you how to make it; and we'll have some to-night!'

And thus the young gentleman astonished his family with the extent of his learning, and proved how a youth of ordinary natural attainments may acquire other knowledge in his University career than what simply pertains to classical literature.

And so much experience had our hero gained during his freshman's term, that when the pleasures of the Long Vacation were at an end, and he had returned to Brazenface, with his firm and fast friend Charles Larkyns, he felt himself entitled to assume a patronising air to the freshmen who then entered, and even sought to impose upon their credulity in ways which his own personal experience suggested.

It was clear that Mr Verdant Green had made his farewell bow as an Oxford Freshman.

*Mr Verdant Green recommences his existence as
an Oxford Undergraduate.*

HE intelligent reader – which epithet I take to be a synonym for everyone who has perused the first part of the Adventures of Mr Verdant Green, – will remember the statement that the hero of the narrative 'had gained so much experience during his Freshman's term, that, when the pleasures of the Long Vacation were at an end, and he had returned to Brazenface with his firm and fast friend Charles Larkyns, he felt himself entitled to assume a patronising air to the Freshmen, who then entered, and even sought to impose upon their credulity in ways which his own personal experience suggested.' And the intelligent reader will further call to mind the fact that the first part of these memoirs concluded with the words – 'it was clear that Mr Verdant Green had made his farewell bow as an Oxford Freshman.'

But, although Mr Verdant Green had of necessity ceased to be 'a Freshman' as soon as he had entered upon his second term of residence – the name being given to students in their first term only – yet this necessity, which, as we all know, *non habet leges*, will occasionally prove its rule by an exception; and if Mr Verdant Green was no longer a Freshman in name, he still continued to be one by nature. And the intelligent reader will perceive when he comes to study these veracious memoirs, that, although their hero will no longer display those peculiarly virulent symptoms of freshness which drew towards him so much friendly sympathy during the earlier part of his University career, yet that he will still, by his innocent simplicity and credulity, occasionally evidence the truth of the Horatian maxim,

> Quo semel est imbuta recens, servabit odorem
> Testa diu,*

which, when *Smart*-ly translated, means, 'A cask will long preserve the flavour, with which, when new, it was once impregnated'; and which, when rendered in the Saxon vulgate, signifieth, 'What is bred in the bone will come out in the flesh.'

It would, indeed, take more than a Freshman's term – a two months' residence in Oxford – to remove the simple gaucheries of the country Squire's hobbodehoy, and convert the girlish youth, the pupil of that Nestor of Spinsters, Miss Virginia Verdant, into the MAN whose school was the University, whose Alma Mater was Oxonia herself. We do not cut our wise teeth in a day; some people, indeed, are so unfortunate as never to cut them at all; at the best, two months is but a brief space in which to get through this sapient teething operation, a short time in which to graft our cutting on the tree of Wisdom, more especially when the tender plant happens to be a Verdant Green. The golden age is past when the full-formed goddess of Wisdom sprang from the brain of Jove complete in all her parts. If our Vulcans nowadays were to trepan the heads of our Jupiters, they would find nothing in them! In these degenerate times it will take more than one splitting headache to produce *our* wisdom.

So it was with our hero. The splitting headache, for example, which had wound up the pleasures of Mr Smalls's 'quiet party', had taught him that the good things of this life were not given to be abused, and that he could not exceed the bounds of temperance and moderation without being made to pay the penalty of the trespass. It had taught him that kind of wisdom which even 'makes fools wise'; for it had taught him Experience. And yet, it was but a portion of that lesson of Experience which it is sometimes so hard to learn, but which, when once got by heart, is like the catechism of our early days – it is never forgotten, it directs us, it warns us, it advises us; it not only adorns the

---

* Horace, Ep. Lib. I. ii., 69.

tale of our life, but it points the moral which may bring that tale to a happy and peaceful end.

Experience! Experience! What will it not do? It is a staff which will help us on when we are jostled by the designing crowds of our Vanity Fair. It is a telescope that will reveal to us the dark spots on what seemed to be a fair face. It is a finger-post to show us whither the crooked paths of worldly ways will lead us. It is a scar that tells of the wound which the soldier has received in the battle of life. It is a lighthouse that warns us off those hidden rocks and quicksands where the wrecks of long past joys that once smiled so fairly, and were loved so dearly, now lie buried in all their ghastliness, stripped of grace and beauty, things to shudder at and dread. Experience! Why, even Alma Mater's doctors prescribe it to be taken in the largest quantities! 'Experientia – *dose it!*' they say: and very largely some of us have to pay for the dose. But the dose does us good; and (for it is an allopathic remedy), the greater the dose, the greater is the benefit to be derived.

The two months' allopathic dose of Experience which had been administered to Mr Verdant Green, chiefly through the agency of those skilful professors, Messrs Larkyns, Fosbrooke, Smalls, and Bouncer, had been so far beneficial to him, that, in the figurative Eastern language of the last-named gentleman, he had not only been 'sharpened up no end by being well rubbed against University bricks', but he had, moreover, 'become so considerably wide-awake, that he would very soon be able to take the shine out of the old original Weazel, whom the pages of History had recorded as never having been discovered in a state of somnolence.'

Now, as Mr Bouncer was a gentleman of considerable experience and was, too, (although addicted to expressions not to be found in 'the Polite Preceptor') quite free from the vulgar habit of personal flattery – or, as he thought fit to express it, in words which would have taken away my Lord Chesterfield's appetite, 'buttering a party to his face in the cheekiest manner' – we may fairly presume, on this strong evidence, that Mr Verdant Green had really gained a considerable amount of experience during his Freshman's term, although there were still left in his character and conduct many marks of viridity which 'Time's effacing fingers', assisted by Mr Bouncer's instructions, would gradually remove. However, Mr Verdant Green had, at any rate, ceased to be 'a Freshman' in name; and had received that University promotion, which Mr Charles Larkyns commemorated by the following *affiche*, which our hero, on his return from his first morning chapel in the Michaelmas term, found in a conspicuous position on his oak:

COMMISSION SIGNED BY THE VICE-CHANCELLOR OF THE UNIVERSITY OF OXFORD

MR VERDANT GREEN to be an Oxford Undergraduate, *vice* Oxford Freshman, SOLD OUT.

It is generally found to be the case, that the youthful Undergraduate first seeks to prove he is no longer a 'Freshman', by endeavouring to impose on the credulity of those young gentlemen who come up as Freshmen in his second term. And, in this, there is an analogy between the biped and the quadruped; for, the wild, gambolling, schoolboy elephant, when he has been brought into a new circle, and has been trained to new habits, will take pleasure in ensnaring and deluding his late companions in play.

The 'sells' by which our hero had been 'sold out' as a Freshman, now formed a stock in trade for the Undergraduate, which his experience enabled him to dispose of (with considerable interest) to the most credulous members of the generations of Freshmen who came up after him. Perhaps no Freshman had ever gone through a more severe course of hoaxing – to survive it – than Mr Verdant Green; and yet, by a system of retaliation, only paralleled by the quadrupedal case of the before-mentioned elephant, and the biped-beadle case of the illustrious Mr Bumble, who after having his own ears boxed by the late Mrs Corney, relieved his feelings by boxing the ears of the small boy who opened the gate for him – our hero took the greatest delight in seeking every opportunity to play off upon a Freshman some one of those numerous hoaxes which had been so successfully practised on himself. And while, in referring to the early part of his University career, he omitted all mention of such anecdotes as displayed his own personal credulity in the strongest light – which anecdotes the faithful historian has thought fit to record – he nevertheless dwelt with extreme pleasure on the reminiscences of a few isolated facts, in which he himself appeared in the character of the hoaxer.

These facts, when neatly garnished with a little fiction, made very palatable dishes for University entertainment, and were served up by our hero, when he went 'down into the country', to select parties of relatives and friends (N.B. – Females preferred). On such occasions, the following hoax formed Mr Verdant Green's *pièce de résistance*.

CHAPTER II

Mr Verdant Green does as he has been done by.

ONE morning, Mr Verdant Green and Mr Bouncer were lounging in the venerable gateway of Brazenface. The former gentleman, being of an amiable, tame-rabbit-keeping disposition, was making himself very happy by whistling popular airs to the Porter's pet bullfinch, who was laboriously engaged on a small tread-mill, winding up his private supply of water. Mr Bouncer, being of a more volatile temperament, was amusing himself by asking the Porter's opinion on the foreign policy of Great Britain, and by making very audible remarks on the passers-by. His attention was at length riveted by the appearance on the other side of the street, of a modest-looking young gentleman, who appeared to be so ill at ease in his frock-coat and 'stick-up' collars as to lead to the strong presumption that he wore those articles of manly dress for the first time.

'I'll bet you a bottle of blacking, Gig-lamps,' said little Mr Bouncer, as he directed our hero's attention to the stranger, 'that this respected party is an intending Freshman. Look at his customary suits of solemn black, as Othello, or Hamlet, or some other swell, says in Shakespeare. And, besides his black go-to-meeting bags, please to observe', continued the little gentleman, in the tone of a wax-work showman, 'please to *h*observe the pecooliarity *h*of the hair-chain, likewise the straps of the period. Look! he's coming this way. Gig-lamps, I vote we take a rise out of the youth. Hem! Good morning! Can we have the pleasure of assisting you in anything?'

'Yes, sir! thank you, sir,' replied the youthful stranger, who was flushing like a girl up to the very roots of his curly, auburn hair; 'perhaps, sir, you can direct me to Brazenface College, sir?'

'Well, sir! it's not at all improbable, sir, but what I could, sir;' replied Mr Bouncer; 'but, perhaps, sir, you'll first favour me with your name, and your business there, sir.'

'Certainly, sir!' rejoined the stranger; and, while he fumbled at his card-case, the experienced Mr Bouncer whispered to our hero, 'Told you he was a sucking Freshman, Gig-lamps! He has got a brand new card-case, and says "sir" at the sight of the academicals.' The card handed to Mr Bouncer, bore the name of 'MR JAMES PUCKER'; and, in smaller characters in the corner of the card, were the words, '*Brazenface College, Oxford.*'

'I came, sir,' said the blushing Mr Pucker, 'to enter for my matriculation examination, and I wished to see the gentleman who will have to examine me, sir.'

'The doose you do!' said Mr Bouncer sternly; 'then young man, allow me to say, that you've regularly been and gone and done it, and put your foot in it most completely.'

'How-ow-ow, how, sir?' stammered the dupe.

'How?' replied Mr Bouncer, still more sternly; 'do you mean to brazen out your offence by asking how? What *could* have induced you, sir, to have had printed on this card the name of this College, when you've not a prospect of belonging to it – it may be for years, it may be for never, as the bard says. You've committed a most grievous offence against the University statutes, young gentleman; and so this gentleman here – Mr Pluckem, the junior examiner – will tell you!' and with that, little Mr Bouncer nudged Mr Verdant Green, who took his cue with astonishing aptitude, and glared through his glasses at the trembling Mr Pucker, who stood blushing, and bowing, and heartily repenting that his school-boy vanity had led him to invest four-and-sixpence in '100 cards, and plate, engraved with name and address.'

'Put the cards in your pocket, sir, and don't let me see them again!' said our hero in his newly-confirmed title of the junior examiner; quite rejoiced at the opportunity afforded him of proving to his friend that *he* was no longer a Freshman.

'He forgives you for the sake of your family, young man!' said Mr Bouncer with pathos; 'you've come to the right shop, for *this* is Brazenface; and you've come just at the right time, for here is the gentleman who will assist Mr Pluckem in examining you;' and Mr Bouncer pointed to Mr Four-in-hand Fosbrooke, who was coming up the street on his way from the Schools, where he was making a very laudable (but as it proved, futile) endeavour 'to get through his smalls', or, in other words, to pass his Little-go examination. The hoax which had been suggested to the ingenious mind of Mr Bouncer, was based upon the fact of Mr Fosbrooke's being properly got-up for his sacrifice in a white tie, and a pair of very small bands – the two articles, which, with the usual academicals, form the costume demanded by Alma Mater of all her children when they take their places in her Schools. And, as Mr Fosbrooke was far too politic a gentleman to irritate the Examiners by appearing in a 'loud' or sporting costume, he had carried out the idea of clerical character suggested by the bands and choker, by a quiet, gentlemanly suit of black, which, he had fondly hoped, would have softened his Examiners' manners, and not permitted them to be brutal.

Mr. Four-in-hand Fosbrooke, therefore, to the unsophisticated eye of the blushing Mr Pucker, presented a very fine specimen of the Examining Tutor; and this impression on Mr Pucker's mind was heightened by Mr Fosbrooke, after a few minutes' private conversation with the other two gentlemen, turning to him and saying, 'It will be extremely inconvenient to me to examine you now; but as you probably wish to return home as soon as possible, I will endeavour to conclude the business at once – this gentleman, Mr Pluckem,' pointing to our hero, 'having kindly promised to assist me. Mr Bouncer, will you have the goodness to follow with the young gentleman to my rooms?'

Leaving Mr Pucker to express his thanks for this great kindness, and Mr Bouncer to plunge him into the depths of trepidation by telling him terrible *stories* of the Examiner's fondness for rejecting the candidates for examination, Mr Fosbrooke and our hero ascended to the rooms of the former, where they hastily cleared away cigar-boxes and pipes, turned certain French pictures with their faces to the wall, and covered over with an outspread *Times* a regiment of porter and spirit bottles which had just been smuggled in, and were drawn up rank-and-file on the sofa. Having made this preparation, and furnished the table with pens, ink, and scribble-paper, Mr Bouncer and the victim were admitted.

'Take a seat, sir,' said Mr Fosbrooke, gravely; and Mr Pucker put his hat on the ground, and sat down at the table in a state of blushing nervousness. 'Have you been at a public school?'

'Yes, sir,' stammered the victim; 'a very public one, sir; it was a boarding-school, sir; forty boarders, and thirty day-boys, sir; I was a day-boy, sir, and in the first class.'

'First class of an uncommon slow train!' muttered Mr Bouncer.

'And are you going back to the boarding-school?' asked Mr Verdant Green, with the air of an assistant judge.

'No, sir,' replied Mr Pucker, 'I have just done with it; quite done with school, sir, this last half; and papa is going to put me to read with a clergyman until it is time for me to come to college.'

'Refreshing innocence!' murmured Mr Bouncer; while Mr Fosbrooke and our hero conferred together, and hastily wrote on two sheets of the scribble-paper.

'Now, sir,' said Mr Fosbrooke to the victim, after a paper had been

completed, 'let us see what your Latin writing is like. Have the goodness to turn what I have written into Latin; and be very careful, sir,' added Mr Fosbrooke, sternly, 'be very careful that it is Cicero's Latin, sir!' and he handed Mr Pucker a sheet of paper, on which he had scribbled the following:

TO BE TRANSLATED INTO PROSE-Y LATIN, IN THE MANNER OF CICERO'S ORATIONS
AFTER DINNER.

If, therefore, any on your bench, my luds, or in this assembly, should entertain an opinion that the proximate parts of a mellifluous mind are for ever conjoined and unconnected, I submit to you, my luds, that it will of necessity follow, that such clandestine conduct being a mere nothing – or, in the noble language of our philosophers, bosh – every individual act of overt misunderstanding will bring interminable limits to the empiricism of thought, and will rebound in the very lowest degree to the credit of the malefactor.

TO BE TURNED INTO LATIN AFTER THE MANNER OF THE ANIMALS OF TACITUS.

She went into the garden to cut a cabbage to make an apple-pie. Just then a great she-bear, coming down the street, poked its nose into the shop-window. 'What! no soap?' So he died, and she (very imprudently) married the barber. And there were present at the wedding the Joblillies, and the Piccannies, and the Gobelites, and the great Panjandrum himself, with the little button on top. So they all set to playing Catch-who-catch-can, till the gunpowder ran out at the heels of their boots.

It was well for the purposes of the hoaxers that Mr Pucker's trepidation prevented him from making a calm perusal of the paper; and he was nervously doing his best to turn the nonsensical English word by word into equally nonsensical Latin, when his limited powers of Latin writing were brought to a full stop by the untranslateable word 'Bosh.' As he could make nothing of this, he wiped the perspiration from his forehead, and gazed appealingly at the benignant features of Mr Verdant Green. The appealing gaze was answered by our hero ordering Mr Pucker to hand in his paper for examination, and to endeavour to answer the questions which he and his brother examiner had been writing down for him.

Mr Pucker took the two papers of questions, and read as follows:

HISTORY.

1. Draw a historical parallel (after the manner of Plutarch) between Hannibal and Annie Laurie.
2. What internal evidence does the Odyssey afford, that Homer sold his Trojan war-ballads at three yards an obolus?
3. Show the strong presumption there is, that Nox was the god of battles.
4. State reasons for presuming that the practice of lithography may be traced back to the time of Perseus and the Gorgon's head.
5. In what way were the shades on the banks of the Styx supplied with spirits?
6. Show the probability of the College Hornpipe having been used by the students of the Academia; and give passages from Thucydides and Tennyson in support of your answer.
7. Give a brief account of the Roman Emperors who visited the United States, and state what they did there.

8. Show from the redundancy of the word γᾶς in Sophocles, that gas must have been used by the Athenians; also state, if the expression οἱ βάρβαροι would seem to signify that they were close shavers.

9. Show from the words 'Hoc erat in votis', (Sat. VI., Lib. II.,) that Horace's favourite wine was hock, and that he meant to say 'he always voted for hock.'

10. Draw a parallel between the Children in the Wood and Achilles in the Styx.

11. When it is stated that Ariadne, being deserted by Theseus, fell in love with Bacchus, is it the poetical way of asserting that she took to drinking to drown her grief?

12. Name the *prima donnas* who have appeared in the operas of Virgil and Horace since the 'Virgilii Opera' and 'Horatii Opera' were composed.'

EUCLID, ARITHMETIC, and ALGEBRA.

1. 'The extremities of a line are points.' Prove this by the rule of railways.

2. Show the fallacy of defining an angle, as 'a worm at one end and a fool at the other'.

3. If one side of a triangle be produced, what is there to prevent the other two sides from also being brought forward?

4. Let A and B be squares having their respective boundaries in E and W ends, and let C and D be circles moving in them; the circle D will be superior to the circle C.

5. In equal circles, equal figures from various squares will stand upon the same footing.

6. If two parts of a circle fall out, the one part will cut the other.

7. Describe a square which shall be larger than Belgrave Square.

8. If the gnomon of a sun-dial be divided into two equal, and also into two unequal parts, what would be its value?

9. Describe a perpendicular triangle having the squares of the semi-circle equal to half the extremity between the points of section.

10. If an Austrian florin is worth 5.61 francs, what will be the value of Pennsylvanian bonds? Prove by rule-of-three inverse.

11. If seven horses eat twenty-five acres of grass in three days, what will be their condition on the fourth day? Prove by practice.

12. If a coach-wheel, $6\frac{5}{30}$ in. diameter and $5\frac{9}{47}$ in. circumference, makes $240\frac{4}{19}$ revolutions in a second, how many men will it take to do the same piece of work in ten days?

13. Find the greatest common measure of a quart bottle of Oxford port.

14. Find the value of a 'bob', a 'tanner', a 'joey', and a 'tizzy'.

15. Explain the common denominators 'brick', 'trump', 'spoon', 'muff', and state what was the greatest common denominator in the last term.

16. Reduce two academical years to their lowest terms.
17. Reduce a Christ Church tuft to the level of a Teddy Hall man.
18. If a freshman A have any mouth x, and a bottle of wine y, show how many applications of x to y will place $y+y$ before A.'

Mr Pucker did not know what to make of such extraordinary and unexpected questions. He blushed, attempted to write, fingered his curls, tried to collect his faculties, and then appeared to give himself over to despair; whereupon little Mr Bouncer was seized with an immoderate fit of coughing which had well nigh brought the farce to its *dénouement*.

'I'm afraid, young gentleman,' said Mr Four-in-hand Fosbrooke, as he carelessly settled his white tie and bands, 'I am afraid, Mr Pucker, that your learning is not yet up to the Brazenface standard. We are particularly cautious about admitting any gentleman whose acquirements are not of the highest order. But we will be as lenient to you as we are able, and give you one more chance to retrieve yourself. We will try a little *viva voce*, Mr Pucker. Perhaps, sir, you will favour me with your opinions on the Fourth Punic War, and will also give me a slight sketch of the constitution of ancient Heliopolis.'

Mr Pucker waxed, if possible, redder and hotter than before, he gasped like a fish out of water; and, like Dryden's prince, 'unable to conceal his pain', he

> Sigh'd and look'd, sigh'd and look'd,
> Sigh'd and look'd, and sigh'd again.

But all was to no purpose: he was unable to frame an answer to Mr Fosbrooke's questions.

'Ah, sir,' continued his tormentor, 'I see that you will not do for us yet awhile, and I am therefore under the painful necessity of rejecting you. I should advise you, sir, to read hard for another twelve months, and endeavour to master those subjects in which you have now failed. For, a young man, Mr Pucker, who knows nothing about the Fourth Punic War, and the constitution of ancient Heliopolis, is quite unfit to be enrolled among the members of such a learned college as Brazenface. Mr Pluckem quite coincides with me in this decision.' (Here Mr Verdant Green gave a Burleigh nod.) 'We feel very sorry for you, Mr Pucker, and also for your unfortunate family; but we recommend you to add to your present stock of knowledge, and to keep those visiting-

cards for another twelvemonth.' And Mr Fosbrooke and our hero –
disregarding poor Mr Pucker's entreaties that they would consider his
pa and ma, and would please to matriculate him this once, and he
would read very hard, indeed he would – turned to Mr Bouncer and
gave some private instructions, which caused that gentleman immediately to vanish, and seek out Mr Robert Filcher.

Five minutes after, that excellent Scout met the dejected Mr Pucker
as he was crossing the Quad on his way from Mr Fosbrooke's rooms.

'Beg your pardon, sir,' said Mr Filcher, touching his forehead; for,
as Mr Filcher, after the manner of his tribe, never was seen in a head-
covering, he was unable to raise his hat or cap; 'beg your pardon, sir!
but was you a lookin' for the party as examines the young gents for
their matrickylation?'

'Eh? – no! I have just come from him,' replied Mr Pucker dolefully.

'Beg your pardon, sir,' remarked Mr Filcher, 'but his rooms ain't
that way at all. Mr Slowcoach, as is the party you *ought* to have seed,
has *his* rooms quite in a hopposite direction, sir; and he's the honly
party as examines the matrickylatin' gents.'

But I *have* been examined,' observed Mr Pucker, with the air of a
plucked man: 'and I am sorry to say that I was rejected, and'...

'I dessay, sir,' interrupted Mr Filcher; 'but I think it's a 'oax, sir!'

'A what?' stammered Mr
Pucker.

'A 'oax – a sell;' replied the
Scout, confidentially. 'You
see, sir, I think some of the
gents have been makin' a little
game of you, sir; they often
does with fresh parties like
you, sir, that seem fresh and
hinnocent like; and I dessay
they've been makin' believe to
examine you, sir, and a
pretendin' that you wasn't
clever enough. But they don't
mean no harm, sir; it's only
their play, bless you!'

'Then', said Mr Pucker, whose countenance had been gradually clearing with every word the scout spoke; 'then I'm not really rejected, but have still a chance of passing my examination?'

'Percisely so, sir,' replied Mr Filcher; 'and – hexcuse me, sir, for a hintin' of it to you – but, if you would let me adwise you, sir, you wouldn't go for to mention anythin' about the 'oax to Mr Slowcoach; *he* wouldn't be pleased, sir, and *you'd* only get laughed at. If you like to go to him now, sir, I know he's in his rooms, and I'll show you the way there with the greatest of pleasure.'

Mr Pucker, immensely relieved in mind, gladly put himself under the scout's guidance, and was admitted into the presence of Mr Slowcoach. In twenty minutes after this he issued from the examining tutor's rooms with a joyful countenance, and again encountered Mr Robert Filcher.

'Hope you've done the job this time, sir,' said the scout.

'Yes.' replied the radiant Mr Pucker; 'and at two o'clock I am to see the Vice-Chancellor; and I shall be able to come to college this time next year.'

'Werry glad of it, indeed, sir!' observed Mr Filcher, with genuine emotion, and an eye to future perquisities; 'and I suppose, sir, you didn't say a word about the 'oax?'

'Not a word!' replied Mr Pucker.

'Then, sir,' said Mr Filcher, with enthusiasm, 'hexcuse me, but you're a trump, sir! And Mr Fosbrooke's compliments to you, sir, and he'll be 'appy if you'll come up into his rooms, and take a glass of wine after the fatigues of the examination. And – hexcuse me again, sir, for a hintin' of it to you, but of course you can't be aweer of the customs of the place, unless somebody tells you on 'em – I shall be werry glad to drink your werry good health, sir.'

Need it be stated that the blushing Mr Pucker, delirious with joy at the sudden change in the state of affairs, and the delightful prospect of being a member of the University, not only tipped Mr Filcher a five-shilling piece, but also paid a second visit to Mr Fosbrooke's rooms, where he found that gentleman in his usual costume, and by him was introduced to the Mr Pluckem, who now bore the name of Mr Verdant Green? Need it be stated that the nervous Mr Pucker blushed and laughed, and laughed and blushed, while his two pseudo-examiners took wine with him in the most friendly manner, Mr Bouncer pronouncing him to be 'an out-and-outer, and no mistake!'? And need it be stated that, after this undergraduate display of hoaxing, Mr Verdant Green would feel exceedingly offended were he still to be called 'an Oxford Freshman'?

CHAPTER III

Mr Verdant Green endeavours to keep his Spirits up by pouring Spirits down.

IT was the evening of the fifth of November; the day which the Protestant youth of England dedicate to the memory of that martyr of gunpowder, the firework Fawkes, and which the youth of Oxford, by a three months' anticipation of the calendar, devote to the celebration of those scholastic sports for which the day of St Scholastica the Virgin was once so famous.*

Rumour with its hundred tongues had spread far and wide the news, that a more than ordinary demonstration would be made of the might of Town, and that this demonstration would be met by a corresponding increase of prowess on the side of Gown. It was darkly whispered that the purlieus of Jericho would send forth champions to the fight. It was mentioned that the Parish of St Thomas would be powerfully represented by its Bargee lodgers. It was confidently

---

*Town and Gown disturbances are of considerable antiquity. Fuller and Matthew Paris give accounts of some which occurred as early as the year 1238. These disputes not unfrequently terminated fatally to some of the combatants. One of the most serious Town and Gown rows on record took place on the day of St Scholastica the Virgin, February 10th, 1345, when several lives were lost on either side. The University was at that time in the Lincoln diocese; and Grostête, the Bishop, placed the townspeople under an interdict, from which they were not released till 1357, and then only on condition that the mayor and sixty of the chief burgesses should, on every anniversary of the day of St Scholastica, attend St Mary's Church and offer up mass for the souls of the slain scholars; and should also individually present an offering of one penny at the high altar. They, moreover, paid a yearly fine of 100 marks to the University, with the penalty of an additional fine of the same sum for every omission in attending at St Mary's. This continued up to the time of the Reformation, when it gradually fell into abeyance. In the fifteenth year of Elizabeth, however, the University asserted their claim to all arrears. The matter being brought to trial, it was decided that the town should continue the annual fine and penance, though the arrears were forgiven. The fine was yearly paid on the 10th of February up to our own time: the mayor and chief burgesses attended at St Mary's, and made the offering at the conclusion of the litany, which, on that occasion, was read from the altar. This was at length put an end to by Convocation in the year 1825.

reported that St Aldate's* would come forth in all its olden strength. It was told as a fact that St Clement's had departed from the spirit of clemency, and was up in arms. From an early hour of the evening, the Townsmen had gathered in threatening groups; and their determined aspect, and words of chaff, had told of the coming storm. It was to be a tremendous Town and Gown!

The Poet has forcibly observed–

> Strange that there should such diff'rence be,
> 'Twixt Tweedledum and Tweedledee!

But the difference between Town and Gown, is not to be classed with the Tweedledum and Tweedledee difference. It is something more than a mere difference of two letters. The lettered Gown lorded it over the unlettered Town: the plebeian Town was perpetually snubbed by the aristocratic Gown. If Gown even wished to associate with Town, he could only do so under certain restrictions imposed by the statutes; and Town was thus made to feel exceedingly honoured by the gracious condescension of Gown. But Town, moreover, maintained its existence that it might contribute to the pleasure and amusements, the needs and necessities, of Gown. And very expensively was Town occasionally made to pay for its existence; so expensively indeed, that if it had not been for the great interest which Town assumed on Gown's account, the former's business-life would have soon failed. But, on many accounts, or rather, *in* many accounts, Gown was deeply indebted to Town; and, although Gown was often loth to own the obligation, yet Town never forgot it, but always placed it to Gown's credit. Occasionally, in his early freshness, Gown would seek to compensate Town for his obliging favours; but Town would gently run counter to this wish, and preferred that the evidences of Gown's friendly intercourse with him should accumulate, until he could, with renewed interest (as we understand from the authority of an aged pun), obtain his payments by Degrees.

When Gown was absent, Town was miserable: it was dull; it did nothing; it lost its customer-y application to business. When Gown returned, there was no small change – the benefit was a sovereign one

---

*Corrupted by Oxford pronunciation (which makes Magdalen *Maudlin* into St *Old's*).

to Town. Notes, too, passed between them; of which those received by Town were occasionally of intrinsic value. Town thanked Gown for these – even thanked him when his civility had only been met by checks – and smirked, and fawned, and flattered; and Gown patronised Town, and was offensively condescending. What a relief then must it have been to the pent-up feelings of Town, when the Saturnalia of a Guy Fawkes day brought its usual licence, and Town could stand up against Gown and try a game of fisticuffs! And if, when there was a cry 'To arms!' we could always settle the dispute in an English fashion with those arms with which we have been supplied by nature, there would then, perhaps, be fewer weeping widows and desolate orphans in the world than there are just at present.

On the evening of the fifth of November, then, Mr Bouncer's rooms were occupied by a wine-party; and, among the gentlemen assembled, we noticed (as newspaper reporters say) Mr Verdant Green, Mr Charles Larkyns, Mr Fosbrooke, Mr Smalls, and Mr Blades. The table was liberally supplied with wine; and a 'desert at eighteen-pence per head' – as Mr Bouncer would afterwards be informed through the medium of his confectioner's bill; – and, while an animated conversation was being held on the expected Town and Gown, the party were fortifying themselves for the *émeute* by a rapid consumption of the liquids before them. Our hero, and some of the younger ones of the party, who had not yet left off their juvenile likings, were hard at work at the dessert in that delightful, disregardless-of-dyspepsia manner, in which boys so love to indulge, even when they have passed into University *men*. As usual, the *bouquet* of the wine was somewhat interfered with by those narcotic odours, which, to a smoker, are as the gales of Araby the Blest.

Mr Blades was conspicuous among the party, not only from his dimensions – or, as he phrased it, from 'his breadth of beam' – but also from his free-and-easy costume. 'To get himself into wind', as he alleged, Mr Blades had just been knocking the wind out of the Honourable Flexible Shanks (youngest son of the Earl of Buttonhole), a Tuft from Christ Church, who had left his luxurious rooms in the Canterbury Quad chiefly for the purpose of preparing himself for the forthcoming Town and Gown, by putting on the gloves with his boating friend. The bout having terminated by Mr Flexible Shanks having been sent backwards into a tray of wine-glasses with which Mr Filcher was just entering the room, the gloves were put aside, and the combatants had an amicable set-to at a bottle of Carbonell's 'Forty-four', which Mr Bouncer brought out of a wine-closet in his bed-room for their especial delectation. Mr Blades, who was of opinion that, in dress, ease should always be consulted before elegance, had not resumed that part of his attire of which he had divested himself for fistianic purposes; and, with a greater display of linen than is usually to be seen in society, was seated comfortably in a lounging chair, smoking the pipe of peace. Since he had achieved the proud feat of placing the Brazenface boat at the head of the river, Mr Blades had gained increased renown, more especially in his own college, where he was regarded in the light of a tutelary river deity; and, as training was not going on, he was now enabled to indulge in a second glass of wine, and also in the luxury of a cigar. Mr Blades's shirt-sleeves were turned up so as to display the anatomical proportion of his arms; and little Mr Bouncer, with the grave aspect of a doctor feeling a pulse, was engaged in fingering his deltoid and biceps muscles, and in uttering panegyrics on his friend's torso-of-Hercules condition.

'My gum, Billy!' (it must be observed, *en passant*, that, although the name given to Mr Blades at an early age was Frank, yet that when he was not called 'old Blades', he was always addressed as 'Billy', it being a custom which has obtained in universities, that wrong names should be familiarly given to certain gentlemen, more as a mark of friendly intimacy than of derision or caprice.) 'My gum, Billy!' observed Mr Bouncer, 'you're as hard as nails! What an extensive assortment of muscles you've got on hand – to say nothing about the arms. I wish I'd got such a good stock in trade for our customers to-night; I'd soon sarve 'em out, and make 'em sing peccavi.'

'The fact is', said Mr Flexible Shanks, who was leaning smoking against the mantelpiece behind him, 'Billy is like a respectable family of bivalves – he is nothing but mussels.'

'Or like an old Turk', joined in Mr Bouncer, 'for he's a regular Mussulman.'

'Oh! Shanks! Bouncer!' cried Charles Larkyns, 'what stale jokes! Do open the window, somebody – it's really offensive.'

'Ah!' said Mr Blades, modestly, 'you only just wait till Footlights brings the Pet, and then you'll see real muscles.'

'It was rather a good move,' said Mr Cheke, a gentleman-commoner of Corpus, who was lounging in an easy-chair, smoking a meerschaum through an elastic tube a yard long – 'it was rather a good move of yours, Fossy,' he said, addressing himself to Mr Four-in-hand Fosbrooke, 'to secure the Pet's services. The feller will do us some service, and will astonish the *hoi polloi* no end.'

'Oh! how prime it *will* be,' cried little Mr Bouncer, in ecstasies with the prospect before him, 'to see the Pet pitching into the cads, and walking into their small affections with his one, two, three! And don't I just pity them when he gets them into Chancery! Were you ever in Chancery, Gig-lamps?'

'No, indeed!' replied the innocent Mr Verdant Green; 'and I hope that I shall always keep out of it: lawsuits are so very disagreeable and expensive.'

Mr Bouncer had only time to remark *sotto voce* to Mr Flexible Shanks, 'it is so jolly refreshing to take a rise out of old Gig-lamps!' when a knock at the oak was heard; and, as Mr Bouncer roared out, 'Come in!' the knocker entered. He was rather dressy in his style of costume, and wore his long dark hair parted in the middle. Opening the door, and striking into an attitude, he exclaimed in a theatrical tone and manner: 'Scene, Mr Bouncer's rooms in Brazenface; in the centre a table, at which Mr B. and party are discovered drinking log-juice, and smoking cabbage-leaves. Door, left, third entrance; enter the Putney Pet. Slow music; lights half-down.' And standing on one side, the speaker motioned to a second gentleman to enter the room.

There was no mistaking the profession of this gentleman; even the inexperience of Mr Verdant Green did not require to be informed that the Putney Pet was a prizefighter. 'Bruiser' was plainly written in his personal appearance, from his hard-featured, low-browed, battered, hang-dog face, to his thickset frame, and the powerful muscular development of the upper part of his person. His close-cropped thatch of hair was brushed down tightly to his head, but was permitted to burst into the luxuriance of two small ringlets, which dangled in front of each huge ear, and were as carefully curled and oiled as though they had graced the face of beauty. The Pet was attired in a dark olive-green

cutaway coat, buttoned over a waistcoat of a violent-coloured plaid, a pair of white cord trousers that fitted tightly to the leg, and a white-spotted blue handkerchief, which was twisted round a neck that might have served as a model for the Minotaur's. In his mouth, the Pet cherished, according to his wont, a sprig of parsley; small fragments of which herb he was accustomed to chew and spit out, as a pleasing relief to the monotony of conversation.

The Pet, after having been proclaimed victor in more than one of those playfully frolicsome 'Frolics of the Fancy', in which nobly born but ignobly-minded 'Corinthians' formerly invested so much interest and money, had at length matched his powers against the gentleman who bore the title of 'the champion of the ring'; but, after a protracted contest of two hours and a half, in which one hundred and nineteen rounds had been fought, the Pet's eyes had been completely closed up by an amusing series of blows from the heavy fists of the more skilful champion; and as the Pet, moreover, was so battered and bruised, and was altogether so 'groggy' that he was barely able to stand up to be knocked down, his humane second had thrown up the sponge in acknowledgment of his defeat. But though unable to deprive the champion of his belt, yet – as *Tintinnabulum's Life* informed its readers on the following Sunday, in its report of this 'matchless encounter' – the Putney Pet had 'established a reputation'; and a reputation *is* a reputation, even though it be one which may be offensive to the nostrils. Retiring, therefore, from the more active public duties of his profession, he took unto himself a wife and a beershop – for it seems to be a freak of 'the Fancy', when they retire from one public line to go into another – and placing the former in charge of the latter, the Pet came forth to the world as a 'Professor of the noble art of Self-defence'.

It was in this phase of his existence, that Mr Fosbrooke had the pleasure of forming his acquaintance. Mr Fosbrooke had received a card, which intimated that the Pet would have great pleasure in giving him '*lessons in the noble and manly art of Self-defence, either at the gentleman's own residence, or at the Pet's spacious Sparring Academy*, 5, *Cribb Court, Drury Lane, which is fitted up with every regard to the comfort and convenience of his pupils. Gloves are provided. N.B. – Ratting sports at the above crib every evening. Plenty of rats always on hand. Use of the Pit gratis.*' Mr Fosbrooke, having come to the wise conclusion that every Englishman ought to know how to be able to use his fists in case of need, and being quite of the opinion of the gentleman who said, 'my son should even learn to box, for do we not meet with imposing toll-keepers, and insolent cabmen? and, as he can't call them out, he should be able to knock them down',* at once put himself under the Pet's tuition; and, as we have before seen, still kept up his practice with the gloves, when he had got to his own rooms at Brazenface.

But the Pet had other Oxford pupils than Mr Fosbrooke; and he took such an affectionate interest in their welfare, that he came down from Town two or three times in each term, to see if his pupils' practice had made them perfect in the art. One of the Pet's pupils was the gentleman who had now introduced him to Mr Bouncer's rooms. His name was Foote, but he was commonly called 'Footelights'; the addition having been made to his name by way of *sobriquet* to express his unusual fondness for the stage, which amounted to so great a passion, that his very conversation was redolent of 'the footlights'. He

---

* *A Bachelor of Arts*, Act I.

had only been at St John's a couple of terms, and Mr Fosbrooke had picked up his acquaintance through the medium of the Pet, and had afterwards made him known to most of the men who were now assembled at Mr Bouncer's wine.

'Your servant, gents!' said the Pet, touching his forehead, and making a scrape with his leg, by way of salutation.

'Hullo, Pet!' returned Mr Bouncer; 'bring yourself to an anchor, my man.' The Pet accordingly anchored himself by dropping on to the edge of a chair, and placing his hat underneath it; while Huz and Buz smelt suspiciously round his legs, and looked at him with an expression of countenance which bore a wonderful resemblance to that which they gazed upon.

'Never mind the dogs; they're amiable little beggars,' observed Mr Bouncer, 'and they never bite anyone except in play. Now then, Pet, what sort of liquors are you given to? Here are Claret liquors, Port liquors, Sherry liquors, egg-flip liquors, Cup liquors. You pays your money, and you takes your choice!'

'Well, sir, thankee!' replied the Pet, 'I ain't no ways pertikler, but if you *have* sich a thing as a glass o' sperrits, I'd prefer that – if not objectionable.'

'In course not, Pet! always call for what you like. We keep all sorts of liquors, and are allowed to get drunk on the premises. Ain't we, Giglamps?' Firing this raking shot as he passed our hero, little Mr Bouncer dived into the cupboard which served as his wine-bin, and brought therefrom two bottles of brandy and whiskey which he set before the Pet. 'If you like gin or rum, or cherry-brandy, or old-tom, better than these liquors,' said Mr Bouncer, astonishing the Pet with the resources of a College wine-cellar, 'just say the word, and you shall have them. "I can call spirits from the vasty deep"; as Shikspur says. How will you take it, Pet? Neat, or adulterated? Are you for *callidum cum*, or *frigidum sine* – for hot-with, or cold-without?'

'I generally takes my sperrits 'ot, sir – if not objectionable;' replied the Pet deferentially. Whereupon Mr Bouncer seizing his speaking-trumpet, roared through it from the top of the stairs, 'Rob-ert! Robert!' But, as Mr Filcher did not answer the summons, Mr Bouncer threw up the window of his room, and bellowed out 'Rob-ert' in tones which must have been perfectly audible in the High Street. 'Doose take the feller, he's always over at the Buttery;' said the incensed gentleman.

'I'll go up to old Sloe's room, and get his kettle,' said Mr Smalls; 'he teas all day long to keep himself awake for reading. If he don't mind, he'll blow himself up with his gunpowder tea before he can take his double-first.'

By the time Mr Smalls had reappeared with the kettle, Mr Filcher had thought it prudent to answer his master's summons.

'Did you call, sir?' asked the scout, as though he was doubtful on that point.

'Call!' said Mr Bouncer, with great irony; 'oh, no! of course not! I should rather think not! Do you suppose that you are kept here that parties may have the chance of hollering out their lungs for you? Don't answer me, sir! but get some hot water, and some more glasses; and be quick about it.' Mr Filcher was gone immediately; and, in three minutes, everything was settled to Mr Bouncer's satisfaction, and he gave Mr Filcher further orders to bring up coffee and anchovy toast, at half-past eight o'clock. 'Now, Pet, my beauty!' said the little

gentleman, 'you just walk into the liquors; because you've got some toughish work before you, you know.'

The Pet did not require any pressing, but did as he was told; and, bestowing a collective nod on the company, drank their healths with the prefatory remark, 'I looks to-*wards* you gents!'

'Will you poke a smipe, Pet?' asked Mr Bouncer, rather enigmatic-ally; but, as he at the same time placed before the Pet a 'yard of clay' and a box of cigars, the professor of the art of self-defence perceived that he was asked to smoke a pipe.

'That's right, Pet!' said the Honourable Flexible Shanks, con-descendingly, as the prizefighter scientifically filled the bowl of his pipe; 'I'm glad to see you join us in a bit of smoke. We're all *Baccy-*nalians now!'

'Shanks, you're incorrigible!' said Charles Larkyns; 'and don't you remember what *the Oxford Parodies* say?' and in his clear, rich voice, Mr Larkyns sang the two following verses to the air of 'Love not':

> Smoke not, smoke not, your weeds nor pipes of clay;
>   Cigars they are made from leaves of cauliflowers;
> Things that are doomed no duty e'er to pay;
>   Grown, made, and smoked in a few short hours.
>   Smoke not – smoke not!
>
> Smoke not, smoke not, the weed you smoke may change
>   The healthfulness of your stomachic tone;
> Things to the eye grow queer and passing strange;
>   All thoughts seem undefined – save one – to be alone!
>   Smoke not – smoke not!

'I know what you're thinking about, Gig-lamps,' said Mr Bouncer, as Charles Larkyns ceased his parody amid an approving clatter of glasses; 'you were thinking of your first weed on the night of Smalls's quiet party: weren't you now, old feller? Ah, you've learnt to poke a smipe, beautiful, since then. Pet, here's your health. I'll give you a toast and sintiment, gentlemen. May the Gown give the Town a jolly good hiding!' The sentiment was received with great applause, and the toast was drunk with all the honours, and followed by the customary but inappropriate chorus, 'For he's a jolly good fellow!' without the singing of which Mr Bouncer could not allow any toast to pass.

'How many cads could you lick at once, one off and the other on?' asked Mr Fosbrooke of the Pet, with the air of Boswell when he wanted to draw out the Doctor.

'Well, sir,' said the Pet, with the modesty of true genius, 'I wouldn't be pertickler to a score or so, as long as I'd got my back well up agin some'ut, and could hit out.'

'What an effective tableau it would be!' observed Mr Foote, who had always an eye to dramatic situations. 'Enter the Pet, followed by twenty townspeople. First T.P. – *Yield, traitor!* Pet – *Never! the man who would yield when ordered to do so, is unworthy the name of a Pet and an Englishman!* Floors the twenty T.P.'s one after the other. Tableau, blue fire. Why, it would surpass the British sailor's broadsword combat for six, and bring down the house.'

'Talking of bringing down,' said Mr Blades, 'did you remember to bring down a cap and gown for the Pet, as I told you?'

'Well, I believe those *were* the stage directions,' answered Mr Foote; 'but, really, the wardrobe was so ill provided that it would only supply a cap. But perhaps that will do for a super.'

'If by a super you mean a supernumerary, Footelights,' said Mr Cheke, the gentleman-commoner of Corpus, 'then the Pet isn't one. He's the leading character of what you would call the *dramatis personae.*'

'True,' replied Mr Foote, 'he's cast for the hero; though he will create a new *rôle* as the walking-into-them gentleman.'

'You see, Footelights,' said Mr Blades, 'that the Pet is to lead our forces; and we depend upon him to help us on to victory: and we must put him into academicals, not only because the town cads must think he is one of us, but also because the proctors might otherwise deprive us of his services – and old Towzer, the Senior Proctor, in particular, is sure to be all alive. Who's got an old gown?'

'I will lend mine with pleasure,' said Mr Verdant Green.

'But you'll want it yourself,' said Mr Blades.

'Why, thank you,' faltered our hero, 'I'd rather, I think, keep within college. I can see the – the fun – yes, the fun – from the window.'

'Oh, blow it, Gig-lamps!' ejaculated Mr Bouncer, 'you'll never go to do the mean, and show the white feather, will you?'

'Music expressive of trepidation,' murmured Mr Foote, by way of parenthesis.

'But', pursued our hero, apologetically, 'there will be, I dare say, a large crowd.'

'A very powerful cast, no doubt,' observed Mr Foote.

'And I may get my – yes, my spectacles broken; and then' . . .

'And then, Gig-lamps,' said Mr Bouncer, 'why, and then you shall be presented with another pair as a testimonial of affection from yours truly. Come, Gig-lamps, don't do the mean! a man of your standing, and with a chest like that!' and the little gentleman sounded on our hero's shirt-front, as doctors do when they stethoscope a patient. 'Come, Gig-lamps, old feller, you mustn't refuse. You didn't ought to was, as Shakespeare says.'

'Pardon me! Not Shakespeare, but Wright, in the *Green Bushes*', interrupted Mr Foote, who was as painfully anxious as Mr Payne Collier himself that the text of the great poet should be free from corruptions.

So Mr Verdant Green, reluctantly, it must be confessed, suffered himself to be persuaded to join that section of the Gown which was to be placed under the leadership of the redoubted Pet; while little Mr Bouncer, who had gone up into Mr Sloe's rooms, and had vainly endeavoured to persuade that gentleman to join in the forthcoming *mêlée*, returned with an undergraduate's gown, and forthwith invested the Pet with it.

'I don't mind this 'ere mortar-board, sir,' remarked the professor of the noble art of self-defence, as he pointed to the academical cap which surmounted his head, 'I don't mind the mortar-board, sir; but I shall never be able to do nothink with this 'ere toggery on my shudders. I couldn't use my mawleys no how!' And the Pet illustrated his remark in a professional manner, by sparring at an imaginary opponent in a feeble and unscientific fashion.

'But you can tie the tail-curtain round your shoulders – like this!' said Mr Fosbrooke, as he twisted his own gown tightly round him. But the Pet had taken a decided objection to the drapery: 'The costume would interfere with the action,' as Mr Foote remarked, 'and the management of a train requires great practice.'

'You see, sir,' said the Pet, 'I ain't used to the feel of it, and I couldn't go to business properly, or give a straight nosender no how. But the mortar-board ain't of so much consekyence.' So a compromise was made; and it was agreed that the Pet was to wear the academicals until he had arrived at the scene of action, where he could then pocket the gown, and resume it on any alarm of the Proctor's approach.

'Here, Gig-lamps, old feller! get a priming of fighting-powder!' said little Mr Bouncer to our hero, as the party were on the point of sallying forth; 'it'll make you hit out from your shoulder like a steam-engine with the chill off.' And, as Mr Bouncer whispered to Charles Larkyns

So he kept his spirits up
By pouring spirits down,

Verdant – who felt extremely nervous, either from excitement or from fear, or from a pleasing mixture of both sensations – drank off a deep draught of something which was evidently not drawn from Nature's spring or the college pump; for it first took away his breath, and made his eyes water; and it next made him cough, and endeavour to choke himself; and it then made his face flush, and caused him to declare that 'the first snob who 'sulted him should have a sound whopping.'

'Brayvo, Gig-lamps!' cried little Mr Bouncer, as he patted him on the shoulder; 'come along! You're the right sort of fellow for a Town and Gown, after all!'

CHAPTER IV

Mr Verdant Green discovers the difference between Town and Gown.

IT was ten minutes past nine, and Tom,* with sonorous voice, was ordering all College gates to be shut, when the wine party, which had just left Mr Bouncer's room, passed round the corner of St Mary's, and dashed across the High. The Town and Gown had already begun.

As usual, the Town had taken the initiative; and, in a dense body, had made their customary sweep of the High Street, driving all before them. After this gallant exploit had been accomplished to the entire satisfaction of the oppidans, the Town had separated into two or three portions, which had betaken themselves to the most probable fighting points, and had gone where glory waited them, thirsting for the blood, or, at any rate, for the bloody noses of the gowned aristocrats. Woe betide the luckless Gownsman, who, on such an occasion, ventures abroad without an escort, or trusts to his own unassisted powers to defend himself! He is forthwith pounced upon by some score of valiant Townsmen, who are on the watch for these favourable opportunities for a display of their personal prowess, and he may consider himself very fortunate if he is able to get back to his college with nothing worse than black eyes and bruises. It is so seldom that the members of the Oxford snobocracy have the privilege afforded them of using their fists on the faces and persons of the members of the Oxford aristocracy, that when they *do* get the chance they are unwilling to let it slip through their fingers. Dark tales have, indeed, been told, of solitary and unoffending undergraduates having, on such occasions, not only received a severe handling from those same fingers, but also having been afterwards, through their agency, bound by their

---

* The great bell of Christ Church. It tolls 101 times each evening at ten minutes past nine o'clock (there being 101 students on the foundation) and marks the time for the closing of the college gates. 'Tom' is one of the lions of Oxford. It formerly belonged to Osney Abbey, and weighs about 17,000 pounds, being more than double the weight of the great bell of St Paul's.

own leading strings to the rails of the Radcliffe, and there left ignominiously to struggle, and shout for assistance. And darker tales still have been told of luckless gownsmen having been borne 'leg and wing' fashion to the very banks of the Isis, and there ducked, amidst the jeers and taunts of their persecutors. But such tales as these are of too dreadful a nature for the conversation of gownsmen, and are very properly believed to be myths scandalously propagated by the Town.

The crescent moon shone down on Mr Bouncer's party, and gave ample light 'To light *them* on *their* prey'. A noise and shouting – which quickly made our hero's Bob-Acreish resolutions ooze out at his fingers' ends – was heard coming from the direction of Oriel Street; and a small knot of gownsmen, who had been cut off from a larger body, appeared, manfully retreating with their faces to the foe, fighting as they fell back, but driven by superior numbers up the narrow street, by St Mary's Hall, and past the side of Spiers's shop into the High Street.

'Gown to the rescue!' shouted Mr Blades, as he dashed across the street; 'come on, Pet! here we are in the thick of it, just in the nick of time!' and, closely followed by Charles Larkyns, Mr Fosbrooke, Mr Smalls, Mr Bouncer, Mr Flexible Shanks, Mr Cheke, Mr Foote, and our hero, and the rest of the party, they soon plunged *in medias res*.

The movement was particularly well-timed, for the small body of gownsmen were beginning to get roughly handled; but the succour afforded by the Pet and his party soon changed the aspect of affairs; and, after a brief skirmish, there was a temporary cessation of hostilities. As reinforcements poured in on either side, the mob which represented the Town, wavered, and spread themselves across on each side of the High, while a huge, lumbering bargeman, who appeared to be the generalissimo of their forces, delivered himself of a brief but energetic speech, in which he delivered his opinion of gownsmen in general, and his immediate foes in particular, in a way which would have to be expressed in proper print chiefly by blanks, and which would have assuredly entailed upon him a succession of five-shilling fines, had he been in a court of justice, and before a magistrate.

'Here's a pretty blank, I don't think!' he observed in conclusion, as he pointed to Mr Verdant Green, who was nervously settling his spectacles, and wishing himself safe back in his own rooms; 'I wouldn't give a blank for such a blank blank. I'm blank, if he don't look as though he'd swaller'd a blank codfish, and had bust out into blank barnacles!' As the bargee was apparently regarded by his party as a gentleman of infinite humour, his highly-flavoured blank remarks were received by them with shouts of laughter; while our hero obtained far more of the *digito monstrari* share of public notice than he wished for.

For some brief space, the warfare between the rival parties of Town and Gown continued to be one merely of words – a mutual discharge of *epea pteroenta* (*vulgariter* 'chaff'), in which a small amount of sarcasm was mingled with a large share of vituperation. At length, a slang rhyme of peculiar offensiveness was used to a Wadham gentleman, which so exasperated him that he immediately, by way of a forcible reply, sent his fist full into the speaker's face. On this, a collision took place between those who formed the outside of the crowd; and the Gowns flocked together to charge *en masse*. Mr Verdant Green was not quite aware of this sudden movement, and, for a moment, was cut off from the rest. This did not escape the eyes of the valiant bargee, who had already singled out our hero as the one whom he could most easily punish, with the least chance of getting quick returns for his small profits. Forthwith, therefore, he rushed to his victim, and aimed a heavy blow at him, which Verdant only half avoided by stooping. Instinctively doubling his fists, our hero found that Necessity was, indeed, the mother of Invention; and, with a passing thought of what would be his mother's and Aunt Virginia's feelings could they see him fighting in the public streets with a common bargeman, he contrived to guard off the second blow. But at the next furious lunge of the bargee he was not quite so fortunate, and, receiving that gentleman's heavy fist full in his forehead, he staggered backwards, and was only prevented from measuring his length on the pavement by falling against the iron gates of St Mary's. The delighted bargee was just on the point of putting the *coup de grâce* to his attack, when, to Verdant's inexpressible delight and relief, his lumbering antogonist was sent sprawling by a well-directed blow on his right ear. Charles Larkyns,

who had kept a friendly eye on our hero, had spied his condition, and had sprung to his assistance. He was closely followed by the Pet, who had divested himself of the gown which had encumbered his shoulders, and was now freely striking out in all directions. The fight had become general, and fresh combatants had sprung up on either side.

'Keep close to me, Verdant,' said Charles Larkyns – quite unnecessarily, by the way, as our hero had no intention of doing otherwise until he saw a way to escape; 'keep close to me, and I'll take care you are not hurt.'

'Here ye are!' cried the Pet, as he set his back against the stone-work flanking the iron gates of the church, immediately in front of one of

the curiously twisted pillars of the porch;* 'come on, half a dozen of ye, and let me have a rap at your smellers!' and he looked at the mob in the 'Come one, come all defiant' fashion of Fitz-James; while Charles Larkyns and Verdant set their backs against the church gates, and prepared for a rush.

The bargee came up furious, and hit out wildly at Charles Larkyns; but science was more than a match for brute force; and, after receiving two or three blows which caused him to shake his head in a don't-like-it sort of way, he endeavoured to turn his attention to Mr Verdant

* The porch was erected in 1637 by order of Archbishop Laud. In the centre of the porch is a statue of the Virgin with the Child in her arms, holding a small crucifix, which at the time of its erection gave such offence to the Puritans that it was included in the articles of impeachment against the Archbishop. The statue remains to this day.

Green, who, with head in air, was taking the greatest care of his spectacles, and endeavouring to ward off the indiscriminate lunges of half a dozen townsmen. The bargee's charitable designs on our hero were, however, frustrated by the opportune appearance of Mr Blades and Mr Cheke, the gentleman-commoner of Corpus, who, in their turn, were closely followed by Mr Smalls and Mr Flexible Shanks; and Mr Blades exclaiming, 'There's a smasher for your ivories, my fine fellow!' followed up the remark with a practical application of his fist to the part referred to; whereupon the bargee fell back with a howl, and gave vent to several curse-ory observations, and blank remarks.

All this time the Pet was laying about him in the most determined manner; and, to judge from his professional observations, his scientific acquirements were in full play. He had agreeable remarks for each of his opponents; and, doubtless, the punishment which they received from his stalwart arms came with more stinging force when the parts affected were pointed out by his illustrative language. To one gentleman he would pleasantly observe, as he tapped him on the chest, 'Bellows to mend for you, my buck!' or else, 'There's a regular rib-roaster for you!' or else, in the still more elegant imagery of the Ring, 'There's a squelcher in the bread-basket, that'll stop *your* dancing, my kivey!' While to another he would cheerfully remark, 'Your head-rails were loosened there, wasn't they?' or, 'How about the kissing-trap?' or, 'That draws the bung from the beer-barrel I'm a thinkin'.' While to another he would say, as a fact not to be disputed, 'You napp'd it heavily on your whisker-bed, didn't you?' or, 'That'll raise a tidy mouse on your ogle, my lad!' or, 'That'll take the bark from your nozzle, and distil the Dutch pink for you, won't it?' While to another he would mention as an interesting item of news, 'Now we'll tap your best October!' or, 'There's a crack on your snuff-box!' or, 'That'll damage your potato-trap!' Or else he would kindly inquire of one gentleman, 'What d'ye ask a pint for your cochineal dye?' or would amiably recommend another that, as his peepers were a goin' fast, he'd best put up the shutters, because the early-closing movement ought to be follered out. All this was done in the cheeriest manner; while, at the same time, the Pet proved himself to be not only a perfect master of his profession, but also a skilful adept in those figures of speech, or 'nice derangements of epitaphs', as Mrs Malaprop calls them, in which the admirers of the fistic art so much delight. At every blow, a fresh opponent either fell or staggered off; the supremacy of the Pet was complete, and his claim to be considered a Professor of the noble and manly art of Self-defence was triumphantly established. 'The Putney Pet' was a decidedly valuable acquisition to the side of Gown.

Soon the crowd became thinner, as those of the Town who liked to give, but not to receive hard blows, stole off to other quarters; and the Pet and his party would have been left peaceably to themselves. But this was not what they wanted, as long as fighting was going on elsewhere; even Mr Verdant Green began to feel desperately courageous as the Town took to their heels, and fled; and, having performed prodigies of valour in almost knocking down a small cad who had had the temerity to attack him, our hero felt himself to be a hero indeed, and announced his intention of pursuing the mob, and sticking close to Charles Larkyns – taking especial care to do the latter.

> All the savage soul of *fight* was up;

and the Gown following the scattered remnant of the flying Town, ran them round by All Saints' Church, and up the Turl.

Here another Town and Gown party had fought their way from the Corn-market; and the Gown, getting considerably the worst of the conflict, had taken refuge within Exeter College by the express order of the Senior Proctor, the Revd Thomas Tozer, more familiarly known

as 'old Towzer.' He had endeavoured to assert his proctorial authority over the mob of the townspeople; but the *profanum vulgus* had not only scoffed and jeered him, but had even torn his gown, and treated his velvet sleeves with the indignity of mud; while the only fireworks which had been exhibited on that evening had been let off in his very face. Pushed on, and hustled by the mob, and only partially protected by his Marshal and Bulldogs,* he was saved from further indignity by the arrival of a small knot of gownsmen, who rushed to his rescue. Their number was too small, however, to make head against the mob, and the best that they could do was to cover the Proctor's retreat. Now, the Revd Thomas Tozer was short, and inclined to corpulence, and, although not wanting for courage, yet the exertion of defending himself from a superior force, was not only a fruitless one, but was, moreover, productive of much unpleasantness and perspiration. Deeming, therefore, that discretion was the better part of valour, he fled (like those who tended, or *ought* to have attended to, the flocks of Mr Norval, Sen.) 'for safety and for succour', and, being rather short of the necessary article of wind, by the time that he had reached Exeter College, he had barely breath enough left to tell the porter to keep the gate shut until he had assembled a body of gownsmen to assist him in capturing those daring ringleaders of the mob who had set his authority at defiance. This was soon done; the call to arms was made, and every Exeter man who was not already out, ran to 'old Towzer's' assistance.

'Now, porter,' said Mr Tozer, 'unbar the gate without noise, and I will look forth to observe the position of the mob. Gentlemen, hold yourselves in readiness to secure the ringleaders.'

The porter undid the wicket, and the Revd Thomas Tozer cautiously put forth his head. It was a rash act; for, no sooner had his nose appeared round the edge of the wicket, than it received a flattening blow from the fist of an active gentleman who, like a clever cricketer, had been on the lookout for an opportunity to get in to his adversary's wicket.

'Oh, this is painful! this is very painful!' ejaculated Mr Tozer, as he rapidly drew in his head. 'Close the wicket directly, porter, and keep

---

* The Marshal is the Proctor's chief officer. The name of 'Bull-dogs' is given to the two inferior officers who attend the Proctor in his nightly rounds.

it fast.' It was like closing the gates of Hougomont. The active gentleman who had damaged Mr Tozer's nose threw himself against the wicket, his comrades assisted him, and the porter had some difficulty in obeying the Proctor's orders.

'Oh, this is painful!' murmured the Revd Thomas Tozer, as he applied a handkerchief to his bleeding nose; 'this is painful, this is very painful! this is exceedingly painful, gentlemen!'

He was immediately surrounded by sympathising undergraduates, who begged him to allow them at once to charge the Town; but 'old Towzer's' spirit seemed to have been aroused by the indignity to which he had been forced so publicly to submit, and he replied that, as soon as the bleeding had ceased, he would lead them forth in person. An encouraging cheer followed this courageous resolve, and was echoed from without by the derisive applause of the Town.

When Mr Tozer's nose had ceased to bleed, the signal was given for the gates to be thrown open; and out rushed Proctor, Marshall, Bulldogs, and undergraduates. The Town was in great force, and the fight became desperate. To the credit of the Town, be it said, they discarded bludgeons and stones, and fought, in John Bull fashion, with their

fists. Scarcely a stick was to be seen. Singling out his man, Mr Tozer made at him valiantly, supported by his Bull-dogs, and a small band of Gownsmen. But the heavy gown and velvet sleeves were a grievous hindrance to the Proctor's prowess; and, although supported on either side by his two attendant Bull-dogs, yet the weight of his robes made poor Mr Tozer almost as harmless as the blind King of Bohemia between his two faithful knights at the battle of Crecy; and, as each of the party had to look to, and fight for himself, the Senior Proctor soon found himself in an awkward predicament.

The cry of 'Gown to the rescue!' therefore, fell pleasantly on his ears; and the reinforcement headed by Mr Charles Larkyns and his party, materially improved the aspect of affairs on the side of Gown. Knocking down a cowardly fellow, who was using his heavy-heeled boots on the body of a prostrate undergraduate, Mr Blades, closely followed by the Pet, dashed in to the Proctor's assistance; and never in a Town and Gown was assistance more timely rendered; for the Revd Thomas Tozer had just received his first knock-down blow! By the help of Mr Blades the fallen chieftain was quickly replaced upon his legs; while the Pet stepped before him, and struck out skilfully right and left. Ten more minutes of scientific pugilism, and the fate of the battle was decided. The Town fled every way; some round the corner by Lincoln College; some up the Turl towards Trinity; some down Ship Street; and some down by Jesus College, and Market Street. A few of the more resolute made a stand in Broad Street; but it was of no avail; and they received a sound punishment at the hands of the Gown, on the spot, where, some three centuries before, certain mitred gownsmen had bravely suffered martyrdom.*

Now, the Revd Thomas Tozer was a strict disciplinarian, and, although he had so materially benefited by the Pet's assistance, yet, when he perceived that that pugilistic gentleman was not possessed of the full complement of academical attire, the duties of the Proctor rose superior to the gratitude of the Man; and, with all the sternness of an ancient Roman Father, he said to the Pet, 'Why have you not on your gown, sir?'

---

* The *exact* spot where Archbishop Cranmer and Bishops Ridley and Latimer suffered martyrdom is not known. 'The most likely supposition is, that it was in the town ditch, the site of which is now occupied by the houses in Broad Street, which are immediately opposite the gateway of Balliol College, or the footpath in front of them, where an extensive layer of wood-ashes is known to remain.' – (Parker.)

'I ax your pardon, guv'nor!' replied the Pet, deferentially; 'I didn't so much care about the mortar-board, but I couldn't do nothin' nohow with the t'other thing, so I pocketted him; but some cove must have gone and prigged him, for he ain't here.'

'I am unable to comprehend the nature of your language, sir,' observed the Revd Thomas Tozer, angrily; for, what with his own excitement, and the shades of evening which had stolen over and obscured the Pet's features, he was unable to read that gentleman's character and profession in his face, and therefore came to the conclusion that he was being chaffed by some impudent undergraduate. 'I don't in the least understand you, sir; but I desire at once to know your name, and college, sir!'

The Putney Pet stared. If the Revd Thomas Tozer had asked him for the name of his Academy, he would have been able to have referred him to his spacious and convenient Sparring Academy, 5, Cribb Court, Drury Lane; but the enquiry for his 'college', was, in the language of his profession, a 'regular floorer.' Mr Blades, however, stepped forward, and explained matters to the Proctor, in a satisfactory manner.

'Well, well!' said the pacified Mr Tozer to the Pet; 'you have used your skill very much to our advantage, and displayed pugilistic powers not unworthy of the athletes and xystics of the noblest days of Rome. As a palaestrite you would have gained palms in the gymnastic exercise of the Circus Maximus. You might even have proved a formidable rival to Dares, who, as you, Mr Blades, will remember, caused the death of Butes at Hector's tomb. You will remember, Mr Blades, that Virgil makes mention of his 'humeros latos', and says

> nec quisquam ex agmine tanto
> Audet adire virum, manibusque inducere cæstus.*

which, in our English idiom, would signify, that everyone was afraid to put on the gloves with him. And, as your skill', resumed Mr Tozer, turning to the Pet, 'has been exercised in defence of my person, and in upholding the authority of the University, I will overlook your offence in assuming that portion of the academical attire, to which you gave the offensive epithet of 'mortar-board'; more especially, as you

* Æn., Book v, 378.

acted at the suggestion and bidding of those who ought to have known better. And now, go home, sir, and resume your customary head-dress; and – stay! here's five shillings for you.'

'I'm much obleeged to you, guv'nor,' said the Pet, who had been listening with considerable surprise to the Proctor's quotations and comparisons, and wondering whether the gentleman named Dares, who caused the death of beauties, was a member of the P.R., and whether they made it out a case of manslaughter against him? and if the gaining palms in a circus was the customary 'flapper-shaking' before 'toeing the scratch for business'? – 'I'm much obleeged to you, guv'nor,' said the Pet, as he made a scrape with his leg: 'and, whenever you *does* come up to London, I 'ope you'll drop in at Cribb Court, and have a turn with the gloves!' And the Pet, very politely, handed one of his professional cards to the Revd Thomas Tozer.

A little later than this, a very jovial supper party might have been seen assembled in a principal room at *The Roebuck*. To enable them to be back within their college walls, and save their gates, before the hour of midnight should arrive, the work of consuming the grilled bones and welch-rabbits was going on with all reasonable speed, the heavier articles being washed down by draughts of 'heavy'. After the cloth was withdrawn, several songs of a miscellaneous character were sung by 'the professional gentlemen present', including, 'by particular request', the celebrated 'Marble Halls' song of our hero, which was given with more coherency than on a previous occasion, but was no less energetically led in its 'you-loved-me-still-the-same' chorus by Mr Bouncer. The Pet was proudly placed on the right hand of the chairman, Mr Blades; and, when his health was proposed, 'with many thanks to him for the gallant and plucky manner in which he had led on the Gown to a glorious victory', the 'three times three,' and the 'one cheer more,' and the 'again', and 'again', and the 'one other little un!' were uproariously given (as Mr Foote expressed it) 'by the whole strength of the company, assisted by Messrs Larkyns, Smalls, Fosbrooke, Flexible Shanks, Cheke, and Verdant Green.'

The forehead of the last-named gentleman was decorated with a patch of brown paper, from which arose an aroma, as though of vinegar. The battle of 'Town and Gown' was over; and Mr Verdant Green was among the number of the wounded.

CHAPTER V

Mr Verdant Green is favoured with Mr Bouncer's Opinions regarding an Undergraduate's Epistolary Communications to his Maternal Relative.

'COME in, whoever you are! don't mind the dogs!' shouted little Mr Bouncer, as he lay, in an extremely inelegant attitude, in a red  morocco chair, which was considerably the worse for wear, chiefly on account of the ill-usage it had to put up with, in being made to represent its owner's antagonist, whenever Mr Bouncer thought fit to practise his fencing. 'Oh! it's you and Gig-lamps, is it, Charley? I'm just refreshing myself with a weed, for I've been desperately hard at work.'

'What! Harry Bouncer devoting himself to study? But this is the age of wonders,' said Charles Larkyns, who entered the room in company with Mr Verdant Green, whose forehead still betrayed the effects of the blow he had received a few nights before.

'It ain't reading that I meant,' replied Mr Bouncer, 'though that always *does* floor me, and no mistake! and what's the use of their making us peg away so at Latin and Greek, I can't make out. When I go out into society, I don't want to talk about those old Greek and Latin birds that they make us get up. I don't want to ask any old dowager I happen to fall in with at a tea-fight, whether she believes all the crammers that Herodotus tells us, or whether she's well up in the naughty tales and rummy nuisances that we have to pass no end of our years in getting by heart. And when I go to a ball, and do the

light fantastic, I don't want to
ask my partner what she thinks
about Euripides, or whether
she prefers Ovid's *Metamor-
phoses* to Ovid's *Art of Love*,
and all that sort of thing; and as
for requesting her to do me a
problem of Euclid, instead of
working me any glorified
slippers or woolleries, I'd scorn
the *h*action. I ain't like you,
Charley, and I'm not *guv* in the
classics: I saw too much of the
beggars while I was at Eton to
take kindly to 'em; and just let
me once get through my
Greats, and see if I don't
precious soon drop the acquaintance of those old classical
parties!'

'No you won't, old fellow!'
said Charles Larkyns; 'you'll find that they'll stick to you through life,
just like poor relations, and you won't be able to shake them off. And
you ought not to wish to do so, more especially as, in the end, you will
find them to have been very rich relations.'

'A sort of "O my prophetic soul, my uncle!"' I suppose, Master
Charley,' observed Mr Bouncer; 'but what I meant when I said that
I had been hard at work, was that I had been writing a letter; and,
though I say it that ought not to say it, I flatter myself it's no end of
a good letter.'

'Is it a love-letter?' asked Charles Larkyns, who was leaning against
the mantel-piece, amusing himself with a cigar which he had taken
from Mr Bouncer's box.

'A love-letter?' replied the little gentleman, contemptuously – 'my
gum! no; I should rayther think not! I may have done many foolish
things in my life, but I can't have the tender passion laid to my charge.
No! I've been writing my letter to the Mum: I always write to her once

a term.' Mr Bouncer, it must be observed, always referred to his maternal relative (his father had been long dead) by the epithet of 'the Mum'.

'Once a term!' said our hero, in a tone of surprise; 'why I always write home once or twice every week.'

'You don't mean to say so, Gig-lamps!' replied Mr Bouncer, with admiration. 'Well, some fellers have what you call a genius for that sort of thing, you see, though what you can find to tell 'em I can't imagine. But if I'd gone at that pace I should have got right through the Guide Book by this time, and then it would have been all U P, and I should have been obleeged to have invented another dodge. You don't seem to take, Gig-lamps?'

'Well, I really don't know what you mean,' answered our hero.

'Why,' continued Mr Bouncer, 'you see, there's only the Mum and Fanny at home: Fanny's my sister, Gig-lamps – a regular stunner – just suit you! – and they, you understand, don't care to hear about wines, and Town and Gowns, and all that sort of thing; and, you see, I ain't inventive and that, and can't spin a yarn about nothing; so, as soon as ever I came up to Oxford, I invested money in a Guide Book; and I began at the beginning, and I gave the Mum three pages of Guide Book in each letter. Of course, you see, the Mum imagines it's all my own observation; and she thinks no end of my letters, and says that they make her know Oxford almost as well as if she lived here; and she, of course, makes a good deal of me; and as Oxford's the place where I hang out, you see, she takes an interest in reading something about the jolly old place.'

'Of course,' observed Mr Verdant Green; 'my mamma – mother, at least – and sisters, always take pleasure in hearing about Oxford; but your plan never occurred to me.'

'It's a first-rater, and no mistake,' said Mr Bouncer, confidently, 'and saves a deal of trouble. I think of taking out a patent for it – "Bouncer's Complete Letter-Writer" – or get some literary swell to put it into a book, "with a portrait of the inventor"; it would be sure to sell. You see, it's what you call amusement blended with information; and that's more than you can say of most men's letters to the Home department.'

'Cocky Palmer's, for instance,' said Charles Larkyns, 'which always contained a full, true, and particular account of his Wheatley doings. He used to go over there, Verdant, to indulge in the noble sport of cock-fighting, for which he had a most unamiable and unenviable weakness; that was the reason why he was called "Cocky" Palmer. His elder brother – who was a Pembroke man – was distinguished by the pronomen "Snuffy", to express his excessive partiality for that titillating compound.'

'And Snuffy Palmer', remarked Mr Bouncer, 'was a long sight better feller than Cocky, who was in the very worst set in Brazenface. But Cocky did the Wheatley dodge once too often, and it was a good job for the King of Oude when his friend Cocky came to grief, and had to take his name off the books.'

'You look as though you wanted a translation of this,' said Charles Larkyns to our hero, who had been listening to the conversation with some wonderment, understanding about as much of it as many persons who attend the St James's Theatre understand the dialogue of the French Plays. 'There are College *cabalia*, as well as Jewish; and College surnames are among these. "The King of Oude" was a man of the name of Towlinson, who always used to carry into Hall with him a bottle of *The King of Oude's Sauce*, for which he had some mysterious liking, and without which he professed himself unable to get through his dinner. At one time he was a great friend of Cocky Palmer's, and used to go with him to the cock-fights at Wheatley – that village just on the other side Shotover Hill – where we did a "constitutional" the other day. Cocky, as our respected friend says, "came to grief", but was allowed to save himself from expulsion by voluntarily, or rather in-voluntarily, taking his name off the books. When his connection with Cocky had thus been ruthlessly broken, "the King" got into a better set, and retrieved his character.'

'The moral of which, my beloved Gig-lamps,' observed Mr Bouncer, 'is that there are as many sets of men in a College as there are of quadrilles in a ball-room, and that it's just as easy to take your place in one as it is in another; but, that when you've once taken up your position, you'll find it ain't an easy thing, you see, to make a change for yourself, till the set is broken up. Whereby, Gig-lamps, you may comprehend what a grateful bird you ought to be, for Charley's having put you into the best set in Brazenface.'

Mr Verdant Green was heard to murmur, 'sensible of honour –
grateful for kindness – endeavours to deserve' – and the other broken
sentiments which are commonly made use of by gentlemen who get
up on their legs to return thanks for having been 'tea-potted'.

'If you like to hear it,' said Mr Bouncer, 'I'll read you my letter to

the Mum. It ain't very
private; and I flatter myself,
Gig-lamps, that it'll serve you
as a model.'

'Let's have it by all means,
Harry,' said Charles Larkyns.
'It must be an interesting
document; and I am curious
to hear what it is that you consider a model for epistolary
communication from an un-
dergraduate to his maternal
relative.'

'Off she goes then,' observed Mr Bouncer; 'lend me
your ears – list, list, O list! as the recruiting-sergeant or some other
feller says in the Play: "Now, my little dears! look straight for'ard –
blow your noses, and don't brathe on the glasses!"' and Mr Bouncer
read the letter, interspersing it with explanatory observations:

"*My dearest mother, I have been quite well since I left you, and I hope
you and Fanny have been equally salubrious.* – That's doing the civil,
you see: now we pass on to statistics. – *We had rain the day before
yesterday, but we shall have a new moon to-night.* – You see, the Mum
always likes to hear about the weather, so I get that out of the Al-
manack. Now we get on to the more interesting part of the letter. – *I
will now tell you a little about Merton College.* – That's where I had just
got to. We go right through the Guide Book, you understand. – *The
history of this establishment is of peculiar importance, as exhibiting the
primary model of all the collegiate bodies in Oxford and Cambridge.
The statutes of Walter de Merton had been more or less copied by all other
founders in succession; and the whole constitution of both Universities, as
we now behold them, may be, not without reason, ascribed to the liberality*

and munificence of this truly great man. – Truly great man! that's no end good, ain't it? observed Mr Bouncer, in the manner of the 'mobled queen is good' of Polonius. – *His sagacity and wisdom led him to profit by the spirit of the times; his opulence enabled him to lay the foundation of a nobler system; and the splendour of his example induced others, in subsequent ages, to raise a superstructure at once attractive and solid.* – That's piling it up mountaynious, ain't it? – *The students were no longer dispersed through the streets and Yanes of the city, dwelling in insulated houses, halls, inns, or hostels, subject to dubious control and precarious discipline.* – That's stunnin', isn't it? just like those *Times* fellers write. – *But placed under the immediate superintendence of tutors and governors, and lodged in comfortable chambers. This was little less than an academic revolution; and a new order of things may be dated from this memorable era. Love to Fanny; and, believe me your affectionate Son, Henry Boun-cer.* – If the Mum don't say that's first-rate, I'm a Dutchman! You see, I don't write very close, so that this respectably fills up three sides of a sheet of note-paper. Oh, here's something over the leaf. – *P.S. I hope Stump and Rowdy have got something for me, because I want some tin very bad.* – That's all! Well, Gig-lamps! don't you call that quite a model letter for a University man to send to his tender parient?"

'It certainly contains some interesting information,' said our hero, with a Quaker-like indirectness of reply.

'It seems to me, Harry,' said Charles Larkyns, 'that the pith of it, like a lady's letter, lies in the postscript – the demand for money.'

'You see,' observed the little gentleman in explanation, 'Stump and Rowdy are the beggars that have got all my property till I come of age next year; and they only let me have money at certain times, because it's what they facetiously call *tied-up*: though *why* they've tied it up, or *where* they've tied it up, I haven't the smallest idea. So, though I tick for nearly everything – for men at College, Gig-lamps, go upon tick as naturally as the crows do on the sheep's backs – I sometimes am rather hard up for ready dibs; and then I give the Mum a gentlemanly hint of this, and she tips me. By the way,' continued Mr Bouncer, as he re-read his postscript, 'I must alter the word "tin" into "money", or else she'll be taking it literally, just as she did with the ponies. Know what a pony is, Gig-lamps?'

'Why, of course I do,' replied Mr Verdant Green; 'besides which,

I have kept one: he was an Exmoor pony – a bay one, with a long tail.'

'Oh, Gig-lamps! You'll be the death of me some fine day,' faintly exclaimed little Mr Bouncer, as he slowly recovered from an exhausting fit of laughter. 'You're as bad as the Mum was. A pony means twenty-five pound, old feller. But the Mum didn't know that; and when I wrote to her and said, "I'm very short; please to send me two ponies" (meaning, of course, that I wanted fifty pound) what must she do, but write back and say, that, with some difficulty, she had procured for me two Shetland ponies, and that, as I was short, she hoped they would suit my size. And, before I had time to send her

another letter, the two little beggars came. Well, I couldn't ride them both at once, like the fellers do at Astley's; so I left one at Tollitt's, and I rode the other down the High, as cool as a cucumber. You see, though I ain't a giant, and that, yet I was big for the pony; and as Shelties are rum-looking little beggars, I dare say we look'd rather queer and original. But the Proctor happened to see me; and he cut up so doosid rough

about it, that I couldn't show on the Shelties any more; and Tollitt was obliged to get rid of them for me.'

'Well, Harry,' said Charles Larkyns, 'it is to Tollitt's that you must now go, as you keep your horse there. We want you to join us in a ride.'

'What!' cried out Mr Bouncer, 'old Gig-lamps going outside an Oxford hack once more! Why, I thought you'd made a vow never to do so again?'

'Why, I certainly did so,' replied Mr Verdant Green; 'but Charles Larkyns, during the holidays – the vacation at least – was kind enough to take me out several rides; so I have had a great deal of practice since last term.'

'And you don't require to be strapped on, or to get inside and pull down the blinds?' inquired Mr Bouncer.

'Oh dear, no!'

The fact was, that during the long vacation Charles Larkyns had paid considerable attention to our hero's equestrian exercises; not so much, it must be confessed, out of friendship for his friend, as that he might have an opportunity of riding by the side of that friend's fair sister Mary, for whom he entertained something more than a partiality. And herein, probably, Mr Charles Larkyns showed both taste and judgment. For there may be many things less pleasant in this world than cantering down a green Warwickshire lane – on some soft summer's day when the green is greenest and the blossoms brightest

– side by side with a charming girl whose nature is as light and sunny as the summer air and the summer sky. Pleasant it is to watch the flushing cheek glow rosier than the rosiest of all the briar-roses that stoop to kiss it. Pleasant it is to look into the lustrous light of tender eyes and to see the loosened ringlets reeling with the motion of the ride. Pleasant it is to canter on from lane to lane over soft moss, and springy turf, between the high honeysuckle hedges, and the broad-branched beeches that meet overhead in a tangled embrace. But pleasanter by far than all is it, to hug to one's heart the darling fancy that she who is cantering on by your side in all the witchery of her maiden beauty, holds you in her dearest thoughts, and dowers you with all her wealth of love. Pleasant rides indeed, pleasant fancies, and pleasant day-dreams, had the long vacation brought to Charles Larkyns!

'Well, come along, Verdant,' said Mr Larkyns, 'we'll go to Charley Symonds's and get our hacks. You can meet us, Harry, just over the Maudlin Bridge; and we'll have a canter along the Henley road.'

So Mr Verdant Green and his friend walked into Holywell Street, and passed under the archway up to Symonds's stables. But the nervous trepidation which our hero had felt in the same place on a previous occasion returned with full force when his horse was led out in an exuberantly playful and 'fresh' condition. The beast he had bestridden during his long vacation rides, with his sister and his (and sister's) friend, was a cob-like steed, whose placidity of temper was fully equalled by its gravity of demeanour; and who would as soon have thought of flying over a five-bar gate as he would of kicking up his respectable heels both behind and before in the low-lived manner recorded of the Ethiopian 'Old Joe'. But, if Charley Symonds's hacks had been of this pacific and easy-going kind, it is highly probable that Mr C. S. and his stud would not have acquired that popularity which they had deservedly achieved. For it seems to be a *sine-qua-non* with an Oxford hack, that to general showiness of exterior, it must add the power of enduring any amount of hard riding and rough treatment in the course of the day which its *pro-tem* proprietor may think fit to inflict upon it; it being an axiom which has obtained, as well in Universities as in other places, that it is of no advantage to hire a hack unless you get out of him as much as you can for your money; you won't want to use him tomorrow, so you don't care about over-riding him today.

But, all this time, Mr Verdant Green is drawing on his gloves, in the nervous manner that tongue-tied gentlemen go through the same performance during the conversational spasms of the first set of quadrilles; the groom is leading out the exuberantly playful quadruped

on whose back Mr Verdant Green is to disport himself; Charles
Larkyns is mounted; the November sun is shining brightly on the
perspective of the yard and stables, and the tower of New College; the
dark archway gives one a peep of Holywell Street; while the cold blue
sky is flecked with gleaming pigeons.

At last, Mr Verdant Green has scrambled into his saddle, and is
riding cautiously down the yard, while his heart beats in an alarming-
like way. As they ride under the archway, there, in the little room
underneath it, is Mr Four-in-hand Fosbrooke, selecting his particular
tandem-whip from a group of some two score of similar whips kept
there in readiness for their respective owners.

'Charley, you're a beast!' says Mr Fosbrooke, politely addressing
himself to Mr Larkyns; 'I wanted Bouncer to come with me in the cart
to Abingdon, and I find that the little man is engaged to you.' Upon
which, Mr Fosbrooke playfully raising his tandem-whip, Mr Verdant
Green's horse plunges, and brings his rider's head into concussion
with the lamp which hangs within the gateway; whereupon, the hat

falls off, and our hero is within an ace of following his hat's example.

By a powerful exertion, however, he recovers his proper position in the saddle, and proceeds in an agitated and jolted condition, by Charles Larkyns's side, down Holywell Street, past the Music Room,* and round by the Long Wall, and over Magdalen Bridge. Here they

are soon joined by Mr Bouncer, mounted, according to the custom of small men, on one of Tollitt's tallest horses, of ever-so-many hands high. As by this time our hero has got more accustomed to his steed, his courage gradually returns, and he rides on with his companions very pleasantly, enjoying the magnificent distant view of his University. When they have passed Cowley, some very tempting fences are met with; and Mr Bouncer and Mr Larkyns, being unable to resist their fascinations, put their horses at them, and leap in and out of the road in an insane Vandycking kind of way, while an excited agriculturalist, whose smock-frock heaves with indignation, pours down denunciations on their heads.

'Blow that bucolical party!' says Mr Bouncer; 'he's no right to interfere with the enjoyments of the animals. If they break the fences, it ain't their faults; it's the fault of the farmers for not making the fences strong enough to bear them. Come along, Gig-lamps! put your beast at that hedge! he'll take you over as easy as if you were sitting in an arm-chair.'

But Mr Verdant Green has doubts about the performance of this piece of equestrian upholstery; and, thinking that the arm-chair would soon become a reclining one, he is firm in his refusal to put the leaping powers of his steed to the test. But having, afterwards, obtained some 'jumping powder' at a certain small road-side hostelry to which Mr Bouncer has piloted the party, our hero, on his way back to Oxford,

* Now used for the Museum of the Oxford Architectural Society.

screws up his courage sufficiently to gallop his steed desperately at a ditch which yawns, a foot wide, before him. But to his immense astonishment – not to say, disgust – the obtuse-minded quadruped gives a leap which would have taken him clear over a canal; and our hero, not being prepared for this very needless display of agility, flies

off the saddle at a tangent, and finds that his 'vaulting ambition' had o'erleap'd itself, and fallen on the other side – of the ditch.

'It ain't your fault, Gig-lamps!' says Mr Bouncer, when he has galloped after Verdant's steed, and has led it up to him, and when he has ascertained that his friend is not in the least hurt, but has only broken – his glasses; 'it ain't your fault, Gig-lamps, old feller! it's the clumsiness of the hack. He tossed you up, and couldn't catch you again!'

And so our hero rides back to Oxford. But, before the Term has ended, he has become more accustomed to Oxford hacks, and has made himself acquainted with the respective merits of the stables of Messrs Symonds, Tollitt, and Pigg; and has, moreover, ridden with the drag, and, in this way hunted the fabled foxes of Bagley Wood, and Whichwood Forest.

CHAPTER VI

*Mr Verdant Green feathers his oars with skill
and dexterity.*

NOVEMBER is not always the month of fog and mist and dullness. Oftentimes there are brilliant exceptions to that generally-received

rule of depressing weather, which, in this month (according to our lively neighbours), induces the natives of our English metropolis to leap in crowds from the Bridge of Waterloo. There are in November, days of calm beauty, which are peculiar to that month – that kind of calm beauty which is so often seen as the herald of decay.

But, whatever weather the month may bring to Oxford, it never brings gloom or despondency to Oxford men. They are a happily constituted set of beings, and can always create their own amusements; they crown Minerva with flowers without heeding her influenza, and never seem to think that the rosy-bosomed Hours may be laid up with bronchitis. Winter and summer appear to be pretty much the same to them: reading and recreation go hand-in-hand all the year round; and, among other pleasure, that of boating finds as many votaries in cold November, as it did in sunny June – indeed, the chillness of the air, in the former month, gives zest to an amusement which degenerates to hard labour in the dog-days. The classic Isis in the month of November, therefore, whenever the weather is anything like favourable, presents an animated scene. Eight-oars pass along, the measured pull of the oars in the rowlocks marking the time in musical cadence with their plashing dip in the water; perilous skiffs flit like fire-flies over the glassy surface of the river; men lounge about in the house-boats and barges, or gather together at King's, or Hall's, and industriously promulgate small talk and tobacco-smoke. All is gay and bustling. Although the feet of the strollers in the Christ Church meadows rustle through the sere and yellow leaf, yet rich masses of brown and russet foliage still hang upon the trees, and light up into

gold in the sun. The sky is of a cold but bright blue; the distant hills and woods are mellowed into sober purplish-gray tints, but over them the sun looks down with that peculiar red glow which is only seen in November.

It was one of these bright days of 'the month of gloom', that Mr Verdant Green and Mr Charles Larkyns being in the room of their friend Mr Bouncer, the little gentleman enquired, 'Now then! what are you two fellers up to! I'm game for anything, I am! from pitch-and-toss to manslaughter.'

'I'm afraid', said Charles Larkyns, 'that we can't accommodate you in either amusement, although we are going down to the river, with which Verdant wishes to renew his acquaintance. Last term, you remember, you picked him up in the Gut, when he had been played with at pitch-and-toss in a way that very nearly resembled man-slaughter.'

'I remember, I remember, how old Gig-lamps floated by!' said Mr Bouncer; 'you looked like a half-bred mermaid, Gig-lamps.'

'But the gallant youth,' continued Mr Larkyns, 'undismayed by the perils from which he was then happily preserved, has boldly come forward and declared himself a worshipper of Isis, in a way worthy of the ancient Egyptians, or of Tom Moore's Epicurean.'

'Well! stop a minute you fellers,' said Mr Bouncer; 'I must have my beer first: I can't do without my Bass relief. I'm like the party in the old song, and I likes a drop of good beer.' And as he uncorked a bottle of Bass, little Mr Bouncer sang, in notes as musical as those produced from his own tin horn –

> 'Twixt wet and dry I always try
>   Between the extremes to steer;
> Though I always shrunk from getting – intoxicated,
>   I was always fond of my beer!
>   For I likes a drop of good beer!
>   I'm particularly partial to beer!
>   Porter and swipes
>   Always give me the – stomach-ache!
>   But that's never the case with beer!

'Bravo, Harry!' cried Charles Larkyns; 'you roar as an' 'twere any nightingale. It would do old Bishop Still's heart good to hear you; and "sure *I* think, that *you* can drink with any that wears a hood", or that *will* wear a hood when you take your Bachelor's, and put on your gown.' And Charles Larkyns sang, rather more musically than Mr Bouncer had done, from that song which, three centuries ago, the Bishop had written in praise of good ale –

> Let back and side go bare, go bare,
>   Both hand and foot go cold:
> But, belly, God send thee good ale enough,
>   Whether it be new or old.

They were soon down at the river side, where Verdant was carefully put into a tub (alas! the dear, awkward, safe, old things are fast passing away; they are giving place to suicidal skiffs, and will soon be numbered among the boats of other days!) – and was started off with almost as much difficulty as on his first essay. The tub – which was, indeed, his old friend the *Sylph* – betrayed an awkward propensity for veering round towards Folly Bridge, which our hero at first failed to overcome; and it was not until he had performed a considerable amount of crab-catching, that he was enabled to steer himself in the proper direction. Charles Larkyns had taken his seat in an outrigger skiff (so frail and shaky that it made Verdant nervous to look at it), and, with one or two powerful strokes, had shot ahead, backed water, turned, and pulled back round the tub long before Verdant had succeeded in passing that eccentric mansion, to which allusion has before been made, as possessing in the place of cellars, an ingenious system of small rivers to

thoroughly irrigate its foundation – a hydropathic treatment which may (or may not) be agreeable in Venice, but strikes one as being decidedly cold and comfortless when applied to Oxford, at any rate, in the month of November. Walking on the lawn which stretched from this house towards the river, our hero espied two extremely pretty young ladies, whose hearts he endeavoured at once to take captive by displaying all his powers in that elegant exercise in which they saw him engaged. It may reasonably be presumed that Mr Verdant Green's hopes were doomed to be blighted.

Let us leave him, and take a look at Mr Bouncer.

Mr Bouncer had been content to represent the prowess of his college in the cricket-field, and had never aspired to any fame as an oar. The exertions, as well as the fame, of aquatic honours, he had left to Mr Blades, and those others like him, who considered it a trifle to pull down to Iffley and back again, two or three times a day, at racing pace with a fresh spurt put on every five minutes. Mr Bouncer, too, had an antipathy to eat beefsteaks otherwise than in the state in which they are usually brought to table; and, as it seemed a *sine qua non* with the gentleman who superintended the training for the boat-races, that his pupils should daily devour beefsteaks which had merely looked at the fire, Mr Bouncer, not having been brought up to cannibal habits, was unable to conform himself to this, and those other vital principles which seemed to regulate the science of aquatic training. The little gentleman moreover, did not join with the 'Torpids' (as the second boats of a college are called), either, because he had a soul above them – he would be *aut Cæsar, aut nullus*; either in the eight, or nowhere – or else, because even the Torpids would cause him more trouble and pleasurable pain than would be agreeable to him. When Mr Bouncer sat down on any hard substance, he liked to be able to do so without betraying any emotion that the action caused him personal discomfort; and he had noticed that many of the Torpids – not to mention one or two of the eight – were more particular than young men usually are about having a very easy, soft, and yielding chair to sit on.

Mr Bouncer, too, was of opinion that continued blisters were both unsightly and unpleasant; and that rawness was bad enough when taken in conjunction with beefsteaks, without being extended to one's own hands. He had also a summer passion for ices and creams, which were forbidden luxuries to one in training – although (paradoxical as it may seem to say so) they trained on Isis! He had also acquired a bad habit of getting up in one day, and going to bed in the next – keeping late hours, and only rising early when absolutely compelled to do so in order to keep morning chapel – a habit which the trainer would have interfered with considerably to the little gentleman's advantage. He had also an amiable weakness for pastry, port, claret, 'et *hock* genus omne'; and would have felt it a cruelty to have been deprived of his daily modicum of 'smoke'; and in all these points, boat-training would have materially interfered with his comfort.

Mr Bouncer, therefore, amused himself equally as much to his own satisfaction as if he had been one of the envied eight, by occasionally paddling about with Charles Larkyns in an old pair-oar, built by Davis and King, and bought by Mr Bouncer of its late Brazenfacian proprietor, when that gentleman, after a humorous series of plucks, rustications, and heavy debts, had finally been compelled to migrate to the King's Bench, for that purification of purse and person commonly designated 'whitewashing'. When Charles Larkyns and his partner did not use their pair-oar, the former occupied his outrigger skiff; and the latter, taking Huz and Buz on board a sailing boat, tacked up and down the river with great skill, the smoke gracefully curling from his meerschaum or short black pipe – for Mr Bouncer disapproved of smoking cigars at those times when the wind would have assisted him to get through them.

'Hullo, Gig-lamps! here we are! as the clown says in the panter-mime,' sang out the little gentleman as he came up with our hero, who was performing some extraordinary feats in full sight of the University crew, who were just starting from their barge; 'you get no end of exercise out of your tub, I should think, by the style you work those paddles. They go in and out beautiful! Splish, splash; splish, splash! You must be one of the *wherry* identical Row-brothers-row, whose voices kept tune and whose oars kept time, you know. You ought to go and splish-splash in the Freshman's River, Gig-lamps – but I forgot – you ain't a freshman now, are you, old feller? Those swells in the University boats look as though they were bursting with envy – not to say, with laughter,' added Mr Bouncer, *sotto voce*. 'Who taught you to do the dodge in such a stunning way, Gig-lamps?'

'Why, last term, Charles Larkyns did,' responded Mr Verdant Green, with the freshness of a Freshman still lingering lovingly upon him. 'I've not forgotten what he told me – to put in my oar deep, and to bring it out with a jerk. But though I make them go as deep as I can, and jerk them out as much as possible, yet the boat *will* keep turning round, and I can't keep it straight at all; and the oars are very heavy and unmanageable, and keep slipping out of the rowlocks ... '

'Commonly called *rullocks*' put in Mr Bouncer, as a parenthetical correction, or marginal note on Mr Verdant Green's words.

'And when the Trinity boat went by, I could scarcely get out of their way; and they said very unpleasant things to me; and, altogether, I can assure you that it has made me very hot.'

'And a capital thing, too, Gig-lamps, this cold November day,' said Mr Bouncer; 'I'm obliged to keep my coppers warm with this pea-coat, and my pipe. Charley came alongside me just now, on purpose to fire off one of his poetical quotations. He said that I reminded him of Beattie's *Minstrel*:

> Dainties he heeded not, nor gaud, nor toy,
> Save one short pipe.

I think that was something like it. But you see, Gig-lamps, I haven't got a figure-head for these sort of things like Charley has, so I couldn't return his shot; but since then, to me deeply pondering, as those old Greek parties say, a fine sample of our superior old crusted jokes has come to hand; and when Charley next pulls alongside, I shall tell him

that I am like that beggar we read
about in old Slowcoach's lecture
the other day, and that, if I had
been in the humour, I could have
sung out, Io Bacche!* *I owe baccy*
– d'ye see, Gig-lamps? Well, old
feller! you look rather puffed, so
clap on your coat; and, if there's a
rope end, or a chain, in your tub,
and you'll just pay it out here, I'll
make you fast astern, and pull you
down the river; and then you'll be
in prime condition to work yourself up again. The wind's in our
back, and we shall get on jolly.'

So our hero made fast the tub to
his friend's sailing-boat, and was
towed as far as the Haystack.
During the voyage Mr Bouncer ascertained that Mr Charles Larkyns
had improved some of the shining hours of the long vacation considerably to Mr Verdant Green's benefit, by teaching him the art of swimming – a polite accomplishment of which our hero had been hitherto
ignorant. Little Mr Bouncer, therefore, felt easier in his mind, if any
repetition of his involuntary bath in the Gut should befal our hero;
and, after giving him (wonderful to say) some correct advice regarding
the management of the oars, he cast off the *Sylph*, and left her and our
hero to their own devices. But, profiting by the friendly hints which
he had received, Mr Verdant Green made considerable progress in the
skill and dexterity with which he feathered his oars; and he sat in his
tub looking as wise as Diogenes may (perhaps) have done in *his*. He
moreover pulled the boat back to Hall's without meeting with any
accident worth mentioning; and when he had got on shore he was
highly complimented by Mr Blades and a group of boating gentlemen
'for the admirable display of science which he had afforded them'.
Mr Verdant Green was afterwards taken alternately by Charles

* 'Si collibuisset, ab ovo
Usque ad mala citaret, Io Bacche!' – Hor. *Sat.* Lib. 1. 3.

Larkyns and Mr Bouncer in their pair-oar; so that, by the end of the term, he at any rate knew more of boating than to accept as one of its fundamental rules, 'put your oar in deep, and bring it out with a jerk.'

In the first week in December he had an opportunity of pulling over a fresh piece of water. One of those inundations occurred to which Oxford is so liable, and the meadow-land to the south and west of the city was covered by the flood. Boats plied to and from the railway station in place of omnibuses; the Great Western was not to be seen for water; and, at the Abingdon Road bridge, at Coldharbour, the rails were washed away, and the trains brought to a standstill. The Isis was amplified to the width of the Christ Church meadows; the Broad Walk had a peep of itself upside down in the glassy mirror; the windings of the Cherwell could only be traced by the trees on its banks. There was 'Water, water everywhere'; and a disagreeable quantity of it too, as those Christ Church men whose ground-floor rooms were towards the meadows soon discovered. Mr Bouncer is supposed to have brought out one of his 'fine, old, crusted jokes', when he asserted in reference to the inundation, that 'Nature had assumed a lake complexion.' Posts and rails, and hay, and a miscellaneous collection of articles, were swept along by the current, together with the bodies of hapless sheep and pigs. But, in spite of these incumbrances, boats of all descriptions were to be seen sailing, pulling, skiffing, and punting, over the flooded meadows.

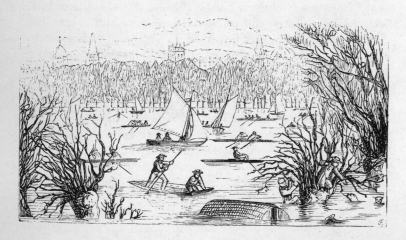

Numerous were the disasters, and many were the boats that were upset.

Indeed, the adventures of Mr Verdant Green would probably have here terminated in a misadventure, had he not (thanks to Charles Larkyns) mastered the art of swimming; for he was in Mr Bouncer's sailing-boat, which was sailing very merrily over the flood, when its merriness was suddenly checked by its grounding on the stump of a lopped pollard willow, and forthwith capsizing. Our hero, who had been sitting in the bows, was at once swept over by the sail, and, for a moment, was in great peril; but, disengaging himself from the cordage, he struck out, and swam to a willow whose friendly boughs and top had just formed an asylum for Mr Bouncer, who in great anxiety was coaxing Huz and Buz to swim to the same ark of safety.

Mr Verdant Green and Mr Bouncer were speedily rescued from their position, and were not a little thankful for their escape.

CHAPTER VII

Mr Verdant Green partakes of a Dove-tart and a Spread Eagle.

'HULLO, Gig-lamps, you lazy beggar!' said the cheery voice of little Mr Bouncer, as he walked into our hero's bedroom one morning towards the end of term, and found Mr Verdant Green in bed, though sufficiently awakened by the sounding of Mr Bouncer's octaves for the purposes of conversation; 'this'll never do, you know, Gig-lamps! Cutting chapel to do the downy! Why, what do you mean, sir? Didn't you ever learn in the nursery what happened to old Daddy Longlegs when he wouldn't say his prayers?'

'Robert *did* call me,' said our hero, rubbing his eyes; 'but I felt tired, so I told him to put in an *æger*.'

'Upon my word, young 'un,' observed Mr Bouncer, 'you're a-coming it, you are! and only in your second term, too. What makes you wear a nightcap, Gig-lamps? Is it to make your hair curl, or to keep your venerable head warm? Nightcaps ain't healthy; they are only fit for long-tailed babbies, and old birds that are as bald as coots; or else for gents that grease their wool with "thine incomparable oil, Macassar", as the noble poet justly remarks.'

'It ain't always pleasant', continued the little gentleman, who was perched up on the side of the bed, and seemed in a communicative disposition, 'it ain't always pleasant to turn out for morning chapel, is it, Gig-lamps? But it's just like the eels with their skinning: it goes against the grain at first, but you soon get used to it. When I first came up, I was a frightful lazy beggar, and I got such a heap of impositions for not keeping my morning chapels, that I was obliged to have three fellers constantly at work writing 'em out for me. This was rather expensive, you see; and then the dons threatened to take away my term altogether, and bring me to grief, if I didn't be more regular. So I was obliged to make a virtuous resolution, and I told Robert that he was to insist on my getting up in a morning, and I should tip him at the end of term if he succeeded. So at first he used to come and hammer

at the door; but that was no go. So then he used to come in and shake me, and try to pull the clothes off; but, you see, I always used to prepare for him, by taking a good supply of boots and things to bed with me; so I was able to take shies at the beggar till he vanished, and left me to snooze peaceably. You see, it ain't every feller as likes to have a Wellington boot at his head; but that rascal of a Robert is used to those trifles, and I was obliged to try another dodge. This you know was only of a morning when I was in bed. When I had had my

breakfast, and got my imposition, and become virtuous again, I used to slang him awful for having let me cut chapel; and then I told him that he must always stand at the door until he heard me out of bed. But, when the morning came, it seemed running such a risk, you see, to one's lungs and all those sort of things to turn out of the warm bed into the cold chapel, that I would answer Robert when he hammered at the door; but instead of getting up, I would knock my boots against the floor, as though I was out of bed, don't you see, and was padding about. But that wretch of a Robert was too old a bird to be caught with this dodge; so he used to sing out, "You must show a leg, sir!" and, as he kept on hammering at the door till I *did* – for, you see, Gig-lamps, he was looking out for the tip at the end of term, so it made him persevere – and as his beastly hammering used, of course, to put a stopper on my going to sleep again, I used to rush out in a frightful state of wax, and show a leg. And then, being well up, you see, it was no use doing the downy again, so it was just as well to make one's *twilight* and go to chapel. Don't gape, Gig-lamps; it's beastly rude, and I haven't done yet. I'm going to tell you another dodge – one of old Small's. He invested money in an alarum, with a string from it tied on to the bed-clothes, so as to pull them off at whatever time you chose to set it. But I never saw the fun of being left high and dry on your bed: it would be a shock to the system which I couldn't stand. But even this dreadful expedient would be better than posting an *æger*; which, you know, you didn't ought to was, Gig-lamps. Well, turn out, old feller! I've told Robert to take your commons* into my room. Smalls and Charley are coming, and I've got a dove-tart and a spread-eagle.'

'Whatever are they?' asked Mr Verdant Green.

'Not know what they are!' cried Mr Bouncer; 'why a dove-tart is what mortals call a pigeon-pie. I ain't much in Tennyson's line, but it strikes me that dove-tarts are more poetical than the other thing; spread-eagle is a barn-door fowl smashed out flat, and made jolly with mushroom sauce, and no end of good things. I don't know how they squash it, but I should say that they sit upon it; I dare say, if we were to enquire, we should find that they kept a fat feller on purpose. But you just come, and try how it eats.' And, as Mr Verdant Green's

---

*The rations of bread, butter, and milk, supplied from the buttery. The breakfast-giver tells his scout the names of those *in*-college men who are coming to breakfast with him. The scout then collects their commons, which thus forms the substratum of the entertainment. The other things are of course supplied by the giver of the breakfast, and are sent in by the confectioner. As to the knives and forks and crockery, the scout produces them from his common stock.

bedroom barely afforded standing room, even for one, Mr Bouncer walked into the sitting-room, while his friend arose from his couch like a youthful Adonis, and proceeded to bathe his ambrosial person, by taking certain sanatory measures in splashing about in a species of tub – a performance which Mr Bouncer was wont to term 'doing tumbies'.

'What'll you take for your letters, Gig-lamps?' called out the little gentleman from the other room; 'the Post's in, and here are three for you. Two are from women, – young uns I should say, from the regular ups and downs, and right angles: they look like billyduxes. Give you a bob for them, at a venture! they may be funny. The other is suspiciously like a tick, and ought to be looked shy on. I should advise you not to open it, but to pitch it in the fire: it may  save a fit of the blues. If you want any help over shaving just say so, Gig-lamps, will you, before I go; and then I'll hold your nose for you, or do anything else that's civil and accommodating. And, when you've done your tumbies, come in to the dove-tart and the spread-eagle.' And off went Mr Bouncer, making terrible noises with his post-horn, in his strenuous but futile endeavours to discover the octaves.

Our hero soon concluded his 'tumbies' and his dressing (not including the shaving), and made his way to Mr Bouncer's rooms, where he did full justice to the dove-tart, and admired the spread-eagle so much, that he thought of bribing the confectioner for the recipe to take home as a Christmas-box for his mother.

'Well, Gig-lamps,' said Mr Bouncer, when breakfast was over, 'to spare the blushes on your venerable cheeks, I won't even so much as refer to the billyduxes; but, I'll only ask, what was the damage of the tick?'

'Oh! it was not a bill,' replied Mr Verdant Green; 'it was a letter about a dog from the man of whom I bought Mop last term.'

'What! Filthy Lucre?' cried Mr Bouncer; 'well, I thought, somehow, I knew the fist! he writes just as if he'd learnt from imitating his dogs' hind-legs. Let's have a sight of it if it ain't private and confidential!'

'Oh dear no! on the contrary, I was going to show it to you, and ask your advice on the contents.' And Verdant handed to Mr Bouncer a letter, which had been elaborately sealed with the aid of a key, and was directed high up in the left-hand corner to 'Virdon grene esqre braisenface collidge Oxford.'

'You look beastly lazy, Charley!' said Mr Bouncer to Mr Charles Larkyns; 'so, while I fill my pipe, just spit out the letter, *pro bono*.' And Charles Larkyns, lying in Mr Bouncer's easiest lounging chair, read as follows:

Onnerd sir i tak the libbaty of a Dressin of you in respex of A dog which i wor sorry For to ear of your Loss in mop which i had The pleshur of Sellin of 2 you onnerd sir A going astray And not a turnin hup Bein of A unsurtin Tempor and guv to A folarin of strandgers which wor maybe as ow You wor a lusein on him onnerd Sir bein Overdogd at this ere present i can let you have A rale good teryer at A barrging which wold giv sattefacshun onnered Sir it wor 12 munth ago i Sold to Bounser esqre a red smooth air terier Dog anserin 2 nam of Tug as wor rite down goodun and No mistake onnerd Sir the purpurt Of this ere is too say as ow i have a Hone brother to Tug black tann and ful ears and If you wold like him i shold bee prowd too wate on you onnerd Sir he wor by robbingsons Twister out of mister jones of abingdons Fan of witch brede Bounser esqre nose on the merritts onnerd Sir he is very Smal and smooth air and most xlent aither for wood Or warter a liter before Tug onnerd Sir is nam is Vermin and he hant got his nam by no mistake as No Vermin not even poll katts can live long before him onnerd Sir I considders as vermin is very sootble compannion for a Gent indors or hout and bein lively wold give amoosement i shall fele it A plesure a waitin on you onnerd Sir opin you will pardin the libbaty of a Dressin of you but my head wor ful of vermin and i wishd to tel you

onnerd Sir yures
2 komand j. Looker.

'The nasty beggar!' said Mr Bouncer, in reference to the last paragraph. 'Well, Gig-lamps! Filthy Lucre doesn't tell fibs when he says that Tug came of a good breed: but he was so doosid pugnacious, that he was always having set-to's with Huz and Buz, in the coal-shop

just outside the door here; and so, as I'd nowhere else to stow them, I was obliged to give Tug away. Dr What's-his-name says, "Let dogs delight to bark and bite, for 'tis their nature to." But then, you see, it's only a delight when they bite *somebody else's* dog; and if Dr What's-his-name had had a kennel of his own, he wouldn't have took it so coolly; and, whether it was their nature so to do or not, he would'nt have let the little beggars, that he fork'd out thirteen bob a-year for to the government, amuse themselves by biting each other, or tearing out each other's eyes; he'd have turn'd them over, don't you see, to his neighbours' dogs, and have let them do the biting department on *them*. And, altogether, Gig-lamps, I'd advise you to let Filthy Lucre's Vermin alone, and have nothing to do with the breed.'

So Mr Verdant green took his friend's advice, and then took himself off to learn boxing at the hands, and gloves, of the Putney Pet; for our hero, at the suggestion of Mr Charles Larkyns, had thought it advisable to receive a few lessons in the fistic art, in order that he might be the better able to defend himself, should he be engaged in a second Town and Gown. He found the Pet in attendance upon Mr Foote;

and, by their mutual aid, speedily mastered the elements of the Art of Self-defence.

Mr Foote's rooms at St John's were in the further corner to the right-hand side of the Quad, and had windows looking into the gardens. When Charles had held his Court at St John's, and when the loyal College had melted down its plate to coin into money for the King's necessities, the Royal visitor had occupied these very rooms. But it was not on this account alone that they were the show rooms of the College, and that tutors sent their compliments to Mr Foote, with the request that he would allow a party of friends to see his rooms. It was chiefly on account of the lavish manner in which Mr Foote had furnished his rooms, with what he theatrically called 'properties', that made them so sought out; and country lionisers of Oxford, who took their impressions of an Oxford student's room from those of Mr Foote, must have entertained very highly coloured ideas of the internal aspect of the sober-looking old Colleges.

The sitting-room was large and lofty, and was panelled with oak throughout. At the further end was an elaborately carved book-case of walnut wood, filled with books gorgeously bound in every tint of morocco and vellum, with their backs richly tooled in gold. It was currently reported in the College that 'Footelights' had given an order for a certain number of *feet* of books – not being at all proud as to their contents – and had laid down the sum of a thousand pounds (or thereabouts) for their binding. This might have been scandal; but the fact of his father being a Colossus of (the iron) Roads, and indulging his son and heir in every expense, gave some colour to the rumour.

The panels were covered with the choicest engravings (all proofs-before-letters), and with water-colour drawings by Cattermole, Cox, Fripp, Hunt, and Frederick Tayler – their wide, white margins being sunk in light gilt frames. Above these gleamed groups of armour, standing out effectively (and theatrically), against the dark oak panels, and full of 'reflected lights', that would have gladdened the heart of Maclise. There were couches of velvet, and lounging chairs of every variety and shape. There was a Broadwood's grand pianoforte, on which Mr Foote, although uninstructed, could play skilfully. There were round tables and square tables, and writing tables; and there were side tables with statuettes, and Swiss carvings, and old china, and gold apostle-spoons, and lava ware, and Etruscan vases, and a swarm of Spiers's elegant knick-knackeries. There were reading-stands of all sorts; Briarean-armed brazen ones that fastened on to the chair you sat in, sloping ones to rest on the table before you, elaborately carved in open work, and an upright one of severe Gothic, like a lectern, where you were to stand and read without contracting your chest. Then there were all kinds of stands to hold books: sliding ones, expanding ones, portable ones, heavy fixture ones, plain mahogany ones, and oak ones made glorious by Margetts with the arms of Oxford and St John's carved and emblazoned on the ends.

Mr Foote's rooms were altogether a very gorgeous instance of a Collegian's apartment; and Mr Foote himself was a very striking example of the theatrical undergraduate. Possessing great powers of mimicry and facial expression, he was able to imitate any peculiarities which were to be observed either in Dons or Undergraduates, in Presidents or Scouts. He could sit down at his piano, and give you – after the manner of Theodore Hook, or John Parry – a burlesque opera; singing high up in his head for the prima donna, and going down to his boots for the *basso profondo* of the great Lablache. He

could also draw corks, saw wood, do a bee in a handkerchief, and make monkeys, cats, dogs, a farm-yard, or a full band, with equal facility. He would also give you Mr Keeley, in 'Betsy Baker'; Mr Paul Bedford, as 'I believe you my bo-o-oy!' Mr Buckstone, as Cousin Joe, and 'Box and Cox'; or Mr Wright, as Paul Pry, or Mr Felix Fluffy. Besides the comedians, Mr 'Footelights' would also give you the leading tragedians, and would favour you (through his nose) with the popular burlesque imitation of Mr Charles Kean, as *Hablet*. He would fling himself down on the carpet, and grovel there, as Hamlet does in the play-scene, and would exclaim, with frantic vehemence, 'He poisods hib i' the garded, for his estate. His dabe's Godzago: the story is extadt, ad writted id very choice Italiad. You shall see adod, how the burderer gets the love of Godzago's wife.' Moreover, as his room possessed the singularity of a trap-door leading down into a wine-cellar, Mr 'Footelights' was thus enabled to leap down into the aperture, and carry on the personation of Hamlet in Ophelia's grave. As the theatrical trait in his character was productive of much amusement, and as he was also considered to be one of those hilarious fragments of masonry, popularly known as 'jolly bricks', Mr Foote's society was greatly cultivated; and Mr Verdant Green struck up a warm friendship with him.

But the Michaelmas term was drawing to its close. Buttery and kitchen books were adding up their sums total; bursars were preparing for battels;* witless men were cramming for Collections;† scouts and bedmakers were looking for tips; and tradesmen were hopelessly expecting their little accounts. And, in a few days, Mr Verdant Green might have been seen at the railway station, in company with Mr Charles Larkyns and Mr Bouncer, setting out for the Manor Green, *via* London – this being, as is well known, the most direct route from Oxford to Warwickshire.

Mr. Bouncer, who when travelling was never easy in his mind unless Huz and Buz were with him in the same carriage, had placed these two interesting specimens of the canine species in a small light box, partially ventilated by means of holes drilled through the top. But Huz and Buz, not much admiring this contracted mode of conveyance, and probably suffering from incipient asphyxia, in spite of the

---

*Battels are the accounts of the expenses of each student. It is stated in Todd's *Johnson* that this singular word is derived from the Saxon verb, meaning 'to count or reckon'. But it is stated in the *Gentleman's Magazine* for 1792, that the word may probably be derived from the Low-German word *bettahlen*, 'to pay', whence may come our English word *tale* or *score*.

† College Terminal Examinations.

admonitory kicks against their box, gave way to dismal howls, at the very moment when the guard came to look at the tickets.

'Can't allow dogs in here, sir! they must go in the locker,' said the guard.

'Dogs?' cried Mr Bouncer, in apparent astonishment 'they're rabbits!'

'Rabbits!' ejaculated the guard, in his turn. 'Oh, come, sir! what makes rabbits bark?'

'What makes 'em bark? Why, because they've got the pip, poor beggars!' replied Mr Bouncer, promptly. At which the guard graciously laughed, and retired; probably thinking that he should, in the end, be a gainer if he allowed Huz and Buz to journey in the same first-class carriage with their master.

CHAPTER VIII

Mr Verdant Green spends a Merry Christmas and a Happy New Year.

CHRISTMAS had come; the season of kindness, and hospitality; the season when the streams of benevolence flow full in their channels; the season when the Honourable Miss Hyems indulges herself with ice, while the vulgar Jack Frost regales himself with cold-without. Christmas had come, and had brought with it an old fashioned winter; and, as Mr Verdant Green stands with his hands in his pockets, and gazes from the drawing-room of his paternal mansion, he looks forth upon a white world.

The snow is everywhere. The shrubs are weighed down by masses of it; the terrace is knee-deep in it; the plaster Apollo, in the long-walk, is more than knee-deep in it, and is furnished with a surplice and wig, like a half-blown Bishop. The distant country looks the very ghost of a landscape: the white-walled cottages seem part and parcel of the snow-drifts around them – drifts that take every variety of form, and are swept by the wind into fairy wreaths, and fantastic caves. The old mill-wheel is locked fast, and gemmed with giant icicles; its slippery stairs are more slippery than ever. Golden gorse and purple heather are now all of a colour; orchards puts forth blossoms of real snow; the gently swelling hills look bright and dazzling in the wintry sun; the grey church tower has grown from grey to white; nothing looks black, except the swarms of rooks that dot the snowy fields, or make their caws (long as any Chancery-suit) to be heard from among the dark branches of the stately elms that form the avenue to the Manor Green.

It is a rare busy time for the intelligent Mr Mole the gardener! He is always sweeping at that avenue, and, do what he will, he cannot keep it clear from snow. As Mr Verdant Green looks forth upon the white world, his gaze is more particularly directed to this avenue, as though the form of the intelligent Mr Mole was an object of interest. From time to time Mr Verdant Green consults his watch in a nervous manner, and is utterly indifferent to the appeals of the robin-redbreast who is hopping about outside, in expectation of the dinner which has been daily given to him.

Just when the robin, emboldened by hunger, has begun to tap fiercely with his bill against the window-pane, as a gentle hint that the smallest donations of crumbs of comfort will be thankfully received, – Mr Verdant Green, utterly oblivious of robins in general, and of the sharp pecks of this one in particular, takes no notice of the little redbreast waiter with the bill, but, slightly colouring up, fixes his gaze upon the lodgegate through which a group of

ladies and gentlemen are passing. Stepping back for a moment, and stealing a glance at himself in the mirror, Mr Verdant Green hurriedly arranges and disarranges his hair – pulls about his collar – ties and unties his neck-handkerchief – buttons and then unbuttons his coat – takes another look from the window – sees the intelligent Mr Mole (besom in hand) salaaming the party, and then makes a rush for the vestibule, to be at the door to receive them.

Let us take a look at them as they come up the avenue. *Place aux dames*, is the proper sort of thing; but as there is no rule without its exception, and no adage without its counter-proverb, we will give the gentlemen the priority of description.

Hale and hearty, the picture of amiability and gentlemanly feeling, comes the rector, Mr Larkyns, sturdily crunching the frozen snow, which has defied all the besom powers of the intelligent Mr Mole. Here, too, is Mr Charles Larkyns, and, moreover, his friend Henry Bouncer, Esq., who has come to Christmas at the Rectory. Following in their wake is a fourth gentleman attired in the costume peculiar to clergymen, dissenting ministers, linen-drapers' assistants, and tavern waiters. He happens to belong to the first-named section, and is no less a person than the Revd Josiah Meek, B.A., (St Christopher's Coll., Oxon.) – who, for the last three months, has officiated as Mr Larkyns's curate. He appears to be of a peace-loving, lamb-like disposition; and, though sportive as a lamb when occasion requires, is yet of timid ways and manners. He is timid, too, in voice – speaking in a feeble treble; he is timid, too, in his address – more particularly as regards females; and he has mild-looking whiskers, that are far too timid to assume any decided or obtrusive colour, and have fallen back on a generalised whitey-brown tint. But, though timid enough in society, he was bold and energetic in the discharge of his pastoral duties, and had already won the esteem of everyone in the parish. So Verdant had been told, when, on his return from college, he had asked his sisters how they liked the new curate. They had not only heard of his good deeds, but they had witnessed many of them in their visits to the schools and among the poor. Mary and Fanny were loud in his praise; and if Helen said but little, it was perhaps because she thought the more; for Helen was now of the susceptible age of 'sweet seventeen', an age that not only feels warmly but thinks deeply; and, who shall say what feelings and thoughts may lie beneath the pure waters of that sea of maidenhood whose surface is so still and calm? Love alone can tell – Love, the bold diver, who can cleave that still surface, and bring up into the light of Heaven the rich treasures that are of Heaven's own creation.

With the four gentlemen come two ladies – young ladies, moreover, who, as penny-a-liners say, are 'possessed of considerable personal attractions'. These are the Misses Honeywood, the blooming daughters of the rector's only sister; and they have come from the far land of the North, and are looking as fresh and sweet as their own heathery hills. The roses of health that bloom upon their cheeks have been brought into full blow by the keen, sharp breeze; the shepherd's plaid shawls drawn tightly around them give the outline of figures that gently swell into the luxuriant line of beauty and grace. Altogether, they are damsels who are pleasant to the eye, and very fair to look upon.

Since they had last visited their uncle four years had passed, and, in that time, they had shot up to womanhood, although they were not yet out of their teens. Their father was a landed proprietor living in north Northumberland; and, like other landed proprietors who live under the shade of the Cheviots, was rich in his flocks, and his herds, and his men-servants and his maid-servants, and his he-asses and his she-asses, and was quite a modern patriarch. During the past summer, the rector had taken a trip to Northumberland, in order to see his sister, and refresh himself with a clergyman's fortnight at Honeywood Hall, and he would not leave his sister and her husband until he had extracted from them a promise that they would bring down their two eldest daughters and Christmas in Warwickshire. This was accordingly agreed to, and, more than that, acted upon; and little

Mr Bouncer and his sister Fanny were asked to meet them; but, to relieve the rector of a superfluity of lady guests, Miss Bouncer's quarters had been removed to the Manor Green.

It was quite an event in the history of our hero and his sisters. Four years ago, they, Kitty and Patty Honeywood, were mere chits, for whom dolls had not altogether lost their interest, and who considered it as promotion when they sat in the drawing-room on company evenings, instead of being shown up at dessert. Four years at this period of life makes a vast change in young ladies, and the Green and Honeywood girls had so altered since last they met, that they had almost needed a fresh introduction to each other. But a day's intimacy made them bosom friends; and the Manor Green soon saw such revels as it had not seen for many a long year.

Every night there were (in the language of the play-bills of provincial theatres) 'singing and dancing, with a variety of other entertainments'; the 'other entertainments' occasionally consisting (as is scandalously affirmed) of a very favourite class of entertainment – popular at all times, but running mad riot at the Christmas season – wherein two performers of either sex take their places beneath a white-berried bough, and go through a species of dance, or *pas de fascination*, accompanied by mysterious rites and solemnities that have been

scrupulously observed, and handed down to us, from the earliest age.

Mr Verdant Green, during the short – alas! *too* short – Christmas week, had performed more polkas than he had ever danced in his life; and, under the charming tuition of Miss Patty Honeywood, was fast becoming a proficient in the *valse à deux temps*. As yet, the whirl of the dance brought on a corresponding rotatory motion of the brain, that made everything swim before his spectacles in a way which will be easily understood by all bad travellers who have crossed from Dover to Calais with a chopping sea and a gale of wind. But Miss Patty Honeywood was both good-natured and persevering: and she allowed our hero to dance on her feet without a murmur, and watchfully guided him when his giddy vision would have led them into contact with foreign bodies.

It is an old saying, that Gratitude begets Love. Mr Verdant Green had already reached the first part of this dangerous creation, for he felt grateful to the pretty Patty for the good-humoured trouble she bestowed on the awkwardness, which he now, for the first time, began painfully to perceive. But, what his gratitude might end in, he had perhaps never taken the trouble to inquire. It was enough to Mr

Verdant Green that he enjoyed the present; and, as to the future, he
fully followed out the Horatian precept –

> Quid sit futurum cras, fuge quærere
> ... nec dulcis amores
>   Sperne, puer, neque tu choreas.

It was perhaps ungrateful in our hero to prefer Miss Patty Honeywood to Miss Fanny Bouncer, especially when the latter was staying
in the house, and had been so warmly recommended to his notice by
her vivacious brother. Especially, too, as there was nothing to be
objected to in Miss Bouncer, saving the fact the some might have
affirmed she was a trifle too much inclined to *embonpoint*, and was

indeed a bouncer in person as well as in name. Especially, too, as Miss
Fanny Bouncer was both good-humoured and clever, and, besides
being mistress of the usual young-lady accomplishments, was a clever
proficient in the fascinating art of photography, and had brought her
camera and chemicals, and had not only calotyped Mr Verdant Green,
but had made no end of duplicates of him, in a manner that was
suggestive of the deepest admiration and affection. But these sort of
likings are not made to rule, and Mr Verdant Green could see Miss
Fanny Bouncer approach without betraying any of those symptoms of

excitement, under the influence of which we had the privilege to see him, as he gazed from the window of his paternal mansion, and then, on beholding the approaching form of Miss Patty Honeywood, rush wildly to the vestibule.

The party had no occasion to ring, for the hall door was already opened for them, and Mr Verdant Green was soon exchanging a delightful pressure of the hand with the blooming Patty.

'We were such a formidable party', said that young lady, as she laughed merrily, and thereby disclosed to the enraptured gazer a remarkably even set of white teeth ('All her own, too!' as little Mr Bouncer afterwards remarked to the enraptured gazer); 'we were such a formidable party', said Miss Patty, 'that papa and mamma declared they would stay behind at the Rectory, and would not join in such a visitation.'

Mr Verdant Green replies, 'Oh dear! I am very sorry', and looks remarkably delighted – though it certainly may not be at the absence of the respected couple; and he then proclaims that everything is ready, and that Miss Bouncer and his sisters had found out some capital words.

'What a mysterious communication, Verdant!' remarks the rector, as they pass into the house. But the rector is only to be let so far into the secret as to be informed that, at the evening party which is to be held at the Manor Green that night, a charade or two will be acted, in order to diversify the amusements. The Misses Honeywood are great adepts in this sort of pastime; so, also, are Miss Bouncer and her brother. For although the latter does not shine as a mimic, yet, as he is never deserted by his accustomed coolness, he has plenty of the *nonchalance* and readiness which is a requisite for charade acting. The Misses Honeywood and Mr Bouncer have therefore suggested to Mr Verdant Green and his sisters, that to get up a little amateur performance would be 'great fun'; and the suggestion has met with a warm approval.

The drawing-room at the Manor Green opened by large folding-doors to the library; so (as Mr Bouncer observed to our hero), 'there you've got your stage and your drop-scene as right as a trivet; and, if you stick a lot of candles and lights on each side of the doors in the library, there you'll have a regular flare-up that'll show off your venerable gig-lamps no end.'

So charades were determined on; and, when words had been hunted up, a council of war was called. But, as the ladies and gentlemen hold their council with closed doors, we cannot intrude upon them. We must therefore wait till the evening, when the result of their deliberations will be publicly manifested.

CHAPTER IX

Mr Verdant Green makes his first appearance on any Boards.

I T is the last night of December. The old year, worn out and spent with age, lies a-dying, wrapped in sheets of snow.

A stern stillness reigns around. The steps of men are muffled; no echoing footfalls disturb the solemn nature of the time. The little runnels weep icy tears. The dark pines hang out their funeral plumes,  and nod with their weight of snow. The elms have thrown off their green robes of joy, and, standing up in gaunt nakedness, wildly toss to heaven their imploring arms. The old year lies a-dying.

Silently through the snow steal certain carriages to the portals of the Manor Green; and, with a ringing of bells and a banging of steps, the occupants disappear in a stream of light that issues from the hall door. Mr Green's small sanctum to the right of the hall has been converted into a cloak-room, and is fitted up with a ladies'-maid and a looking-glass, in a manner not to be remembered by the oldest inhabitant.

There the finishing stroke of ravishment is given to the toilette disarranged by a long drive through the impending snow. There Miss Parkington (whose papa has lately revived his old school friendship with Mr Green) discovers, to her unspeakable disgust, that the ten mile drive through the cold has invested her cheek with purple tints, and given to her *retroussé* (ill-natured people call it 'pug') nose a hue that mocks 'the turkey's crested fringe'. There, too, Miss Waters (whose paternities had hitherto only been on morning-call terms with the Manor Green people, but had brushed up their acquaintance now that there was a son of marriageable years and heir to an independent fortune) discovers to her dismay that the joltings received during a six-mile drive through snowed-up lanes, have somewhat deteriorated the very full-dress aspect of her attire, and considerably flattened its former balloon-like dimensions. And there, too, Miss Brindle (whose family have been hunted up for the occasion) makes the alarming discovery that, in the lurch which their hack-fly had made at the cross roads, her brother Alfred's patent boots had not only dragged off some

yards (more or less) of her flounces, but had also – to use her own mystical language – 'torn her skirt at the gathers!'

All, however, is put right as far as possible. A warm at the sanctum's fire diminishes the purple in Miss Parkington's cheeks; and the maid, by some hocus-pocus peculiar to her craft, again inflates Miss Waters into a balloon, and stitches up Miss Brindle's flounces and 'gathers'. The ladies join their respective gentlemen, who have been cooling their toes and uttering warm anathemas in the hall; and the party sail, arm-in-arm, into the drawing-room, and forthwith fall to lively remarks on that neutral ground of conversation, the weather. Mr Verdant Green is there, dressed with elaborate magnificence; but he continues in a state of listless apathy, and is indifferent to the 'lively' rattle of the balloon-like Miss Waters, until John the footman (who is suffering from influ-

enza) rouses him into animation by the magic talisman 'Bister, Bissies, an' the Biss 'Oneywoods'; when he beams through his spectacles in the most benign and satisfied manner. The Misses Honeywood are as blooming as usual: the cold air, instead of spoiling their good looks, has but improved their healthy style of beauty; and they smile, laugh, and talk in a perfectly easy, unaffected, and natural manner. Mr Verdant Green at once makes his way to Miss Patty Honeywood's side, and, gracefully standing beside her, coffee-cup in hand, plunges headlong into the depths of a tangled conversation.

Meanwhile, the drawing-room of the Manor Green becomes filled in a way that has not been seen for many a long year; and the intelligent Mr Mole, the gardener (who has been impressed as an odd man for the occasion, and is served up in a pseudo-livery to make him more presentable), sees more 'genteel' people than have, for a long time, been visible to his naked eye. The intelligent Mr Mole, when he has afterwards been restored to the bosom of Mrs Mole and his family, confides to his equally intelligent helpmate that, in his opinion, 'Master has guv the party to get husbands for the young ladies' – an opinion which, though perhaps not founded on fact so far as it related to the party which was the subject of Mr Mole's remark, would doubtless be applicable to many similar parties given under somewhat similar circumstances.

It is not improbable that the intelligent Mr Mole may have based his opinion on a circumstance – which, to a gentleman of his sagacity, must have carried great weight – namely, that whenever in the course of the evening the hall was made the promenade for the loungers and dancers, he perceived, firstly, that Miss Green was invariably accompanied by Mr Charles Larkyns; secondly, that the Revd Josiah Meek kept Miss Helen dallying about the wine and lemonade tray much longer than was necessary for the mere consumption of the cooling liquids; and thirdly, that Miss Fanny, who was a pert, talkative miss of sixteen, was continually to be found there with either Mr Henry Bouncer or Mr Alfred Brindle dancing attendance upon her. But, be this as it may, the intelligent Mr Mole was impressed with the conviction that Mr Green had called his young friends together as to a matrimonial auction, and that his daughters were to be put up without reserve, and knocked down to the highest bidder.

All the party have arrived. The weather has been talked over for the last time (for the present); a harp, violin, and a cornet-à-piston from the county town, influenced by the spirit of gin-and-water, are heard discoursing most eloquent music in the dining-room, which has been cleared out for the dance. Miss Patty Honeywood, accepting the offer of Mr Verdant Green's arm, swims joyously out of the room; other ladies and gentlemen pair, and follow: the ball is opened.

A polka follows the quadrille; and, while the dancers rest awhile from their exertions, or crowd around the piano in the drawing-room to hear the balloon-like Miss Waters play a firework piece of music, in which execution takes the place of melody, and chromatic scales are discharged from her fingers like showers of rockets, Mr Verdant Green mysteriously weeds out certain members of the party, and vanishes with them upstairs.

When Miss Waters has discharged all her fireworks, and has descended from the throne of her music-stool, a set of Lancers is formed; and, while the usual mistakes are being made in the figures, the dancers find a fruitful subject of conversation in surmises that a charade is going to be acted. The surmise proves to be correct: for

when the set has been brought to an end with that peculiar in-and-out tum-tum-tiddle-iddle-tum-tum movement which characterises the last figure of *Les Lanciers*, the trippers on the light fantastic toe are requested to assemble in the drawing-room, where the chairs and couches have been pulled up to face the folding doors that lead into the library. Mr Verdant Green appears; and, after announcing that the word to be acted will be one of three syllables, and that each syllable will be represented by itself, and that then the complete word will be given, throws open the folding doors for

SCENE I. *Syllable* I. – Enter the Misses Honeywood, dressed in fashionable bonnets and shawls. They are shown in by a footman (Mr Bouncer) attired in a peculiarly ingenious and effective livery, made by pulling up the trousers to the knee, and wearing the dress-coat inside out, so as to display the crimson silk linings of the sleeves: the effect of Mr Bouncer's appearance is considerably heightened by a judicious outlay of flour sprinkled over his hair. Mr Bouncer (as footman) gives the ladies chairs, and inquires, 'What name shall I be pleased to say, mem?' Miss Patty answers in a languid and fashionable voice, 'The Ladies Louisa and Arabella Mountfidget'. Mr Bouncer evaporates with a low bow, leaving the ladies to play with their parasols, and converse. Lady Arabella (Miss Patty) then expresses a devout wish that Lady Trotter (wife of Sir Lambkin Trotter, Bart.), in whose house they are supposed to be, will not keep them waiting as long as she detained her aunt, Lady Bellwether, when the poor old lady fell asleep from sheer fatigue, and was found snoring on the sofa. Lady Louisa then falls to an inspection of the card-tray, and reads the paste-boards of some high-sounding titles not to be found in Debrett, and expresses wonder as to where Lady Trotter can have picked up the Duchess of Ditchwater's card, as she (Lady Louisa) is morally convinced that her Grace can never have condescended to have even sent in her card by a footman. Becoming impatient at the non-appearance of Lady Trotter, Miss Patty Honeywood then rings the bell, and, with much asperity of manner, inquires of Mr Bouncer (as footman) if Lady Trotter is informed that the Ladies Louisa and Arabella Mountfidget are waiting to see her? Mr Bouncer replies, with a footman's bow, and a footman's *h*exasperation of his h's, 'Me lady is haweer hof your ladyships' visit; but me lady is at present hunable to happear: me lady, 'owever, has give me a message, which she hasks me to deliver to your ladyships.' 'Then why don't you deliver it at once,' says Miss Patty, 'and not waste the valuable time of the Ladies Louisa and Arabella Mountfidget? What *is* the message?' 'Me lady', replies Mr Bouncer, 'requests me to present her compliments to your ladyships, and begs me to hinform you that me lady is a cleaning of herself!' Amid great laughter from the audience, the Ladies Mountfidget toss their heads and flutter grandly out of the room, followed by the floured footman; while Mr Verdant Green, unseen by those in front, pushes-to the folding doors, to show that the first syllable is performed.

Praises of the acting, and guesses at the word, agreeably fill up the time till the next scene. The Revd Josiah Meek, who is not much used to charades, confides to Miss Helen Green that he surmises the word to be, either 'visitor' or 'impudence;' but, as the only ground to this surmise rests on these two words being words of three syllables, Miss Helen gently repels the idea, and sagely observes, 'we shall see more in the next scene.'

SCENE II. *Syllable* 2. – The folding-doors open, and discover Mr Verdant Green, as a sick gentleman, lying on a sofa, in a dressing-gown, with pillows under his head, and Miss Patty Honeywood in attendance upon him. A table, covered with glasses and medicine bottles, is drawn up to the sufferer's couch in an inviting manner. Miss Patty informs the sufferer that the time is come for him to take his draught. The sufferer groans in a dismal manner, and says, 'Oh! is it, my dear?' She replies, 'Yes! you must take it now'; and sternly pours some sherry wine out of the medicine bottle into a cup. The sufferer makes piteous faces, and exclaims, 'It is so nasty, I can't take it, my love!' (It is to be observed that Mr Verdant Green, skilfully taking advantage of the circumstance that Miss Patty Honeywood is supposed to represent the wife of the sufferer, plentifully besprinkles his conversation with endearing epithets.) When, after much persuasion and groaning, the sufferer has been induced to take his medicine, his spouse announces the arrival of the doctor; when, enter Mr Bouncer, still floured as to his head, but wearing spectacles, a long black coat, and a shirt-frill, and having his dress otherwise altered so as to represent a medical man of the old school. The doctor asks what sort of a night his patient has had, inspects his tongue with professional gravity, feels his pulse, looks at his watch, and mysteriously shakes his head. He then commences thrusting and poking Mr Verdant Green in various parts of his body – after the manner of doctors with their victims, and farmers with their beasts – enquiring between each poke, 'Does that hurt you?' and being answered by a convulsive 'Oh!' and a groan of agony. The doctor then prescribes a draught to be taken every half-hour, with the pills and blister at bed-time; and, after covering his two fellow-actors with confusion, by observing that he leaves his patient in admirable hands, and, that in an affection of the heart, the application of lip-salve and warm treatment will give a decided tone to the system, and produce soothing and grateful emotions – takes his leave; and the folding-doors are closed on the blushes of Miss Patty Honeywood, and Mr Verdant Green.

More applause: more agreeable conversation: more ingenious speculations. The Revd Josiah Meek is now of opinion that the word is

either 'medicine' or 'suffering.' Miss Helen still sagely observes, 'we shall see more in the next scene.'

SCENE III. *Syllable* 3. – Mr Verdant Green discovered sitting at a table furnished with pens and ink, books, and rolls of paper. Mr Verdant Green wears on his head a Chelsea pensioner's cocked-hat (the 'property' of the Family, as Mr Footelights would have said), folded into a shovel shape; and is supposed to accurately represent the outside of a London publisher. To him enter Mr Bouncer – the flour off his head – coat buttoned tightly to the throat, no visible linen, and wearing in his face and appearance generally, 'the garb of humility.' Says the publisher 'Now, sir, please to state your business, and be quick about it: I am much engaged in looking over for the press a work of a distinguished author, which I am just about to publish.' Meekly replies the other, as he holds under his arm an immense paper packet: 'It is about a work of my own, sir, that I have now ventured to intrude upon you. I have here, sir, a small manuscript' (producing his roll of a book), 'which I am ambitious to see given to the world through the medium of your printing establishment.' To him, the publisher – 'Already am I inundated with manuscripts on all possible subjects, and cannot undertake to look at any more for some time to come. What is the nature of your manuscript?' Meekly replies the other – 'The theme of my work, sir, is a History of England before the Flood. The subject is both new and interesting. It is to be presumed that our beloved country existed before the Flood: if so, it must have had a history. I have therefore endeavoured to fill up what is lacking in the annals of our land, by a record of its antediluvian state, adapted to the meanest comprehension, and founded on the most baseless facts. I am desirous, sir, to see myself in print. I should like my work, sir, to appear in large letters; in very large letters, sir. Indeed, sir, it would give me joy, if you would condescend to print it altogether in capital letters; my *magnum opus* might then be called with truth, a capital work.' To him, the publisher – 'Much certainly depends on the character of the printing.' Meekly the author – 'Indeed, sir, it does. A great book, sir, should be printed in great letters. If you will permit me, I will show you the size of the letters in which I should wish my book to be printed.' Mr Bouncer then points out in some books on the table, the printing he most admires; and, beseeching the publisher to read over his manuscript, and think favourably of his History of England before the Flood, makes his bow to Mr Verdant Green and the Chelsea pensioner's cocked hat.

More applause, and speculations. the Revd Josiah Meek confident that he has discovered the word. it must be either 'publisher' or 'authorship.' Miss Helen still sage.

SCENE IV. *The Word.* – Miss Bouncer discovered with her camera, arranging her photographic chemicals. She soliloquises. 'There! now, all is ready for my sitter.' She calls the footman (Mr

Verdant Green), and says, 'John, you may show the Lady Fitz-Canute upstairs.' The footman shows in Miss Honeywood, dressed in an antiquated bonnet and mantle, waving a huge fan. John gives her a chair, into which she drops, exclaiming, 'What an insufferable toil it is to ascend to these elevated Photographic rooms;' and makes good use of her fan. Miss Bouncer then fixes the focus of her camera, and begs the Lady Fitz-Canute to sit perfectly still, and to call up an agreeable smile to her face. Miss Honeywood thereupon disposes her face in ludicrous 'wreathed smiles'; and Miss Bouncer's head disappears under the velvet hood of the camera. 'I am afraid', at length says Miss Bouncer, 'I am afraid that I shall not be able to succeed in taking a likeness of your ladyship this morning.' 'And why, pray?' asks her ladyship with haughty surprise. 'Because it is a gloomy day,' replies the Photographer, 'and much depends upon the rays of light.' 'Then procure the rays of light!' 'That is more than I can do.' 'Indeed! I suppose if the Lady Fitz-Canute wishes for the rays of light, and condescends to pay for the rays of light, she can obtain the rays of light.' Miss Bouncer considers this too *exigeant*, and puts her sitter off by promising to complete a most fascinating portrait of her on some more favourable day. Lady Fitz-Canute appears to be somewhat mollified at this, and is graciously pleased to observe, 'Then I will undergo the fatigue of ascending to these elevated Photographic rooms at some future period. But, mind, when I next come, that you procure the rays of light!' So she is shown out by Mr Verdant Green, and the folding-doors are closed amid applause, and the audience distract themselves with guesses as to the word.

'Photograph' is a general favourite, but is found not to agree with the three first scenes, although much ingenuity is expended in endeavouring to make them fit the word. the curate makes a headlong rush at the word 'Daguerreotype,' and is confident that he has solved the problem, until he is informed that it is a word of more than three syllables. Charles Larkyns has already whispered the word to Mary Green; but they keep their discovery to themselves. At length, the Revd Josiah Meek, in a moment of inspiration, hits upon the word, and proclaims it to be CALOTYPE ('Call–oh!–type'); upon which Mr Alfred Brindle declares to Miss Fanny Green that he had fancied it must be that, all along, and, in fact, was just on the point of saying it:

and the actors, coming in in a body, receive the violet-crowns and laurel-wreaths of praise as the meed of their exertions. Perhaps the Misses Honeywood and Mr Bouncer receive larger crowns than the others, but Mr Verdant Green gets his due share, and is fully satisfied with his first appearance on 'the boards'.

Dancing then succeeds, varied by songs from the young ladies, and discharges of chromatic fireworks from the fingers of Miss Waters, for whom Charles Larkyns does the polite, in turning over the leaves of her music. Then some carol-singers come to the hall-door, and the bells of the church proclaim, in joyful peals, the birth of the New Year; a new year of hopes, and joys, and cares, and griefs, and unions, and

partings; a new year of which, who then present shall see the end? who shall be there to welcome in its successor? who shall be absent, laid in the secret places of the earth? Ah, *who?* For, even in the midst of revelry and youth, the joy-peals of those old church bells can strike the key-note of a wail of grief.

Another charade follows, in which new actors join. Then comes a merry supper, in which Mr Alfred Brindle, in order to give himself courage to appear in the next charade, takes more champagne than is good for him; in which, too (probably, from similar champagney reasons), Miss Parkington's unfortunately self-willed nose again assumes a more roseate hue than is becoming to a maiden; in which, too, Mr Verdant Green being called upon to return thanks for 'the ladies' – (toast, proposed in eloquent terms by H. Bouncer, Esq., and drunk 'with the usual honours',) – is so alarmed at finding himself upon his legs, that his ideas altogether vanish, and in great confusion of utterance, observes, 'I–I–ladies and gentlemen–feel–I–I–a–feel–assure you–grattered and flattified–I mean, flattered and gratified–being called on–return thanks–I–I–a–the ladies–give a larm to chife–I mean, charm to life – (*applause*) – and–a–a–grace by their table this presence – I mean–a–a(*applause*) – and joytened our eye–I mean, heightened our joy, to-night – (*applause*) – in their name – thanks – honour.' Mr Verdant Green takes advantage of the applause which follows these incoherent remarks, and sits down, covered with confusion, but thankful that the struggle is over.

More dancing follows. Our hero performs prodigies in the *valse à deux temps*, and twirls about until he has not a leg left to stand upon. The harp, the violin, and the cornet-à-piston, from the county-town, play mechanically in their sleep, and can only be roused by repeated applications of gin-and-water. Carriages are ordered round; wraps are in requisition; the mysterious rites under the white-berried bush are stealthily repeated for the last time; the guests depart, as it were, in a heap, the Rectory party being the last to leave. The intelligent Mr Mole, who has fuddled himself by an injudicious mixture of the half-glasses of wine left on the supper-table, is exasperated with the butler for not allowing him to assist in putting away the silver; and declares that he (the butler) is 'a hold himage', for which he (the intelligent Mr M.) 'don't care a button!' and, as the epithet 'image' appears to wondrously offend the butler, Mr Mole is removed from further consequences by his intelligent wife, who is waiting to conduct her lord and master home.

At length, the last light is out in the Manor Green. Mr Verdant Green is lying uncomfortably upon his back and is waltzing through Dreamland with the blooming Patty Honeywood.

CHAPTER X

Mr Verdant Green enjoys a real Cigar.

THE Christmas vacation passed rapidly away; the Honeywood family returned to the far North; and, once more, Mr Verdant Green found himself within the walls of Brazenface. He and Mr Bouncer had together gone up to Oxford, leaving Charles Larkyns behind to keep a grace-term.

Charles Larkyns had determined to take a good degree. For some time past, he had been reading steadily; and, though only a few hours in each day may be given to books – yet, when that is done, with regularity and painstaking, a real and sensible progress is made. He knew that he had good abilities, and he had determined not to let them remain idle any longer, but to make that use of them for which they were given to him. His examination would come on during the next term; and he hoped to turn the interval to good account, and be able in the end to take a respectable degree. He was destined for the Bar; and, as he had no wish to be a briefless Barrister, he knew that college honours would be of great advantage to him in his after career. He, at once, therefore, set bodily to work to read up his subjects; while his father assisted him in his labours, and Mary Green smiled a kind approval.

Meanwhile, his friends, Mr Verdant Green and Mr Henry Bouncer, were enjoying Oxford life, and disporting themselves among the crowd of skaters in the Christ Church meadows. And a very different scene did the meadows present to the time when they had last skimmed over its surface. Then, the green fields were covered with sailing-boats, out-riggers, and punts, and Mr Verdant Green had nearly come to an untimely end in the waters. But now the scene was changed! Jack Frost had stepped in, and had seized the flood in his frozen fingers, and had bound it up in an icy breast-plate.

And a capital place did the meadows make for any Undergraduate who was either a professed skater, or whose skating education (as in the case of our hero) had been altogether neglected. For the water was only of a moderate depth; so that, in the event of the ice giving way, there was nothing to fear beyond a slight and partial ducking. This was especially fortunate for Mr Verdant Green, who, after having experienced total submersion and a narrow escape from drowning on that very spot, would never have been induced to again commit himself to the surface of the deep, had he not been fully convinced that the deep had now subsided into a shallow. With his breast fortified by this resolution, he therefore fell a victim to the syren tongue of Mr Bouncer, when that gentleman observed to him with sincere feeling, 'Giglamps, old fellow! it would be a beastly shame, when there's such jolly ice, if you did not learn to skate; especially, as I can show you the trick.'

For Mr Bouncer was not only skilful with his hands and arms, but could also perform feats with his feet. He could not only dance quadrilles in dress boots in a ball-room, but he could also go through the figures on the ice in a pair of skates. He could do the outside edge at a more acute angle than the generality of people; he could cut figures of eight that were worthy of Cocker himself, he could display spread-eagles that would have astonished the Fellows of the Zoological Society. He could skim over the thinnest ice in the most don't-care way, and, when at full speed, would stoop to pick up a stone. He would take a hop-skip-and-a-jump, and would vault over walking-sticks, as easily as if he were on dry land – an accomplishment which he had learnt of the Count Doembrownski, a Russian gentleman, who, in his own country, lived chiefly on skates, and, in this country, on pigeons, and whose short residence in Oxford was suddenly brought to a full stop by the arbitrary power of the Vice-Chancellor. So, Mr Verdant Green was persuaded to purchase and put on a pair of skates, and to make his first appearance as a skater in the Christ Church meadows, under the auspices of Mr Bouncer.

The sensation of first finding yourself on a pair of skates is peculiar. It is not unlike the sensation which must have been felt by the young bear, when he was dropped from his mamma's mouth, and, for the first time, told to walk. The poor little bear felt, that it was all very well to say 'walk' – but how was he to do it? Was he to walk with his right fore-leg only? or with his left fore-leg? or with both his fore-legs? or was he to walk with his right hind-leg? or with his left hind-leg? or with both his hind-legs? or was he to make a combination of hind and fore-legs, and walk with all four at once? or what was he to do? So he tried each of these ways; and they all failed. Poor little bear!

Mr Verdant Green felt very much in the little bear's condition. He was undecided whether to skate with his right leg, or with his left leg, or with both legs. He tried his right leg, and immediately it glided off

at right angles with his body, while his left leg performed a similar and spontaneous movement in the contrary direction. Having captured his left leg, he put it cautiously forwards, and immediately it twisted under him, while his right leg amused itself by describing an altogether unnecessary circle. Obtaining a brief mastery over both legs, he put them forwards at the same moment, and they fled from beneath him, and he was flung – bump! – on his back. Poor little bear!

But, if it is hard to make a start in a pair of skates when you are in a perpendicular position, how much is the difficulty increased when your position has become a horizontal one! You raise yourself on your knees, you assist yourself with your hands, and, no sooner have you got one leg right, then away slides the other, and down you go. It is like the movement in that scene with the pair of short stilts, in which the French clowns are so amusing, and it is almost as difficult to perform. Mr Verdant Green soon found that though he might be ambitious to excel in the polite accomplishment of skating, yet that his ambition was destined to meet with many a fall. But he persevered, and perseverance will achieve wonders, especially when aided by the tuition of such an indefatigable gentleman as Mr Bouncer.

'You get on stunningly, Gig-lamps,' said the little gentleman, 'and haven't been on your beam ends more than once a minute. But I should advise you, old fellow, to get your sit-upons seated with wash-leather – just like the eleventh hussars do with their cherry-coloured pants. It'll come cheaper in the end, and may be productive of comfort. And now, after all these exciting ups and downs, let us go and have a quiet hand at billiards.' So the two friends strolled up the High, where they saw two Queensmen 'confessing their shame', as Mr Bouncer phrased it, by standing under the gateway of their college; and went on to Bickerton's, where they found all the tables occupied, and Jonathan playing a match with Mr Fluke of Christ Church. So, after watching the celebrated marker long enough to inspire them with a desire to accomplish similar feats of dexterity, they continued their walk to Broad Street, and turning up a yard opposite to the Clarendon, found that Betteris had an upstairs room at liberty. Here they accomplished several pleasing mathematical problems with the balls, and

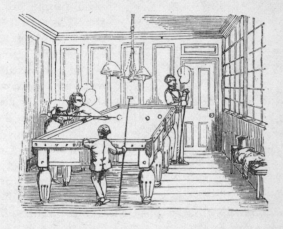

contributed their modicum towards the smoking of the ceiling of the room.

Since Mr Verdant Green had acquired the art of getting through a cigar without making himself ill, he had looked upon himself as a genuine smoker; and had, from time to time, bragged of his powers as regarded the fumigation of 'the herb Nicotiana, commonly called tobacco' (as the Oxford statute tersely says). This was an amiable weakness on his part that had not escaped the observant eye of Mr Bouncer, who had frequently taken occasion, in the presence of his friends, to defer to Mr Verdant Green's judgment in the matter of cigars. The train of adulation being thus laid, an opportunity was only needed to fire it. It soon came.

'Once upon a time,' as the story-books say, it chanced that Mr Bouncer was consuming his minutes and cigars at his tobacconist's, when his eye lighted for the thousandth time on the roll of cabbage-leaves, brown paper, and refuse tobacco, which being done up into the form of a monster cigar (a foot long, and of proportionate thickness), was hung in the shop-window, and did duty as a truthful token of the commodity vended within. Mr Bouncer had looked at this implement

nine hundred and ninety nine times, without its suggesting anything else to his mind, than its being of the same class of art as the monster mis-representations outside wild-beast shows; but he now gazed upon it with new sensations. In short, Mr Bouncer took such a fancy to the thing, that he purchased it, and took it off to his rooms – though he did not mention this fact to his friend, Mr Verdant Green, when he saw him soon afterwards, and spoke to him of his excellent judgement in tobacco.

'A taste for smoke comes natural, Gig-lamps!' said Mr Bouncer. 'It's what you call a *nascitur non fit*; and, if you haven't the gift, why you can't purchase it. Now, you're a judge of smoke; it's a gift with you, don't you see; and you could no more help knowing a good weed from a bad one, than you could help waggling your tail if you were a baa-lamb.'

Mr Verdant Green bowed, and blushed, in acknowledgment of this delightful flattery.

'Now, there's old Footelights, you know; he's got an uncle, who's a governor, or some great swell, out in Barbadoes. Well, every now and then the old trump sends Footelights no end of a box of weeds; not common ones, you understand, but regular tip-toppers; but they're quite thrown away on poor Footelights, who'd think as much of cabbage-leaves as he would of real Havannahs, so he's always obliged to ask somebody else's opinion about them. Well, he's got a sample of a weed of a most terrific kind – *Magnifico Pomposo* is the name – no end uncommon, and at least a foot long. We don't meet with 'em in England because they're too expensive to import. Well, it wouldn't do to throw away such a weed as this on anyone; so Footelights wants to have the opinion of a man who's really a judge of what a good weed is. I refused, because my taste has been rather out of order lately; and Billy Blades is in training for Henley, so he's obliged to decline; so I told him of you, Gig-lamps, and said, that if there was a man in Brazenface that could tell him what his Magnifico Pomposo was worth, that man was Verdant Green. Don't blush, old feller! you can't help having a

fine judgment, you know; so don't be ashamed of it. Now, you just wine with me this evening; Footelights and some more men are coming; and we're all anxious to hear your opinion about these new weeds, because, if it's favourable we can club together, and import a box.' Mr Bouncer's victim, being perfectly unconscious of the trap laid for him, promised to come to the wine, and give his opinion on this weed of fabled size and merit.

When the evening and company had come, he was rather staggered at beholding the dimensions of the pseudo-cigar; but, rashly judging that to express surprise would be to betray ignorance, Mr Verdant Green inspected the formidable monster with the air of a connoisseur, and smelt, pinched, and rolled his tongue round it, after the manner of the best critics. If this was a diverting spectacle to the assembled guests of Mr Bouncer, how must the humour of the scene have been increased, when our hero, with great difficulty, lighted the cigar, and, with still greater difficulty, held it in his mouth, and endeavoured to smoke it! As Mr Foote afterwards observed, 'it was a situation for a screaming farce.'

'It doesn't draw well!' faltered the victim, as the bundle of rubbish went out for the fourth time.

'Why, that's always the case with the Barbadoes baccy!' said Mr Bouncer; 'it takes a long pull, and a strong pull, and a pull all together to get it to make a start; but when once it does go, it goes beautiful – like a house a-fire. But you can't expect it to be like a common threepenny weed. Here! let me light him for you, Gig-lamps; I'll give the beggar a dig in his ribs, as a gentle persuader.' Mr Bouncer thereupon poked his pen-knife through the rubbish, and after a time induced it to 'draw'; and Mr Verdant Green pulled at it furiously, and made his eyes water with the unusual cloud of smoke that he raised.

'And now, what d'ye think of it, my beauty?' inquired Mr Bouncer. 'It's something out of the common, ain't it?'

'It has a beautiful ash!' observed Mr Smalls.

'And diffuses an aroma that makes me long to defy the trainer, and smoke one like it!' said Mr. Blades.

'So pray give me your reading – at least, your opinion – on my Magnifico Pomposo!' asked Mr Foote.

'Well,' answered Mr Verdant Green, slowly – turning very pale as he spoke – 'at first, I thought it was be-yew-tiful; but, altogether, I think–that–the Barbadoes tobacco–doesn't quite–agree with–my stom ... ' the speaker abruptly concluded by dropping the cigar, putting his handkerchief to his mouth, and rushing into Mr Bouncer's bed-room. The Magnifico Pomposo had been too much for him, and had produced sensations accurately interpreted by Mr Bouncer, who forthwith represented in expressive pantomime, the actions of a distressed voyager, when he feebly murmurs 'Steward!'

To atone for the 'chaffing' which he had been the means of inflicting on his friend, the little gentleman, a few days afterwards, proposed to take our hero to the Chipping Norton Steeple-chase, Mr Smalls and Mr Fosbrooke making up the quartet for a tandem. It was on their return from the races, that, after having stopped at the *Bear* at Woodstock 'to wash out the horses' mouths', and having done this so effectually that the

horses had appeared to have no mouths left, and had refused to answer the reins, and had smashed the cart against a house, which had seemed to have danced into the middle of the road for their diversion – and, after having put back to the *Bear*, and prevailed upon that animal to lend them a nondescript vehicle of the 'pre-adamite buggy' species, described by Sidney Smith – that, much time having been consumed by the progress of this chapter of accidents, they did not reach Peyman's Gate until a late hour; and Mr Verdant Green found that he was once more in difficulties. For they had no sooner got through the gate, than the wild octaves from Mr Bouncer's post-horn were suddenly brought to a full stop, and Mr Fosbrooke, who was the 'waggoner', was brought to Woh! and was compelled to pull up in obedience to the command of the Proctor, who, as on a previous occasion, suddenly appeared from behind the toll-house, in company with his marshall and bull-dogs.

The sentence pronounced on our hero the next day, was, 'Sir! – You will translate all your lectures; have your name crossed on the buttery and kitchen books; and be confined to chapel, hall, and college.'

This sentence was chiefly annoying, inasmuch as it somewhat interfered with the duties and pleasures attendant upon his boating practice. For, wonderful to relate. Mr Verdant Green had so much improved in the science, that he was now 'Number 3' of his college 'Torpid', and was in hard training. The Torpid races commenced on 10 March, and were continued on the following days. Our hero sent his father a copy of *Tintinnabulum's Life*, which – after informing the

Manor Green family that 'the boats took up positions in the following order: 'Brasenose, Exeter 1, Wadham, Balliol, St John's, Pembroke, University, Oriel, Brazenface, Christ Church 1, Worcester, Jesus, Queen's, Christ Church 2, Exeter 2' – proceeded to enter into particulars of each day's sport, of which it is only necessary to record such as gave interest to our hero's family.

'First day. ... Brazenface refused to acknowledge the bump by Christ Church (1) before they came to the Cherwell. There is very little doubt but that they were bumped at the Gut and the Willows. ...

'Second day. ... Brazenface rowed pluckily away from Worcester. ...

'Third day. ... A splendid race between Brazenface and Worcester; and, at the flag, the latter were within a foot; they did not, however, succeed in bumping. The cheering from the Brazenface barge was vociferous. ...

'Fourth day. ... Worcester was more fortunate, and succeeded in making the bump at the Cherwell, in consequence of No. 3 of the Brazenface boat fainting from fatigue.'

Under 'No. 3' Mr Verdant Green had drawn a pencil line, and had written 'V.G.' He shortly after related to his family the gloomy particulars of the bump, when he returned home for the Easter vacation.

CHAPTER XI

Mr Verdant Green gets through his Smalls.

DESPITE the hindrance which the *grande passion* is supposed to bring to the student, Charles Larkyns had made very good use of the opportunities afforded him by the leisure of his grace-term. Indeed, as he himself observed,

> Who hath not owned, with rapture-smitten frame,
> The power of *grace*?

And as he felt that the hours of his grace-term had not been wasted in idleness, but had been turned to profitable account, it is not at all unlikely that his pleasures of hope regarding his Degree-examination, and the position his name would occupy in the Class-list, were of a roseate hue. He therefore, when the Easter vacation had come to an end, returned to Oxford in high spirits, with our hero and his friend Mr Bouncer, who, after a brief visit to 'the Mum', had passed the remainder of the vacation at the Manor Green. During these few holiday weeks, Charles Larkyns had acted as private tutor to his two friends, and had, in the language of Mr Bouncer, 'put them through their paces uncommon'; for the little gentleman was going in for his Degree, *alias* Great-go, *alias* Greats, and our hero for his first examination *in literis humanioribus*, *alias* Responsions, *alias* Little-go, *alias* Smalls. Thus the friends returned to Oxford mutually benefited; but, as the time for examination drew nearer and still nearer, the fears of Mr Bouncer rose in a gradation of terrors, that threatened to culminate in an actual panic.

'You see', said the little gentleman, 'the Mum's set her heart on my getting through, and I must read like the doose. And I haven't got the head, you see, for Latin and Greek; and that beastly Euclid altogether stumps me; and I feel as though I should come to grief. I'm blowed', the little gentleman would cry, earnestly and sadly, 'I'm blow'd if I don't think they must have given me too much pap when I was a babby, and softened my brains! or else, why can't I walk into these classical parties just as easy as you, Charley, or old Gig-lamps there? But I can't, you see: my brains are addled. They say it ain't a bad thing for reading to get your head shaved. It cools your brains, and gives full play to what you call your intellectual faculties. I think I shall try the dodge, and get a gent's real head of hair, till after the exam; and then, when I've stumped the examiners, I can wear my own luxuriant locks again.'

And, as Mr Bouncer professed, so did he; and, not many days after, astonished his friends and the University generally by appearing in a wig of curly black hair. It was a pleasing sight to see the little gentleman with a scalp like a billiard ball, a pipe in his mouth, and the wig mounted on a block, with books spread before him, endeavouring to

persuade himself that he was working up his subjects. It was still more pleasing to view him, in moments of hilarity, divest himself of his wig, and hurl it at the scout, or any other offensive object that appeared before him. And it was a sight not to be forgotten by the beholders, when, after too recklessly partaking of an indiscriminate mixture of egg-flip, sangaree, and cider-cup, he feebly threw his wig at the spectacles of Mr Verdant Green, and, overbalanced by the exertion, fell back into the coal-scuttle, where he lay, bald-headed and helpless, laughing and weeping by turns, and caressed by Huz and Buz.

But the shaving of his head was not the only feature (or, rather, loss of feature) that distinguished Mr Bouncer's reading for his degree.

The gentleman with the limited knowledge of the cornet-à-piston, who had the rooms immediately beneath those of our hero and his friend, had made such slow progress in his musical education, that he had even now scarcely got into his 'Cottage near a Wood'. This gentleman was Mr Bouncer's Frankenstein. He was always riding up when he was not wanted. When Mr Bouncer felt as if he could read, and sat down to his books, wigless and determined, the doleful legend of the cottage near a wood was forced upon him in an unpleasingly obtrusive and distracting manner. It was in vain that Mr Bouncer sounded his octaves in all their discordant variations; the gentleman had no ear, and was not to be put out of his cottage on any terms: Mr. Bouncer's notices of ejectment were always disregarded. He had hoped that the ears of Mr Slowcoach (whose rooms were in the angle of the quad) would have been pierced by the noise, and that he would have put a stop to the nuisance; but, either from its being too customary a custom, or that the ears of Mr Slowcoach had grown callous, the nuisance was suffered to continue unreproved.

Mr Bouncer resolved, therefore, on some desperate method of calling attention to one nuisance, by creating another of a louder description; and, as his octaves appeared to fail in this – notwithstanding the energy and annoying ability that he threw into them – he conceived the idea of setting up a drum! The plan was no sooner thought of than carried out. He met with an instrument sufficiently large and formidable for his purpose, hired it, and had it stealthily conveyed into college (like another Falstaff) in a linen 'buck-basket'. He waited his opportunity; and, the next time that the gentleman in the rooms beneath took his cornet to his cottage near a wood, Mr Bouncer, stationed on the landing above, played a thundering accompaniment on his big drum.

The echoes from the tightened parchment rolled round the quad, and brought to the spot a rush of curious and excited undergraduates. Mr Bouncer, after taking off his wig in honour of the air, then treated them to the National Anthem, arranged as a drum solo for two sticks, the chorus being sustained by the voices of those present; when in the midst of the entertainment, the reproachful features of Mr Slowcoach appeared upon the scene. Sternly the tutor demanded the reason of the strange hubbub; and was answered by Mr Bouncer, that, as one

gentleman was allowed to play *his* favourite instrument whenever he chose, for his own but no one else's gratification, he could not see why he (Mr Bouncer) might not also, whenever he pleased, play for *his* own gratification his favourite instrument – the big drum. This specious excuse, although logical, was not altogether satisfactory to Mr Slowcoach; and, with some asperity, he ordered Mr Bouncer never again to indulge in, what he termed (in reference probably to the little gentleman's bald head), 'such an indecent exhibition'. But, as he further ordered that the cornet-à-piston gentleman was to instrumentally enter into his cottage near a wood, only at stated hours in the afternoon, Mr Bouncer had gained his point in putting a stop to the nuisance so far as it interfered with his reading; and, thenceforth, he might be seen on brief occasions persuading himself that he was furiously reading and getting up his subjects by the aid of those royal roads to knowledge, variously known as cribs, crams, plugs, abstracts, analyses, or epitomes.

But, besides the assistance thus afforded to him *out* of the schools, Mr Bouncer, like many others, idle as well as ignorant, intended to assist himself when *in* the schools by any contrivance that his ingenuity could suggest, or his audacity carry out.

'It's quite fair', was the little gentleman's argument, 'to do the examiners in any way that you can, as long as you only go in for a pass. Of course, if you were going in for a class, or a scholarship, or anything of that sort, it would be no end mean and dirty to crib; and the gent that did it ought to be kicked out of the society of gentlemen. But when you only go in for a pass, and ain't doing anyone any harm by a little bit of cribbing, but choose to run the risk to save yourself the bother of being ploughed, why then, I think, a feller's bound to do what he can for himself. And, you see, in my case, Gig-lamps, there's the Mum to be considered; she'd cut up doosid, if I didn't get through; so I must crib a bit, if it's only for *her* sake.'

But although the little gentleman thus made filial tenderness the excuse for his deceit, and the salve for his conscience, yet he could neither persuade Mr Verdant Green to follow his example, nor to be a convert to his opinions; nor would he be persuaded by our hero to relinquish his designs.

'Why, look here, Gig-lamps!' Mr Bouncer would say; 'how *can* I relinquish them, after having had all this trouble? I'll put you up to a few of my dodges – free, gratis, for nothing. In the first place, Gig-lamps, you see here's a small circular bit of paper, covered with Peloponnesian and Punic wars, and no end of dates – written small and short, you see, but quite legible – with the chief things done in red ink. Well, this gentleman goes in the front of my watch, under the glass; and, when I get stumped for a date, out comes the watch; I look at the time of day – you understand – and down goes the date. Here's another dodge!' added the little gentleman – who might well have been called 'the Artful Dodger' – as he produced a shirt from a drawer. 'Look here, at the wristbands! Here are all the Kings of Israel and Judah, with their dates and prophets, written down in India-ink, so as to wash out again. You twitch up the cuff of your coat, quite accidentally, and then you book your king. You see, Gig-lamps, I don't like to trust, as some fellows do, to having what you want, written down small and shoved into a quill, and passed to you by some man sitting in the schools; that's dangerous, don't you see. And I don't like to hold cards in my hand; I've improved on that, and invented a first-rate dodge of my own, that I intend to take out a patent for. Like all truly great inventions, it's no end simple. In the first place, look straight afore you, my little dear, and you will see this pack of cards – all made of a size, nice to hold in the palm of your hand; they're about all sorts of rum things – everything that I want. And you see that each beggar's got a hole drilled in him. And you see, here's a longish string with a little bit of hooked wire at the end, made so that I can easily hang the card on it. Well, I pass the string up my coat sleeve, and down under my waistcoat; and here, you see, I've got the wire end in the palm of my hand. Then, I slip out the card I want, and hook it onto the wire, so that I can have it just before me as I write. Then, if any of the examiners look suspicious, or if one of them comes round to spy, I just pull the bit of string that hangs under the bottom of my waistcoat, and away flies the card up my coat sleeve; and when the examiner comes

round, he sees that my hand's never moved, and that there's nothing in it! So he walks off satisfied; and then I shake the little beggar out of my sleeve again, and the same game goes on as before. And when the string's tight, even straightening your body is quite sufficient to hoist the card into your sleeve, without moving either of your hands. I've got an Examination-coat made on purpose, with a heap of pockets, in which I can stow my cards in regular order. These three pockets', said Mr Bouncer, as he produced the coat, 'are entirely for Euclid. Here's each problem written right out on a card; they're laid regularly in order, and I turn them over in my pocket, till I get hold of the one I want, and then take it out, and work it. So you see, Gig-lamps, I'm safe to get through! – it's impossible for them to plough me, with all these contrivances. That's a consolation for a cove in distress, ain't it, old feller?'

Both our hero and Charles Larkyns endeavoured to persuade Mr Bouncer that his conduct would, at the very least, be foolhardy, and that he had much better throw his pack of cards into the fire, wash the

Kings of Israel and Judah off his shirt, destroy his strings and hooked wires, and keep his Examination-coat for a shooting one. But all their arguments were in vain, and the infatuated little gentleman, like a deaf adder, shut his ears at the voice of the charmer.

What between the Cowley cricketings, and the Isis boatings, Mr Verdant Green only read by spasmodic fits; but, as he was very fairly up in his subjects – thanks to Charles Larkyns and the rector – and as the Little-go was not such a very formidable affair, or demanded a scholar of first-rate calibre, the only terrors that the examination could bring him were those which were begotten of nervousness. At length the lists were out; and our hero read among the names of candidates, that of

GREEN, *Verdant, è Coll. Æn. Fac.*

There is a peculiar sensation on first seeing your name in print. Instances are on record where people have taken a world of trouble merely that they may have the pleasure of perusing their names 'among the fashionable present' at the Countess of So-and-so's evening reception; and cases are not wanting where young ladies and gentlemen have expended no small amount of pocket-money in purchasing copies of *The Times* (no reduction, too, being made on taking a quantity!) in order that their sympathising friends might have the pride of seeing their names as coming out at drawing-rooms and *levées*. When a young M.P. has stammered out his *coup-d'essai* in the House, he views, with mingled emotions, his name given to the world, for the first time, in capital letters. When young authors and artists first see their names in print, is it not a pleasure to them? When Ensign Dash sees himself gazetted, does he not look on his name with a peculiar sensation, and forthwith send an impression of the paper to Master Jones, who was flogged with him last week for stealing apples? When Mr. Smith is called to the Bar, and Mr Robinson can dub himself M.R.C.S., do they not behold their names in print with feelings of rapture? And when Miss Brown has been to her first ball, does she not anxiously await the coming of the next county newspaper, in order to have the happiness of reading her name there?

But, different to these are the sensations that attend the seeing your name first in print in a College examination-list. They are, probably, somewhat similar to the sensations you would feel on seeing your name in a death-warrant. Your blood runs hot, then cold, then hot again; your pulse goes at fever pace; the throbbing arteries of your brow almost jerk your cap off. You know that the worst is come – that the law of the Dons, which altereth not, has fixed your name there, and

that there is no escape. The courage of despair then takes possession of your soul, and nerves you for the worst. You join the crowd of nervous fellow-sufferers who are thronging round the buttery-door to examine the list, and you begin with them calmly to parcel out the names by sixes and eights, and then to arrive at an opinion when your day of execution will be. If your name comes at the head of the list, you wish that you were 'YOUNG, *Carolus, è Coll. Vigorn.*' that you might have a reprieve of your sentence. If your name is at the end of the list, you wish that you were 'ADAMS, *Edvardus Jacobus, è Coll. Univ.*' that you might go in at once, and be put out of your misery. If your name is in the middle of the list, you wish that it were elsewhere: and then you wish that it were out of the list altogether.

Through these varying shades of emotion did Mr Verdant Green pass, until at length they were all lost in the deeper gloom of actual entrance into the schools. When once there, his fright soon passed away. Reassured by the kindly voice of the examiner, telling him to read over his Greek before construing it, our hero recovered his equanimity, and got through his *viva voce* with flying colours; and, on glancing over his paper-work, soon saw that the questions were within his scope, and that he could answer most of them. Without hazarding his success by making 'bad shots', he contented himself by answering those questions only on which he felt sure; and, when his examination was over, he left the schools with a pretty safe conviction that he was safe, 'and was well through his smalls'.

He could not but help, however, feeling some anxiety on the subject, until he was relieved from all further fears, by the arrival of Messrs Fosbrooke, Smalls, and Blades, with a slip of paper (not unlike those which Mr Levi, the sheriff's officer, makes use of), on which was written and printed as follows:

GREEN, VERDANT è COLL. ÆN. FAC.
Quæstionibus Magistrorum Scholarum in Parviso pro forma respondit.
Ita testamur, { GULIELMUS SMITH,
ROBERTUS JONES.

Junii 7, 18–.

Alas for Mr Bouncer! Though he had put in practice all the ingenious plans which were without a doubt to ensure his success; and though he had worked his cribs with consummate coolness, and had not been discovered; yet, nevertheless, his friends came to him empty-handed. The infatuated little gentleman had either trusted too much to his own astuteness, or else he had over-reached himself, and had used his card-knowledge in wrong places; or, perhaps, the examiners may have suspected his deeds from the nature of his papers, and may have refused to pass him. But whatever might be the cause, the little gentleman had to defer taking his degree for some months at least. In a word – and a dreadful word it is to all undergraduates – Mr Bouncer was PLUCKED! He bore his unexpected reverse of fortune very philosophically, and professed to regret it only for 'the Mum's' sake; but he seemed to feel that the dons of the college would look shy upon him, and he expressed his opinion that it would be better for him to migrate to the Tavern.*

But, while Mr Bouncer was thus deservedly punished for his

---

*A name given to New Inn Hall, not only from its title, 'New Inn', but also because the buttery is open all day, and the members of the Hall can call for what they please at any hour, the same as in a tavern.

idleness and duplicity, Charles Larkyns was rewarded for all his toil. He did even better than he had expected: for, not only did his name appear in the second class, but the following extra news concerning him was published in the daily papers, under the very appropriate heading of 'University *Intelligence*'.

OXFORD, June 9. – The Chancellor's prizes have been awarded as follows:– Latin Essay, Charles Larkyns, Commoner of Brazenface. The Newdigate Prize for English Verse was also awarded to the same gentleman.

His writing for the prize-poem had been a secret. He had conceived the idea of doing so when the subject had been given out in the previous 'long': he had worked at the subject privately, and, when the day (1 April) on which the poems had to be sent in, had come, he had watched his opportunity, and secretly dropped through the wired slit in the door of the registrar's office at the Clarendon, a manuscript poem, distinguished by the motto:

> Oh for the touch of a vanish'd hand
> And the sound of a voice that is still.

We may be quite sure that there was great rejoicing at the Manor Green and the rectory, when the news arrived of the success of Charles Larkyns and Mr Verdant Green.

CHAPTER XII

Mr Verdant Green and his Friends enjoy the Commemoration.

THE Commemoration had come; and, among the people who were drawn to the sight from all parts of the country, the Warwickshire coach landed in Oxford our friends Mr Green, his two eldest daughters, and the rector – for all of whom Charles Larkyns had secured very comfortable lodgings in Oriel Street.

The weather was of the finest; and the beautiful city of colleges looked at its best. While the rector met with old friends, and heard his son's praises, and renewed his acquaintance with his old haunts of study, Mr Green again lionised Oxford in a much more comfortable and satisfactory manner than he had previously done at the heels of a professional guide. As for the young ladies, they were charmed with everything; for they had never before been in an University town, and all things had the fascination of novelty. Great were the luncheons held in Mr Verdant Green's and Charles Larkyns's rooms; musical was the laughter that floated merrily through the grave old quads of Brazenface; happy were the two hearts that held converse with each other in those cool cloisters and shady gardens. How a few flounces and bright girlish smiles can change the aspect of the sternest homes of knowledge! How sunlight can be brought into the gloomiest nooks of learning by the beams that irradiate happy girlish faces, where the light of love and truth shines out clear and joyous! How the appearance of the Commemoration week is influenced in a way thus described by one of Oxonia's poets:

Peace! for in the gay procession brighter forms are borne along –
Fairer scholars, pleasure-beaming, float amid the classic throng.
Blither laughter's ringing music fills the haunts of men awhile,
And the sternest priests of knowledge blush beneath a maiden's smile.
Maidens teach a softer science – laughing Love his pinions dips,
Hush'd to hear fantastic whispers murmur'd from a pedant's lips.

Oh, believe it, throbbing pulses flutter under folds of starch,
And the Dons are human-hearted if the ladies' smiles be arch.

Thanks to the influence of Charles Larkyns and his father, the party
were enabled to see all that was to be seen during the Commemoration
week. On the Saturday night they went to the amateur concert at the
Town Hall, in aid of which, strange to say, Mr Bouncer's proffer of
his big drum had been declined. On the Sunday they went, in the
morning, to St Mary's to hear the Bampton lecture; and, in the afternoon, to the magnificent choral service at New College. In the evening
they attended the customary 'Show Sunday' promenade in Christ

Church Broad Walk, where, under the delicious cool of the luxuriant
foliage, they met all the rank, beauty, and fashion that were assembled
in Oxford; and where, until Tom 'tolled the hour for retiring', they
threaded their way amid a miscellaneous crowd of Dons and Doctors,
and Tufts and Heads of Houses –

> With prudes for Proctors, dowagers for Deans,
> And bright girl-graduates with their golden hair.

On the Monday they had a party to Woodstock and Blenheim; and in
the evening went, on the Brazenface barge, to see the procession of

boats, where the Misses Green had the satisfaction to see their brother pulling in one of the fifteen Torpids that followed immediately in the wake of the other boats. They concluded the evening's entertainments in a most satisfactory manner, by going to the ball at the Town Hall.

Indeed, the way the two young ladies worked was worthy of all credit, and proved them to be possessed of the most vigorous constitutions; for, although they danced till an early hour in the morning, they not only, on the next day, went to the anniversary sermon for the Radcliffe, and after that to the horticultural show in the Botanical Gardens, and after that to the concert in the Sheldonian Theatre, but – as though they had not had enough to fatigue them already – they must, forsooth – Brazenface being one of the ball-giving colleges – wind up the night by accepting the polite invitation of Mr Verdant Green and Mr Charles Larkyns to a ball given in their college hall. And how many polkas these young ladies danced, and how many waltzes they waltzed, and how many ices they consumed, and how

many too susceptible partners they drove to the verge of desperation, it would be improper, if not impossible, to say.

But, however much they might have been fagged by their exertions of feet and features, it is certain that, by ten of the clock the next morning, they appeared, quite fresh and charming to the view, in the ladies' gallery in the Theatre. There – after the proceedings had been opened by the undergraduates in *their* peculiar way, and by the Vice-Chancellor in *his* peculiar way – and, after the degrees had been conferred, and the public orator had delivered an oration in a tongue not understood of the people, our friends from Warwickshire had the delight of beholding Mr Charles Larkyns ascend the rostrums to deliver, in their proper order, the Latin Essay and the English Verse.

He had chosen his friend Verdant to be his prompter; so that the well-known 'gig-lamps' of our hero formed, as it were, a very focus of attraction: but it was well for Mr Charles Larkyns that he was possessed of self-control and a good memory, for Mr Verdant Green was far too nervous to have prompted him in any efficient manner. We may be sure that, in all that bevy of fair women, at least one pair of bright eyes kindled with rapture, and one heart beat with exulting joy, when the deafening cheers that followed the poet's description of the moon, the sea, and woman's love (the three ingredients which are apparently necessary for the sweetening of all prize-poems), rang through the Theatre and made its walls re-echo to the shouting. And we may be sure that, when it was all over, and when the Commemoration had come to an end, Charles Larkyns felt rewarded for all his hours of labour by the deep love garnered up in his heart by the trustful affection of one who had become as dear to him as life itself!

It was one morning after they had all returned to the Manor Green that our hero said to his friend 'How I *do* wish that this day week were come!'

'I dare say you do,' replied the friend; 'and I dare say that the pretty Patty is wishing the same wish.' Upon which Mr Verdant Green not only laughed but blushed!

For it seemed that he, together with his sisters, Mr Charles Larkyns, and Mr Bouncer, were about to pay a long-vacation visit to Honeywood Hall, in the county of Northumberland; and the young man was naturally looking forward to it with all the ardour of a first and consuming passion.

PART III

MARRIED AND DONE FOR

CHAPTER I

Mr Verdant Green travels North.

ULY: fierce and burning! A day to tinge the green corn with a golden hue. A day to scorch grass into hay between sunrise and sunset. A day in which to rejoice in the cool thick masses of trees, and to lie on one's back under their canopy, and look dreamily up, through its rents, at the peep of hot, cloudless, blue sky. A day to sit on shady banks upon yielding cushions of moss and heather, from whence you gaze on bright flowers blazing in the blazing sun, and rest your eyes again upon your book to find the lines swimming in a radiance of mingled green and red. A day that fills you with amphibious feelings, and makes you desire to be even a dog, that you might bathe and paddle and swim in every roadside brook and pond, without the exertion of dressing and undressing, and yet with propriety. A day that sends you out by willow-hung streams, to fish, as an excuse for idleness. A day that drives you dinnerless from smoking joints, and plunges you thirstfully into barrels of beer. A day that induces apathetic listlessness and total prostration of energy, even under the aggravating warfare of gnats and wasps. A day that engenders pity for the ranks of ruddy haymakers, hotly marching on under the merciless glare of the noonday sun. A day when the very air, steaming up from the earth, seems to palpitate with the heat. A day when Society has left its cool and pleasant country-house, and finds itself baked and burnt up in Town, condemned to ovens of operas, and fiery furnaces of *levées* and drawing-rooms. A day when even ice is warm, and perspiring visitors to the Zoological Gardens envy the hippopotamus living in his bath. A day when a hot, frizzling, sweltering smell ascends from the ground, as though it was the earth's great ironing day. And – above all – a day that converts a railway traveller into a martyr, and a first-class carriage into a moving representation of the Black Hole of Calcutta.

So thought Mr Verdant Green, as he was whirled onward to the far North, in company with his three sisters, Miss Bouncer, and Mr Charles Larkyns. Being six in number, they formed a snug (and hot) family party, and filled the carriage, to the exclusion of little Mr Bouncer, who, nevertheless, bore this temporary and unavoidable separation with a tranquil mind, inasmuch as it enabled him to ride in a second-class carriage, where he could the more conveniently indulge in the furtive pleasures of the Virginian weed. But, to keep up his connection with the party, and to prove that his interest in them could not be diminished by a brief and enforced absence, Mr Bouncer paid them flying visits at every station, keeping his pipe alight by a puff into the carriage, accompanied with an expression of his full conviction that Miss Fanny Green had been smoking, in defiance of the company's by-laws. These rapid interviews were enlivened by Mr Bouncer informing his friends that Huz and Buz (who were panting in a locker) were as well as could be expected, and giving any other interesting particulars regarding himself, his fellow-travellers, or the country in general, that could be compressed into the space of sixty seconds or thereabouts; and the visits were regularly and ruthlessly brought to an abrupt termination by the angry 'Now, then, sir!' of the guard, and the reckless thrusting of the little gentleman into his second-class carriage, to the endangerment of his life and limbs, and the exaggerated display of authority on the part of the railway official.

Mr Bouncer's mercurial temperament had enabled him to get over the little misfortune that had followed upon his examination for his degree; but he still preserved a memento of that hapless period in the shape of a wig of curly black hair. For he found, during the summer months, such coolness from his shaven poll, that, in spite of 'the Mum's' entreaties, he would not suffer his own luxuriant locks to grow, but declared that, till the winter at any rate, he would wear his gent's real head of hair; and in order that our railway party should not forget the reason for its existence, Mr Bouncer occasionally favoured them with a sight of his bald head, and also narrated to them, with great glee, how, when a very starchy lady of a certain age had left their carriage, he had called after her upon the platform – holding out his wig as he did so – that she left some of her property behind her; and how the passengers and porters had grinned, and the starchy lady had lost all her stiffening through the hotness of her wrath.

York at last! A half-hour's escape from the hot carriage, and a hasty dinner on cold lamb and cool salad in the pleasant refreshment-room hung round with engravings. Mr Bouncer's dinner is got over with incredible rapidity, in order that the little gentleman may carry out his humane intention of releasing Huz and Buz from their locker, and giving them their dinner and a run on the remote end of the platform, at a distance from timid spectators; which design is satisfactorily performed, and crowned with a douche bath from the engine-pump. Then, away again to the rabbit-hole of a locker, the smoky second-class carriage, and the stuffy first-class; incarcerated in which black hole, the plump Miss Bouncer, notwith-standing that she has removed her bonnet and all superfluous coverings, gets hot-ter than ever in the afternoon sun, and is seen, ever and anon, to pass over

her glowing face a handkerchief cooled with the waters of Cologne. And, when the man with the grease-pot comes round to look at the tires of the wheels, the sight of it increases her warmth by suggesting a desire (which cannot be gratified) for lemon ice. Nevertheless, they have with them a variety of cooling refreshments, and their hot-house fruit and strawberries are most acceptable. The Misses Green have wisely followed their friend's example, in the removal of bonnets and mantles; and, as they amuse themselves with books and embroidery, the black hole bears, as far as possible, a resemblance to a boudoir. Charles Larkyns favours the company with extracts from *The Times*; reads to them the last number of Dickens's new tale, or directs their attention to the most note-worthy points on their route. Mr Verdant Green is seated *vis-à-vis* to the plump Miss Bouncer, and benignantly beams upon her through his glasses, or musingly consults his *Bradshaw* to count how much nearer they have crept to their destination, the while his thoughts have travelled on in the very quickest of express trains, and have already reached the far North.

Thus they journey: crawling under the stately old walls of York; then, with a rush and a roar, sliding rapidly over the level landscape, from whence they can look back upon the glorious Minster towers standing out grey and cold from the sunlit plain. Then, to Darlington; and on by porters proclaiming the names of stations in uncouth Dunelmian tongue, informing passengers that they have reached 'Faweyill' and 'Fensoosen', instead of 'Ferry Hill' and 'Fence Houses', and terrifying nervous people by the command to 'Change here for Doom!' when only the propinquity of the palatinate city is signified. And so, on by the triple towers of Durham that gleam in the sun with a ruddy orange hue; on, leaving to the left that last resting-place of Bede and St Cuthbert, on the rock

> Where his cathedral, huge and vast,
> Looks down upon the Wear.

On, past the wonderfully out-of-place 'Durham monument', a Grecian temple on a naked hill among the coal-pits; on, with a double curve, over the Wear, laden with its Rhine-like rafts; on, to grimy Gateshead and smoky Newcastle, and, with a scream and a rattle, over the wonderful High Level (then barely completed), looking down with a sort of self-satisfied shudder upon the bridge, and the Tyne, and the fleet of colliers, and the busy quays, and the quaint timber-built houses with their overlapping storeys, and picturesque black and white gables. Then on again, after a cool delay and brief release from the black hole; on, into Northumbrian ground, over the Wansbeck; past

Morpeth; by Warkworth, and its castle, and hermitage; over the Coquet stream, beloved by the friends of gentle Izaak Walton; on, by the sea-side – almost along the very sands – with the refreshing sea-breeze, and the murmuring splash of the breakers – the Misses Green giving way to childish delight at this their first glimpse of the sea; on, over the Aln, and past Alnwick; and so on, still further North, to a certain little station, which is the terminus of their railway journey, and the signal of their deliverance from the black hole.

There, on the platform is Mr Honeywood, looking hale and happy, and delighted to receive his posse of visitors; and there, outside the little station, is the carriage and dog-cart, and a spring-cart for the luggage. Charles Larkyns takes possession of the dog-cart, in company with Mary and Fanny Green, and little Mr Bouncer; while Huz and Buz, released from their weary imprisonment, caracole gracefully around the vehicle. Mr Honeywood takes the reins of his own carriage; Mr Verdant Green mounts the box beside him; Miss Bouncer and Miss Helen Green take possession of the open interior of the carriage; the spring-cart, with the servants and luggage, follows in the rear; and off they go.

But, though the two blood-horses are by no means slow of action, and do, in truth, gallop apace like fiery-footed steeds, yet to Mr Verdant Green's anxious mind they seem to make but slow progress; and the magnificent country through which they pass offers but slight charms for his abstracted thoughts; until (at last) they come in sight of a broken mountain-range, and Mr Honeywood, pointing with his whip, exclaims, 'Yon's the Cheevyuts, as they say in these parts; there are the Cheviot Hills; and there, just where you see that gleam of light on a white house among some trees – there is Honeywood Hall.'

Did Mr Verdant Green remove his eyes from that object of attraction, save when intervening hills, for a time, hid it from his view? did he, when they neared it, and he saw its landscape beauties bathed in the golden splendours of a July sunset, did he think it a very paradise that held within its bowers the Peri of his heart's worship? did he – as they passed the lodge, and drove up an avenue of firs – did he scan the windows of the house, and immediately determine in his own mind which was HER window, oblivious to the fact that SHE might sleep on the other side of the building? did he, as they pulled up at the door, scrutinise the female figures who were there to receive them, and experience a feeling made up of doubt and certainty, that there was one who, though not present, was waiting near with a heart beating as anxiously as his own? did he make wild remarks, and return incoherent answers, until the long-expected moment had come that brought him face to face with the adorable Patty? did he envy Charles Larkyns for possessing and practising the cousinly privilege of bestowing a kiss upon her rosy cheeks? and did he, as he pressed her hand, and marked the heightened glow of her happy face, did he feel within his heart an exultant thrill of joy as the fervid thought fired his brain – one day she may be mine?

Perhaps!

CHAPTER II

*Mr Verdant Green delivers Miss Patty Honeywood from
the Horns of a Dilemma.*

EVEN if Mr Verdant Green
had not been filled with the
peculiarly pleasurable sensations to which allusion has
just been made, it is yet exceedingly probable that he
would have found his visit to
Honeywood Hall one of those
agreeable and notable events
which the memory of after-
years invests with the *couleur de rose*.

In the first place – even if Miss Patty was left out of the question
– everyone was so particularly attentive to him, that all his wants, as
regarded amusement and occupation, were promptly supplied, and
not a minute was allowed to hang heavily upon his hands. And, in the
second place, the country, and its people and customs, had so much
freshness and peculiarity, that he could not stir abroad without meeting with novelty. New ideas were constantly received; and other sensations of a still more delightful nature were daily deepened. Thus the
time passed pleasantly away at Honeywood Hall, and the hours chased
each other with flying feet.

Mr. Honeywood was a squire, or laird; and though the prospect
from the Hall was far too extensive to allow of his being monarch of
all that he surveyed, yet he was the proprietor of no inconsiderable
portion. The small village of Honeybourn – which brought its one
wide street of long, low, lime-washed houses hard by the Hall – owned
no other master than Mr. Honeywood; and all its inhabitants were, in
one way or other, his labourers. They had their own blacksmith,
shoemaker, tailor, and carpenter; they maintained a general shop of the
tea-coffee-tobacco-and-snuff genus; and they lived as one family,

entirely independent of any other village. In fact, the villages in that district were as sparingly distributed as are 'livings' among poor curates, and, when met with, were equally as small; and so it happened, that as the landowners usually resided, like Mr Honeywood, among their own people, a gentleman would occasionally be as badly off for a neighbour, as though he had been a resident in the backwoods of Canada. This evil, however, was productive of good, in that it set aside the possibility of a deliberate interchange of formal morning-calls, and obliged neighbours to be hospitable to each other, *sans cérémonie*, and with all good fellowship. To drive fifteen, twenty, or even five-and-twenty miles, to a dinner party was so common an occurrence, that it excited surprise only in a stranger, whose wonderment at this voluntary fatigue would be quickly dispelled on witnessing the hearty hospitality and friendly freedom that made a north country visit so enjoyable, and robbed the dinner party of its ordinary character of an English solemnity.

Close to Honeybourn village was the Squire's model farm, with its wide-spreading yards and buildings, and its comfortable bailiff's house. In a morning at sunrise, when our Warwickshire friends were yet in bed, such of them as were light sleepers would hear a not very melodious fanfare from a cow's horn – the signal to the village that the day's work was begun, which signal was repeated at sunset. This old custom possessed uncommon charms for Mr Bouncer, whose only regret was that he had left behind him his celebrated tin horn. But he took to the cow-horn with the readiness of a child to a new plaything; and, having placed himself under the instruction of the Northumbrian Kœnig, was speedily enabled to sound his octaves and go the complete

unicorn (as he was wont to express it, in his peculiarly figurative eastern language) with a still more astounding effect than he had done on his former instrument. The little gentleman always made a point of thus signalling the times of the arrival and departure of the post – greatly to the delight of small Jock Muir, who, girded with his letter-bag, and mounted on a highly-trained donkey, rode to and fro to the neighbouring post-town.

Although Mr Verdant Green was not (according to Mr Bouncer) 'a bucolical party', and had not any very amazing taste for agriculture, he nevertheless could not but feel interested in what he saw around him. To one who was so accustomed to the small enclosures and timbered hedge-rows of the midland counties, the country of the Cheviots appeared in a grand, though naked aspect, like some stalwart gladiator of the stern old times. The fields were of large extent; and it was no uncommon sight to see, within one boundary fence, a hundred acres of wheat, rippling into mimic waves, like some inland sea. The flocks and herds, too, were on a grand scale; men counted their sheep, not by tens, but by hundreds. Everything seemed to be influenced, as it were, by the large character of the scenery. The green hills, with their short sweet grass, gave good pasture for the fleecy tribe, who were dotted over the sward in almost countless numbers; and Mr Verdant Green was as much gratified with 'the silly sheep' as with anything else that he witnessed in that land of novelty. To see the shepherd, with his bonnet and grey plaid, and long slinging step, walking first, and the flock following him – to hear him call the sheep by name, and to perceive how he knew them individually, and how they each and all would answer to his voice, was a realisation of Scripture reading, and a northern picture of Eastern life.

The head shepherd, old Andrew Graham – an active youth whose long snowy locks had been bleached by the snows of eighty winters – was an especial favourite of Mr Verdant Green's, who would never tire of his company, or of his anecdotes of his marvellous dogs. His cottage was at a distance from the village, up in a snug hollow of one of the hills. There he lived, and there had been brought up his six sons, and as many daughters. Of the latter, two were out at service in noble families of the county; one was maid to the Misses Honeywood, and the three others were at home. How they and the other inmates of the cottage were housed, was a mystery; for, although old Andrew was of a superior condition in life to the other cottagers of Honeybourn, yet his domicile was like all the rest in its arrangements and accommodation. It was one moderately large room, fitted up with cupboards, in which, one above another, were berths, like to those on board a steamer. In what way the morning and evening toilettes were performed was a still greater mystery to our Warwickshire friends; nevertheless, the good-looking trio of damsels were always to be found neat, clean, and presentable; and, as their mother one day proudly remarked, they were 'douce, sonsy bairns, wi' weel-faur'd nebs; and, for puir folks, would be weel tochered'. Upon which our hero said 'Indeed!' which, as he had not the slightest idea what the good woman meant, was, perhaps, the wisest remark that he could have made.

One of them was generally to be found spinning at her muckle wheel, retiring and advancing to the music of its cheerful hum, the while her spun thread was rapidly coiled up on the spindle. The others, as they busied themselves in their household duties, or brightened up the delf and pewter, and set it out on the shelf to its best advantage, would join in some plaintive Scotch ballad, with such good taste and skill that our friends would frequently love to linger within hearing, though out of sight. But these artless ditties were sometimes specially sung for them when they paid the cottage-room

a visit, and sat around its canopied, projecting fireplace. For old Andrew was a great smoker; and little Mr Bouncer was exceedingly fond of waylaying him on his return home, and 'blowing a cloud' with so loquacious and novel a companion. And Mr Verdant Green sometimes joined him in these visits; on which occasions, as harmony was the order of the day, he would do his best to further it by singing 'Marble Halls', or any other song that his limited repertoire could boast; while old Andrew would burst into 'Tullochgorum', or do violence to 'get up and bar the door'.

It must be confessed, that the conversation at such times was sustained not without difficulty. Old Andrew, his wife, and the major portion of his family, were barely able to understand the language of their guests, whom they persisted in generalising as 'cannie Soothrons'; while the guests, on their part, could not altogether arrive at the meaning of observations that were couched in the most incomprehensible *patois* that was ever invented. It was 'neither fish, flesh, nor good red herring', although it was flavoured with the Northumbrian burr, and mixed with a species of Scotch; and the historian of these pages would feel almost as much difficulty in setting down this north-Northumbrian dialect, as he would do were he to attempt to reduce to words the bird-like chatter of the Bosjesmen.

When, for example, the bewigged Mr Bouncer – 'the laddie wi' the black pow', as they called him – was addressed as 'Hinny! jist come ben, and crook yer hough on the settle, and het yersen by the chimney-lug', it was as much by action as by word that he understood an invitation to be seated; though the 'wet yer thrapple wi' a drap o' whuskie, mon!' was easier of comprehension when accompanied with the presentation of the whiskey-horn. In like manner, when Mr Verdant Green's arrival was announced by the furious barking of the faithful dogs, the apology that 'the camstary breutes of dougs would not steek their clat-

terin' gabs', was accepted as an ample explanation, more from the dogs being quieted than from the lucidity of the remark that explained their uproar.

There was one class of lady-labourers, peculiar to that part of the country, who were called Bondagers – great strapping damsels of three or four woman-power, whose occupation it was to draw water, and perform some of the rougher duties attendant upon agricultural pursuits. The sturdy legs of these young ladies were equipped in greaves of leather, which protected them from the cutting attacks of stubble, thistles, and all other lacerating specimens of botany, and their

exuberant figures were clad in buskins, and many-coloured garments, that were not long enough to conceal their greaves and clod-hopping boots. Altogether, these young women, when engaged at their ordinary avocations by the side of a spring, formed no unpicturesque subject for the sketcher's pencil, and might have been advantageously transferred to canvas by many an artist who travels to greater distances in search of lesser novelties.*

But many peculiar subjects for the pencil might there have been found. One day when they were all going to see the ewe-milking (which of itself would have furnished material for a host of sketches), they suddenly came upon the following scene. Round by the gable of a cottage was seated a shock-headed rustic Absalom, and standing over

---

*In north-Northumberland, farm-labourers are usually hired by the year – from Whitsunday to Whitsunday – and are paid mostly in kind; so many bolls of oats, barley, and peas; so much flax and wheat; the keep of a cow; and the addition of a few pounds in money. Every hind or labourer is bound, in return for his house, to provide a woman-labourer to the farmer, for so much a day throughout the year – which is usually tenpence a day in summer, and eightpence in winter; and as it often happens that he has none of his own family fit for the work, he has to hire a woman, at large wages, to do it. As the demand is greater than the supply there is not always a strict enquiry into the 'bondager's' character. As with the case of hop-pickers – whom these bondagers somewhat resemble both socially and morally – they are oftentimes the inhabitants of densely-populated towns, who are tempted to live a brief agricultural life, not so much from the temptation of the wages, as from the desire to pass a summer-time in the country.

him was another rustic, who, with a pair of shears, was acting as an amateur Tonson, and was earnestly engaged in reducing the other's profuse head of hair; an occupation upon which he busied himself with more zeal than discretion. Of this little scene Miss Patty Honeywood forthwith made a memorandum.

For Miss Patty possessed the enviable accomplishment of sketching from nature; and, leaving the beaten track of young-lady figure-artists, who usually limit their efforts to chalk-heads and crayon smudges, she boldly launched into the more difficult, but far more pleasing undertaking of delineating the human form divine from the very life. Mr Verdant Green found this sketching from nature to be so pretty a pastime, that though unable of himself to produce the feeblest specimen of art, he yet took the greatest delight in watching the facility with which Miss Patty's taper fingers transferred to paper the *vraisemblance* of a pair of sturdy Bondagers, or the miniature reflection of a grand landscape. Happily for him, also, by way of an excuse for bestowing his company upon Miss Patty, he was enabled to be of some use to her in carrying her sketching-block and box of moist watercolours, or in bringing to her water from a neighbouring spring, or in sharpening her pencils. On these occasions Verdant would have preferred their being left to the sole enjoyment of each other's company; but this was not so to be, for they were always favoured with the attendance of at least a third person.

But (at last!) on one happy day, when the bright sunshine was reflected in Miss Patty Honeywood's bright-beaming face, Mr Verdant Green found himself wandering forth, 'All in the blue, unclouded weather', with his heart's idol, and no third person to intrude upon their duet. The alleged purport of the walk was that Miss Patty might sketch the ruined church of Lasthorpe, which was about two miles distant from the Hall. To reach it they had to follow the course of the Swirl, which ran through the Squire's grounds.

The Swirl was a brawling, picturesque stream; at one place narrowing into threads of silver between lichen-covered stones and fragments of rock; at another place flowing on in deep pools –

> Wimpling, dimpling, staying never –
> Lisping, gurgling, ever going,

> Sipping, slipping, ever flowing,
> Toying round the polish'd stone;*

fretting 'in rough, shingly shallows wide', and then 'bickering down the sunny day'. On one day, it might, in places, and with the aid of stepping-stones, be crossed dryshod; and within twenty-four hours it might be swelled by mountain torrents into a river wider than the Thames at Richmond. This sudden growth of the 'Infant of the weeping hills' was the reason why the high road was carried over the Swirl by a bridge of ten arches – a circumstance which had greatly excited little Mr Bouncer's ideas of the ridiculous when he perceived the narrow stream scarcely wide enough to wet the sides of one of the arches of the great bridge that straggled over it, like a railway viaduct over a canal. But, ere his visit to Honeywood Hall had come to an end, the little gentleman had more than once seen the Swirl swollen to its fullest dimensions, and been enabled to recognise the use of the bridge, and the full force of the local expression – 'the waeter is grit'.

As Verdant and Miss Patty made their way along the bank of this most changeable stream, they came upon Mr Charles Larkyns knee-

deep in it, equipped in his wading-boots and fishing-dress, and industriously whipping the water for trout. The Swirl was a famous trout-stream, and Mr Honeywood's coachman was a noted fisherman, and was accustomed to pass many of his nights fishing the stream with a white moth. It appeared that the finny inhabitants of the Swirl were as fond of whitebait as are Cabinet Ministers and London aldermen; for the coachman's deeds of darkness invariably resulted in the production of a fine dish of freshly-caught trout for the breakfast-table.

'It must be hard work,' said Verdant to his friend, as they stopped awhile to watch him; 'it must be hard work to make your way against

---

*Thomas Aird.

the stream, and to clamber in and out among the rocks and stones.'

'Not at all hard work,' was Charles Larkyns's reply, 'but play. Play, too, in more senses than one. See! I have just struck a fish. Watch, while I play him. "The play's the thing!" Wait awhile and you'll see me land him, or I'm much mistaken.'

So they waited awhile and watched this fisherman at play, until he had triumphantly landed his fish, and then they pursued their way.

Miss Patty had great conversational abilities and immense power of small talk, so that Verdant felt quite at ease in her society, and found his natural timidity and quiet bashfulness to be greatly diminished, even if they were not altogether put on one side. They were always such capital friends, and Miss Patty was so kind and thoughtful in making Verdant appear to the best advantage, and in looking over any little *gaucheries* to which his bashfulness might give birth, that it is not to be wondered at if the young gentleman should feel great delight in her society, and should seek for it at every opportunity. In fact, Miss Patty Honeywood was beginning to be quite necessary to Mr Verdant Green's happy existence. It may be that the young lady was not altogether ignorant of this, but was enabled to read the young man's state of mind, and to judge pretty accurately of his inward feelings, from those minute details of outward evidence which womankind are so quick to mark, and so skilful in tracing to their true source. It may be, also, that the young lady did not choose either to check these feelings or to alter this state of mind – which she certainly ought to have done if she was solicitous for her companion's happiness, and was unable to increase it in the way that he wished.

But, at any rate, with mutual satisfaction for the present, they strolled together along the Swirl's rocky banks, and passing into a large enclosure, they advanced midway through the fields to a spot which seemed a suitable one for Miss Patty's purpose. The brawling stream made a good foreground for the picture, which, on the one side, was shut in by a steep hill rising precipitously from the water's rough bed, and on the other side opened out into a mountainous landscape, having in the near view the ruined church of Lasthorpe, with the still more ruinous minister's house, a fir plantation, and a rude bridge; with a middle distance of bold, sheep-dotted hills; and for a background the 'sow-backed' Cheviot itself.

Miss Patty had made her outline of this scene, and was preparing to wash it in, when, as her companion came up from the stream with a little tin can of water, he saw, to his equal terror and amazement, a huge bull of the most uninviting aspect stealthily approaching the seated figure of the unconscious young lady. Mr Verdant Green looked hastily around and at once perceived the danger that menaced his fair friend. It was evident that the bull had come up from the further end of the large enclosure, the while they had been too occupied to observe his stealthy approach. No one was in sight save Charles Larkyns, who was too far off to be of any use. The nearest gate was about a hundred and fifty yards distant; and the bull was so placed that he could overtake them before they would be able to reach it. Overtake them! – yes! But suppose they separated? then, as the brute could not go two ways at once, there would be a chance for one of them to get through the gate in safety. Love, which induces people to take extraordinary steps, prompted Mr Verdant Green to jump at a conclusion. He determined, with less display but more sincerity than melodramatic heroes, to save Miss Patty, or 'perish in the attempt'.

She was seated on the rising bank altogether ignorant of the presence of danger; and, as Verdant returned to her with the tin can of water, she received him with a happy smile, and a gush of pleasant small talk, which our hero immediately repressed by saying, 'Don't be frightened – there is no danger – but there is a bull coming towards us. Walk quietly to that gate, and keep your face towards him as much as possible, and don't let him see that you are afraid of him. I will take off his attention till you are safe at the gate, and then I can wade through the stream and get out of his reach.'

Miss Patty had at once sprung to her feet, and her smile had changed to a terrified expression. 'Oh, but he will hurt you!' she cried, 'do come with me. It is papa's bull Roarer; he is very savage. I can't think what brings him here – he is generally up at the bailiff's. Pray do come, I can take care of myself.'

Miss Patty in her agitation and anxiety had taken hold of Mr Verdant Green's hand; but, although the young gentleman would at any other time have very willingly allowed her to retain possession of it, on the present occasion he disengaged it from her clasp, and said, 'Pray don't lose time, or it will be too late for both of us. I assure you that I can easily take care of myself. Now do go, pray; quietly, but quickly.' So Miss Patty, with an earnest, searching gaze into her companion's face, did as he bade her, and retreated with her face to the foe.

In a few seconds, however, the object of her movement had dawned upon Mr Roarer's dull understanding, upon which discovery he set up a bellow of fury, and stamped the ground in very undignified wrath. But, more than this, like a skilful general who has satisfactorily worked out the forty-seventh proposition of the First Book of Euclid, and knows therefrom that the square of the hypotenuse equals both that of the base and perpendicular, he unconsciously commenced the solution of the problem, by making a galloping charge in the direction of the gate to which Miss Patty was hastening. Thereupon, Mr Verdant Green, perceiving the young lady's peril, deliberately ran towards Mr Roarer, shouting and brandishing the sketch-book. Mr Roarer paused in wonder and perplexity. Mr Verdant Green shouted and advanced; Miss Patty steadily retreated. After a few moments of indecision Mr Roarer abandoned his design of pursuing the petticoats, and resolved that the gentleman should be his first victim. Accordingly he sounded his trumpet for the conflict, gave another roar and a stamp, and then ran towards Mr Verdant Green, who, having picked up a large stone, threw it dexterously into Mr Roarer's face, which brought that broad-chested gentleman to a stand-still of astonishment and a search for the missile. Of this Mr Verdant Green took advantage, and made a Parthian retreat. Glancing towards Miss Patty he saw that she was within thirty yards of the gate, and in a minute or two would be in safety – saved through his means!

A bellow from Mr Roarer's powerful lungs prevented him for the present from pursuing this delightful theme. In another moment the bull charged, and Mr Verdant Green – braced up, as it were, to energetic proceedings by the screams with which Miss Patty had now begun to shrilly echo Mr Roarer's deep-mouthed bellowings – waited for his approach, and then, as the bull rushed on him – like a massive rock hurled forward by an avalanche – he leaped aside, nimble as a doubling hare. As he did so, he threw down his wide-awake, which the irate Mr Roarer forthwith fell upon, and tossed, and tossed, and tore into shreds. By this time, Verdant had reached the bank of the Swirl; but before he could proceed further, the bull was upon him again. Verdant was prepared for this, and had taken off his coat. As the bull dashed heavily towards him, with head bent wickedly to the ground, Verdant again doubled, and, with the dexterity of a matador, threw his coat upon the horns. Blinded by this, Mr Roarer's headlong career was temporarily checked; and it was three minutes before he had torn to shreds the imaginary body of his enemy; but this three minutes' pause was of very great importance, and in all probability prevented the memoirs of Mr Verdant Green from coming to an untimely end at this portion of the narrative.

Miss Patty's continued screams had been signals of distress that had not only brought up Charles Larkyns, but four labourers also, who were working in a field within ear-shot. This *corps de reserve* ran up to the spot with all speed, shouting as they did so, in order to distract Mr Roarer's attention. By this time Mr Verdant Green had waded into the water, and was making the best of his way across the Swirl, in order that he might reach the precipitous hill to the right; up this he could scramble and bid defiance to Mr Roarer. But there is many a slip 'tween cup and lip. Poor Verdant chanced to make a stepping-stone of a treacherous boulder, and fell headlong into the water; and ere he could regain his feet, the bull had plunged with a bellow into the stream, and was within a yard of his prostrate form, when . . .

When you may imagine Mr Verdant Green's delight and Miss Patty Honeywood's thankfulness at seeing one of the labourers run into the stream, and strike the bull a heavy stroke with a sharp hoe, the pain of which wound caused Mr Roarer to suddenly wheel round and engage with his new adversary, who followed up his advantage, and cut into his enemy with might and main. Then Charles Larkyns and the other three labourers came up, and the bull was prevented from doing an injury to anyone until a farm-servant had arrived upon the scene with a strong halter, when Mr Roarer, somewhat spent with wrath, and suffering from considerable depression of animal spirits, was conducted to the obscure retirement and littered ease of the bull-house.

This little adventure has been recorded here, inasmuch as from it was forged, by the hand of Cupid, a golden link in our hero's chain of fate; for to this occurrence Miss Patty attached no slight importance. She exalted Mr Verdant Green's conduct on this occasion into an act of heroism worthy to be ranked with far more notable deeds of valour. She looked upon him as a Bayard who had chivalrously risked his life in the cause of – love, was it? or only of – a lady. Her gratitude, she considered, ought to be very great to one who had, at so great a venture, preserved her from so horrible a death. For that she would have been dreadfully gored, and would have lost her life, if she had not been rescued by Mr Verdant Green, Miss Patty had most fully and unalterably decided – which, certainly, might have been the case.

At any rate, our hero had no reason to regret that portion of his life's drama in which Mr Roarer had made his appearance.

CHAPTER III

Mr Verdant Green studies ye Manners and Customs of ye Natyves.

MISS Patty Honeywood was not only distinguished for unlimited powers of conversation, but was also equally famous for her equestrian abilities. She and her sister were the first horsewomen in that part of the county; and, if their father had permitted, they would have been delighted to ride to hounds, and to cross-country with the foremost flight, for they had pluck enough for anything. They had such light hands and good seats, and in every respect rode so well, that, as a matter of course, they looked well – never better, perhaps, than – when on horseback. Their bright, happy faces – which were far more beautiful in their piquant irregularities of feature, and gave one far more pleasure in the contemplation than if they had been moulded in the coldly chiselled forms of classic beauty – appeared with no diminution of charms, when set off by their pretty felt riding-hats; and their full, firm, and well-rounded figures were seen to the greatest advantage when clad in the graceful dress that passes by the name of a riding-habit.

Every morning, after breakfast, the two young ladies were accustomed to visit the stables, where they had interviews with their respective steeds – steeds and mistresses appearing to be equally gratified thereby. It is perhaps needless to state that during Mr Verdant Green's sojourn at Honeywood Hall, Miss Patty's stable calls were generally made in his company.

Such rides as they took in those happy days – wild, picnic sort of rides, over country equally as wild and removed from formality – rides by duets and rides in duodecimos; sometimes a solitary couple or two; sometimes a round dozen of them, scampering and racing over the hill and heather, with startled grouse and black-cock skirring up from under the very hoofs of the equally startled horses; rides by tumbling streams, like the Swirl – splashing through them, with pulled-up or draggled habits – then cantering on 'over bank, bush, and scaur', like so many fair Ellens and young Lochinvars – clambering up very precipices, and creeping down break-neck hills – laughing and talking, and singing, and whistling, and even (so far as Mr Bouncer was concerned) blowing cows' horns! What vagabond, rollicking rides were those! What a healthy contrast to the necessarily formal, groom-attended canter on Society's Rotten Row!

A legion of dogs accompanied them on these occasions; a miscellaneous pack composed of Masters Huz and Buz (in great spirits at finding themselves in such capital quarters), a black Newfoundland (answering to the name of 'Nigger'), a couple of Setters (with titles from the heathen mythology – 'Juno' and 'Flora'), a ridiculous-looking, bandy-legged otter-hound (called 'Gripper'), a wiry, rat-catching terrier ('Nipper'), and two silky-haired, long-backed, short-legged, sharp-nosed, bright-eyed, pepper-and-salt Skye-terriers, who respectively answered to the names of 'Whisky' and 'Toddy', and were the property of the Misses Honeywood. The lordly shepherd's dogs, whom they encountered on their journeys, would have nothing to do with such a medley of unruly scamps, but turned from their overtures of friendship with patrician disdain. They routed up rabbits; they turned out hedgehogs; and, at their approach, they made the game fly with a WHIRR-R-R-R arranged as a *diminuendo*.

These free-and-easy equestrian expeditions were not only agreeable to Mr Verdant Green's feelings, but they were also useful to him as so many lessons of horsemanship, and so greatly advanced him in the practice of that noble science, that the admiring Squire one day said to him – 'I'll tell you what, Verdant! before we've done with you, we shall make you ride like a Shafto!' At which high eulogium Mr Verdant Green blushed, and made an inward resolution that, as soon as he had returned home, he would subscribe to the Warwickshire hounds, and make his appearance in the field.

On Sundays the Honeywood party usually rode and drove to the church of a small market-town, some seven or eight miles distant. If it was a wet day, they walked to the ruined church of Lasthope – the place Miss Patty was sketching when disturbed by Mr Roarer. Last-hope was in lay hands; and its lay rector, who lived far away, had so little care for the edifice, or the proper conduct of divine service, that

he allowed the one to continue in its ruins, and suffered the other to be got through anyhow or not at all – just as it happened. Clergymen were engaged to perform the service (there was but one each day) at the lowest price of the clerical market. Occasionally it was announced, in the vernacular of the district, that there would be no church, 'because the priest had gone for the sea-bathing', or because the waters were out, and the priest could not get across. As a matter of course, in consequence of the uncertainty of finding anyone to perform the service when they had got to church, and of the slovenly way in which the service was scrambled through when they had got a clergyman there, the congregation generally preferred attending the large Presbyterian meeting-house, which was about two miles from Last-hope. Here, at any rate, they met with the reverse of coldness in the conduct of the service.

Mr Verdant Green and his male friends strayed there one Sunday for curiosity's sake, and found a minister of indefatigable eloquence and enviable power of lungs, who had arrived at such a pitch of heat, from the combined effects of the weather and his own exertions, that in the very middle of his discourse – and literally in the heat of it – he paused to divest himself of his gown, heavily braided with serge and velvet, and, hanging it over the side of the pulpit ('the pilput', his congregation called it), mopped his head with his handkerchief, and then pursued his theme like a giant refreshed. At this stage in the proceedings, little Mr Bouncer became in a high state of pleasurable excitement, from the expectation that the minister would next divest himself of his coat, and would struggle through the rest of his argument in his shirt-sleeves; but Mr Bouncer's improper wishes were not gratified.

The sermon was so extremely metaphorical, was founded on such abstruse passages, and was delivered in so broad a dialect, that it was *caviare* to Mr Verdant Green and his friends; but it seemed to be far otherwise with the attentive and crowded congregation, who relieved their minister at intervals by loud bursts of singing, that were impressive from their fervency though not particularly harmonious to a delicately-musical ear. Near to the close of the service there was a collection, which induced Mr Bouncer to whisper to Verdant – as an axiom deduced from his long experience – that 'you never come to a strange place, but what you are sure to drop in for a collection'; but, on finding that it was a weekly offering, and that no one was expected to give more than a copper, the little gentleman relented, and cheerfully dropped a piece of silver into the wooden box. It was astonishing to see the throngs of people, that, in so thinly inhabited a district, could be assembled at this meeting-house. Though it seemed almost incredible to our midland-county friends, yet not a few of these poor, simple, earnest-minded people would walk from a distance of fifteen miles, starting at an early hour, coming by easy stages, and bringing with them their dinner, so as to enable them to stay for the afternoon service. On the Sunday mornings the red cloaks and grey plaids of these pious men and women might be seen dotting the green hillsides, and slowly moving towards the gaunt and grim red brick meeting-house. And around it, on great occasions, were tents pitched for the between-service accommodation of the worshippers.

Both they and it contrasted, in every way, with the ruined church of Lasthope, whose worship seemed also to have gone to ruin with the uncared-for edifice. Its aisles had tumbled down, and their material had been rudely built up within the arches of the nave. The church was thus converted into the non-ecclesiastical form of a parallelogram, and was fitted up with the very rudest and ugliest of deal enclosures, which were dignified with the name of pews, but ought to have been termed pens.

During the time of Mr Verdant Green's visit, the service at this ecclesiastical ruin was performed by a clergyman who had apparently been selected for the duty from his harmonious resemblance to the place; for he also was an ecclesiastical ruin – a schoolmaster in holy orders, who, having to slave hard all through the working-days of the week, had to work still harder on the day of rest. For, first, the Ruin had to ride his stumbling old pony a distance of twelve miles (and twelve *such* miles!) to Lasthope, where he stabled it (bringing the feed of corn in his pocket, and leading it to drink at the Swirl) in the dilapidated stable of the tumbled-down rectory-house. Then he had to get through the morning service without any loss of time, to enable him to ride eight miles in another direction (eating his sandwich dinner as he went along), where he had to take the afternoon duty and occasional services at a second church. When this was done, he might find his way home as well as he could, and enjoy with his family as much of the day of rest as he had leisure and strength for. The stipend that the Ruin received for his labours was greatly below the wages given to a butler by the lay rector, who pocketed a very nice income by this respectable transaction. But the butler was a stately edifice in perfect repair, both outside and in, so far as clothes and food went; and the parson was an ill-conditioned ruin left to moulder away in an obscure situation, without even the ivy of luxuriance to make him graceful and picturesque.

Mr Honeywood's family were the only 'respectable' persons who occasionally attended the Ruin's ministrations in Lasthope church. The other people who made up the scanty congregation were old Andrew Graham and his children, and a few of the poorer sort of Honeybourn. They all brought their dogs with them as a matter of course. On entering the church the men hung up their bonnets on a row of pegs provided for that purpose, and fixed, as an ecclesiastical ornament, along the western wall of the church. They then took their places in their pens, accompanied by their dogs, who usually behaved with remarkable propriety, and, during the sermon, set their masters an example of watchfulness. On one occasion the proceedings were interrupted by a rat hunt; the dogs gave tongue, and leaped the pews in the excitement of the chase – their masters followed them and laid about them with their sticks – and when with difficulty order had been restored, the service was proceeded with. It must be confessed that Mr Bouncer was so badly disposed as to wish for a repetition of this scene; but (happily) he was disappointed.

The choir at Lasthope Church was centred in the person of the clerk, who apparently sang tunes of his own composing, in which the congregation joined at their discretion, though usually to different airs. The result was a discordant struggle, through which the clerk bravely maintained his own until he had exhausted himself, when he shut up his book and sat down, and the congregation had to shut up also. During the singing the intelligence of the dogs was displayed in their giving a stifled utterance to howls of anguish, which were repeated *ad libitum* throughout the hymn; but as this was a customary proceeding it attracted no attention, unless a dog expressed his sufferings more loudly than was wont, when he received a clout from his master's staff that silenced him, and sent him under the pew-seat, as to a species of ecclesiastical St Helena.

Such was Lasthope Church, its Ruin, and its service; and, as may be imagined from these notes which the veracious historian has thought fit to chronicle, Mr Verdant Green found that his Sundays in Northumberland produced as much novelty as the week-days.

CHAPTER IV

Mr Verdant Green endeavours to say Snip to someone's Snap.

THERE was a gate in the kitchen-garden of Honeywood Hall, that led into an orchard; and in this orchard there was a certain apple-tree that had assumed one of those peculiarities of form to which the children of Pomona are addicted. After growing upright for about a foot and a half, it had suddenly shot out at right angles, with a gentle upward slope for a length of between three and four feet, and had then again struck up into the perpendicular. It thus formed a natural orchard seat, capable of holding two persons comfortably – provided that they regarded a close proximity as comfortable sitting.

One day Miss Patty directed Verdant's attention to this vagary of nature. 'This is one of my favourite haunts,' she said. 'I often steal here on a hot day with some work or a book. You see this upper branch makes quite a little table, and I can rest my book upon it. It is so pleasant to be under the shade here, with the fruit or blossoms over one's head; and it is so snug and retired, and out of the way of everyone.'

'It is very snug – and very retired,' said Mr Verdant Green; and he thought that now would be the very time to put in execution a project that had for some days past been haunting his brain.

'When Kitty and I', said Miss Patty, 'have any secrets we come here and tell them to each other while we sit at our work. No one can hear what we say; and we are quite snug all to ourselves.'

Very odd, thought Verdant, that they should fix on this particular spot for confidential communications, and take the trouble to come here to make them, when they could do so in their own rooms at the house. And yet it isn't such a bad spot either.

'Try how comfortable a seat it is!' said Miss Patty.

Mr Verdant Green began to feel hot. He sat down, however, and tested the comforts of the seat, much in the same way as he would try the spring of a lounging chair, and apparently with a like result, for he said, 'Yes, it *is* very comfortable – very comfortable indeed.'

'I thought you'd like it,' said Miss Patty; 'and you see how nicely the branches droop all round: they make it quite an arbour. If Kitty had been here with me I think you would have had some trouble to have found us.'

'I think I should; it is quite a place to hide in,' said Verdant. But the young lady and gentleman must have been speaking with the spirit of ostriches, and have imagined that, when they had hidden their heads, they had altogether concealed themselves from observation; for the branches of the apple-tree only drooped low enough to conceal the upper part of their figures, and left the rest exposed to view. 'Won't you sit down, also?' asked Verdant, with a gasp and a sensation in his head as though he had been drinking champagne too freely.

'I'm afraid there's scarcely room for me,' pleaded Miss Patty.

'Oh yes, there is, indeed! pray sit down.'

So she sat down on the lower part of the trunk. Mr Verdant Green glanced rapidly round and perceived that they were quite alone, and partly shrouded from view. The following highly interesting conversation then took place.

He. 'Won't you change places with me? you'll slip off.'

She. 'No – I think I can manage.'

He. 'But you can come closer.'

She. 'Thanks.' (*She comes closer.*)

He. Isn't that more comfortable?'

She. 'Yes – very much.'

He. (*Very hot, and not knowing what to say*) 'I–I think you'll slip!'

She. 'Oh no! it's very comfortable indeed.'

(That is to say – thinks Mr Verdant Green – that sitting BY ME is very comfortable. Hurrah!)

She. 'It's very hot, don't you think?'

He. 'How very odd! I was just thinking the same.'

She. 'I think I shall take my hat off – it is so warm. Dear me! how stupid! – the strings are in a knot.'

He. 'Let me see if I can untie them for you.'

She. 'Thanks! no! I can manage.' (*But she cannot.*)

He. 'You'd better let me try! now do!'

She. 'Oh thanks! but I'm sorry you should have the trouble.'

He. 'No trouble at all. Quite a pleasure.'

(In a very hot condition of mind and fingers, Mr Verdant Green then endeavoured to release the strings from their entanglement. But all in vain: he tugged, and pulled, and only made matters worse. Once or twice in the struggle his hands touched Miss Patty's chin; and no highly-charged electrical machine could have imparted a shock greater than that tingling sensation of pleasure which Mr Verdant Green experienced when his fingers, for the fraction of a second, touched Miss Patty's soft dimpled chin. Then there was her beautiful neck, so white, and with such blue veins! he had an irresistible desire to stroke it for its very smoothness – as one loves to feel the polish of marble, or the glaze of wedding-cards – instead of employing his hands in fumbling at the brown ribands, whose knots became more complicated than ever. Then there was her happy rosy face, so close to which his own was brought; and her bright, laughing, hazel eyes, in which, as he timidly looked up, he saw little daguerreotypes of himself. Would that he could retain such a photographer by his side through life! Miss Bouncer's camera was as nothing compared with the *camera lucida* of those clear eyes, that shone upon him so truthfully, and mirrored for him such pretty pictures. And what with these eyes, and the face, and the chin, and the neck, Mr Verdant Green was brought into such an irretrievable state of mental excitement that he was perfectly unable to render Miss Patty the service he had proffered. But, more than that, he as yet lacked sufficient courage to carry out his darling project.

At length Miss Patty herself untied the rebellious knot, and took off her hat. The highly interesting conversation was then resumed.

She. 'What a frightful state my hair is in!' (*Loops up an escaped lock*.) 'You must think me so untidy. But out in the country, and in a place like this where no one sees us, it makes one careless of appearance.'

He. 'I like "a sweet neglect", especially in – in some people; it suits them so well. I – 'pon my word, it's very hot!'

She. 'But how much hotter it must be from under the shade. It is so pleasant here. It seems so dream-like to sit among the shadows and look out upon the bright landscape.'

He. 'It *is* – very jolly – soothing, at least!' (*A pause*.) 'I think you'll slip. Do you know, I think it will be safer if you will let me' (*here his courage fails him. He endeavours to say* 'put my arm round your waist', *but his tongue refuses to speak the words; so he substitutes*) 'change places with you.'

She. (*Rises, with a look of amused vexation.*) 'Certainly! if you so particularly wish it.' (*They change places.*) 'Now, you see, you have lost by the change. You are too tall for that end of the seat, and it did very nicely for a little body like me.'

He. (*With a thrill of delight and a sudden burst of strategy.*) 'I can hold on to this branch, if my arm will not inconvenience you.'

She. 'Oh no! not particularly:' (*he passes his right arm behind her, and takes hold of a bough*) 'but I should think it's not very comfortable for you.'

He. 'I couldn't be more comfortable, I'm sure.' (*Nearly slips off the tree, and doubles up his legs into an unpicturesque attitude highly suggestive of misery. – A pause.*) 'And do you tell your secrets here?'

She. 'My secrets? Oh, I see – you mean, with Kitty. Oh, yes! if this tree could talk, it would be able to tell such dreadful stories.'

He. 'I wonder if it could tell any dreadful stories of – *me?*'

She. 'Of you? Oh, no! Why should it? We are only severe on those we dislike.'

He. 'Then you don't dislike me?'

She. 'No! – why should we?'

He. 'Well – I don't know – but I thought you might. Well, I'm glad of that – I'm *very* glad of that. 'Pon my word, it's *very* hot! don't you think so?'

She. 'Yes! I'm burning. But I don't think we should find a cooler place.' (*Does not evince any symptoms of moving.*)

He. 'Well, p'raps we shouldn't.' (*A pause*) 'Do you know that I'm very glad you don't dislike me; because, it wouldn't have been pleasant to be disliked by you, would it?'

She. 'Well – of course, I can't tell. It depends upon one's own feelings.'

He. 'Then you don't dislike me?'

She. 'Oh dear, no! why should I?'

He. 'And if you don't dislike me, you must like me?'

She. 'Yes – at least – yes, I suppose so.'

At this stage of the proceedings, the arm that Mr Verdant Green had passed behind Miss Patty thrilled with such a peculiar sensation that his hand slipped down the bough, and the arm consequently came against Miss Patty's waist, where it rested. The necessity for saying something, the wish to make that something the something that was bursting his heart and brain, and the dread of letting it escape his lips – these three varied and mingled sensations so distracted poor Mr Verdant Green's mind, that he was no more conscious of what he was giving utterance to than if he had been talking in a dream. But there was Miss Patty by his side – a very tangible and delightful reality – playing (somewhat nervously) with those rebellious strings of her hat, which loosely hung in her hand, while the dappled shadows flickered on the waving masses of her rich brown hair – so something must be said; and, if it should lead to *the* something, why, so much the better.

Returning, therefore, to the subject of like and dislike, Mr Verdant Green managed to say, in a choking, faltering tone, 'I wonder how much you like me – very much?'

She. 'Oh, I couldn't tell – how should I? What strange questions you ask! You saved my life; so, of course, I am very, very grateful; and I hope I shall always be your friend.'

He. 'Yes, I hope so indeed – always – and something more. Do you hope the same?'

She. 'What do you mean? Hadn't we better go back to the house?'

He. 'Not just yet – it's so cool here – at least, not cool exactly, but hot – pleasanter, that is – much pleasanter here. *You* said so, you know, a little while since. Don't mind me; I always feel hot when – when I'm out of doors.'

She. 'Then we'd better go indoors.'

He. 'Pray don't – not yet – do stop a little longer.'

And the hand that had been on the bough of the tree, timidly seized Miss Patty's arm, and then naturally, but very gently, fell upon her waist. A thrill shot through Mr Verdant Green, like an electric flash, and, after traversing from his head to his heels, probably passed out safely at his boots – for it did him no harm, but, on the contrary, made him feel all the better.

'But', said the young lady, as she felt the hand upon her waist – not that she was really displeased at the proceeding, but perhaps she thought it best, under the circumstances, to say something that should have the resemblance of a veto–'but it is not necessary to hold me a prisoner.'

'It's *you* that hold *me* a prisoner!' said Mr Verdant Green, with a sudden burst of enthusiasm and blushes, and a great stress upon the pronouns.

'Now you are talking nonsense, and, if so, I must go!' said Miss Patty. And she also blushed; perhaps it was from the heat. But she removed Mr Verdant Green's hand from her waist and he was much too frightened to replace it.

'Oh! *do* stay a little!' gasped the young gentleman, with an awkward sensation of want of employment for his hands. 'You said that secrets were told here. I don't want to talk nonsense; I don't indeed; but the truth. *I've* a secret to tell you. Should you like to hear it?'

'Oh yes!' laughed Miss Patty. 'I like to hear secrets.'

Now, how very absurd it was in Mr Verdant Green wasting time in beating about the bush in this ridiculously timid way! Why could he not at once boldly secure his bird by a straight-forward shot? She did not fly out of his range – did she? And yet, here he was making himself unnecessarily hot and uncomfortable, when he might, by taking it coolly, have been at his ease in a moment. What a foolish young man! Nay, he still further lost time and evaded his purpose, by saying once again to Miss Patty – instead of immediately replying to her observation – ''Pon my word, it's uncommonly hot! don't you think so?'

Upon which Miss Patty replied, with some little chagrin, 'And was that your secret?' If she had lived in the Elizabethan era she could have adjured him with a 'Marry, come up!' which would have brought him to the point without any further trouble; but living in a Victorian age, she could do no more than say what she did, and leave the rest of her meaning to the language of the eyes.

'Don't laugh at me!' urged the bashful and weak-minded young man; 'don't laugh at me! If you only knew what I feel when you laugh at me, you'd ...'

'Cry, I dare say!' said Miss Patty, cutting him short with a merry smile, and (it must be confessed) a most wickedly-roguish expression about those bright flashing hazel eyes of hers. 'Now, you haven't told me this wonderful secret!'

'Why,' said Mr Verdant Green, slowly and deliberately – feeling that his time was coming on, and cowardly anxious still to fight off the fatal words – 'you said that you didn't dislike me; and, in fact, that you liked me very much; and ...'

But here Miss Patty cut him short again. She turned sharply round upon him, with those bright eyes and that merry face, and said, 'Oh! how *can* you say so? I never said anything of the sort!'

'Well', said Mr Verdant Green, who was now desperate, and mentally prepared to take the dreaded plunge into that throbbing sea that beats upon the strand of matrimony, 'whether *you* like *me* very much or not, *I* like *you* very much! – very much indeed! Ever since I saw you, since last Christmas, I've – I've liked you – very much indeed.'

Mr Verdant Green, in a very hot

and excited state, had, while he was speaking, timidly brought his hand once more to Miss Patty's waist; and she did not interfere with its position. In fact, she was bending down her head, and was gazing intently on another knot that she had wilfully made in her hat-strings; and she was working so violently at that occupation of untying the knot, that very probably she might not have been aware of the situation of Mr Verdant Green's hand. At any rate, her own hands were too much busied to suffer her to interfere with his.

At last the climax had arrived. Mr Verdant Green had screwed his courage to the sticking point, and had resolved to tell the secret of his love. He had got to the very edge of the precipice, and was on the point of jumping over head and ears into the stream of his destiny, and of bursting into any excited form of words that should make known his affection and his designs, when – when a vile perfume of tobacco, a sudden barking rush of Huz and Buz, and the horrid voice of little Mr Bouncer, dispelled the bright vision, dispersed his ideas, and prevented the fulfilment of his purpose.

'Holloa, Gig-lamps!' roared the little gentleman, as he removed a short pipe from his mouth, and expelled an ascending curl of smoke; 'I've been looking for you everywhere! Here we are – as Hamlet's uncle said – all in the orchard! I hope he's not been pouring poison in *your* ear, Miss Honeywood; he looks rather guilty. The Mum – I mean your mother – sent me to find you. The luncheon's been on the table more than an hour!'

Luckily for Mr Verdant Green and Miss Patty Honeywood, little Mr Bouncer rattled on without waiting for any reply to his observations, and thus enabled the young lady to somewhat recover her presence of mind, and to effect a hasty retreat from under the apple tree, and through the garden gate.

'I say, old feller,' said Mr Bouncer, as he criticised Mr Verdant Green's countenance over the bowl of his pipe, 'you look rather in a stew! What's up? My gum!' cried the little gentleman, as an idea of the truth suddenly flashed upon him; 'you don't mean to say you've been doing the spooney – what you call making love – have you?'

'Oh!' groaned the person addressed, as he followed out the train of his own ideas; 'if you *had* but have come five minutes later – or not at all! It's most provoking!'

'Well! you're a grateful bird, I don't think!' said Mr Bouncer. ' Cut after her into luncheon, and have it out over the cold mutton and pickles!'

'Oh no!' responded the luckless lover; 'I can't eat – especially before the others! I mean – I couldn't talk to her before the others. Oh! I don't know what I'm saying.'

'Well, I don't think you do, old feller!' said Mr Bouncer, puffing away at his pipe. 'I'm sorry I was in the road, though! because, though I fight shy of those sort of things myself, yet I don't want to interfere with the little weaknesses of other folks. But come and have a pipe, old feller, and we'll talk matters over, and see what pips are on the cards, and what's the state of the game.'

Now, a pipe was Mr Bouncer's panacea for every kind of indisposition, both mental and bodily.

CHAPTER V

Mr Verdant Green meets with the Green-eyed Monster.

ENTION had frequently been made by the members of the Honeywood family, but more especially by Miss Patty, of a cousin – a male cousin – to whom they all seemed to be exceedingly partial – far more partial, as Mr Verdant Green thought, with regard to Miss Patty, than he would have wished her to have been. This cousin was Mr Frederick Delaval, a son of their father's sister. According to their description, he possessed good looks, and an equivalently good fortune, with all sorts of accomplishments, both useful and ornamental; and was, in short (in their eyes at least), a very admirable Crichton of the nineteenth century.

Mr Verdant Green had heard from Miss Patty so much of her cousin Frederick, and of the pleasure they were anticipating from a visit he had promised shortly to make to them, that he had at length begun to suspect that the young lady's maiden meditations were not altogether 'fancy free', and that her thoughts dwelt upon this handsome cousin far more than was palatable to Mr Verdant Green's feelings. In the most unreasonable manner, therefore, he conceived a violent antipathy to Mr Frederick Delaval, even before he had set eyes upon him, and considered that the Honeywood family had, one and all, greatly overrated him. But these suppositions and suspicions made him doubly anxious to come to an understanding with Miss Patty before the arrival of the dreaded Adonis; and it was this thought that had helped to nerve him through the terrors of the orchard scene, and which, but for Mr Bouncer's *malapropos* intrusion, would have brought things to a crisis.

However, after he had had a talk with Mr. Bouncer, and had been fortified by that little gentleman's pithy admonitions to 'go in and win', and to 'strike while the iron's hot', and that 'faint heart never won a nice young 'ooman', he determined to seek out Miss Patty at once, and bring to an end their unfinished conversation. For this purpose he returned to the hall, where he found a great commotion, and a carriage at the door; and out of the carriage jumped a handsome young man, with a black moustache, who ran up to the open hall-door (where Miss Patty was standing with her sister), seized Miss Kitty by the hand, and placed his moustache under her nose, and then seized Miss Patty by *her* hand, and removed the moustache to beneath *her* nose! And all this unblushingly and as a matter of course, out in the sunshine, and before the servants! Mr Verdant Green retreated without having been seen, and plunging into the shrubbery, told his woes to the evergreens, and while he listened to 'The dry-tongued laurel's pattering talk', he thought, 'It is as I feared! I am nothing more to her than a simple friend.' Though, why he so morosely arrived at this idea it would be hard to say. Perhaps other jealous lovers have been similarly unreasonable and unreasoning in their conclusions, and, of their own accord, run to the dark side of the cloud, when they might have pleasantly remained within its silver lining.

But when Frederick Delaval had been seen, and heard, and made acquaintance with, Verdant, who was much too simple-hearted to dislike anyone without just grounds for so doing, entered (even after half an hour's knowledge) into the band of his admirers; and that same evening, in the drawing room, while Miss Kitty was playing one of Schulhoff's mazurkas, with her moustached cousin standing by her side, and turning over the music-leaves, Verdant privately declared, over a chess board, to Miss Patty, that Mr Frederick Delaval was the handsomest and most delightful man he had ever met. And when Miss Patty's eyes sparkled at this proof of his truth and disinterestedness, Verdant mistook the bright signals; and further misconstruing the cause why (as they continued to speak of her cousin) she made a most egregious blunder, that caused her opponent to pronounce the word 'Mated!' he regarded it as a fatal omen, more especially as Mr Frederick came to her side at that very moment; and when the young lady laughed, and said, 'What a goose I am! whatever could I have been thinking of?' he thought within himself (persisting in his illogical and perverse conclusions), 'It is very plain what she is thinking about! I was afraid that she loved him, and now I know it.' So he put up the chess-men, while she went to the piano with her cousin; and he even wished that Mr Bouncer had interrupted their apple-tree conversation

at its commencement; but was thankful to him for coming in time to save him from the pain of being rejected in favour of another. Then, in five minutes, he changed his mind, and had decided that it would have spared him much misery if he could have heard his fate from his Patty's own lips. Then he wished that he had never come to Northumberland at all, and began to think how he should spend his time in the purgatory that Honeywood Hall would now be to him.

When they separated for the night, HE again placed his moustache beneath HER nose. Mr Verdant Green turned away his head at such a sickly exhibition. It was a presumption upon cousinship. Charles Larkyns did not kiss her; and he was equally as much her cousin as Frederick Delaval.

And yet, when the young men went into the back kitchen for a pipe and a chat before going to bed, Verdant was so delighted with that handsome cousin Frederick, that he thought, 'If I was a girl, I should think as *she* does.'

'And why should she not love him?' meditated the poor fellow, when he was lying awake in his bed that self-same night, rendered sleepless by the pain of his new wound; 'why should she not love him? how could she do otherwise? thrown together as they have been from children – speaking to each other as "Patty" and "Fred" – kissing each other – and being as brother and sister. Would that they were so! How he kept near her all the evening – coming to her even when she was playing chess with *me*, then singing with her, and playing her accompaniments. She said that no one could play her accompaniments like *he* could – he had such good taste, and such a firm, delicate touch. Then, when they talked about sketching, she said how she had missed him, and that she had been reserving the view from Brankham Law, in order that they might sketch it together. Then he showed her his last drawings – and they were beautiful. What can I do against this?' groaned poor Verdant, from under the bed-clothes; 'he has accomplishments, and I have none; he has good looks, and I haven't; he has a moustache and a pair of whiskers – and I have only a pair of spectacles! I cannot shine in society, and win admiration, like he does; I have nothing to offer her but my love. Lucky fellow! he is worthier of her than I am – and I hope they will be very happy.' At which thought, Verdant felt highly the reverse, and went off into dismal dreams.

In the morning, when Miss Patty and her cousin were setting out for the hill called Brankham Law, Verdant, who had retreated to a garden-seat beneath a fine old cedar, was roused from a very abstracted perusal of 'The Dream of Fair Women', by the apparition of one who, in his eyes, was fairer than them all.

'I have been searching for you everywhere,' said Miss Patty. 'Mamma said that you were not riding with the others, so I knew that you must be somewhere about. I think I shall lock up my *Tennyson*, if it takes you so much out of our society. Won't you come up Brankham Law with Frederick and me?'

'Willingly if you wish it,' answered Verdant, though with an unwilling air; 'but of what use can I be? Othello's occupation is gone. Your cousin can fill my place much better than if I were there.'

'How very ungrateful you are!' said Miss Patty; 'you really deserve a good scolding! I allow you to watch me when I am painting, in order that you may gain a lesson, and just when you are beginning to learn something, then you give up. But, at any rate, take Fred for your master, and come and watch *him*; he *can* draw. If you were to go to any of the great men to have a lesson of them, all that they would do would be to paint before you, and leave you to look on and pick up what knowledge you could. I know that *I* cannot draw anything worth looking at . . . '

'Indeed, but . . . '

'But Fred', continued Miss Patty, who was going at too great a pace to be stopped, 'but Fred is as good as many masters that you would meet with; so it will be an advantage to you to come and look over him.'

'I think I should prefer to look over you.'

'Now you are paying compliments, and I don't like them. But, if you will come, you will really be useful. You see I am mercenary in my wishes, after all. Here is Fred with a load of sketching materials; won't you take pity on him, and relieve him of my share of his burden?'

If I could take *you* off his hands, thought Verdant, I should be better pleased. But Miss Patty won the day; and Verdant took possession of her sketching-block and drawing materials, and set off with them to Brankham Law.

Frederick Delaval was a yachtsman, and owner of the *Fleur-de-lys*, a cutter yacht, of fifty tons. Besides being inclined to amateur nautical pursuits, he was also partial to an amateur nautical costume; and he further dressed the character of a yachtsman by slinging round him his telescope, which was protected from storms and salt water by a leathern case. This telescope was, in a moment, uncased and brought to bear upon everybody and everything, at every opportunity, in proper nautical fashion, being used by him for distant objects as other people would use an eyeglass for nearer things. And no sooner had they arrived at the grassy *plateau* that marked the summit of Brankham Law, than the telescope was unslung, and its proprietor swept the horizon – for there was a distant view of the ocean – in search of the *Fleur-de-lys*.

'I am afraid', he said, 'that we shall not be able to make her out; the distance is almost too great to distinguish her from other vessels, although the whiteness of her sails would assist us to a recognition. If the skipper got under way at the hour I told him, he ought about this time to be rounding the headland that you see stretching out yonder.'

'I think I see a white sail in that direction,' said Miss Patty, as she shaded her eyes with her hand, and looked out earnestly in the required quarter.

'My dear Patty,' laughed her cousin, 'if you knew anything of nautical matters, you would see that it was not a cutter yacht, for she has more than one mast; though, certainly, as you saw her, she seemed to have but one, for she was just coming about, and was in stays.'

'In stays!' exclaimed Miss Patty; 'why what singular expressions you sailors have!'

'Oh yes!' said Frederic Delaval, 'and some vessels have waists – like young ladies. But now I think I see the *Fleur-de-lys*! that gaff tops'l yard was never carried by a coasting vessel. To be sure it is! the skipper knows how to handle her; and, if the breeze holds, she will soon reach her port. Come and have a look at her, Patty, while I rest the glass for you.' So he balanced it on his shoulder, while Miss Patty looked through it with her one eye, and placed her fingers upon the other – after the manner of young ladies when they look through a telescope; and then burst into such animated, but not thoughtful observations, as 'Oh! I can see it quite plainly. Oh! it is rolling about so! Oh! there are two little men in it! Oh! one of them's pulling a rope! Oh! it all seems to be brought so near!' as if there had been some doubt on the matter, and she had expected the telescope to make things invisible. Miss Patty was quite in childish delight at watching the *Fleur-de-lys's* movements, and seemed to forget all about the proposed sketch, although Mr Verdant Green had found her a comfortable rock seat, and had placed her drawing materials ready for use.

'How happy and confiding they are!' he thought, as he gazed upon them thus standing together; 'they seem to be made for each other. He is far more fitted for her than I am. I wonder if I shall ever see them after they are – married. *I* shall never be married.' And, after this morbid fashion, the young gentleman took a melancholy pleasure in arranging his future.

It was about this time that the divine afflatus – which had lain almost dormant since his boyish 'Address to the Moon' – was again manifested in him by the production of numberless poetical effusions, in which his own poignant anguish and Miss Patty's incomparable attractions were brought forward in verses of various degrees of mediocrity. They were also equally varied in their style and treatment; one being written in a fierce and gloomy Byronic strain, while another followed the lighter childish style of Wordsworth. To this latter class, perhaps, belonged the following lines, which, having accidentally fallen into the hands of Mr Bouncer, were pronounced by him to be 'no end good! first-rate fun!' for the little gentleman put a highly erroneous construction upon them, and, to the great laceration of the author's feelings, imagined them to be altogether of a comic tendency. But, when Mr Verdant Green wrote them, he probably thought that 'deep meaning lieth oft in childish play':

Pretty Patty Honeywood,
   fresh, and fair, and plump,
Into your affections
   I should like to jump!
Into your good graces
   I should like to steal;
That you lov'd me truly
   I should like to feel.

Pretty Patty Honeywood,
   You can little know
How my sea of passion
   Unto you doth flow;
How it ever hastens,
   With a swelling tide,
To its strand of happiness
   At thy darling side.

Pretty Patty Honeywood,
   Would that you and I
Could ask the surpliced parson
   Our wedding knot to tie!
Oh! my life of sunshine
   Then would be begun,
Pretty Patty Honeywood,
   When you and I were one.

But by far his greatest poetical achievement was his 'Legend of the Fair Margaret', written in Spenserian metre, and commenced at this period of his career, though never completed. The plot was of the most dismal and intricate kind. The Fair Margaret was beloved by two young men, one of whom (Sir Frederico) was dark, and (necessarily, therefore) as badly disposed a young man as you would desire to keep out of your family circle, and other (Sir Verdour) was light, and (consequently) as mild and amiable as any given number of maiden aunts could wish. As a matter of course, therefore, the Fair Margaret perversely preferred the dark Sir Frederico, who had poisoned her ears, and told her the most abominable falsehoods about the good and innocent Sir Verdour; when just as Sir Frederico was about to forcibly carry away the Fair Margaret . . .

Why, just then, circumstances over which Mr Verdant Green had no control, prevented the *dénouement*, and the completion of 'the Legend'.

CHAPTER VI

Mr Verdant Green joins a Northumberland Picnic.

SOME weeks had passed away very pleasantly to all – pleasantly even to Mr Verdant Green; for, although he had not renewed his apple-tree conversation with Miss Patty, and was making progress with his 'Legend of the Fair Margaret', yet – it may possibly have been that the exertion to make 'dove' rhyme with 'love,' and 'gloom' with 'doom,' occupied his mind to the exclusion of needless sorrow – he contrived to make himself mournfully amiable, even if not tolerably happy, in the society of the fair enchantress.

The Honeywood party were indeed a model household; and rode, and drove, and walked, and fished, and sketched, as a large family of brothers and sisters might do – perhaps with a little more piquancy than is generally found in the home-made dish.

They had had more than one little friendly picnic and excursion, and had seen Warkworth, and grown excessively sentimental in its hermitage; they had lionised Alnwick, and gone over its noble castle, and sat in Hotspur's chair, and fallen into raptures at the Duchess's bijou of a dairy, and viewed the pillared *passant* lion, with his tail blowing straight out (owing, probably, to the breezy nature of his position), and seen the Duke's herd of buffaloes tearing along their park with streaming manes; and they had gone back to Honeywood Hall, and received Honeywood guests, and been entertained by them in return.

But the Squire was now about to give a picnic on a large scale; and as it was important, not only in its dimensions and preparations, but also in bringing about an occurrence that in no small degree affected

Mr Verdant Green's future life, it becomes his historian's duty to chronicle the event with the fulness that it merits. The picnic, moreover, deserves mention because it possessed an individuality of character, and was unlike the ordinary solemnities attending the picnics of every-day life.

In the first place, the party had to reach the appointed spot – which was Chillingham – in an unusual manner. At least half of the road that had to be traversed was impassable for carriages. Bridgeless brooks had to be crossed; and what were called 'roads' were little better than the beds of mountain torrents, and in wet weather might have been taken for such. Deep channels were worn in them by the rush of impetuous streams, and no known carriage-springs could have lived out such ruts. Carriages, therefore, in this part of the country, were out of the question. The Squire did what was usual on such occasions: he appointed, as a rendezvous, a certain little inn at the extremity of the carriageable part of the road, and there all the party met, and left their chariots and horses. They then – after a little preparatory picnic, for many of them had come from long distances – took possession of certain wagons that were in waiting for them.

These wagons, though apparently of light build, were constructed for the country, and were capable of sustaining the severe test of the rough roads. Within them were lashed hay-sacks, which, when covered with railway rugs, formed sufficiently comfortable seats, on which the divisions of the party sat *vis-à-vis*, like omnibus travellers. Frederick Delaval and a few others, on horses and ponies, as outriders, accompanied the wagon procession, which was by no means deficient in materials for the picturesque. The teams of horses were turned out to their best advantage, and decorated with flowers. The fore horse of each team bore his collar of little brass bells, which clashed out a wild music as they moved along. The ruddy-faced wagoners were in their shirt-sleeves, which were tied round with ribbons; they had gay ribbons also on their hats and whips, and did not lack bouquets and flowers for the further adornment of their persons. Altogether they were most theatrical-looking fellows, and appeared perfectly prepared to take their places in the *Sonnambula*, or any other opera in which decorated rustics have to appear and unanimously shout their joy and grief at the nightly rate of two shillings per head. The light summer dresses of the ladies helped to make an agreeable variety of colour, as the wagons moved slowly along the dark heathery hills, now by the side of a brawling brook, and now by a rugged road.

The joltings of these same roads were, as little Mr Bouncer feelingly remarked, facts that must be felt to be believed. For, when the wheel of any vehicle is suddenly plunged into a rut or hole of a foot's depth, and from thence violently extracted with a jerk, plunge, and wrench, to be again dropped into another hole or rut, and withdrawn from thence in a like manner, and when this process is being simultaneously repeated, with discordant variations, by other three wheels attached to the self-same vehicle, it will follow, as a matter of course, that the result of this experiment will be the violent agitation and commingling of the movable contents of the said vehicle; and, when these contents chance to take the semblance of humanity, it may readily be imagined what must have been the scene presented to the view as the picnic

wagons, with their human freight, laboured through the mountain roads that led towards Chillingham. But all this only gave zest to the day's enjoyment; and, if Miss Patty Honeywood was unable to maintain her seat without assistance from her neighbour, Mr Verdant Green, it is not at all improbable but that she approved of his kind attention, and that the other young ladies who were similarly situated accepted similar attentions with similar gratitude.

In this way they literally jogged along to Chillingham, where they alighted from their novel carriages and four, and then leisurely made their way to the castle. When they had sufficiently lionised it, and had strolled through the gardens, they went to have a look at the famous Wild Cattle. Our Warwickshire friends had frequently had a distant view of them; for the cattle kept together in a herd, and as their park was on the slope of a dark hill, they were visible from afar off as a moving white patch on the landscape. On the present occasion they found that the cattle, which numbered their full herd of about a hundred strong, were quietly grazing on the border of their pine wood, where a few of their fellow-tenants, the original red-deer, were lifting their enormous antlers. From their position the picnic party were unable to obtain a very near view of them; but the curiosity of the young ladies was strongly excited, and would not be allayed without a closer acquaintance with these formidable but beautiful creatures. And it therefore happened that, when the courageous Miss Bouncer proposed that they should make an incursion into the very territory of the Wild Cattle, her proposition was not only seconded, but was carried almost unanimously. It was in vain that Mr Honeywood, and the seniors and chaperones of the party, reminded the younger people of the grisly head they had just seen hanging up in the lodge, and those straight sharp horns that had gored to death the brave keeper who had risked his own life to save his master's friend; it was in vain that Charles Larkyns, fearful for his Mary's sake, quoted the 'Bride of Lammermoor', and urged the improbability of another Master of Ravenswood starting out of the bushes to the rescue of a second Lucy Ashton; it was in vain that anecdotes were told of the fury of these cattle – how they would single out some aged or wounded companion, and drive him out of the herd until he miserably died, and how they would hide themselves for days within their dark pine-wood, where no one dare attack them; it was in vain that Mr Verdant Green reminded Miss Patty Honeywood of her narrow escape from Mr Roarer, and warned her that her then danger was now increased a hundredfold; all in vain, for Miss Patty assured him that the cattle were as peaceable as they were beautiful, and that they only attacked people in self-defence when provoked or molested. So, as the young ladies were positively bent upon having a nearer view of the milk-white herd, the greater number of the gentlemen were obliged to accompany them.

It was no easy matter to get into the Wild Cattle's enclosure, as the boundary fence was of unusual height, and the difficulty of its being scaled by ladies was proportionately increased. Nevertheless, the fence and the difficulty were alike surmounted, and the party were safely landed within the park. They had promised to obey Mr Honeywood's advice, and to abstain from that mill-stream murmur of conversation in which a party of young ladies usually indulge, and to walk quietly among the trees, across an angle of the park, at some two or three hundred yards' distance from the herd, so as not to unnecessarily attract their attention; and then to scale the fence at a point higher up the hill. Following this advice, they walked quietly across the mossy grass, keeping behind trees, and escaping the notice of the cattle. They had reached midway in their proposed path, and, with silent admiration, were watching the movements of the herd as they placidly grazed at a short distance from them, when Miss Bouncer, who was addicted to uncontrollable fits of laughter at improper seasons, was so tickled at some *sotto voce* remark of Frederick Delaval's, that she burst into a hearty ringing laugh, which, ere she could smother its noise with her handkerchief, had startled the watchful ears of the monarch of the herd.

The Bull raised his magnificent head, and looked round in the direction from whence the disturbance had proceeded. As he perceived it, he sniffed the air, made a rapid movement with his pink-edged ears, and gave an ominous bellow. This signal awoke the attention of the other bulls, their wives, and children, who simultaneously left off grazing and commenced gazing. The bovine monarch gave another bellow, stamped upon the ground, lashed his tail, advanced about twenty yards in a threatening manner, and then paused, and gazed fixedly upon the picnic party and Miss Bouncer, who too late regretted her malapropos laugh.

'For heaven's sake!' whispered Mr Honeywood, 'do not speak; but get to the fence as quietly and quickly as you can.'

The young ladies obeyed, and forbore either to scream or faint – for the present. The Bull gave another stamp and bellow, and made a second advance. This time he came about fifty yards before he paused, and he was followed at a short distance, and at a walking pace, by the rest of the herd. The ladies retreated quietly, the gentlemen came after them, but the park-fence appeared to be at a terribly long distance, and it was evident that if the herd made a sudden rush upon them, nothing could save them – unless they could climb the trees; but this did not seem very practicable. Mr Verdant Green, however, caught at the probability of such need, and anxiously looked round for the most likely tree for his purpose.

The Bull had made another advance, and was gaining upon them. It seemed curious that he should stand forth as the champion of the herd, and do all the roaring and stamping, while the other bulls remained mute, and followed with the rest of the herd, yet so it was; but there seemed no reason to disbelieve the unpleasant fact that the monarch's example would be imitated by his subjects. The herd had now drawn so near, and the young ladies had made such a comparatively slow retreat, that they were yet many yards distant from the boundary fence, and it was quite plain that they could not reach it before the advancing milk-white mass would be hurled against them. Some of the young ladies were beginning to feel faint and hysterical, and their alarm was more or less shared by all the party.

It was now, by Charles Larkyns's advice, that the more active gentlemen mounted on to the lower branches of the wide-spreading trees, and, aided by others upon the ground, began to lift up the ladies to places of security. But, the party being a large one, this caring for its more valued but less athletic members was a business that could not be transacted without the expenditure of some little time and trouble, more, as it seemed, than could now be bestowed; for, the onward movement of the Chillingham Cattle was more rapid than the corresponding upward movement of the Northumbrian picnickers. And, even if Charles Larkyns's plan should have a favourable issue, it did not seem a very agreeable prospect to be detained up in a tree, with a century of bulls bellowing beneath, until casual assistance should arrive; and yet, what was this state of affairs when compared with the terrors of that impending fate from which, for some of them at least, there seemed no escape? Mr Verdant Green fully realised the horrors of this alternative when he looked at Miss Patty Honeywood, who had not yet joined those ladies who, clinging fearfully to the boughs, and crouching among the branches like roosting guinea-fowls, were for the present in comparative safety, and out of the reach of the cattle.

The monarch of the herd had now come within forty yards' distance, and then stopped, lashing his tail and bellowing defiance, as he appeared to be preparing for a final rush. Behind him, in a dense phalanx, white and terrible, were the rest of the herd. Suddenly, and before the snowy Bull had made his advance, Frederick Delaval, to the wondering fear of all, stepped boldly forth to meet him. As has been said, he was one of the equestrians of the party, and he carried a heavy-handled whip, furnished with a long and powerful lash. He wrapped this lash round his hand, and walked resolutely towards the Bull, fixing his eyes steadily upon him. The Bull chafed angrily, and stamped upon the ground, but did not advance. The herd, also, were motionless; but their dark, lustrous eyes were centred upon Frederick Delaval's advancing figure. The members of the picnic party were also watching him with intense interest. If they could, they would have prevented his purpose; for to all appearance he was about to lose his own life in order that the rest of the party might gain time to reach a place of safety. The very expectation of this prevented many of the ladies availing themselves of the opportunity thus so boldly purchased, and they stood transfixed with terror and astonishment, breathlessly awaiting the result.

They watched him draw near the wild white Bull, who stood there yet, foaming and stamping up the turf, but not advancing. His huge horned head was held erect, and his mane bristled up, as he looked upon the adversary who thus dared to brave him. He suffered Frederick Delaval to approach him, and only betrayed a consciousness of his presence by his heavy snorting, angry lashing of the tail, and quick motion of his bright eye. All this time the young man had looked the Bull steadfastly in the front, and had drawn near him with an equal and steady step. Suppressed screams broke from more than one witness of his bravery, when he at length stood within a step of his huge adversary. He gazed fixedly into the Bull's eyes, and, after a moment's pause, suddenly raised his riding-whip, and lashed the animal heavily over the shoulders. The Bull tossed round, and roared with fury. The whole herd became agitated, and other bulls trotted up to support their monarch.

Still looking him steadfastly in the eyes, Frederick Delaval again raised his heavy whip, and lashed him more severely than before. The wild Bull butted down, swerved round, and dashed out with his heels. As he did so, Frederick again struck him heavily with the whip, and, at the same time, blew a piercing signal on the boatswain's whistle that he usually carried with him. The sudden shriek of the whistle appeared to put the *coup de grâce* to the young man's bold attack, for the animal had no sooner heard it than he tossed up his head and threw forward his ears, as though to ask from whence the novel noise proceeded. Frederick Delaval again blew a piercing shriek on the whistle; and when the wild Bull heard it, and once more felt the stinging lash of the heavy whip, he swerved round, and with a bellow of pain and fury trotted back to the herd. The young man blew another shrill whistle, and cracked the long lash of his whip until its echoes reverberated like so many pistol-shots. The wild Bull's trot increased to a gallop, and he and the whole herd of the Chillingham Cattle dashed rapidly away from the picnic party, and in a little time were lost to view in the recesses of their forest.

'Thank God!' said Mr Honeywood; and it was echoed in the hearts of all. But the Squire's emotion was too deep for words, as he went to meet Frederick Delaval, and pressed him by the hand.

'Get the women outside the park as quickly as possible,' said Frederick, 'and I will join you.'

But when this was done, and Mr Honeywood had returned to him, he found him lying motionless beneath the tree.

CHAPTER VII

Mr Verdant Green has an Inkling of the Future.

MONG other things that Mr Honeywood had thoughtfully provided for the picnic was a flask of pale brandy, which, for its better preservation, he had kept in his own pocket. This was fortunate, as it enabled the Squire to make use of it for Frederick Delaval's recovery. He had fainted: his concentrated courage and resolution had borne him bravely up to a certain point, and then his overtaxed energies had given way when the necessity for their exertion was removed. When he had come to himself, he appeared to be particularly thankful that there had not been a spectator of (what he deemed to be) his unpardonable foolishness in giving way to a weakness that he considered should be indulged in by none other than faint-hearted women; and he earnestly begged the Squire to be silent on this little episode in the day's adventure.

When they had left the Wild Cattle's park, and had joined the rest of the party, Frederick Delaval received the hearty thanks that he so richly deserved; and this, with such an exuberant display of feminine gratitude as to lead Mr Bouncer to observe, that, if Mr Delaval chose to take a mean advantage of his position, he could have immediately proposed to two-thirds of the ladies, without the possibility of their declining his offer: at which remark Mr Verdant Green experienced an uncomfortable sensation, as he thought of the probable issue of events if Mr Delaval should partly act upon Mr Bouncer's suggestion, by selecting one young lady – his cousin Patty – and proposing to her. This reflection became strengthened into a determination to set the matter at rest, decide his doubts, and put an end to his suspense, by taking the first opportunity to renew with Miss Patty that most interesting apple-tree conversation that had been interrupted by Mr Bouncer at such a critical moment.

The picnic party, broken up into couples and groups, slowly made their way up the hill to Ros Castle – the doubly-intrenched British fort on the summit – where the dinner was to take place. It was a rugged road, running along the side of the park, bounded by rocky banks, and shaded by trees. It was tenanted as usual by a Faw gang – a band of gipsies, whose wild and gay attire, with their accompaniments of tents, carts, horses, dogs, and fires, added picturesqueness to the scene. With the characteristic of their race – which appears to be a shrewd mixture of mendicity and mendacity – they at once abandoned their business of tinkering and peg-making; and, resuming their other business of fortune-telling and begging, they judiciously distributed themselves among the various divisions of the picnic party.

Mr Verdant Green was strolling up the hill lost in meditation, and so inattentive to the wiles of Miss Eleonora Morkin, and her sister Letitia Jane (two fascinating young ladies who were bent upon turning the picnic to account), that they had left him, and had forcibly attached themselves to Mr Poletiss (a soft young gentleman from the neighbourhood of Wooler), when a gipsy woman, with a baby at her back and two children at her heels, singled out our hero as a not unlikely victim, and began at once to tell his fate, dispensing with the aid of stops:

'May the heavens rain blessings on your head my pretty gentleman give the poor gipsy a piece of silver to buy her a bit for the bairns and I can read by the lines in your face my pretty gentleman that you're born to ride in a golden coach and wear buckles of diemints and that your heart's opening like a flower to help the poor gipsy to get her a trifle for her poor famishing bairns that I see the tears of pity astanding like pears in your eyes my pretty gentleman and may you never know the want of the shilling that I see you're going to give the poor gipsy who will send you all the rich blessings of heaven if you will but cross her hand with the bright pieces of silver that are not half so bright as the sweet eyes of the lady that's awaiting and athinking of you my pretty gentleman.'

This unpunctuated exhortation of the dark-eyed prophetess was here diverted into a new channel by the arrival of Miss Patty Honeywood, who had left her cousin Frederick, and had brought her sketch-book to the spot where 'the pretty gentleman' and the fortune-teller were standing.

'I do so want to draw a real gipsy,' she said. 'I have never yet sketched one; and this is a good opportunity. These little brownies of children, with their Italian faces and hair, are very picturesque in their rags.'

'Oh! do draw them!' said Verdant enthusiastically, as he perceived that the rest of the party had passed out of sight. 'It is a capital opportunity, and I dare say they will have no objection to be sketched.'

'May the heavens be the hardest bed you'll have to lie on my pretty rosebud', said the unpunctuating descendants of John Faa, as she addressed herself to Miss Patty; 'and you're welcome to take the poor gipsy's pictur and to cross her hand with the shining silver while she reads the stars and picks you out a prince of a husband and twelve pretty bairns like the . . . '

'No, no!' said Miss Patty, checking the gipsy in her bounteous promises. 'I'll give you something for letting me sketch you, but I won't have my fortune told. I know it already; at least as much as I care

to know.' A speech which Mr Verdant Green interpreted thus:
Frederick Delaval has proposed, and has been accepted.

'Pray don't let me keep you from the rest of the party,' said Miss
Patty to our hero, while the gipsy shot out fragments of persuasive
oratory. 'I can get on very well by myself.' 'She wants to get rid of me,'
thought Verdant. 'I dare say her cousin is coming back to her.' But he
said, 'At any rate let me stay until Mr Delaval rejoins you.'

'Oh! he is gone on with the rest, like a polite man. The Miss
Maxwells and their cousins were all by themselves.'

'But *you* are all by *yourself*; and, by your own showing, I ought to
prove my politeness by staying with you.'

'I suppose that is Oxford logic,' said Miss Patty, as she went on with
her sketch of the two gipsy children. 'I wish these small persons would
stand quiet. Put your hands on your stick, my boy, and not before your
face. – But there are the Miss Morkins, with one gentleman for the
two; and I dare say you would much rather be with Miss Eleonora.
Now, wouldn't you?' and the young lady, as she rapidly sketched the
figures before her, stole a sly look at the enamoured gentleman by her
side, who forthwith protested, in an excited and confused manner, that
he would rather stand near her for one minute than walk and talk for
a whole day with the Miss Morkins; and then, having made this (for
him) unusually strong avowal, he timidly blushed, and retired within
himself.

'Oh yes! I dare say,' said Miss Patty; 'but I don't believe in compliments. If you choose to victimise yourself by staying here, of course
you can do so. – Look at me, little girl; you needn't be frightened; I
shan't eat you. – And perhaps you can be useful. I want some water
to wash-in these figures; and if they were literally washed in it, it would
be very much to their advantage, wouldn't it?'

Of course it would; and of course Mr Verdant Green was delighted
to obey the command. 'What spirits she is in!' he thought, as he dipped
the little can of water into the spring. 'I dare say it is because she and
her cousin Frederick have come to an understanding.'

'If you are anxious to hear a fortune told', said Miss Patty, 'here is
the old gipsy coming back to us, and you had better let her tell yours.'

'I am afraid that I know it.'

'And do you like the prospect of it?'

'Not at all!' and as he said this Mr Verdant Green's countenance
fell. Singularly enough, a shade of sadness also stole over Miss Patty's
sunny face. What could he mean?

A somewhat disagreeable silence was broken by the gipsy most
volubly echoing Miss Patty's request.

'You had better let her tell you your fortune,' said the young lady;
'perhaps it may be an improvement on what you expected. And I shall
be able to make a better sketch of her in her true character of a fortune-
teller.'

Then, like as Martivalle inspected Quentin Durward's palm, according to the form of the mystic arts which he practised, so the
swarthy prophetess opened her Book of Fate, and favoured Mr Verdant Green with choice extracts from its contents. First, she told the
pretty gentleman a long rigmarole about the stars, and a planet that
ought to have shone upon him, but didn't. The she discoursed of a
beautiful young lady, with a heart as full of love as a pomegranate was
full of seeds – painting, in pretty exact colours, a lively portraiture of
Miss Patty, which was no very difficult task, while the fair original was
close at hand; nevertheless, the infatuated pretty gentleman was
deeply impressed with the gipsy narrative, and began to think that the

practice and knowledge of the occult sciences may, after all, have been handed down to the modern representatives of the ancient Egyptians. He was still further impressed with this belief when the gipsy proceeded to tell him that he was passionately attached to the pomegranate-hearted young lady, but that his path of true love was crossed by a rival – a dark man.

Frederick Delaval! This is really most extraordinary! thought Mr Verdant Green, who was not familiar with a fortune-teller's stock in trade; and he waited with some anxiety for the further unravelling of his fate.

The cunning gipsy saw this, and broadly hinted that another piece of silver placed upon the junction of two cross lines in the pretty gentleman's right palm would materially propitiate the stars, and assist in the happy solution of his fortune. When the hint had been taken she pursued her romantic narrative. Her elaborate but discursive summing-up comprehended the triumph of Mr Verdant Green, the defeat of the dark man, the marriage of the former to the pomegranate-hearted young lady, a yellow carriage and four white horses with long tails, and, last but certainly not least, a family of twelve children: at which childish termination Miss Patty laughed, and asked our hero if that was the fate that he had dreaded?

Her sketch being concluded, she remunerated her models so munificently as to draw upon her head a rapid series of the most wordy and incoherent blessings she had ever heard, under cover of which she effected her escape, and proceeded with her companion to rejoin the others. They were not very far in advance. The gipsies had beset them at divers points in their progress, and had made no small number of them yield to their importunities to cross their hands with silver. When the various members of the picnic party afterwards came to compare notes as to the fortunes that had been told them, it was discovered that a remarkable similarity pervaded the fates of all, though their destinies were greatly influenced by the amount expended in crossing the hand; and it was observable that the number of children promised to bless the nuptial tie was also regulated by a sliding-scale of payment – the largest payers being rewarded with the assurance of the largest families. It was also discovered that the description of the favoured lover was invariably the verbal delineation of the lady or gentleman who chanced to be at that time walking with the person whose fortune was being told – a prophetic discrimination worthy of all praise, since it had the pretty good security of being correct in more than one case, and in the other cases there was the chance of the prophecy coming true, however improbable present events would appear. Thus, Miss Eleonora Morkin received, and was perfectly satisfied with, a description of Mr Poletiss; while Miss Letitia Jane Morkin was made supremely happy with a promise of a similarly-described gentleman; until the two sisters had compared notes, when they discovered that the same husband had been promised to both of them – which by no means improved their sororal amiability.

As Verdant walked up the hill with Miss Patty, he thought very seriously on his feelings towards her, and pondered what might be the nature of her feelings in regard to him. He believed that she was engaged to her cousin Frederick. All her little looks, and acts, and words to himself, he could construe as the mere tokens of the friendship of a warm-hearted girl. If she was inclined to a little flirtation, there was then an additional reason for her notice of him. Then he thought that she was of far too noble a disposition to lead him on to a love which she could not, or might not wish to, return; and that she would not have said and done many little things that he fondly recalled, unless she had chosen to show that he was dearer to her than a mere friend. Having ascended to the heights of happiness by this thought, Verdant immediately plunged from thence into the depths of misery, by calling to mind various other little things that she had said and done in connection with her cousin; and he again forced himself into the conviction that in Frederick Delaval he had a rival, and, what was more, a successful one. He determined, before the day was over, to end his tortures of suspense by putting to Miss Patty the plain question whether or no she was engaged to her cousin, and to trust to her kindness to forgive the question if it was an impertinent one. He was unable to do this for the present, partly from lack of courage, and partly from the too close neighbourhood of others of the party; but he concocted several sentences that seemed to him to be admirably adapted to bring about the desired result.

'How abstracted you are!' said Miss Patty to him rather abruptly. 'Why don't you make yourself agreeable? For the last three minutes you have not taken your eyes off Kitty.'·(She was walking just before them, with her cousin Frederick.) 'What were you thinking about?'

Perhaps it was that he was suddenly roused from deep thought, and had no time to frame an evasive reply; but at any rate Mr Verdant Green answered, 'I was thinking that Mr Delaval had proposed, and had been accepted.' And then he was frightened at what he had said; for Miss Patty looked confused and surprised. 'I see that it is so,' he sighed, and his heart sank within him.

'How did you find it out?' she replied. 'It is a secret for the present; and we do not wish any one to know of it.'

'My dear Patty,' said Frederick Delaval, who had waited for them to come up, 'wherever have you been? We thought the gipsies had stolen you. I am dying to tell you my fortune. I was with Miss Maxwell at the time, and the old woman described her to me as my future wife. The fortune-teller was slightly on the wrong tack, wasn't she?' So Frederick Delaval and the Misses Honeywood laughed; and Mr Verdant Green also laughed in a very savage manner; and they all seemed to think it a very capital joke, and walked on together in very capital spirits.

'My last hope is gone!' thought Verdant. 'I have now heard my fate from her own lips.'

CHAPTER VIII

Mr Verdant Green crosses the Rubicon.

HE picnic dinner was laid near to the brow of the hill of Ros Castle, on the shady side of the park wall. In this cool retreat, with the thick summer foliage to screen them from the hot sun, they could feast undisturbed either by the Wild Cattle or the noon-day glare, and drink in draughts of beauty from the wide-spread landscape before them.

The hill on which they were seated was broken up into the most picturesque undulations; here, the rock cropped out from the mossy turf; there, the blaeberries (the bilberries of more southern counties) clustered in myrtle-like bushes. The intrenched hill sloped down to a rich plain, spreading out for many miles, traversed by the Great North road, and dotted over with hamlets. Then came a brown belt of sand, and a broken white line of breakers; and then the sea, flecked with crested waves, and sails that glimmered in the dreamy distance. Holy Island was also in sight, together with the rugged Castle of Bamborough, and the picturesque groups of the Staple and the Farn Islands, covered with sea-birds, and circled with pearls of foam.

The immediate foreground presented a very cheering prospect to hungry folks. The snowy table-cloth – held down upon the grass by fragments of rock against the surprise of high winds – was dappled over with loins of lamb, and lobster salads, and pigeon-pies, and veal cakes, and grouse, and game, and ducks, and cold fowls, and ruddy hams, and helpless tongues, and cool cucumbers, and pickled salmon, and roast-beef of old England, and oyster patties, and venison pasties, and all sorts of pastries and jellies, and custards, and ice: to say nothing of piles of peaches, and nectarines, and grapes, and melons, and pines. Everything had been remembered – even the salt, and the knives and forks, which are usually forgotten at *al-fresco* entertainments. All this was very cheering, and suggestive of enjoyment and creature comforts. Wines and humbler liquids stood around; and, for the especial delectation of the ladies, a goodly supply of champagne lay cooling itself in some ice-pails, under the tilt of the cart that had brought it. This cart-tilt, draped over with loose sacking, formed a very good imitation of a gipsy tent, that did not in the least detract from the rusticity of the scene, more especially as close behind it was burning a gipsy fire, surmounted by a triple gibbet, on which hung a kettle, melodious even then, and singing through its swan-like neck an intimation of its readiness to aid, at a moment's notice, in the manufacture of whisky-toddy.

The dinner was a very merry affair. The gentlemen vied with the servants in attending to the wants of the ladies, and were assiduous in the duties of cutting and carving; while the sharp popping of the champagne, and the heavier artillery of the pale ale and porter bottles, made a pleasant fusillade. Little Mr Bouncer was especially deserving of notice. He sat with his legs in the shape of the letter V inverted, his legs being forced to retain their position from the fact of three dishes of various dimensions being arranged between them in a diminuendo passage. These three dishes he vigorously attacked, not only on his own account, but also on behalf of his neighbours, more especially Miss Fanny Green, who reclined by his side in an oriental posture, and made a table of her lap. The disposition of the rest of the *dramatis personæ* was also noticeable, as also their positions – their sitting *à la* Turk or tailor, and their

dégagés attitudes and costumes. Charles Larkyns had got by Mary Green; Mr Poletiss was placed, sandwich-like, between the two Miss Morkins, who were both making love to him at once; Frederick Delaval was sitting in a similar fashion between the two Miss Honeywoods, who were not, however both making love to him at once; and on the other side of Miss Patty was Mr Verdant Green. The infatuated young man could not drag himself away from his conqueror. Although, from her own confession, he had learnt what he had many times suspected – that Frederick Delaval had proposed and had been accepted – yet he still felt a pleasure in burning his wings and fluttering round his light of love. 'An affection of the heart cannot be cured at a moment's notice,' thought Verdant; 'to-morrow I will endeavour to begin the task of forgetting – to-day, remembrance is too recent; besides, everyone is expected to enjoy himself at a picnic, and I must appear to do the same.'

But it did not seem as though Miss Patty had any intention of allowing those in her immediate vicinity to betake themselves to the dismals, or to the produce of wet-blankets, for she was in the very highest spirits, and insisted, as it were, that those around her should catch the contagion of her cheerfulness. And it accordingly happened that Mr Verdant Green seemed to be as merry as was old King Cole, and laughed and talked as though black care was anywhere else than between himself and Miss Patty Honeywood.

Close behind Miss Patty was the gipsy-tent-looking cart-tilt; and when dinner was over, and there was a slight change of places, while the fragments were being cleared away and the dessert and wine were being placed on the table – that is to say, the cloth – Miss Patty, under pretence of escaping from a ray of sunshine that had pierced the trees and found its way to her face, retreated a yard or so, and crouched beneath the pseudo gipsy-tent. And what so natural but that Mr Verdant Green should also find the sun disagreeable, and should follow his light of love, to burn his wings a little more, and flutter round her fascinations? At any rate, whether natural or no, Verdant also drew back a yard or so, and found himself half within the cart-tilt, and very close to Miss Patty.

The picnic party were stretched at their ease upon the grass, drinking wine, munching fruit, talking, laughing, and flirting, with the blue sea before them and the bluer sky above them, when said the Squire in heroic strain, 'Song alone is wanting to crown our feast! Charles Larkyns, you have not only the face of a singer, but, as we all know, you have the voice of one. I therefore call upon you to set our minstrels an example; and, as a propitiatory measure, I beg to propose your health, with eulogistic thanks for the song you are about to sing!' Which was unanimously seconded amid laughter and cheers; and the pop of the champagne bottles gave Charles Larkyns the key-note for his song. It was suited to the occasion (perhaps it was composed for it?), being a pæan for a picnic, and it stated (in chorus) –

> Then these aids to success
> Should a picnic possess
> For the cup of its joy to be brimming:
> Three things there should shine
> Fair, agreeable, and fine –
> The Weather, the Wine, and the Women!

A rule of picnics which, if properly worked out, could not fail to answer.

Other songs followed; and Mr Poletiss, being a young gentleman of a meek appearance and still meeker voice, lyrically informed the company that 'Oh! he was a pirate bold, the scourge of the wide, wide sea, With a murd'rous thirst for gold, And a life that was wild and free!' And when Mr Poletiss arrived at this point, he repeated the last word two or three times over – just as if he had been King George the Third visiting Whitbread's Brewery –

> 'Grains, grains!' said majesty, 'to fill their crops?
> Grains, grains! that comes from hops – yes, hops, hops, hops!'

So Mr Poletiss sang, 'And a life that was wild and free, free, free, And a life that was wild and free.' To this charming lyric there was a chorus of, 'Then hurrah for the pirate bold, And hurrah for the rover wild, And hurrah for the yellow gold, And hurrah for the ocean's child!' the mild enunciation of which highly moral and appropriate chant appeared to give Mr Poletiss great satisfaction, as he turned his half-shut eyes to the sky, and fashioned his mouth into a smile. Mr Bouncer's love for a chorus was conspicuously displayed on this occasion; and Miss Eleonora and Miss Letitia Jane Morkin added their feeble trebles

to the hurrahs with which Mr Poletiss, in his George the Third fashion, meekly hailed the advantages to be derived from a pirate's career.

But what was Mr Verdant Green doing all this time? The sunbeam had pursued him, and proved so annoying that he had found it necessary to withdraw altogether into the shade of the pseudo gipsy-tent. Miss Patty Honeywood had made such room for him that she was entirely hidden from the rest of the party by the rude drapery of the tent. By the time that Mr Poletiss had commenced his piratical song, Miss Patty and Verdant were deep in a whispered conversation. It was she who had started the conversation, and it was about the gipsy and her fortune-telling.

Just when Mr Poletiss had given his first imitation of King George, and was mildly plunging into his hurrah chorus, Mr Verdant Green – whose timidity, fears, and depression of spirits had somewhat been dispelled and alleviated by the allied powers of Miss Patty and the champagne – was speaking thus: 'And do you really think that she was only inventing, and that the dark man she spoke of was a creature of her own imagination?'

'Of course!' answered Miss Patty; 'you surely don't believe that she could have meant anyone in particular, either in the gentleman's case or in the lady's?'

'But, in the lady's, she evidently described *you*.'

'Very, likely! just as she would have described any other young lady who might have chanced to be with you: Miss Morkin, for example. The gipsy knew her trade.'

'Many true words are spoken in jest. Perhaps it was not altogether idly that she spoke; perhaps I *did* care for the lady she described.'

The sunbeam must surely have penetrated through the tent's coarse covering, for both Miss Patty and Mr Verdant Green were becoming very hot – hotter even than they had been under the apple-tree in the orchard. Mr Poletiss was all this time giving his imitations of George the Third, and lyrically expressing his opinion as to the advantages to be derived from the profession of a pirate; and, as his song was almost as long as 'Chevy Chase', and mainly consisted of a chorus, which was energetically led by Mr Bouncer, there was noise enough made to drown any whispered conversation in the pseudo gipsy-tent.

'But', continued Verdant, 'perhaps the lady she described did not care for me, or she would not have given all her love to the dark man.'

'I think', faltered Miss Patty, 'the gipsy seemed to say that the lady preferred the light man. But you do not believe what she told you?'

'I would have done so a few days ago – if it had been repeated by you.'

'I scarcely know what you mean.'

'Until today I had hoped. It seems that I have built my hopes on a false foundation, and one word of yours has crumbled them into the dust!'

This pretty sentence embodied an idea that he had stolen from his own 'Legend of the Fair Margaret'. He felt so much pride in his property that, as Miss Patty looked slightly bewildered and remained speechless, he reiterated the little quotation about his crumbling hopes.

'Whatever can I have done', said the young lady, with a smile, 'to cause such a ruin?'

'It caused you no pain to utter the words,' replied Verdant; 'and why should it? but, to me, they tolled the knell of my happiness.' (This was another quotation from his 'Legend'.)

'Then hurrah for the pirate bold, And hurrah for the rover wild!' sang the meek Mr Poletiss.

Miss Patty Honeywood began to suspect that Mr Verdant Green had taken too much champagne!

'What *do* you mean?' she said. 'Whatever have I said or done to you that you make use of such remarkable expressions?'

'And hurrah for the yellow gold, And hurrah for the ocean's child!' chorussed Messrs. Poletiss, Bouncer, and Co.

Looking as sentimental as his spectacles would allow, Mr Verdant Green replied in verse –

> 'Hopes that once we've loved to cherish
> May fade and droop, but never perish!

as Shakespeare says.' (Although he modestly attributed this sentiment to the Swan of Avon, it was, nevertheless, another quotation from his own 'Legend'.) 'And it is my case. *I* cannot forget the Past, though *you* may!'

'Really, you are as enigmatical as the Sphinx!' said Miss Patty, who again thought of Mr Verdant Green in connection with champagne. 'Pray condescend to speak more plainly, for I was never clever at finding out riddles.'

'And have you forgotten what you said to me, in reply to a question that I asked you, as we came up the hill?'

'Yes, I have quite forgotten. I dare say I said many foolish things; but what was the particular foolish thing that so dwells on your mind?'

'If it is so soon forgotten, it is not worth repeating.'

'Oh, it is! Pray gratify my curiosity. I am sorry my bad memory should have given you any pain.'

'It was not your bad memory, but your words.'

'My bad words?'

'No, not bad; but words that shut out, a bright future, and changed my life to gloom.' (The 'Legend' again.)

Miss Patty looked more perplexed than ever, while Mr Poletiss politely filled up the gap of silence with an imitation of King George the Third.

'I really do not know what you mean,' said Miss Patty. 'If I have said or done anything that has caused you pain, I can assure you it was quite unwittingly on my part, and I am very sorry for it; but, if you will tell me what it was, perhaps I may be able to explain it away, and disabuse your mind of a false impression.'

'I am quite sure that you did not intend to pain me,' replied Verdant; 'and I know that it was presumptuous in me to think as I did. It was scarcely probable that you would feel as I felt; and I ought to have made up my mind to it, and have borne my sufferings with a patient heart.' (The 'Legend' again!) 'And yet when the shock *does* come, it is very hard to be borne.'

Miss Patty's bright eyes were dilated with wonder, and she again thought of Mr Verdant Green in connection with champagne. Mr Poletiss was still taking his pirate through all sorts of flats and sharps, and chromatic imitations of King George.

'But, what *is* this shock?' asked Miss Patty. 'Perhaps I can relieve it; and I ought to do so if it came through my means.'

'You cannot help me,' said Verdant. 'My suspicions were confirmed by your words, and they have sealed my fate.'

'But you have not yet told me what those words were, and I must really insist upon knowing,' said Miss Patty, who had begun to look very seriously perplexed.

'And, can you have forgotten?' was the reply. 'Do you not remember, that, as we came up the hill, I put a certain question to you about Mr Delaval having proposed and having been accepted?'

'Yes! I remember it very well! And, what then?'

'And, what then!' echoed Mr Verdant Green, in the greatest wonder at the young lady's calmness; 'what then! why, when you told me that he *had* been accepted, was not that sufficient for me to know? – to know that all my love had been given to one who was another's, and that all my hopes were blighted! was not this sufficient to crush me, and to change the colour of my life?' And Verdant's face showed that, though he might be quoting from his 'Legend', he was yet speaking from his heart.

'Oh! I little expected this!' faltered Miss Patty, in real grief, 'I little thought of this. Why did you not speak sooner to someone – to me, for instance – and have spared yourself this misery? If you had been earlier made acquainted with Frederick's attachment, you might then have checked your own. I did not ever dream of this!' And Miss Patty, who had turned pale, and trembled with agitation, could not restrain a tear.

'It is very kind of you thus to feel for me!' said Verdant; 'and all I ask is, that you will still remain my friend.'

'Indeed, I will. And I am sure Kitty will always wish to be the same. She will be sadly grieved to hear of this; for, I can assure you that she had no suspicion you were attached to her.'

'Attached to HER!' cried Verdant, with vast surprise. 'Whatever do you mean?'

'Have you not been telling me of your secret love for her?' answered Miss Patty, who again turned her thoughts to the champagne.

'Love for *her*? No! nothing of the kind.'

'What! and not spoken about your grief when I told you that Frederick Delaval had proposed to her, and had been accepted?'

'Proposed to *her*?' cried Verdant, in a kind of dreamy swoon.

'Yes! to whom else do you suppose he would propose?'

'To *you*!'

'To ME!'

'Yes, to you! Why, have you not been telling me that you were engaged to him?'

'Telling you that *I* was engaged to Fred!' rejoined Miss Patty. 'Why, what could put such an idea into your head? Fred is engaged to Kitty. You asked me if it was not so; and I told you, yes, but that it was a secret at present. Why, then of whom were *you* talking?'

'Of *you*!'

'Of *me*?'

'Yes, of you!' And the scales fell from the eyes of both and they saw their mutual mistake.

There was a silence, which Verdant was the first to break.

'It seems that love is really blind. I now perceive how we have been playing at cross questions and crooked answers. When I asked you about Mr Delaval, my thoughts were wholly of you, and I spoke of you, and not of your sister, as you imagined; and I fancied that you answered not for your sister, but for yourself. When I spoke of my attachment, it did not refer to your sister, but to you.'

'To me?' softly said Miss Patty, as a delicious tremor stole over her.

'To you, and to you alone,' answered Verdant. The great stumbling-block of his doubts was now removed, and his way lay clear before him. Then, after a momentary pause to nerve his determination, and without further prelude, or beating about the bush, he said, 'Patty – my dear Miss Honeywood – I love you! do you love me?'

There it was at last! The dreaded question over which he had passed so many hours of thought, was at length spoken. The elaborate sentences that he had devised for its introduction, had all been forgotten; and his artificial flowers of oratory had been exchanged for those simpler blossoms of honesty and truth: 'I love you – do you love me?' He had imagined that he should put the question to her when they were alone in some quiet room; or, better still, when they were wandering together in some sequestered garden walk or shady lane; and, now, here he had unexpectedly, and undesignedly, found his opportunity at a picnic dinner, with half a hundred people close beside him, and his ears assaulted with a songster's praises of piracy and murder. Strange accompaniments to a declaration of the tender passion! But, like others before him, he had found that there was no such privacy as that of a crowd – the fear of interruption probably adding a spur to determination, while the laughter and busy talking of others assist to fill up awkward pauses of agitation in the converse of the loving couple.

Despite the heat, Miss Patty's cheeks paled for a moment, as Verdant put to her that question. 'Do you love me?' Then a deep blush stole over them, as she whispered 'I do.'

What need for more? what need for pressure of hands or lips, and vows of love and constancy? What need even for the elder and more desperate of the Miss Morkins to maliciously suggest that Mr Poletiss – who had concluded, amid a great display of approbation (probably because it *was* concluded) his mild piratical chant, and his imitations of King George the Third – should call upon Mr Verdant Green, who, as she understood, was a very good singer? 'And, dear me! where could he have gone to, when he was here just now, you know! and, good gracious! why there he was, under the cart-tilt – and well, I never was so surprised – Miss Martha Honeywood with him, flirting now, I dare say? shouldn't you think so?'

No need for this stroke of generalship! No need for Miss Letitia Jane Morkin to prompt Miss Fanny Green to bring her brother out of his retirement. No need for Mr Frederick Delaval to say 'I thought you were never going to slip from your moorings!' Or for little Mr Bouncer to cry, 'Yoicks! unearthed at last!' No need for anything, save the parental sanction to the newly-formed engagement. Mr Verdant Green had proposed, and had been accepted; and Miss Patty Honey-wood could exclaim with Schiller's heroine, '*Ich habe gelebt und geliebet!* – I have lived, and have loved!'

CHAPTER IX

Mr Verdant Green asks Papa.

ISS MORKIN met with her reward before many hours. The picnic party were on their way home, and had reached within a short distance of the inn, where their wagons had to be exchanged for carriages. It has been mentioned that, among the difficulties of the way, they had to drive through bridgeless brooks; and one of these was not half-a-mile distant from the inn.

It happened that the mild Mr Poletiss was seated at the tail end of the wagon, next to the fair Miss Morkin, who was laying violent siege to him, with a battery of words, if not of charms. If the position of Mr Poletiss, as to deliverance from his fair foe, was a difficult one, his position, as to maintaining his seat during the violent throes and tossings to and fro of the wagon, was even more difficult; for Mr Poletiss's mildness of voice was surpassed by his mildness of manner, and he was far too timid to grasp at the side of the wagon by placing his arm behind the fair Miss Morkin, lest it should be supposed that he was assuming the privileged position of a partner in a *valse*. Mr Poletiss, therefore, whenever they jolted through ruts or brooks, held on to his hay hassock, and preserved his equilibrium as best he could.

On the same side of the wagon, but at its upper and safer end, was seated Mr Bouncer, who was not slow to perceive that a very slight *accident* would destroy Mr Poletiss's equilibrium; and the little gentleman's fertile brain speedily concocted a plan, which he forthwith communicated to Miss Fanny Green, who sat next to him. It was this: that when they were plunging through the brook, and everyone was swaying to and fro, and was thrown off their balance, Mr Bouncer should take advantage of the critical moment, and (by accident, of course!) give Miss Fanny Green a heavy push; this would drive her against her next neighbour, Miss Patty Honeywood; who, from the recoil, would literally be precipitated into the arms of Mr Verdant Green, who would be pushed against Miss Letitia Jane Morkin, who would be driven against her sister, who would be propelled against Mr Poletiss, and thus give him that *coup de grâce*, which, as Mr Bouncer hoped, would have the effect of quietly tumbling him out of the wagon, and partially ducking him in the brook. 'It won't hurt him,' said the little gentleman; 'it'll do him good. The brook ain't deep, and a bath will be pleasant such a day as this. He can dry his clothes at the inn, and get some steaming toddy, if he's afraid of catching cold. And it will be such a lark to see him in the water. Perhaps Miss Morkin will take a header, and plunge in to save him; and he will promise her his hand, and a medal from the Humane Society! The wagon will be sure to give a heavy lurch as we come up out of the brook, and what so natural as that we should all be jolted against each other?' It is not necessary to state whether or no Miss Fanny Green seconded or opposed Mr Bouncer's motion; suffice it to say that it was carried out.

They had reached the brook. Miss Morkin was exclaiming, 'Oh, dear! here's another of those dreadful brooks – the last, I hope, for I always feel so timid at water, and I never bathe at the sea-side without shutting my eyes and being pushed into it by the old woman – and, my goodness! here we are, and I feel convinced that we shall all be thrown in by those dreadful wagoners, who are quite tipsy I'm sure – don't you think so, Mr Poletiss?'

But, ere Mr Poletiss could meekly respond, the horses had been quickened into a trot, the wagon had gone down into the brook – through it – and was bounding up the opposite side – everybody was holding tightly to anything that came nearest to hand – when, at that fatal moment, little Mr Bouncer gave the preconcerted push, which was passed on, unpremeditatedly, from one to another, until it had gained its electrical climax in the person of Miss Morkin, who, with a shriek, was propelled against Mr Poletiss, and gave the necessary momentum that toppled him from the wagon into the brook. But, dreadful to relate, Mr Bouncer's practical joke did not terminate at this fixed point. Mr Poletiss, in the suddenness of his fall, naturally struck out at any straw that might save him; and the straw that he caught was the dress of Miss Morkin. She being at that moment off her balance, and the wagon moving rapidly at an angle of 45°, was unable to save herself from following the example of Mr Poletiss, and she also toppled over into the brook. A third victim would have been added to Mr Bouncer's list, had not Mr Verdant Green, with considerable presence of mind, plucked Miss Letitia Jane Morkin from the violent hands that her sister was laying upon her, in making the same endeavours after safety that had been so futilely employed by the luckless Mr Poletiss.

No sooner had he fallen with a splash into the brook, than Miss Eleonora Morkin was not only after but upon him. This was so far fortunate for the lady, that it released her with only a partial wetting, and she speedily rolled from off her submerged companion onto the shore; but it rendered the ducking of Mr Poletiss a more complete one, and he scrambled from the brook, dripping and heavy with wet, like an old ewe emerging from a sheep-shearing tank. The wagon had been immediately stopped, and Mr Bouncer and the other gentlemen had at once sprung down to Miss Morkin's assistance. Being thus surrounded by a male body-guard, the young lady could do no less than go into hysterics, and fall into the nearest gentleman's arms, and as this gentleman was little Mr Bouncer he was partially punished for his

practical joke. Indeed, he afterwards declared that a severe cold which troubled him for the next fortnight was attributable to his having held in his arms the damp form of the dishevelled naiad. On her recovery – which was effected by Mr Bouncer giving way under his burden, and lowering it to the ground – she utterly refused to be again carried in the wagon; and, as walking was perhaps better for her under the circumstances, she and Mr Poletiss were escorted in procession to the inn hard by, where dry changes of costume were provided for them by the landlord and his fair daughter.

As this little misadventure was believed by all, save the privileged few, to have been purely the result of accident, it was not permitted, so Mr Bouncer said, to do as Miss Morkin had done by him – throw a damp upon the party; and as the couple who had taken a watery bath met with great sympathy, they had no reason to complain of the incident. Especially had the fair Miss Morkin cause to rejoice therein, for the mild Mr Poletiss had to make her so many apologies for having been the innocent cause of her fall, and, as a reparation, felt bound to so particularly devote himself to her for the remainder of the evening,

that Miss Morkin was in the highest state of feminine gratification, and observed to her sister, when they were preparing themselves for rest, 'I am quite sure, Letitia Jane, that the gipsy woman spoke the truth, and could read the stars and whatdyecallems as easy as *a b c*. She told me that I should be married to a man with light whiskers and a soft voice, and that he would come to me from over the water; and it's quite evident that she referred to Mr Poletiss and his falling into the brook; and I'm sure if he'd have had a proper opportunity he'd have said something definite tonight.' So Miss Eleonora Morkin laid her head upon her pillow, and dreamt of bride-cake and wedding-favours. Perhaps another young lady under the same roof was dreaming the same thing!

A ball at Honeywood Hall terminated the pleasures of the day. The guests had brought with them a change of garments, and were therefore enabled to make their reappearance in evening costume. This quiet interval for dressing was the first moment that Verdant could secure for sitting down by himself to think over the events of the day. As yet the time was too early for him to reflect calmly on the step he had taken. His brain was in that kind of delicious stupor which we experience when, having been aroused from sleep, we again shut our eyes for a moment's doze. Past, present, and future were agreeably mingled in his fancies. One thought quickly followed upon another; there was no dwelling upon one special point, but a succession of crowding feelings chased rapidly through his mind, all pervaded by that sunny hue that shines out from the knowledge of love returned.

He could not rest until he had told his sister Mary, and made her a sharer in his happiness. He found her just without the door, strolling up and down the drive with Charles Larkyns, so he joined them; and, as they walked in the pleasant cool of the evening down a shady walk, he stammered out to them, with many blushes that Patty Honeywood had promised to be his wife.

'Cousin Patty is the very girl for you!' said Charles Larkyns, 'the very best choice you could have made. She will trim you up and keep you tight, as old Tennyson hath it. For what says "the fat-faced curate Edward Bull?"

> 'I take it, God made the woman for the man
> And for the good and increase of the world.
> A pretty face is well, and this is well,
> To have a dame indoors, that trims us up
> And keeps us tight.'

'Verdant, you are a lucky fellow to have won the love of such a good and honest-hearted girl, and if there is any room left to mould you into a better fellow than what you are, Miss Patty is the very one for the modeller.'

At the same time that he was thus being congratulated on his good fortune and happy prospects, Miss Patty was making a similar confession to her mother and sister, and receiving the like good wishes. And it is probable that Mrs Honeywood made no delay in communicating this piece of family news to her liege lord and master; for when, half an hour afterwards, Mr Verdant Green had screwed up his courage sufficiently to enable him to request a private interview with Mr Honeywood in the library, the Squire most humanely relieved him from a large load of embarrassment, and checked the hems and hums and haws that our hero was letting off like squibs, to enliven his conversation, by saying, 'I think I guess the nature of your errand – to ask my consent to your engagement with my daughter Martha? Am I right?'

And so, by this grateful helping of a very lame dog over a very difficult stile, the diplomatic relations and circumlocutions that are usually observed at horrible interviews of this description were altogether avoided, and the business was speedily brought to a satisfactory termination.

When Mr Verdant Green issued from the library, he felt himself at least ten years older and a much more important person than when he had entered it, so greatly is our bump of self-esteem increased by the knowledge that there is a being in existence who holds us dearer than aught else in the whole wide world. But not even a misogynist would have dared to assert that, in the present instance, love was but an excess of self-love; for if ever there was a true attachment that honestly sprang from the purest feelings of the heart, it was that which existed between Miss Patty Honeywood and Mr Verdant Green.

What need to dwell further on the daily events of that happy time? What need to tell how the several engagements of the two Miss Honeywoods were made known, and how, with Miss Mary Green and Mr Charles Larkyns, there were thus three *bona fide* 'engaged couples' in the house at the same time, to say nothing of what looked like an embryo engagement between Miss Fanny Green and Mr Bouncer? But if this last-named attachment should come to anything, it would probably be owing to the severe aggravation which the little gentleman felt on continually finding himself *de trop* at some scene of tender sentiment.

If, for example, he entered the library, its tenants, perhaps, would be Verdant and Patty, who would be discovered, with agitated expressions, standing or sitting at intervals of three yards, thereby endeavouring to convey to the spectator the idea that those positions had been relatively maintained by them up to the movement of his entering the room, an idea which the spectator invariably rejected. When Mr Bouncer had retired with figurative Eastern apologies from the library, he would perhaps enter the drawing-room, there to find that Frederick Delaval and Miss Kitty Honeywood had sprung into remote positions (as certain bodies rebound upon contact), and were regarding him as an unwelcome intruder. Thence, with more apologies, he would betake himself to the breakfast-room, to see what was going on in that quarter, and there he would flush a third brace of betrotheds, a proceeding that was not much sport to either party. It could hardly be a matter of surprise, therefore, if Mr Bouncer should be seized with the prevailing epidemic, and, from the circumstances of his position, should be driven more than he might otherwise have been into Miss Fanny Green's society. And though the little gentleman had no serious intentions in all this, yet it seemed highly probable that something might come of it, and that Mr Alfred Brindle (whose attentions at the Christmas charade-party at the Manor Green had been of so marked a character) would have to resign his pretensions to Miss Fanny Green's hand in favour of Mr Henry Bouncer.

But it is needless to describe the daily lives of these betrothed couples – how they rode, and sketched, and walked, and talked, and drove, and fished, and shot, and visited, and picnicked – how they went out to sea in Frederick Delaval's yacht, and were overtaken by rough weather, and became so unromantically ill that they prayed to be put on shore again – how, on a chosen day, when the sea was as calm as a duckpond, they sailed from Bamborough to the Longstone, and nevertheless took provisions with them for three days, because, if storms should arise, they might have found it impossible to put back from the island to the shore; but how, nevertheless, they were altogether fortunate, and had not to lengthen out their picnic to such an uncomfortable extent – and how they went over the Lighthouse, and talked about the brave and gentle Grace Darling; and how that handsome, grey-headed old man, her father, showed them the presents that had been sent to his daughter by Queen, and Lords, and Commons, in token of her deed of daring; and how he was garrulous about them and her, with the pardonable pride of a

> fond old man,
> Fourscore and upward,

who had been the father of such a daughter. It is needless to detail all this; let us rather pass to the evening of the day preceding that which should see the group of visitors on their way back to Warwickshire.

Mr Verdant Green and Miss Patty Honeywood have been taking a farewell after-dinner stroll in the garden, and have now wandered into the deserted breakfast-room, under the pretence of finding a water-colour drawing of Honeywood Hall, that the young lady had made for our hero.

'Now, you must promise me', she said to him, 'that you will take it to Oxford.'

'Certainly, if I go there again. But . . . '

'*But*, sir! but I thought you had promised to give up to me on that point. You naughty boy! if you already break your promises in this way, who knows but what you will forget your promise to remember me when you have gone away from here?'

Mr Verdant Green here did what is usual in such cases. He kissed the young lady, and said, 'You silly little woman! as though I *could* forget you!' *et cetera, et cetera.*

'Ah! I don't know,' said Miss Patty.

Mr Verdant Green repeated the kiss and the *et ceteras.*

'Very well, then, I'll believe you,' at length said Miss Patty. 'But I won't love you one bit unless you'll faithfully promise that you will go back to Oxford. Whatever would be the use of your giving up your studies?'

'A great deal of use; we could be married at once.'

'Oh no, we couldn't. Papa is quite firm on this point. You know that he thinks us much too young to be married.'

'But,' pleaded our hero, 'if we are old enough to fall in love, surely we must be old enough to be married.'

'Oxford logic again, I suppose,' laughed Miss Patty, 'but it won't persuade papa, nevertheless. I am not quite nineteen, you know, and papa has always said that I should never be married until I was one-and-twenty. By that time you will have done with college and taken your degree, and I should so like to know that you have passed all your examinations, and are a Bachelor of Arts.'

'But', said Verdant, 'I don't think I shall be able to pass. Examinations are very nervous affairs, and suppose I should be plucked. You wouldn't like to marry a man who had disgraced himself.'

'Do you see that picture?' asked Miss Patty; and she directed Verdant's attention to a small but exquisite oil-painting by Maclise. It was in illustration of one of Moore's melodies, 'Come, rest in this bosom, my own stricken deer!' The lover had fallen upon one knee at his mistress's feet, and was locked in her embrace. With a look of fondest

love she had pillowed his head upon her bosom, as if to assure him, 'Though the herd have all left thee, thy home it is here.'

'Do you see that picture?' asked Miss Patty. 'I would do as she did. If all others rejected you yet would I never. You would still find your home here,' and she nestled fondly to his side.

'But', she said, after one of these delightful pauses which lovers know so well how to fill up, 'you must not conjure up such silly fancies. Charles has often told me how easily you passed your – Little-go, isn't it called? – and he says you will have no trouble in obtaining your degree.'

'But two years is such a tremendous time to wait,' urged our hero, who, like all lovers, was anxious to crown his happiness without much delay.

'If you are resolved to think it long,' said Miss Patty; 'but it will enable you to tell whether you really like me. You might, you know, marry in haste, and then have to repent at leisure.'

And the end of this conversation was, that the fair special-pleader gained her cause, and that Mr Verdant Green consented to return to Oxford, and not to dream of marriage until two years had passed over his head.

The next night he slept at the Manor Green, Warwickshire.

CHAPTER X

Mr Verdant Green is made a Mason.

MR VERDANT GREEN and Mr Bouncer were once more in Oxford, and on a certain morning had turned into the coffee-room of the *Mitre* to 'do bitters,' as Mr Bouncer phrased the act of drinking bitter beer, when said the little gentleman, as he dangled his legs from the table,

'Gig-lamps, old feller! you ain't a Mason.'

'A mason! of course not.'

'And why do you say "of course not"?'

'Why, what would be the use of it?'

'That's what parties always say, my tulip. Be a Mason, and then you'll soon see the use of it.'

'But I am independent of trade.'

'Trade? Oh, I twig. My gum, Gig-lamps! you'll be the death of me some fine day. I didn't mean a mason with a hod of mortar; he'd be a hod-fellow, don't you see? – there's a fine old crusted joke for you – I mean a Mason with a petticut, a freemason.'

'Oh, a freemason. Well, I really don't seem to care much about being one. As far as I can see, there's a great deal of mystery and very little use in it.'

'Oh, that's because you know nothing about it. If you were a Mason you'd soon see the use of it. For one thing, when you go abroad you'd find it no end of a help to you. If you'll stand another tankard of beer I'll tell you an *à propos* tale.'

So when a fresh supply of the bitter beverage had been ordered and brought, little Mr Bouncer, perched upon the table, and dangling his legs, discoursed as follows:

'Last Long, Billy Blades went on to the Continent, and in the course of his wanderings he came across some gentlemen who turned out to be bandits, although they weren't dressed in tall hats and ribbons, and

scarves, and watches, and velvet sit-upons, like you see them in pictures and at theatres; but they were rough customers for all that, and
they laid hands upon Master Billy, and politely asked him for his
money or his life. Billy wasn't inclined to give them either, but he was
all alone, with nothing but his knapsack and a stick, for it was a
frequented road, and he had no idea that there were such things as
banditti in existence. Well, as you're aware, Gig-lamps, Billy's a
modern Hercules, with an unusual development of biceps, and he not
only sent out left and right, and gave them a touch of Hammer Lane
and the Putney Pet combined, but he also applied his shoemaker to
another gentleman's tailor with considerable effect. However, this
didn't get him *kudos*, or mend matters one bit; and, after being
knocked about much more than was agreeable to his feelings, he was
forced to yield to superior numbers. They gagged and blindfolded
him, formed him into a procession, and marched him off; and when
in about half-an-hour they again let him have the use of his eyes and
tongue, he found himself in a rude hut, with his *banditti* friends around
him. They had pistols, and poniards, and long knives, with which they
made threatening demonstrations. They had cut open his knapsack
and tumbled out its contents, but not a *sou* could they find; for Billy,
I should have told you, had left the place where he was staying, for a
few days' walking tour, and he had only taken what little money he
required; of this he had one or two pieces left, which he gave them. But
it wouldn't satisfy the beggars, and they signified to him – for you see,
Gig-lamps, Billy didn't understand a quarter of their lingo – that he
must fork out with his tin unless he wished to be forked into with their
steel. Pleasant position, wasn't it?'

'Extremely.'

'Well, they searched him, and when they found that they really
couldn't get anything more out of him, they made him understand that
he must write to someone for a ransom, and that he wouldn't be
released until the money came. Pleasant again, wasn't it?'

'Excessively. But what has all this to do with freemasonry?'

'Gig-lamps, you're as bad as a girl who peeps at the end of a novel
before she begins to read it. Drink your beer, and let me tell my tale
in my own way. Well, now we come to volume the third, chapter the
last. Master Billy found that there was nothing for it but to obey

orders, so he sent off a note to his banker, stating his requirements. As soon as this business was transacted, the amiable bandits turned to pleasure, and produced a bottle of wine, of which they politely asked Billy to partake. He thought at first that it might be poison, and he wasn't very far wrong, for it was most villainous stuff. However, the

other fellows took to it kindly, and got more amiable than ever over it; so much so that they offered Billy one of his own weeds, and they all got very jolly, and were as thick as thieves. Billy made himself so much at home – he's a beggar that can always adapt himself to circumstances – that at last the chief bandit proposed his health, and then they all shook hands with him. Well, now comes the moral of my story. When the captain of the bandits was drinking Billy's health in this flipper-shaking way, it all at once occurred to Billy to give him the masonic grip. I must not tell you what it was, but he gave it, and, lo and behold! the bandit returned it. Both Billy and the bandit opened their eyes pretty considerably at this. The bandit also opened his arms and embraced his captive; and the long and short of it was that he begged Billy's pardon for the trouble and delay they had caused him, returned him his money and knapsack, and all the weeds that were not smoked, set aside the ransom, and escorted him back to the high road, guaranteeing him a free and unmolested passage if he should come that way again. And all this because Billy was a Mason; so you see, Gig-lamps, what use it is to a feller. But', said Mr Bouncer, as he ended his tale, 'Talking's monstrously dry work. So, I looks to-wards you, Gig-lamps! to which, if you wish to do the correct thing, you should reply "I likewise bows!"' And, little Mr Bouncer, winking affably to his friend, raised the silver tankard to his lips, and kept it there for the space of ten seconds.

'I suppose', said Verdant, 'that the real moral of your story is, that I must become a freemason, because I might travel abroad and be attacked by a scamp who was also a freemason. Now, I think I had better decline joining a society that numbers *banditti* among its members.'

'Oh, but that was an exceptional case. I dare say, if the truth was known, Billy's friend had once been a highly respectable party, and had paid his water-rate and income-tax like any other civilised being. But all Masons are not like Billy's friend, and the more you know of them the more you'll thank me for having advised you to join them. But it isn't altogether that. Every Oxford man who is really a man is a Mason, and that, Gig-lamps, is quite a sufficient reason why *you* should be one.'

So Verdant said, Very well, he had no objection; and little Mr Bouncer promised to arrange the necessary preliminaries. What these were will be seen if we advance the progress of events a few days later.

Messrs Bouncer, Blades, Foote, and Flexible Shanks – who were all Masons, and could affix to their names more letters than members of far more learned societies could do – had undertaken that Mr Verdant Green's initiation into the mysteries of the craft should be altogether a private one. Verdant felt that this was exceedingly kind of them; for, if it must be confessed, he had adopted the popular idea that the admission of members was in some way or other connected with the free use of a red-hot poker, and though he was reluctant to breathe his fears on this point, yet he looked forward to the ceremony with no little dread. He was therefore immensely relieved when he found that, by the kindness of his friends, his initiation would not take place in the presence of the assembled members of the Lodge.

For a week Mr Verdant Green was benevolently left to ponder and speculate on the ceremonial horrors that would attend his introduction to the mysteries of freemasonry, and by the appointed day he had worked himself into such a state of nervous excitement that he was burning more with the fever of apprehension than that of curiosity. There was no help for him, however; he had promised to go through the ordeal, whatever it might be, and he had no desire to be laughed at for having abandoned his purpose through fear.

The Lodge of Cemented Bricks, of which Messrs Bouncer and Co. had promised to make Mr Verdant Green a member, occupied spacious rooms in a certain large house in a certain small street not a hundred miles from the High Street. The ascent to the Lodge-room, which was at the top of the house, was by a rather formidable flight of stairs, up which Mr Verdant Green tremblingly climbed, attended by Mr Bouncer as his *fidus Achates*. The little gentleman, in that figurative Oriental language to which he was so partial, considerately advised his friend to keep up his pecker and never say die; but his exhortation of 'Now, don't you be frightened, Gig-lamps, we shan't hurt you more than we can help' only increased the anguish of our hero's sensations; and when at the last he found himself at the top of the stairs, and before a door which was guarded by Mr Foote, who held a drawn sword, and was dressed in unusually full masonic costume, and looked stern and unearthly in the dusky gloom, he turned back, and would have made his escape had he not been prevented by Mr 'Footelights's' naked weapon. Mr Bouncer had previously cautioned him that he must not in any way evince a recognition of his friends until the ceremonies of the initiation were completed, and that the infringement of this command would lead to his total expulsion from his friends' society. Mr Bouncer had also told him that he must not be surprised at anything that he might see or hear; which, under the circumstances, was very seasonable as well as sensible advice. Mr Verdant Green, therefore, submitted to his fate, and to Mr Footelights's drawn sword.

'The first step, Gig-lamps,' whispered Mr Bouncer, 'is the blind-folding; the next is the challenge, which is in Coptic, the original language, you know, of the members of the first Lodge of Cemented Bricks. Swordbearer and Deputy Past Pantile Foote will do this for you. I must go and put my things on. Remember, you mustn't recog-nise me when you come into the Lodge. Adoo, Samiwel! keep your pecker up.' Mr Verdant Green wrung his friend's hand, pocketed his spectacles, and submitted to be blindfolded.

Mr Footelights then took him by the hand, and knocked three times at the door. A voice, which Verdant recognised as that of Mr Blades, inquired, 'Kilaricum luricum tweedlecum twee?'

To which Mr Footelights replied, 'Astrakansa siphonia bostrukizon!' and laid the cold steel against Mr Verdant Green's cheek in a way which made that gentleman shiver.

Mr Blades's voice then said, 'Swordbearer and Deputy Past Pantile, pass in the neophyte who seeks to be a Cemented Brick,' and Mr Verdant Green was thereupon guided into the room.

'Gropelos tolery lol! remove the handkerchief,' said the voice of Mr Blades.

The glare from numerous wax-lights, reflected as it was from polished gold, silver, and marble, affected Mr Verdant Green's band-aged eyes, and prevented him for a time from seeing anything dis-tinctly, but on Mr Foote motioning to him that he might resume his spectacles, he was soon enabled by their aid to survey the scene. Around him stood Mr Bouncer, Mr Blades, Mr Flexible Shanks, and Mr Foote. Each held a drawn and gleaming sword; each wore aprons, scarves, or mantles; each was decorated with mystic masonic jewellery; each was silent and preternaturally serious. The room was large and was furnished with the greatest splendour, but its contents seemed strange and mysterious to our hero's eyes.

'Advance the neophyte! Oodiny dulipy sing!' said Mr Blades, who walked to the other end of the room, stepped upon a daïs, ascended his throne, and laid aside the sword for a sceptre. Mr Foote and Mr Flexible Shanks then took Mr Verdant Green by either shoulder, and escorted him up the room with their drawn swords turned towards him, while Mr Bouncer followed, and playfully prodded him in the rear.

In front of Mr Blades's throne there was a species of altar, of which the chief ornaments were a large sword, a skull and cross-bones, illuminated by a great wax light placed in a tall silver candlestick. Silver globes and pillars stood upon the daïs on either side of the throne; and luxuriously-velveted chairs and rows of seats were ranged around. Before the altar-like erection a small funereal black and white carpet was spread upon the black and white lozenged floor; and on this carpet were arranged the following articles: a money chest, a ballot box (very like Miss Bouncer's camera), two pairs of swords, three little mallets, and a skull and cross-bones – the display of which emblems of mortality confirmed Mr Verdant Green in his previously-formed opinion, that the Lodge-room was a veritable chamber of horrors, and he would willingly have preferred a visit to that 'lodge in some vast wilderness', for which the poet sighed, and to have foregone all those promised benefits that were to be derived from Freemasonry.

But wishing could not save him. He had no sooner arrived in front of the skull and cross-bones than the procession halted, and Mr Blades, rising from his throne, said, 'Let the Sword-bearer and Deputy Past Pantile, together with the Provincial Grand Mortar-board, do their duty! Ramohun roy azalea tong! Produce the poker! Past Grand Hodman, remain on guard!'

Mr Foote and Mr Flexible Shanks removed their hands and swords from Mr Verdant Green, and walked solemnly down the room, leaving little Mr Bouncer standing beside our hero, and holding the drawn sword above his head. Mr Foote and Mr Flexible Shanks returned, escorting between them the poker. It was cold! that was a relief. But how long was it to remain so?

'Past Grand Hodman!' said Mr Blades, 'instruct the neophyte in the primary proceedings of the Cemented Bricks.'

At Mr Bouncer's bidding, Mr Verdant Green then sat down upon the lozenged floor, and held his knees with his hands. Mr Flexible Shanks then brought to him the poker, and said, 'Tetrao urogallus orygometra crex!' The poker was then, by the assistance of Mr Foote, placed under the knees and over the arms of Mr Verdant Green, who thus sat like a trussed fowl, and equally helpless.

'Recite to the neophyte the oath of the Cemented Bricks!' said Mr Blades.

'Ramphastidinæ toco scolopendra tinnunculus cracticornis bos!' exclaimed Mr Flexible Shanks.

'Do you swear to obey through fire and water, and bricks and mortar, the words of this oath?' asked Mr Blades from his throne.

'You must say, I do!' whispered Mr Bouncer to Mr Verdant Green, who accordingly muttered the response.

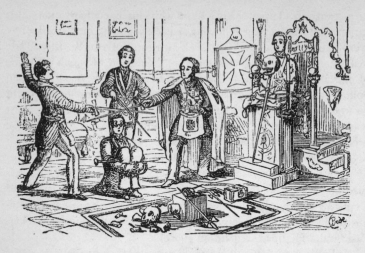

'Let the oath be witnessed and registered by Swordbearer and Deputy Past Pantile, Provincial Grand Mortar-board, and Past Grand Hodman!' said Mr Blades; and the three gentlemen thus designated stood on either side of and behind Mr Verdant Green, and, with theatrical gestures, clashed their swords over his head.

'Keemo kimo lingtum nipcat! let him rise,' said Mr Blades; and the poker was thereupon withdrawn from its position, and Mr Verdant Green, being untrussed, but somewhat stiff and cramped, was assisted upon his legs.

He hoped his troubles were now at an end; but this pleasing delusion was speedily dispelled, by Mr Blades saying – 'The next part of the ceremonial is the delivery of the red-hot poker. Let the poker be heated!'

Mr Verdant Green went chill with dread as he watched the terrible instrument borne from the room by Mr Foote and Mr Flexible Shanks, while Mr Bouncer resumed his guard over him with the drawn sword. All was quiet save a smothered sound from the other side of the door, which, under other circumstances, Verdant would have taken for suppressed laughter; but, the solemnity of the proceedings repelled the idea.

At length the poker was brought in, red-hot and smoking, whereupon Mr Blades left his throne and walked to the other end of

the room, and there took his seat upon a second throne, before which was a second altar, garnished – as Mr Verdant Green soon perceived, to his horror and amazement – with a human head (or the representation of one) projecting from a black cloth that concealed the neck, and, doubtless, the marks of decapitation. Its ghastly features were clearly displayed by the aid of a wax light placed in a tall silver candlestick by its side.

Mr Blades received the poker from Mr Foote, and commanded the neophyte to advance. Mr Verdant Green did so, and took up a trembling position to the left of the throne, while Mr Foote and Mr Flexible Shanks proceeded to the organ, which was to the right of the entrance door. Mr Blades then delivered the poker to Mr Verdant Green, who, at first, imagined that he was required to seize it by its red-hot end, but was greatly relieved in his mind when he found that he had merely to take it by the handle, and repeat (as well as he could) a form of gibberish that Mr Blades dictated. Having done this he was desired to transfer the poker to the Past Grand Hodman – Mr Bouncer.

He had just come to the joyful conclusion that the much dreaded poker portion of the business was now at an end, when Mr Blades ruthlessly cast a dark cloud over his gleam of happiness, by saying – 'The next part of the ceremony will be the branding with the red-hot poker. Let the organist call in the aid of music to drown the shrieks of the victim!' and, thereupon, Mr Foote struck up (with the full swell of the organ) a heart-rendering air that sounded like 'the cries of the wounded' from the *Battle of Prague*.

Now, it happened that little Mr Bouncer – like his sister – was subject to uncontrollable fits of laughter at improper seasons. For the last half-hour he had suffered severely from the torture of suppressed mirth, and, now, as he saw Mr Verdant Green's climax of fright at the anticipated branding, human nature could not longer bear up against an explosion of merriment, and Mr Bouncer burst into shouts of laughter, and, with convulsive sobs, flung himself upon the nearest seat. His example was contagious; Mr Blades, Mr Foote, and Mr Flexible Shanks, one after another, joined in the roar, and relieved their pent-up feelings with a rush of uproarious laughter.

At the first Mr Verdant Green looked surprised, and in doubt whether or no this was but a part of the usual proceedings attendant upon the initiation of a member into the Lodge of Cemented Bricks. Then the truth dawned upon him, and he blushed up to his spectacles.

'Sold again, Gig-lamps!' shouted little Mr Bouncer. 'I didn't think we could carry out the joke so far. I wonder if this will be hoax the last for Mr Verdant Green?'

'I hope so indeed!' replied our hero; 'for I have no wish to continue a freshman all through my college life. But I'll give you full liberty to hoax me again – if you can.' And Mr Verdant Green joined good-humouredly in the laughter raised at his own expense.

Not many days after this he was really made a Mason; although the Lodge was not that of the Cemented Bricks, or the forms of initiation those invented by his four friends.

CHAPTER XI

Mr Verdant Green breakfasts with Mr Bouncer, and enters for a Grind.

ITTLE Mr Bouncer had abandoned his intention of obtaining a *licet migrare* to 'the Tavern', and had decided (the Dons being propitious) to remain at Brazenface, in the nearer neighbourhood of his friends. He had resumed his reading for his degree; and, at various odd times, and in various odd ways, he crammed himself for his forthcoming examination with the most confused and confusing scraps of knowledge. He was determined, he said, 'to stump the examiners'.

One day, when Mr Verdant Green had come from morning chapel, and had been refreshed by the perusal of an unusually long epistle from his charming Northumbrian correspondent, he betook himself to his friend's rooms, and found the little gentleman – notwithstanding that he was expecting a breakfast party – still luxuriating in bed. His curly black wig reposed on its block on the dressing table, and the closely shaven skull that it daily decorated shone whiter than the pillow that it pressed; for although Mr Bouncer considered that night-caps might be worn by 'long-tailed babbies', and by 'old birds that were as bald as coots', yet he, being a young bird – though not a baby – declined to ensconce his head within any kind of white covering, after the fashion of the portraits of the poet Cowper. The smallness of Mr Bouncer's dormitory caused his wash-hand-stand to be brought against his bed's head; and the little gentleman had availed himself of this conveniency, to place within the basin a blubbering, bubbling, gurgling hookah, from which a long stem curled in vine-like tendrils, until it found a resting place in Mr Bouncer's mouth. The little gentleman lay comfortably propped on pillows, with his hands tucked under his head, and his knees crooked up to form a rest for a manuscript book of choice 'crams', that had been gleaned by him from those various fields of knowledge from which the true labourer reaps so rich and ripe a store. Huz and Buz reposed on the counterpane, to complete this picture of Reading for a Pass.

'The top o' the morning to you, Gig-lamps!' he said, as he saluted his friend with a volley of smoke – a salute similar as to the smoke, but

superior, in the absence of noise and slightness of expense, to that which would have greeted Mr Verdant Green's approach had he been of the royal blood – 'here I am! sweating away, as usual, for that beastly examination.' (It was a popular fallacy with Mr Bouncer, that he read very hard and very regularly.) 'I thought I'd cut chapel this morning, and coach up for my Divinity paper. Do you know who Hadassah was, old feller?'

'No! I never heard of her.'

'Ha! you may depend upon it, those are the sort of questions that pluck a man,' said Mr Bouncer, who thought – as other like him have thought – that the getting up of a few abstruse proper names would be proof sufficient for a thorough knowledge of the whole subject. 'But I'm not going to let them gulph me a second time; though, they ought not to plough a man who's been at Harrow, ought they, old feller?'

'Don't make bad jokes.'

'So I shall work well at these crams, although, of course, I shall put on my examination coat, and trust a good deal to my cards, and watch papers, and shirt wristbands, and so on.'

'I should have thought', said Verdant, 'that after those sort of crutches had broken down with you once, you would not fly to their support a second time.'

'Oh, I shall though! – I must, you know!' replied the infatuated Mr Bouncer. 'The Mum cut up doosid this last time; you've no idea how she turned on the main, and did the briny! and I must make things sure this time. After all, I believe it was those Second Aorists that ploughed me.'

It is remarkable, that, not only in Mr Bouncer's case, but in many others, also, of a like nature, gentlemen who have been plucked can always attribute their totally-unexpected failures to a Second Aorist, or a something equivalent to 'the salmon', or 'the melted butter', or 'that glass of sherry', which are recognised as the causes for so many morning reflections. This curious circumstance suggests an interesting source of enquiry for the speculative.

'Well!' said Mr Bouncer meditatively; 'I'm not so sorry, after all, that they cut up rough, and ploughed me. It's enabled me, you see, to come back here, and be jolly. I shouldn't have known what to do with myself away from Oxford. A man can't be always going to feeds and tea-fights; and that's all that I have to do when I'm down in the country with the Mum – she likes me, you know, to do the filial, and go about with her. And it's not a bad thing to have something to work at! it keeps what you call your intellectual faculties on the move. I don't wonder at thingumbob crying when he'd no more whatdyecallems to conquer! he was regularly used up, I dare say.'

Mr Bouncer, upon this, rolled out some curls of smoke from the corner of his mouth, and then observed, 'I'm glad I started this hookah! "The judicious Hooker", ain't it, Gig-lamps? It is so jolly, at night, to smoke oneself to sleep, with the tail end of it in one's mouth, and to find it there in the morning, all ready for a fresh start. It makes me get on with my coaching like a house on fire.'

Here there was a rush of men into the adjacent room, who hailed Mr Bouncer as a disgusting Sybarite, and, flinging their caps and gowns into a corner, forthwith fell upon the good fare which Mr Robert Filcher had spread before them; at the same time carrying on a lively conversation with their host, the occupant of the bed-room. 'Well! I suppose I must turn out, and do tumbies!' said Mr Bouncer.

So he got up, and went into his tub; and, presently, sat down comfortably to breakfast, in his shirt-sleeves.

When Mr Bouncer had refreshed his inner man and strengthened himself for his severe course of reading by the consumption of a singular mixture of coffee and kidneys, beef-steaks and beer; and when he had rested from his exertions, and had resumed his pipe – which was not 'the judicious Hooker', but a short clay, smoked to a swarthy hue, and on that account, as well as from its presumed medicatory power, called 'the Black Doctor' – just then, Mr Smalls, and a detachment of invited guests, who had been to an early lecture, dropped in to breakfast. Huz and Buz, setting up a terrific bark, darted towards a minute specimen of the canine species, which, with the aid of a powerful microscope, might have been discovered at the feet of its proud proprietor, Mr Smalls. It was the first dog of its kind imported into Oxford, and it was destined to set on foot a fashion that soon bade fair to drive out of the field those long-haired Skye terriers, with two or three specimens of which species, he entered the room.

'Kill 'em, Lympy!' said Mr Smalls to his pet, who, with an extreme display of pugnacity, was submitting to the curious and minute inspection of Huz and Buz. 'Lympy' was a black and tan terrier, with smooth hair, glossy coat, bead-like eyes, cropped ears, pointed tail, limbs of a cobwebby structure, and so diminutive in its proportions, that its owner was accustomed to carry it inside the breast of his waistcoat, as a precaution, probably, against its being blown away. And it was called 'Lympy', as an abbreviation of 'Olympus', which was the name derisively given to it for its smallness, on the *lucus a non lucendo* principle that miscalls the lengthy 'brief' of the barrister, the 'living' – not-sufficient-to-support-life – of the poor vicar, the uncertain 'certain age', the unfair 'fare,' and the son-ruled 'governor'.

'Lympy' was placed upon the table, in order that he might be duly admired; an exaltation at which Huz and Buz and the Skye terriers chafed with jealousy. 'Be quiet, you beggars! he's prettier than you!' said Mr Smalls; whereupon, a mild punster present propounded the canine query, 'Did it ever occur to a cur to be lauded to the Skyes?' at which there was a shout of indignation, and he was sconced by the unanimous vote of the company.

'Lympy ain't a bad style of dog,' said little Mr Bouncer, as he puffed away at the Black Doctor. 'He'd be perfect, if he hadn't one fault.'

'And what's his fault, pray?' asked his anxious owner.

'There's rather too much of him!' observed Mr Bouncer, gravely. 'Robert!' shouted the little gentleman to his scout; 'Robert! doose take the feller, he's always out of the way when he's wanted.' And, when the performance of a variety of

octaves on the post-horn, combined with the free use of the speaking-trumpet, had brought Mr Robert Filcher to his presence, Mr Bouncer received him with objurgations, and ordered another tankard of beer from the buttery.

In the mean time, the conversation had taken a sporting turn. 'Do you meet Drake's to-morrow?' asked Mr Blades of Mr Four-in-hand Fosbrooke.

'No! the old Berkshire,' was the reply.

'Where's the meet?'

'At Buscot Park. I send my horses to Thompson's, at the Faringdon Road station, and go to meet him by rail.'

'And, what about the Grind?' asked Mr Smalls of the company generally.

'Oh yes!' said Mr Bouncer, 'let us talk over the Grind. Gig-lamps, old feller, you must join.'

'Certainly, if you wish it,' said Mr Verdant Green, who, however, had as little idea as the man in the moon what they were talking about. But, as he was no longer a Freshman, he was unwilling to betray his ignorance on any matter pertaining to college life; so, he looked much wiser than he felt, and saved himself from saying more on the subject, by sipping a hot spiced draught, from a silver cup that was pushed round to him.

'That's the very cup that Four-in-hand Fosbrooke won at the last Grind,' said Mr Bouncer.

'Was it indeed!' safely answered Mr Verdant Green, who looked at the silver cup (on which was engraven a coat of arms with the words 'Brazenface Grind. – Fosbrooke'), and wondered what a 'Grind'

might be. A medical student would have told him that a 'Grind' meant
the reading up for an examination under the tuition of one who was
familiarly termed a 'Grinder' – a process which Mr Verdant Green's
friends would phrase as 'Coaching' under a 'Coach'; but the conversation that followed upon Mr Smalls's introduction of the subject,

made our hero aware, that, to a University man, a Grind did not possess any
reading signification, but a riding one. In
fact, it was a steeplechase, slightly varying in its details according to the college
that patronised the pastime. At Brazenface, 'the Grind' was usually over a
known line of country, marked out with
flags by the gentleman (familiarly known
as Anniseed) who attended to this business, and full of leaps of various kinds,
and various degrees of stiffness. By sweepstakes and subscriptions, a
sum of from ten to fifteen pounds was raised for the purchase of a silver
cup, wherewith to grace the winner's wines and breakfast parties; but,
as the winner had occasionally been known to pay as much as fifteen
pounds for the day's hire of the blood horse who was to land him first
at the goal, and as he had, moreover, to discharge many other little
expenses, including the by no means little one of a dinner to the losers,
the conqueror for the cup usually obtained more glory than profit.

'I suppose you'll enter Tearaway, as before?' asked Mr Smalls of Mr
Fosbrooke.

'Yes! for I want to get him in condition for the Aylesbury steeple-
chase,' replied the owner of Tearaway, who was rather too fond of
vaunting his blue silk and black cap before the eyes of the sporting
public.

'You've not much to fear from this man,' said Mr Bouncer, indicat-
ing (with the Black Doctor) the stalwart form of Mr Blades. 'Billy's too
big in the Westphalias. Gig-lamps, you're the boy to cook Fosbrooke's
goose. Don't you remember what old father-in-law Honeywood told
you – that you might, would, should, and could, ride like a Shafto? and
lives there a man with soul so dead – as Shikspur or some other cove
observes – who wouldn't like to show what stuff he was made of? I can

put you up to a wrinkle,' said the little gentleman, sinking his voice to a whisper. 'Tollitt has got a mare who can lick Tearaway into fits. She is as easy as a chair, and jumps like a cat. All that you have to do is to sit back, clip the pig-skin, and send her at it; and, she'll take you over without touching a twig. He'd promised her to me, but I intend to cut the Grind altogether; it interferes too much, don't you see, with my coaching. So I can make Tollitt keep her for you. Think how well the cup would look on your side-board, when you've blossomed into a parient, and changed the adorable Patty into Mrs Verdant. Think of that, Master Gig-lamps!'

Mr Bouncer's argument was a persuasive one, and Mr Verdant Green consented to be one of the twelve gentlemen, who cheerfully paid their sovereigns to be allowed to make their appearance as amateur jockeys at the forthcoming Grind. After much debate, 'the Wet Ensham course' was decided upon; and three o'clock in the afternoon of that day fortnight was fixed for the start. Mr Smalls gained *kudos* by offering to give the luncheon at his rooms; and the host of the Red Lion, at Ensham, was ordered to prepare one of his very best dinners, for the winding up of the day's sport.

'I don't mind paying for it', said Verdant to Mr Bouncer, 'if I can but win the cup, and show it to Patty, when she comes to us at Christmas.'

'Keep your pecker up, old feller! and put your trust in old beans' was Mr Bouncer's reply.

CHAPTER XII

Mr Verdant Green takes his degree.

DURING the fortnight that intervened between Mr Bouncer's breakfast party and the Grind, Mr Verdant Green got himself into training for his first appearance as a steeple-chase rider, by practising a variety of equestrian feats over leaping-bars and gorse-stuck hurdles; in which he acquitted himself with tolerable success, and came off with fewer bruises than might have been expected. At this period of his career, too, he strengthened his bodily powers by practising himself in those varieties of the 'manly exercises' that found most favour in Oxford.

The adoption of some portion of these was partly attributable to his having been made a Mason; for, whenever he attended the meetings of his Lodge, he had to pass the two rooms where Mr MacLaren conducted his fencing-school and gymnasium. The fencing-room – which was the larger of the two, and was of the same dimensions as the

Lodge-room above it – was usually tenanted by the proprietor and his assistant, (who, as Mr Bouncer phrased it, 'put the pupils through their paces') and re-echoed to the sounds of stampings, and the cries of 'On guard! quick! parry! lunge!' with the various other terms of Defence and Attack, uttered in French and English. At the upper end of the room, over the fire-place, was a stand of curious arms, flanked on either side by files of single-sticks. The centre of the room was left clear for the fencing; while the lower end was occupied by the parallel bars, a regiment of Indian clubs, and a mattress apparatus for the delectation of the sect of jumpers.

Here Mr Verdant Green, properly equipped for the purpose, was accustomed to swing his clubs after the presumed Indian manner, to lift himself off his feet and hang suspended between the parallel bars, to leap the string on to the mattress, to be rapped and thumped with single-sticks and boxing-gloves by anyone else than Mr Blades (who had developed his muscles in a most formidable manner), and to go through his parades of *quarte* and *tierce* with the flannel-clothed assistant.

Occasionally he had a fencing bout with the good-humoured Mr MacLaren, who – professionally protected by his padded leathern *plastron* – politely and obligingly did his best to assure him, both by precept and example, of the truth of the wise old saw, 'mens sana in corpore sano'.

The lower room at MacLaren's presented a very different appearance to the fencing-room. The wall to the right hand, as well as a part of the wall at the upper end, was hung around – not 'With pikes, and guns, and bows', – like the fine old English gentleman's, but, nevertheless, 'With swords, and good old cutlasses', and foils, and fencing masks, and fencing gloves, and boxing gloves, and pads, and belts, and light white shoes. Opposite to the door, was the vaulting-horse, on whose wooden back the gymnasiast sprang at a bound, and over which the tyro (with the aid of the spring-board) usually pitched himself headlong. Then, commencing at the further end, was a series of poles and ropes – the turning pole, the hanging poles, the rings, and the *trapèze* – on either or all of which the pupil could exercise himself; and, if he had the skill so to do, could jerk himself from one to the other, and finally hang himself upon the sloping ladder, before the momentum of his spring had passed away.

Mr. Bouncer, who could do most things with his hands and feet, was a very distinguished pupil of Mr MacLaren's; for the little gentleman was as active as a monkey, and – to quote his own remarkably

H

figurative expression – was 'a great deal livelier than the *Bug and Butterfly*'.*

Mr Bouncer, then, would go through the full series of gymnastic performances, and finally pull himself up the rounds of the ladder, with the greatest apparent ease, much to the envy of Mr Verdant Green, who, bathed in perspiration, and nearly dislocating every bone in his body, would vainly struggle (in attitudes like to those of 'the perspiring frog' of Count Smorltork) to imitate his mercurial friend, and would finally drop exhausted on the padded floor.

And Mr Verdant Green did not confine himself to these indoor amusements; but studied the *Oxford Book of Sports* in various out-of-door ways. Besides his Grinds, and cricketing, and boating, and hunting, he would paddle down to Wyatt's, for a little pistol practice, or to indulge in the exciting amusement of rifle-shooting at empty bottles, or to practise, on the leaping and swinging poles, the lessons he was learning at MacLaren's, or to play at skittles with Mr Bouncer (who was very expert in knocking down three out of the four), or to kick football until he became (to use Mr Bouncer's expression) 'as stiff as a biscuit'.

Or he would attend the shooting parties given by William Brown, Esquire, of University House; where blue-rocks and brown rabbits were turned out of traps for the sport of the assembled bipeds and quadrupeds. The luckless pigeons and rabbits had but a poor chance for their lives; for, if the gentleman who paid for the privilege of the shot missed his rabbit (which was within the bounds of probability)

* A name given to Mr. Hope's Entomological Museum.

the other guns were at once discharged, and the dogs of Town and Gown let slip. And, if any rabbit was nimble and fortunate enough to run this gauntlet with the loss of only a tail or ear, and, Galatea-like, 'fugit ad salices', and rushed into the willow-girt ditches, it speedily fell before the clubs of the 'cads', who were there to watch, and profit by the sports of their more aristocratic neighbours.*

Mr Verdant Green would also study the news of the day, in the floating reading-room of the University Barge; and, from these comfortable quarters, indite a letter to Miss Patty, and look out upon the picturesque river with its moving life of eights and four-oars sweeping past with measured stroke. A great feature of the river picture, just about this time, was the crowd of newly introduced canoes; their occupants, in every variety of bright-coloured shirts and caps, flashing up and down a double paddle, the ends of which were painted in gay colours, or emblazoned with the owner's crest. But Mr Verdant Green, with a due regard for his own preservation from drowning, was content with looking at these cranky canoes, as they flitted, like gaudy dragon-flies, over the surface of the water.

Fain would the writer of these pages linger over these memoirs of Mr Verdant Green. Fain would he tell how his hero did many things

* 'The Vice-Chancellor, by the direction of the Hebdomadal Council, has issued a notice against the practice of pigeon-shooting, &c., in the neighbourhood of the University.' – *Oxford Intelligence*, Dec. 1854.

that might be thought worthy of mention, besides those which have been already chronicled; but, this narrative has already reached its assigned limits, and, even a historian must submit to be kept within reasonable bounds.

The Dramatist has the privilege of escaping many difficulties, and passing swiftly over confusing details, by the simple intimation, that 'An interval of twenty years is supposed to take place between the Acts.' Suffice it, therefore, for Mr Verdant Green's historian to avail himself of this dramatic art, and, in a very few sentences, to pass over the varied events of two years, in order that he may arrive at a most important passage in his hero's career.

The Grind came off without Mr Verdant Green being enabled to communicate to Miss Patty Honeywood, that he was the winner of a silver cup. Indeed, he did not arrive at the winning post until half-an-hour after it had been first reached by Mr Four-in-hand Fosbrooke on his horse *Tearaway*; for, after narrowly escaping a blow from the hatchet of an irate agriculturalist who professed great displeasure at any one presuming to come a galloperin' and a tromplin' over his fences, Mr Verdant Green finally 'came to grief', by being flung into a disagreeably moist ditch. And though, for that evening, he forgot his troubles, in the jovial dinner that took place at the *Red Lion*, yet, the next morning, they were immensely aggravated, when the Tutor told them that he had heard of the steeple-chase, and should expel every gentleman who had taken part in it. The Tutor, however, relented, and did not carry out his threat; though Mr Verdant Green suffered almost as much as if he had really kept it.

The infatuated Mr Bouncer madly persisted (despite the entreaties and remonstrances of his friends) in going into the Schools clad in his examination coat, and padded over with a host of crams. His fate was a warning that similar offenders should lay to heart, and profit by; for the little gentleman was again plucked. Although he was grieved at this on 'the Mum's' account, his mercurial temperament enabled him to thoroughly enjoy the Christmas vacation at the Manor Green, where were again gathered together the same party who had met there the previous Christmas. The cheerful society of Miss Fanny Green did much, probably, towards restoring Mr Bouncer to his usual happy frame of mind; and, after Christmas, he gladly returned to his beloved

Oxford, leaving Brazenface, and migrating ('through circumstances over which he had no control', as he said) to 'the Tavern.' But when the time for his examination drew on, the little gentleman was seized with such trepidation, and 'funked' so greatly, that he came to the resolution not to trouble the examiners again, and to dispense with the honours of a degree. And so, at length, greatly to Mr Verdant Green's sorrow, and 'regretted by all that knew him', Mr Bouncer sounded his final octaves and went the complete unicorn for the last time in a college quad, and gave his last Wine (wherein he produced some 'very old port, my teacakes! – I've had it since last term!') and then, as an undergraduate, bade his last farewell to Oxford, with the parting declaration, that, though he had not taken his degree, yet that he had got through with great *credit*, for that he had left behind him a heap of unpaid bills.

By this time, or shortly after, many of Mr Verdant Green's earliest friends had taken their degrees, and had left college; and their places were occupied by a new set of men, among whom our hero found many pleasant companions, whose names and titles need not be recorded here.

When June had come, there was a 'grand Commemoration,' and this was quite a sufficient reason that the Misses Honeywood should take their first peep at Oxford, at so favourable an opportunity. Accordingly there they came, together with the Squire, and were met by a portion of Mr Verdant Green's family, and by Mr Bouncer; and there were they duly taken to all the lions, and initiated into some of the mysteries of college life. Miss Patty was enchanted with everything that she saw – even carrying her admiration to Verdant's undergraduate gown – and was proudly escorted from college to college by her enamoured swain.

> Pleasant it was, when woods were green,
> And winds were soft and low,

when in a House-boat, and in four-oars, they made an expedition ('a wine and water party', as Mr Bouncer called it) to Nuneham, and, after safely passing through the perils of the pound-locks of Iffley and Sandford, arrived at the pretty thatched cottage, and picnicked in the round-house, and strolled through the nut plantations up to Carfax

hill, to see the glorious view of Oxford, and looked at the Conduit, and Bab's-tree, and paced over the little rustic bridge to the island, where Verdant and Patty talked as lovers love to talk.

Then did Mr Verdant Green accompany his lady-love to Northumberland; from whence, after spending a pleasant month that, all too quickly, came to an end, he departed (*via* Warwickshire) for a continental tour, which he took in the company of Mr and Mrs Charles Larkyns (*née* Mary Green), who were there for the honeymoon.

Then he returned to Oxford; and when the month of May had again come round, he went in for his Degree examination. He passed with flying colours, and was duly presented with that much-prized shabby piece of paper, on which was printed and written the following brief form:

Green Verdant è Coll. Æn. Fac.

Die 28° *Mensis* Maii *Anni* 185 –

Examinatus, prout Statuta requirunt, satisfecit nobis Examinatoribus.

Ita testamur $\left\{\begin{array}{l}\text{J. Smith.}\\\text{Gul. Brown.}\\\text{Jac. L. Jones.}\\\text{R. Robinson}\end{array}\right\}$ *Examinatores in Literis Humanioribus.*

Owing to Mr Verdant Green's having entered upon residence at the time of his matriculation, he was obliged, for the present, to defer the putting on of his gown, and, consequently, of arriving at the *full* dignity of a Bachelor of Arts. Nevertheless, he had taken his Degree *de facto*, if not *de jure*: and he, therefore – for reasons which will appear – gave the usual Degree dinner, on the day of his taking his Testamur.

He also cleared his rooms, giving some of his things away, sending others to Richards's sale-rooms, and resigning his china and glass to the inexorable Mr Robert Filcher, who would forthwith dispose of these gifts (much over their cost price) to the next Freshman who came under his care.

Moreover, as the adorning of college chimney-pieces with the photographic portraits of all the owner's college friends, had just then come into fashion, Mr Verdant Green's beaming countenance and spectacles were daguerreotyped in every variety of Ethiopian distortion; and, being enclosed in miniature frames, were distributed as souvenirs among his admiring friends.

Then, Mr Verdant Green went down to Warwickshire; and, within three months, travelled up to Northumberland on a special mission.

Mr Verdant Green is Married and Done for.

LASTHOPE'S ruined church, since it had become a ruin – which was many a long year ago – had never held within its mouldering walls so numerous a congregation as was assembled therein on one particular September morning, somewhere about the middle of the present century. It must be confessed that this unusual assemblage had not been drawn together to see and hear the officiating clergyman (who had never, at any time, been a special attraction), although that ecclesiastical Ruin was present, and looked almost picturesque in the unwonted glories of a clean surplice and white kid gloves. But, this decorative appearance of the Ruin, coupled with the fact that it was made on a week-day, was a sufficient proof that no ordinary circumstance had brought about this goodly assemblage.

At length, after much expectant waiting, those on the outside of the Church discerned the figure of small Jock Muir mounted on his highly-trained donkey, and galloping along at a tearing pace from the direction of Honeywood Hall. It soon became evident that he was the advance guard of two carriages that were being rapidly whirled along the rough road that led by the rocky banks of the Swirl. Before small Jock drew rein, he had struggled to relieve his own excitement, and that of the crowd, by pointing to the carriages and shouting, 'Yon's the greums, wi' the t'other priest!' the correctness of which assertion was speedily manifested by the arrival of the 'grooms' in question, who were none other than Mr Verdant Green and Mr Frederick Delaval, accompanied by the Revd Mr Larkyns (who was to 'assist' at the ceremony) and their 'best men', who were Mr Bouncer and a cousin of Frederick Delaval's. Which quintet of gentlemen at once went into the Church, and commenced a whispered conversation with the ecclesiastical Ruin. These circumstances, taken in conjunction with the gorgeous attire of the gentlemen, their white gloves, their waistcoats 'equal to any emergency' (as Mr Bouncer had observed), and the bows of white satin ribbon that gave a festive appearance to themselves, their carriage-horses, and postilions – sufficiently proclaimed the fact that a wedding – and that, too, a double one – was at hand.

The assembled crowd had now sufficient to engage their attention by the approach of a very special train of carriages, that was brought to a grand termination by two travelling-carriages, respectively drawn by four greys, which were decorated with flowers and white ribbons, and were bestridden by gay postilions in gold-tasselled caps and scarlet jackets. No wonder that so unusual a procession should have attracted such an assemblage; no wonder that old Andrew Graham (who was there with his well-favoured daughters) should pronounce it 'a brae sight for weak een.'

As the clatter of the carriages announced their near approach to Lasthope Church, Mr Verdant Green – who had been in the highest state of excitement, and had distractedly occupied himself in looking at his watch to see if it was twelve o'clock; in arranging his Oxford-blue tie; in futilely endeavouring to button his gloves; in getting ready, for the fiftieth time, the gratuity that should make the Ruin's heart to leap for joy; in longing for brandy and water; and in attending to the highly-out-of-place advice of Mr Bouncer, relative to the sustaining of his 'pecker' – Mr Verdant Green was thereupon seized with the fearful apprehension that he had lost the ring; and, after an agonising and trembling search in all his pockets, was only relieved by finding it in his glove (where he had put it for safety) just as the double bridal procession entered the church.

Of the proceedings of the next hour or two, Mr Verdant Green never had a clear perception. He had a dreamy idea of seeing a bevy of ladies and gentlemen pouring into the church, in a mingled stream of bright-coloured silks and satins, and dark-coloured broadcloths, and lace, and ribbons, and mantles, and opera cloaks, and bouquets; and, that this bright stream, followed by a rush of dark shepherd's-plaid waves, surged up the aisle, and, dividing confusedly, shot out from their centre a blue coat and brass buttons (in which, by the way, was Mr Honeywood), on the arms of which were hanging two white-robed figures, partially shrouded with Honiton-lace veils, and crowned with orange blossoms.

Mr Verdant Green has a dim remembrance of the party being

marshalled to their places by a confused clerk, who assigned the wrong brides to the wrong bridegrooms, and appeared excessively anxious that his mistake should not be corrected. Mr Verdant Green also had an idea that he himself was in that state of mind in which he would passively have allowed himself to be united to Miss Kitty Honeywood, or to Miss Letitia Jane Morkin (who was one of Miss Patty's bridesmaids), or to Mrs Hannah More, or to the Hottentot Venus, or to anyone in the female shape who might have thought proper to take his bride's place. Mr Verdant Green also had a general recollection of making responses, and feeling much as he did when in for his *viva voce* examination at college; and of experiencing a difficulty when called upon to place the ring on one of the fingers of the white hand held forth to him, and of his probable selection of the thumb for the ring's resting place, had not the bride considerately poked out the proper finger, and assisted him to place the golden circlet in its assigned position. Mr Verdant Green had also a misty idea that the service terminated with kisses, tears, and congratulations; and, that there was a great deal of writing and signing of names in two documentary-looking books; and that he had mingled feelings that it was all over, that he was made very happy, and that he wished he could forthwith project himself into the middle of the next week.

Mr Verdant Green had also a dozy idea that he was guided into a carriage by a hand that lay lovingly upon his arm; and, that he shook a variety of less delicate hands that there were thrust out to him in hearty northern fashion; and, that the two cracked old bells of Last-hope Church made a lunatic attempt to ring a wedding peal, and only succeeded in producing music like to that which attends the hiving of bees; and, that he jumped into the carriage, amid a burst of cheering and God-blessings; and, that he heard the carriage-steps and door shut to with a clang; and that he felt a sensation of being whirled on by moving figures, and sliding scenery; and, that he found the carriage tenanted by one other person, and that person, his WIFE.

'My darling wife! My dearest wife! My own wife!' It was all that his heart could find to say. It was sufficient, for the present, to ring the tuneful changes on that novel word, and to clasp the little hand that trembled under its load of happiness, and to press that little magic circle, out of which the necromancy of Marriage should conjure such wonders and delights.

The wedding breakfast – which was attended, among others, by Mr and Mrs Poletiss (*née* Morkins), and by Charles Larkyns and his wife, who was now

> The mother of the sweetest little maid
> That ever crow'd for kisses –

the wedding breakfast, notwithstanding that it was such a substantial reality, appeared to Mr Verdant Green's bewildered mind to resemble somewhat the pageant of a dream. There was the usual spasmodic gaiety of conversation that is inherent to bridal banquets, and toasts were proclaimed and honoured, and speeches were made – indeed, he himself made one, of which he could not recall a word. Sufficient let it be for our present purpose, therefore, to briefly record the speech of Mr Bouncer, who was deputed to return thanks for the duplicate bodies of bridesmaids.

Mr Bouncer (who with some difficulty checked his propensity to indulge in Oriental figurativeness of expression) was understood to observe, that on interesting occasions like the present, it was the custom for the youngest groomsman to return thanks on behalf of the bridesmaids; and that he, not being the youngest, had considered himself safe from this onerous duty. For though the task was a pleasing one, yet it was one of fearful responsibility. It was usually regarded as a sufficiently difficult and hazardous experiment when one single gentleman attempted to express the sentiments of one single lady; but when, as in the present case, there were ten single ladies, whose unknown opinions had to be conveyed through the medium of one single gentleman, then the experiment became one from which the boldest heart might well shrink. He confessed that he experienced these emotions of timidity on the present occasion. (*Cries of 'Oh!'*) He felt, that to adequately discharge the duties entrusted would require the might of an engine of ten-bridesmaid power. He would say more, but his feelings overcame him. (*Renewed cries of 'Oh!'*) Under these circumstances he thought that he had better take his leave of the subject, convinced that the reply to the toast would be most eloquently conveyed by the speaking eyes of the ten blooming bridesmaids. (*Mr Bouncer resumes his seat amid great approbation.*)

Then the brides disappeared, and after a time made their reappearance in travelling dresses. Then there were tears, and 'doubtful joys', and blessings, and farewells, and the departure of the two carriages-and-four (under a brisk fire of old shoes) to the nearest railway station, from whence the happy couples set out, the one for Paris, the other for the Cumberland Lakes; and it was amid those romantic lakes, with their mountains and waterfalls, that Mr Verdant Green sipped the sweets of the honeymoon, and realised the stupendous fact that he was a married man.

*

The honeymoon had barely passed, and November had come, when Mr Verdant Green was again to be seen in Oxford – a bachelor only in the University sense of the term, for his wife was with him, and they had rooms in the High Street. Mr. Bouncer was also there, and had prevailed upon Verdant to invite his sister Fanny to join them and be properly chaperoned by Mrs Verdant. For, that wedding-day in Northumberland had put an effectual stop to the little gentleman's determination to refrain from the wedded state, and he could now say with Benedick, 'When I said I would die a bachelor, I did not think I should live till I were married.' But Miss Fanny Green had looked so particularly charming in her bridesmaid's dress, that little Mr Bouncer was inspired with the notable idea, that he should like to see her playing first fiddle, and attired in the still more interesting costume of a bride. On communicating this inspiration (couched, it must be confessed, in rather extraordinary language) to Miss Fanny, he found that the young lady was far from averse to assisting him to carry out his idea; and in further conversation with her, it was settled that she should follow the example of her sister Helen (who was 'engaged' to the Revd Josiah Meek, now the rector of a Worcestershire parish), and consider herself as 'engaged' to Mr Bouncer. Which facetious idea of the little gentleman's was rendered the more amusing from its being accepted and agreed to by the young lady's parents and 'the Mum'. So here was Mr Bouncer again in Oxford, an 'engaged' man, in company with the object of his

affections, both being prepared as soon as possible to follow the example of Mr and Mrs Verdant Green.

Before Verdant could 'put on his gown', certain preliminaries had
to be observed. First, he had to call, as a matter of courtesy, on the head
of his college, to whom he had to show his Testamur, and whose
formal permission he requested that he might put on his gown.

'Oh yes!' replied Dr Portman, in his monosyllabic tones, as though
he were reading aloud from a child's primer; 'oh yes, cer-tain-ly! I was
de-light-ed to know that you had pass-ed, and that you have been such
a cred-it to your col-lege. You will o-blige me, if you please, by pre-
sent-ing your-self to the Dean of Arts.' And then Dr Portman shook
hands with Verdant, wished him good morning, and resumed his
favourite study of the Greek particles.

Then, at an appointed hour in the evening, Verdant, in company
with other men of his college, went to the Dean of Arts, who heard
them read through the Thirty-nine Articles, and dismissed them with
this parting intimation – 'Now, gentlemen! I shall expect to see you
at the Divinity School in the morning at ten o'clock. You must come
with your bands and gown, and fees; and be sure, gentlemen, that you
do not forget the fees!'

So in the morning Verdant takes Patty to the Schools, and commits
her to the charge of Mr Bouncer, who conducts her and Miss Fanny
to one of the raised seats in the Convocation House, from whence they
will have a good view of the conferring of Degrees. Mr Verdant Green
finds the precincts of the Schools tenanted by droves of college but-
lers, porters, and scouts, hanging about for the usual fees and old
gowns, and carrying blue bags, in which are the new gowns. Then –
having seen that Mr. Robert Filcher is in attendance with his own
particular gown– he struggles through the Pig-market,* thronged with
bustling Bedels and University Marshals, and other officials. Then, as
opportunity offers, he presents himself to the senior Squire Bedel in
Arts, George Valentine Cox, Esq., who sits behind a table, and, in his
polite and scholarly manner, puts the usual questions to him, and
permits him, on the due payment of all the fees, to write his name in
a large book, and to place 'Fil Gen.'† after his autograph. Then he has

* The derivation of this word has already been given. See Part I, p. 45.
† *i.e.* Filius Generosi – the son of a gentleman of independent means.

to wait some time until the Superior Degrees are conferred, and the Doctors and Masters have taken their seats, and the Proctors have made their apparently insane promenade.*

Then the Deans come into the ante-chamber to see if the men of their respective colleges are duly present, properly dressed, and have faithfully paid the fees. Then, when the Deans, having satisfactorily ascertained these facts, have gone back again into the Convocation House, the Yeoman Bedel rushes forth with his silver 'poker', and summons all the Bachelors, in a very precipitate and far from impressive manner, with 'Now then, gentlemen! please all of you to come in! you're wanted!' Then the Bachelors enter the Convocation House in a troop, and stand in the area, in front of the Vice-Chancellor and the two Proctors. Then are these young men duly quizzed by the strangers present, especially by the young ladies, who, besides noticing their own friends, amuse themselves by picking out such as they suppose to have been reading men, fast men, or slow men – taking the face as the index of the mind. We may be sure that there is a young

* See note, Part I, p.122

married lady present who does not indulge in futile speculations of this sort, but fixes her whole attention on the figure of Mr Verdant Green.

Then the Bedel comes with a pile of Testaments, and gives one to each man; Dr Bliss, the Registrar of the University, administers to them the oath, and they kiss the book. Then the Deans present them to the Vice-Chancellor in a short Latin form; and then the Vice-Chancellor, standing up uncovered, with the Proctors standing on either side, addresses them in these words: 'Domini, ego admitto vos ad lectionem cujuslibet libri Logices Aristotelis; et insuper earum Artium, quas et quatenus per Statuta audivisse tenemini; insuper autoritate mea et totius universitatis, do vobis potestatem intrandi scholas, legendi, disputandi, et reliqua omnia faciendi, quæ ad gradum Baccalaurei in Artibus spectant.'

When the Vice-Chancellor has spoken these remarkable words (which, after three years of university reading and expense, grant so much that has not been asked or wished for), the newly-made Bachelors rush out of the Convocation House in wild confusion, and stand on one side to allow the Vice-Chancellorian procession to pass. Then, on emerging from the Pig-market, they hear St Mary's bells, which sound to them sweeter than ever.

Mrs Verdant Green is especially delighted with her husband's voluminous bachelor's gown and white-furred hood (articles which

Mr Robert Filcher, when helping to put them on his master in the ante-chamber, had declared to be 'the most becomingest things as was ever wore on a gentleman's shoulders'), and forthwith carries him off to be photographed while the gloss of his new glory is yet upon him. Of course, Mr Verdant Green and all the new Bachelors are most profusely 'capped'; and, of course, all this servile homage – although appreciated at its full worth, and repaid by shillings and quarts of buttery beer – of course it is most grateful to the feelings, and is as delightfully intoxicating to the imagination as any incense of flattery can be.

What a pride does Mr Verdant Green feel as he takes his bride through the streets of his beautiful Oxford! how complacently he conducts her to lunch at the confectioner's who had supplied *their* wedding-cake! how he escorts her (under the pretence of making purchases) to every shop at which he has dealt, that he may gratify his innocent vanity in showing off his charming bride! how boldly he catches at the merest college acqaintance, solely that he may have the proud pleasure of introducing 'My wife!'

But what said Mrs Tester, the bed-maker? 'Law bless you sir!' said that estimable lady, dabbing her curtseys where there were stops, like the beats of a conductor's *bâton* – 'Law bless you, sir! I've bin a wife meself, sir. And I knows your feelings.'

And what said Mr Robert Filcher? 'Mr Verdant Green,' said he, 'I'm sorry as how you've done with Oxford, sir, and that we're a-going to lose you. And this I *will* say, sir! if ever there was a gentleman I were sorry to part with, it's you, sir. But I hopes, sir, that you've got a wife as'll be a good wife to you, sir; and make you ten times happier than you've been in Oxford, sir!'

And so say we.